TO DWELL IN DARKNESS

BOOKS BY DEBORAH CROMBIE

To Dwell in Darkness

The Sound of Broken Glass

No Mark Upon Her

Necessary as Blood

Where Memories Lie

Water Like a Stone

In a Dark House

Now May You Weep

And Justice There Is None

A Finer End

Kissed a Sad Goodbye

Dreaming of the Bones

Mourn Not Your Dead

Leave the Grave Green

All Shall Be Well

A Share in Death

TO DWELL IN
DARKNESS

DEBORAH CROMBIE

WILLIAM MORROW
An Imprint of HarperCollinsPublishers

TO DWELL IN DARKNESS. Copyright © 2014 by Deborah Crombie. All rights reserved. Printed in the United States of America. No part of this book may be used or reproduced in any manner whatsoever without written permission except in the case of brief quotations embodied in critical articles and reviews. For information address HarperCollins Publishers, 195 Broadway, New York, NY 10007.

HarperCollins books may be purchased for educational, business, or sales promotional use. For information please e-mail the Special Markets Department at SPsales@harpercollins.com.

FIRST EDITION

Map drawn by Laura Hartman Maestro

ISBN 978-0-06-227160-0 (hardcover)
ISBN 978-0-06-232526-6 (international edition)

14   15   16   17   DIX/RRD   10   9   8   7   6   5   4   3   2   1

TO THE BEST SUPPORT GROUP A WRITER COULD HAVE—
MY FELLOW JUNGLE RED WRITERS: RHYS BOWEN, LUCY BURDETTE,
HALLIE EPHRON, JULIA SPENCER-FLEMING, SUSAN ELIA MACNEAL,
AND HANK PHILLIPPI RYAN. YOUR FRIENDSHIP AND ENCOURAGEMENT
HAVE BEEN A CONTINUING JOY AND PRIVILEGE.

JUNGLE REDS ROCK!

ACKNOWLEDGMENTS

No writer could be more fortunate in the number of friends who have contributed advice, support, and encouragement. Thanks to Kate Charles, Marcia Talley, Gigi Norwood, Steve Ullathorne, Barb Jungr, Abi Grant, and my fellow Jungle Red Writers—Rhys Bowen, Lucy Burdette, Hallie Ephron, Julia Spencer-Fleming, Susan Elia MacNeal, and Hank Phillippi Ryan.

My agent, Nancy Yost, has, as always, been a pillar of support. My terrific editor, Carrie Feron, is more patient with me than I deserve.

Laura Maestro has once again brought the story to life with an enchanting endpaper map, and Victoria Mathews has crossed my *t*'s and dotted my *i*'s.

Kayti and Michael Gage have fed me, poured me wine when appropriate, and egged me on.

Rick Wilson keeps the home fires burning and makes *everything* possible.

And last but certainly not least, a huge thanks to Diane Hale, who has for more than twenty years been brainstorming buddy, first reader, medical expert, advice giver, best friend, and the one who told me repeatedly that yes, I would finish the book.

Any errors are entirely my own.

TO DWELL IN DARKNESS

CHAPTER ONE

Saint Pancras is the patron saint of children, and is invoked against perjury and false witness.

—*Anonymous*

In the first moment of waking, he had no idea who he was.

He floated, his mind rising slowly from the dim pool of sleep. The hard ridge of his own knuckles pressed against his cheekbone—he realized he was lying on his side. When he moved his hand, he felt the scrape of stubble. Experimentally, he ran his tongue around his mouth, then swallowed against the fuzziness and the sour aftertaste of beer.

Sound began to filter in, little bursts like old radio static. Was it girls' voices? For a moment he thought it was his daughters, giggling with their friends. Was he home? But no, there was urgency in this conversation, not laughter. People were arguing. There was a female voice, then a male. He shifted, feeling his sleeping bag slither against his skin, then the press of the hard boards of the old wooden floor beneath him.

Not at home, then. Not in his own bed, beside his wife.

Awareness flooded in. He was in the flat in the Caledonian Road. The smell of frying chicken rose from the takeaway on the ground floor, making his already queasy stomach turn over.

He realized that the hand under his face was icy. The flat was cold.

The voices grew louder, nearer. He picked out Matthew, arrogant, impatient, impassioned. Then Paul, protesting, but sullen with it, beginning to whine.

He would talk to them. Together he and Wren could make them see sense.

Wren. Oh, God.

Memory returned, and with it despair so crushing it took his breath away. Wren was gone.

Now he knew who he was and exactly where he was. He didn't think he could bear it.

And then he remembered what he had to do that day.

London was miserably cold for mid-March. There were a few hardy crocuses showing their heads in the parks and private gardens, but hard frost had nipped the daffodils and turned the early blossoms on the fruit trees crystalline.

Detective Superintendent Duncan Kincaid walked to Southampton Row from Holborn tube station, his coat collar turned up, neck swaddled in a wool scarf, gloved hands shoved deep in his overcoat pockets. The sky was as dark as gunmetal, and when he turned east into Theobald's Road, a blast of wind almost pushed him off his feet. Lowering his head, he trudged on. The weather boffins said the wind was blowing from the Siberian steppes—he wondered if he should consider one of those Russian hats with the earflaps. At least he now understood why the Russians wore the silly-looking things.

He quickened his pace as the concrete bulk of Holborn Police Station came into view. Although its architectural design might have come straight from the Gulag, it at least promised warmth.

Holborn station. His home away from home for more than two weeks now, yet he still felt as displaced as he had on his first awkward day. And as angry.

Returning to Scotland Yard from paternity leave in mid-February, he'd found his office empty. He'd been transferred from his longtime job as head of a homicide liaison team at the Yard to an area major-incident team based here in Holborn. It was a demotion, although he had kept his rank. There had been no warning and no explanation.

His immediate superior, Chief Superintendent Denis Childs, had been called out of the country on a family emergency. That had added a second worry atop the first, as Kincaid and his family had been letting Childs's sister Liz's home in Notting Hill while her husband worked a five-year contract in Singapore.

Kincaid had come to like Liz Davies, although they had communicated only via e-mail. He hoped that the out-of-the-country emergency didn't include her.

With Kincaid's transfer to Holborn, Doug Cullen, Kincaid's detective sergeant, had been moved into a data-entry job at the Yard, ostensibly to accommodate his recovery from a broken ankle. Now Kincaid faced adjusting to a new job without Cullen's capable, nerdy presence.

Losing a good detective sergeant—a partner with whom you spent more hours than you did with your spouse—ranked, in his opinion, close to divorce on the scale of life disruptions, and there'd been no compensating honeymoon with his new team.

As if conjured up by his thoughts, he glimpsed his new detective constable, George Sweeney, trotting down the steps of the LA Fitness gym across the street from the police station. Fresh from his morning workout, Sweeney wore a three-piece suit that was too expensive for a constable's salary, and no overcoat. His short hair was still damp and trendily spiked, his cheeks red from his healthy exertion.

"Morning, Guv'nor," Sweeney said, overly hearty, as they both reached the station entrance. "You look like death warmed over," he added, squinting at Kincaid. "A little too much partying?" Sweeney added with a wink and what came much too close to a nudge. By God, the man was irritating.

"Sick child," Kincaid said shortly. Their three-year-old foster daughter, Charlotte, had a bad cough, and he and Gemma had taken turns to sit up with her.

"Oh, well." Sweeney shrugged. "That means the day can only get better, right, Guv?"

Kincaid felt a sting on his cheek, and then another. The lowering sky had begun to spit sleet.

"I'm not wearing a bloody cardigan," said Andy Monahan.

His face was set in the mulish expression Detective Sergeant Melody Talbot had come to recognize in the less than two months they'd been a couple. It had taken all her powers of persuasion to get him into the trendy clothing shop in Soho.

As Andy studied himself in the mirror, she crossed her fingers behind her back. At least he hadn't taken it off. He lifted a lapel, his lip curling in distaste. "I look like somebody's granddad. All I need is a regimental tie."

In his late twenties, with rumpled blond hair, dark blue eyes, and a face that might be thought pretty if not for its intensity, Andy looked like a rock star girls would swoon over. "You roll up the sleeves, and wear it with a white T-shirt and Levi's," Melody insisted. "And you certainly don't look like my granddad."

He refused the flirtatious bait. "I'll look like Liberace's granddad. The damned thing is baby blue."

"No rhinestones, though," she said, grinning. "And it brings out the color of your eyes. Besides," Melody added, going in for the kill, "you can't possibly let Poppy outdo you. Trust me."

Andy gave her an assessing glance. "You're the woman who wears Super Detective suits to work. I should trust your fashion advice?" But his mouth had relaxed and there was a hint of a twinkle in his blue eyes. "If I buy it, will you come to the gig?"

"I'll be there. I promised I'd come." The gig in question was late that afternoon in the main concourse at St. Pancras International, part of a March festival featuring hot indie pop and rock bands. There would be live radio coverage and a throng of rush-hour commuters. It was a mark of the meteoric success of Andy and his new partner, Poppy Jones, that they were headlining the festival.

Melody knew he was nervous. There were hints that a scout from a major recording label might attend.

"Up front? By the stage?" Andy asked, the cardigan momentarily forgotten.

This was not an argument Melody wanted to have. Not here. Not now. Melody's insistence that she not be seen publicly as Andy's girlfriend had become the biggest point of dissension in their relationship.

She had weight on her side. Both Andy's manager, Tam Moran, and Poppy's manager, Caleb Hart, wanted to make the most of the duo's onstage chemistry, and they did not see their guitarist's romance with a female detective sergeant in the Metropolitan Police as a marketing plus.

Nor did Melody think her bosses on the job would be thrilled.

But it went deeper. Since childhood she'd been obsessive about her privacy, for good reason. Only a few of her closest friends knew that Melody's father owned one of the most successful—and most sensational—national tabloids. If that connection became public, it would mean career suicide for her. Not to mention that she had not told Andy. She was going to have to come clean with him—but not today.

"Not that I'll have any trouble seeing you from the back in that." She gave the sleeve of the cardigan a playful pinch, trying to deflect a row. "Maybe Poppy could be persuaded to color coordinate with a few blue streaks in her hair."

Andy rolled his eyes. "Don't even suggest it." Poppy was already a flower child gone wild without any encouragement.

"Well, come on, then. Are you going to be brave?"

He eyed her speculatively. "Will I get a reward?"

"There's always afters." She gave the sleeve of the cardigan a deliberate caress.

The salesclerk, who'd been eyeing Andy with interest, gave a little tsk of disgust.

"Sorry, mate." Melody winked at the clerk as she slipped the cardigan off Andy's shoulders. "No joy for you. But at least you made a sale."

Detective Inspector Gemma James stared at the report on the computer screen in South London Station's CID room and tried to resist putting her head down on the desk. The hum of voices, the clatter of keyboards, the ringing of phones were all fading into a soporific buzz.

Last night had been the first time Charlotte had been ill since she had come to live with them the previous autumn, and Gemma suspected she and Kincaid had both overreacted to an ordinary childhood cough.

Now she was counting the minutes until she could justify a midafternoon coffee. She stretched, blinked, and tried to refocus on the screen.

Gemma and her colleagues on the South London murder squad suspected a man of having abducted, raped, and murdered a twelve-year-old girl named Mercy Johnson. It was the team's most pressing case. So far, however, they had nothing concrete enough for a search warrant, much less an arrest.

Dillon Underwood was white, middle class, and manipulatively charming, while Mercy had been working class and black. Gemma and her team feared that Underwood's slick plausibility would help his defense, hence the hours spent going over files for something that might give them enough ammunition to at least search his flat and get a DNA profile.

Gemma's detective sergeant, Melody Talbot, had spent the afternoon reinterviewing Underwood's colleagues in hopes of finding a snippet of information they might have missed.

Nor would Melody be coming back to the police station—she'd told Gemma she meant to go on to St. Pancras International, where her guitarist boyfriend was playing a concert.

The thought made Gemma smile. Her tidy, precise, impeccably dressed detective sergeant with a slightly scruffy rock guitarist.

She glanced back to the computer screen and the details of their suspect's life. Twenty-two-year-old Dillon Underwood worked in a local electronics store as a salesclerk and was apparently quite successful at it. Especially, according to the other employees, with female customers. Mercy Johnson had visited the store numerous times in the weeks before her death, daydreaming over the computers, one of which she hoped to talk her single mother into buying for her thirteenth birthday. But they had no footage on the store cameras of Mercy being served by Dillon, only the word of her best friends. Again, circumstantial, and the testimony of two twelve-year-old girls could easily be discredited by the defense.

On the night of Mercy's disappearance, Underwood had witnesses placing him at a busy club in Brixton Road, although it was the sort of place where it would be easy to lose a friend in the throng for an hour or two.

Mercy's body had been found two days later by a dog walker in the scrub on Clapham Common. Underwood had no car, so if he left the club for long enough to meet and kill Mercy, he had done so on foot. And he would have had to agree to meet Mercy on the common.

When the mobile on Gemma's desk vibrated, she grabbed it, hoping it was Duncan. She'd been worried about him since he'd started the new job at Holborn. Not that she hadn't expected it to be an adjustment, but it had been weeks and the situation didn't seem to be improving.

But the call was from Kit, her fourteen-year-old stepson, and when she glanced at the time she saw that it was late enough for the children to be out of school.

Fumbling the phone to her ear, she said, "Hi, love. Is everything all right?"

But it wasn't Kit. Her six-year-old son Toby's voice rang so loudly in her ear that she jerked the phone away.

"Mummy, Mummy. Kit let me use his phone. We found a cat. In the garden. With babies!"

"Babies? Where? What garden?" she asked fuzzily, still trying to switch gears.

"Kittens!" Toby was emphatic. "But they're really little. Like, like pigs."

"Pigs?" Gemma asked. Then she heard Kit's voice in the background, obviously correcting Toby. "Toby, lovey," she said, "let me speak to Kit."

There was the sound of fumbling and Kit came on the line. "Gemma." Her heart sank. When Kit was relaxed or teasing, he called her Mum.

"What's this about a cat in the garden?" She glanced out the window of the CID room at the leaden sky. The temperature was hovering near freezing and she knew the wind was icy.

"You know the shed?"

Their house in Notting Hill backed onto a communal garden, and a small shed in the garden's center housed the grounds-keeping equipment.

"We were out with the dogs," Kit went on, "and they heard

something." Tess was Kit's rescued terrier; Geordie, Gemma's blue roan cocker spaniel. Good hunting instincts, both. "When we got the door open—"

"What about the gardener's lock?" Gemma broke in.

There was a pause, then Kit said, "I used a hammer. We heard crying. We thought it might be a baby or something."

Gemma let it go for the moment. "And?"

"There was a pile of sacking. I made Toby hold the dogs outside. There was a cat in a sort of nest. With four kittens. Gemma, she's so thin. And the kittens are so tiny. I'm afraid they'll die."

"But, Kit, she's not our cat. Maybe she belongs to one of the neighbors—"

"She's starving, Gemma. She can barely lift her head. We have to do something."

Kittens. Oh, heavens. "Okay, Kit, wait a minute," Gemma said, trying to collect herself. "You can't just move her into the house, not with Sid and the dogs, even if she'd let you." She bit her lip, thinking. "Bryony," she said. "Call Bryony."

Bryony Poole was their vet, the very one who had talked her into adopting Geordie. "Bryony will know what to do."

"Will you be home soon?"

She heard the slight quaver in Kit's voice. He tried so hard to be grown-up, but he couldn't bear anything to be helpless or hurt, or worse, abandoned.

"Yes, love," she said. "I'll be home as soon as I can."

Nothing Paul Cole did was ever good enough according to his parents. Nor according to his teachers when he'd been at school. And now, not according to anyone in the group. Not according to Matthew, who thought he was God's gift to the entire world.

And especially not according to Ariel.

She hadn't believed he'd go through with things today, but he was going to prove her wrong.

He shifted his backpack, feeling the sweat break out under his arms even though it was frigging bloody freezing in the upper concourse of St. Pancras International. He stood near the top of the escalators at the north end of the concourse, so that he had a good view of the length of both upper and lower levels. Moving to the glass guard wall, he looked down at the thickening rush-hour crowd. People were pushing and shoving, intent on getting their shopping and making their commuter connections. They were like scurrying rats, never looking up, oblivious to the glory of the sky-blue station vault.

Nor did they care anything about the trains. Beyond Searcys, the yuppie champagne bar that straddled the center of the upper concourse, two sleek yellow Eurostar trains bound for Paris idled on their platforms. The bespoke-suited men and women sipping their after-work bubbly had no clue as to how incredible these trains were or what it took to keep them running. They took everything in their overindulged lives for granted. Well, they might not be quite so complacent when they went to their beds this night.

Paul drew his eyes from the trains and checked his watch, then scanned the lower concourse again. The others should be here soon. Directly below Searcys, he could see musicians setting up for a concert. It was the first act of the station's March music festival. That was one of the reasons they'd chosen this particular day—the crowd gathering to watch the band would concentrate more people in a small area, and the press coverage of the band would be an added bonus.

A slight girl with spiky ginger hair knelt and lifted a bass guitar from a case, while a blond bloke fiddled with an amp. Passersby were starting to stop and watch. Showtime.

Then he saw the group, coming in from the direction of the tube station at the far end of the concourse. Matthew, unmistakable with his height and loping stride, even with a watch cap pulled over his dark curly hair. Cam. Iris. Trish. Lee. And Dean, pulling the flat suitcase that held their placards, ready to be assembled. They wouldn't have much time.

He searched for Ariel but didn't see her with the rest of the group. But she would be there somewhere, he was certain. As would Ryan.

Paul frowned. There was something about Ryan Marsh that had never seemed quite right. And after what had happened with Wren, there'd been a look in his eyes that frightened Paul. Not that he could blame Ryan, God, no. He felt sick just thinking about it. But still, sometimes Ryan made him uneasy. He'd tried to talk to Matthew about it, but Matthew had blown him off, just like Matthew had blown him off that morning. Bloody Matthew always knew bloody best. Except maybe this time he didn't.

The big station clock over the sculpture of "the lovers" ticked round to five thirty. The musicians played a few sound-check bars on their instruments. The crowd in the center of the lower concourse seemed to move and swell like a living thing. The group had separated and wandered into adjacent shops, not wanting to be noticed until the band was in full swing and media cameras were rolling.

Then, after a last tuning of their instruments, the ginger-haired girl spoke into the mic, and the guitarist hit the first bar.

Showtime, indeed.

Heart thudding in his throat, Paul shifted his backpack to one shoulder and stepped to the top of the escalator.

Melody took the tube straight from Brixton to King's Cross/ St. Pancras. There was no way she could have crossed London at rush hour in her car and got to the station in time for Andy and Poppy's concert. Even so, when "person under a train" came over the speaker as the train pulled into Oxford Circus, she felt a moment of panic. She hated being stuck on the tube. When a second announcement advised all passengers on the Central line to reroute, she breathed a sigh of relief.

The accident wasn't on her line. There was nothing she could do, and she couldn't help feeling relieved that the mess wasn't on her watch. She'd dealt with a jumper once, when she was still in uniform, and there weren't many things worse.

She shivered at the memory, in spite of the bodies packed against her in the back of the train car. But she was determined not to let work interfere with her enjoyment of Andy's moment in the limelight—the first of many, she felt sure. And she couldn't wait to see if he had actually worn the blue cardigan.

Seeing her smile, the middle-aged woman squashed beside her smiled back. Nodding, Melody took the small contact as a good omen. Most Londoners weren't too bad, given half a chance. And bless London Transport—they did their best to keep things running.

But when the train idled far longer than normal at Warren Street, then again at Euston, Melody's anxiety rose. Andy would be crushed if she didn't make it. She'd almost decided to get out at Euston and walk the rest of the way when the train doors closed and the train moved out of the station.

When the train pulled into King's Cross, Melody was first out the doors. She sprinted for the Underground ticket barrier, then started for the St. Pancras concourse at a jog. Good thing she'd worn boots that day because of the cold, she thought, rather than her work heels and one of the suits Andy loved to tease her about. Warm and red-cheeked by the time she entered the south end of the station, she stopped a moment to catch her breath.

The music came to her faintly, in intermittent bursts, but she recognized it instantly. Before she met Andy, she'd have been hard-pressed to tell a guitar from a banjo, but now she would know the distinctive sound of Andy's guitar anywhere. And there, on another wave of sound, was Poppy's unique, rich vocal, with Andy singing harmony.

If she stood at the back, perhaps Andy wouldn't notice how late she'd been.

As she came into the concourse proper, she glimpsed, beyond the glass elevator, the crowd gathered round the small temporary stage. Moving closer, she saw the duo clearly—Poppy, in a floaty white top over a short flowered skirt and her usual tights and boots; Andy, resplendent in the sky-blue cardigan, the light glinting from his tousled fair hair and his brilliant red guitar.

Andy hadn't seen her. He and Poppy were into a new song now, both of them playing and singing, their focus intense. Melody felt the same thrill of excitement she'd had the very first time she'd heard them perform. They had something electric together, Andy and Poppy, the whole bigger than the parts, and Melody could feel the energy move through the gathered crowd.

Under the edge of the café arcade to her left, she saw Tam and Caleb, Andy and Poppy's respective managers. They were standing, holding their coffees and watching the stage intently, grinning from ear to ear.

Then something else caught her eye. On her right, near the Marks & Spencer food shop, half a dozen protesters raised placards in unison. As they were facing away from her, she couldn't read the signs, but the group looked harmless enough. Still, she didn't want anything spoiling Andy and Poppy's moment. Looking round, she saw a female uniformed British Transport Police officer walking towards them, radio in hand.

Good. The last thing she wanted was to have to act in an official capacity here. She turned back to the stage as Andy and Poppy's voices rose to a crescendo in the last verse of the song.

She'd raised her hands, ready to applaud, when she heard

a whoosh, then a high, keening wail. Voices rose in frantic screams as Melody whirled round.

She jerked back instinctively, gasping. There, in the open space where the arcade led out to the western taxi rank, burned a ball of fire as bright as a flaring match. And in its center was a human form.

CHAPTER TWO

St. Pancras Old Church is a Church of England parish church in Somers Town, central London. It is dedicated to the Roman martyr Saint Pancras, and is believed by many to be one of the oldest sites of Christian worship in England.
                              —*Wikipedia, St. Pancras Old Church*

Blinded by the flare of light, Melody instinctively threw her arm up to protect her eyes. Then, even as she was blinking and trying to focus, her training kicked in. She yanked her phone from her coat pocket and punched the preprogrammed direct number to Emergency Services Control. The 999 lines would be lighting up like Christmas trees and she couldn't afford to be put on hold. When the dispatcher answered, Melody shouted to make herself heard over the rising clamor in the concourse. "Detective Sergeant Melody Talbot. Emergency. St. Pancras International. Main concourse. A man on fire—possibly a bomb." The music shuddered to a stop and suddenly she could hear herself shouting. "All services on the doub—"

Then, before her eyes, the figure inside the ball of fire collapsed. A wave of hot, chemical smell singed her nose. She realized that the screams weren't only from panic—there were other people on fire, batting frantically at themselves. "Make that multiple victims," she said to Control. "All services. Hurry."

"Stay on the line, Sergeant," said the female dispatcher. "You'll need to keep us updat—"

"I've got to help. Look, I'll put you on speaker." Before the dispatcher could argue, she dropped the phone back in her pocket and fumbled her warrant card out, holding it aloft. Looking round, she couldn't spot the British Transport Police officer she'd glimpsed earlier. She was on her own.

The screams grew louder. Smoke began to billow through the concourse. Andy and Poppy were still on the makeshift stage and Andy's voice reverberated over the sound system. "What the—"

"Andy," she shouted, and saw him searching the crowd for her. She waved her arms, then cupped her hands into a megaphone to make herself heard over the chaos. "Andy! Use the mic. Tell everybody to get out. Then go!"

She saw the relief on his face as he spotted her; then he hesitated. "But you—"

Melody shook her head. "Do it! Get everyone out."

Moving on, she heard Andy an instant later, shouting into the mic, "Get out! Everybody evacuate! Find the nearest exit! Out, now!"

Melody kept on towards the burned figure, still holding her ID up, an ineffective shield. The smoke turned to white fog. People she couldn't see clearly banged into her, making her stagger. Disembodied voices cried and swore. Her foot slipped on something. Looking down, she saw a spilled cup of AMT Coffee, the brown liquid seeping into a trampled supermarket bouquet of pink carnations.

Poppy's voice now echoed Andy's over the sound system, repeating Andy's exhortations. They both sounded impossibly distant. Then she heard Andy growl a response to some unseen punter, "No, it's not a fucking joke, you moron."

The smoke grew thicker. Her nose and eyes were streaming and she began to cough. She caught glimpses of people smacking at blobs of fire on their clothes, in their hair. "Roll!" she shouted. "Smother it. Use your coats, anything." Coughing, she tripped over an abandoned suitcase, banging her shin, fell, then got up again. Her throat burned.

Then, even through the chemical blanket of smoke, the smell hit her. Burned hair. Fat. Meat. Human flesh.

Suddenly there was a man beside her, shouting hoarsely, "Get back! Everybody get back! Don't breathe the smoke!" He pushed at her, a hard shove out of the fog. "I said get the fuck back!"

She grabbed at him, catching his jacket. "I'm a cop! Help me, for God's sake!"

Through a break in the haze she saw his face, soot smudged, now inches from her own. Light brown hair, red-rimmed blue eyes. "Cover your face," he said, nodding an acknowledgment. She saw that he had a blue handkerchief in his hand. "The fire—it's bloody phosphorus."

Holding the handkerchief to his face like a mask, he grabbed her elbow with his other hand. Together they pushed forward, through the knot of people jostling the other way. With her free hand she followed his example, pulling her coat up over her mouth and nose.

Then suddenly the smoke was above them, rising into the pale blue height of the concourse, and Melody saw clearly what lay ahead.

The charred body lay in the pugilist position, arms and legs drawn up in an obscene parody of a boxer. Wisps of smoke still rose from the blackened and tattered skin and clothing. Along the body, little spurts of fire ignited randomly, then winked out, like fireflies on a summer evening.

"Oh, God." The man beside her tightened his grip on her arm until it felt like a vise.

Melody dragged her gaze from the corpse. She met her companion's eyes and saw not just horror, but anguish.

"What the— How did—" His voice was a croak. He shook his head, tried again. "Shit. There's nothing—nothing we can do for him now. Nothing anyone can do for him now."

Duncan Kincaid stood at the door of his office in Holborn Police Station, looking into the CID room and surreptitiously stifling a yawn.

He thought of Scotland Yard with an almost physical stab of longing. There had been slow days in Homicide Liaison, yes, but still there had always been a hum of purposefulness in the building. And he missed having his own office, occupied so comfortably for so long that it had felt like a second home.

He hadn't even bothered moving his books into this one. He felt temporary here. Displaced. Yet the result was a sterile environment that didn't inspire him to spend one moment longer than necessary at work.

So he entertained himself by examining his new detective inspector. Jasmine Sidana was thirty-five years old, and single. This he knew from her personnel file. It also told him that she had a degree from University College London, and that she'd worked her way quickly through the ranks, from uniform to CID, until she'd reached her current position.

She wore the same starched white long-sleeved blouse to work every day, and the same dark knee-length skirt. She apparently didn't drink alcohol, and was conspicuously absent from any after-work fraternizing within the department. She was neat, efficient, and organized to a fault. It was also apparent that she had badly wanted his job, and the promotion that would have gone with it. Sidana made no secret of her resentment, or of the fact that she felt she'd been discriminated against on gender and racial grounds.

"Sir?" said Sidana, even more frostily than usual, looking up from her desk, and he chided himself for having been caught staring.

"Nothing, Detective." Kincaid had yet to solve the problem of what to call her. With most officers in his command, he'd felt comfortable addressing them at least by their surnames, if not their given names. But with Sidana even that felt awkward, and yet he couldn't go round calling her "Detective Inspector" unless it was in a formal meeting.

He sighed, and for the barest instant he thought he saw a flash of concern in her expression. If so, it was quickly replaced by a frown that drew her dark brows together in a formidable line. Point for Sidana, he thought.

He'd slipped his phone from his pocket, intending to ring Gemma, when he heard Sweeney's phone's distinctive text tone—the pop of a bottle opener. Then Sidana's postman's bell, and as they were reaching for their phones, the other mobiles in the room began to chirp and chime and whistle.

Then his phone began to vibrate in his hand.

His was not a text, but a call, and his caller ID informed him it was the borough commander, Chief Superintendent Thomas Faith. "Bugger," Kincaid muttered under his breath, straightening automatically, suddenly wide awake.

"Sir," he answered.

Faith's voice was tight. "Possible bombing. St. Pancras International. SO15 is on it, and the brigade, but I want CID there in full force as well. You'll be liaising with DCI Callery from SO15."

SO15. Counter Terrorism Command. Shit.

Kincaid saw that his team was already on their feet, grabbing jackets and bags. "Any other information, sir?"

"No. Just get there. Report as soon as you know anything." Faith clicked off.

It was only then Kincaid remembered that his friend Andy Monahan was meant to be playing a concert in the St. Pancras concourse.

Taking an involuntary step back, Melody coughed and wiped her streaming eyes. For the first time, she was aware of the wail of sirens above the sounds of the crowd.

"Thank God. Help's coming." She turned, wanting reassurance from her companion as much as she wanted to reassure him.

But he was gone. She could still feel the imprint of his fingers above her elbow where he had gripped her arm. "What the—" She shook her head. Later. She'd think about it later. And he'd been right, there was nothing anyone could do for the poor sod in front of her.

Melody stood for an instant, staring at the burned form on the polished concourse floor.

Suddenly she was transported, once again a green PC at the scene of her first major car crash. The occupants screamed as the car burst into flames, and she caught the scent of singed hair and burning flesh on the hot wind. The smell seemed to lodge itself in her nostrils and on her tongue with a greasy permanence. Bile rose in her throat and she lifted a hand to her mouth.

The gesture, instinctive, brought her back to reality with a jolt. The screams were real. That was a child wailing, a woman sobbing. And that squawking sound was the phone in her coat pocket—she'd left it on speaker and the dispatcher was shouting at her.

Fumbling the phone to her ear, she heard, ". . . situation report! Sergeant Talbot, can you—"

"I'm here." Melody made an effort to take stock of the chaos around her. "One fatality. Some kind of explosive device. Multiple injuries. I need—"

"Are there any other incidents?"

Melody scanned the crowd. "Not that I—"

It was then that she saw Tam. He was rolling on the floor beside one of the overturned café tables, and he was on fire. Caleb Hart was beating at the flames with his coat.

"Hold on," Melody told the dispatcher.

As she ran towards them, a young woman came through the doors from the glass-walled interior of the café. She wore the distinctive black uniform of the café's waitstaff, and she carried a fire extinguisher.

"Here!" Melody shouted as she reached her friends. She registered the waitress's white face and pinched lips, but the girl wielded the extinguisher like a pro. The chemical foam covered Tam's midsection and the last of the flames sputtered out.

"Good thinking," Melody told her, kneeling quickly beside Tam. Looking up, she added, "Can you see who else needs help?" The girl nodded and ran towards another victim.

Turning her attention to Tam, Melody touched his shoulder gently. She couldn't judge the extent of Tam's injuries, but he was pale and sweating, his eyes glazed with shock. His familiar battered cap lay on the floor beside him.

"It just splashed on him, from out of nowhere," said Caleb, his voice rising. He looked frightened but unhurt. "I threw coffee on him. It was cold. I didn't know what else to do."

"You did great, Caleb, just right. Now keep him warm while I get help."

She pulled off her red coat and laid it gently over Tam. He looked up, and she saw recognition flare in his eyes.

"Melody, lass." The words came out in a croak. "Hurts like the devil."

"Shhh." She touched his cheek. "Don't talk. I'm going to get hel—"

She started as a hand grasped her shoulder.

"Melody!" It was Andy, with Poppy right behind him. "Thank God you're all right. I was afraid—" He froze as he saw Tam. "Tam. Oh, shit, man. He's hurt. Is he—"

"He'll be fine," Melody said with more assurance than she felt. She gestured to Poppy. "You two, stay with Tam and Caleb." She knew she should make them evacuate. But she knew she'd be wasting her breath if she tried and she didn't have time to argue. "I've got to deal with this." Involuntarily, she glanced at the corpse, and Andy and Poppy followed her gaze.

"Jesus," Andy whispered.

The color drained from Poppy's face and she swayed.

Melody grabbed them both roughly. "Andy. You've got to help Caleb with Tam. Poppy, listen to me." Poppy's eyes came back to hers and the girl swallowed hard. "Poppy." Melody gave her a little shake. "You help with the injured. If they're mobile, gather them there." She pointed to a clear space near one of the concourse pillars. "I need you. Okay?"

Poppy nodded and moved to help the girl from the café, who had set down her fire extinguisher and was trying to comfort the victims.

Andy gave Melody a long look. "You're the boss." He squeezed her shoulder, then knelt by Caleb and Tam. He tucked Melody's coat gently around his injured friend.

The concourse had begun to clear as the panicked crowd moved towards the exits. Most of those that remained were helping the injured or seemed too shocked to function. A few flames still spluttered here and there.

Melody knew she had to secure the scene and move any

uninjured witnesses out of the station and into some kind of containment area. Where the hell was assistance?

The big station clock in the south end of the upper concourse caught her eye—had it really been less than ten minutes since this had begun?

She realized she still held her phone in her hand. As she was about to ask Control for aid once more, she saw two officers wearing the yellow safety vests of the British Transport Police jogging towards her from the south end of the concourse.

She held up her ID and shouted, "CID!"

The younger man reached her first. "You're the detective sergeant?" He was blond and pink-cheeked, a little short of breath.

"Melody Talbot. Look, where the hell is—"

"Oh, Christ," said the Transport officer, echoing Andy, his eyes fixed on the body beyond Melody. "Control said a fatality, but—"

Melody cut him off. "Give me a report. Where's the bloody fire brigade? Uniformed backup?"

"Brigade's on their way," said the older officer, having caught up. "Traffic's completely shut down with the evacuation from the station. We're on lockdown. Transport's armed unit is gearing up while we wait for SO15."

SO15. Counter Terrorism. The enormity of what had happened began to hit Melody. She'd been reacting, not thinking. Now she drew a breath. "Any other incidents?"

"Nothing reported. We're still clearing the station. But we've had to shut down all services, here and at King's Cross as well, including the tube station. It'll be a hell of a mess." His glance strayed back to the corpse. "The bugger blew himself up?"

"Not a bomb. Some sort of incendiary device. Someone"— she thought again of her vanished companion—"mentioned phosphorus. We've got burn victims that need treatment as soon as possible. I'll secure the scene until the senior investigating officer arrives." It was a bit tricky, she knew, as British Transport had jurisdiction in the station. But she was the only CID officer on hand, and she wasn't turning the scene over to anyone but an investigator.

She just hoped that whoever landed the case knew what the hell they were doing.

CHAPTER THREE

The [St. Pancras Old Church] church is situated on Pancras Road in the London Borough of Camden . . . Largely rebuilt in the Victorian era, it should not be confused with St. Pancras New Church about a kilometer away, on the Euston Road.
—*Wikipedia, St. Pancras Old Church*

Even though the March days were lengthening, the drizzle and heavy gray skies had drawn the dusk in early. The flashing blue lights from the phalanx of emergency vehicles gathered round St. Pancras International threw a pattern on the dark red brick of the great Victorian train station that might, under other circumstances, have seemed festive.

To Duncan Kincaid, it looked like disaster.

It had taken nearly half an hour to mobilize cars and drive the short distance from Holborn Police Station. It was rush hour, and the exodus of evacuees from the railway station, combined with the arrival of the emergency vehicles, had slowed traffic to a standstill. The flood of adrenaline in Kincaid's system made the lights look sharp and jagged round the edges and he drummed his fingers on the car's armrest.

Seething with frustration, Kincaid jumped from the car

when they reached Euston Road, taking Jasmine Sidana with him and leaving DC Sweeney behind the wheel.

"Park it somewhere," he snapped to Sweeney. "Up on the pavement if you have to."

Sidana stayed close to his shoulder as they crossed Euston Road and began pushing their way through the crowd on the pavement. Kincaid had been told to meet his SO15 counterpart at the station's east entrance. As they passed the King's Cross/ St. Pancras Underground station, he saw uniformed officers blocking access.

Turning the corner into Pancras Road, they passed the Costa Coffee and another guarded Underground entrance. The north wind hit them full in the face and Kincaid felt once more the stinging of drops of sleet. The east side of the station stretched ahead of them. Kincaid quickened his pace, dodging pedestrians. Sidana broke into a jog in order to keep up with his long stride. They passed the Eurostar taxi drop-off, which was guarded as well.

Ahead, Kincaid saw two fire brigade engines, another cluster of blue-and-yellow-liveried Met cars, and three ambulances. As they drew nearer, he saw people huddled on the pavement, some sitting on their suitcases, watched over by more uniformed officers. They'd reached the station's main entrance.

The press had got there first. Already reporters shoved against the police cordon, video and still cameras held high, microphones to mouths. Good luck with getting any decent sound in this wind, Kincaid thought, but he wondered if they already knew something he didn't.

He and Sidana showed their IDs to the closest uniformed officer, who let them through.

"SO15?" Kincaid asked.

"Just inside, sir," said the constable, motioning towards the glass doors under the main entrance arches.

The first thing that struck Kincaid as they entered the station proper was the warmth. The second was the emptiness.

This central part of the station, bisecting the long north-south concourses, was normally filled with people rushing to and fro between train lines or grabbing food from the various kiosks and markets.

Now there were only British Transport Police, several in full armed-response gear, firefighters, and a few plainclothes officers.

Kincaid picked out Nick Callery, the DCI from SO15, without an introduction. Silvery-blond hair, cut almost to a buzz. Silvery-gray suit, expensive, no tie, no overcoat. He was trim and moved lightly on his feet, like a boxer. As he saw Kincaid, he broke off his conversation with another officer and came towards him, hand out.

"Callery. Counter Terrorism."

Kincaid introduced himself and Sidana, then said, "What's the situation?"

"Far as we can tell, one nutter burned himself to a crisp. White phosphorus, according to the fire brigade. Nothing else suspicious in the station so far, but we're still clearing." Callery had a trace of a northern accent.

"Other injuries?" Kincaid asked.

"Quite a few. The medics are doing triage now."

"Any ID on the victim?"

"Ha." Callery shook his head. "Not bloody likely. You'll see for yourself. I'll take you—he's up by the Marks and Sparks."

Kincaid felt a clutch of dread. That was where the station set up the temporary concert stage. "Was there a band playing? A duo?" Jasmine Sidana gave him a puzzled look.

Frowning, Callery said, "I saw some equipment. Nothing looked damaged. Can't say about any musicians. They may have been evacuated."

Kincaid had not seen Andy or Poppy among those gathered outside the east entrance, but surely people had left by other exits.

"Luckily, there was a DS on hand who secured the scene

until we could get here," Callery added. "The fire brigade will have hazmat gear for us."

"Right." Kincaid nodded. "Let's see what we've got."

The main concourse looked as eerily empty as the market and ticketing area. The glass-fronted shops were lit but deserted. Here and there, a dropped coat or scarf, bits of food stall debris scattered like confetti, a spilled bag of groceries. Outside the Peyton and Byrne tea shop, a chair had been left overturned.

"No luggage left behind?" Kincaid asked Callery.

"There were a few pieces, but we've had the dogs go over them before we locked them in the station manager's office. Funny how good people are at holding on to their belongings in a crisis."

"You were remarkably quick."

"Most of that's down to British Transport. The dogs were already on hand for the Eurostar luggage." Callery gestured towards the upper concourse, where Kincaid could just glimpse a sleek yellow Eurostar train on the departure platform. "The station manager is already pulling her hair out," Callery went on. "It's not just that it's prime time for international arrivals and departures. Any delay on the domestic lines can back up rail traffic all over the country, but we can't reopen the station until we've cleared the crime scene and made certain there are no other mad buggers hiding in the woodshed. A cluster fuck."

Glancing at Sidana as she walked beside him, Kincaid saw her pinch her lips together in disapproval. He wondered how someone who couldn't tolerate profanity had lasted so long in police work. Callery seemed oblivious to her discomfort.

A uniformed British Transport Police dog handler came towards them, his springer spaniel straining at the end of its lead. The dog worked methodically, checking doorways and left or dropped objects.

"Second pass," the dog handler told Callery, stopping for a moment. "Clear so far."

"Can the dog detect phosphorus?" Kincaid asked.

"She's not trained on it specifically," answered the handler. "But she is trained on fertilizer-based explosives, so I think she'd pick up something. And we want to make sure there are no other nasty surprises." As the dog whined in impatience, the handler moved on.

Ahead, Kincaid saw figures in protective gear, moving around a temporary screen. Then, he caught the first whiff of a strange smell. Burned matches and . . . garlic?

A firefighter came to meet them, pulling off his hood and respirator. "Detective." He nodded at Callery and gave Kincaid a questioning glance.

"Detective Superintendent Kincaid, Camden CID." Kincaid still hesitated when he introduced himself. It seemed odd to say "Camden" rather than "Scotland Yard." "And DI Sidana," he added.

"John Stacey, crew manager," said the firefighter, a burly man with short, thinning hair. "The good news is that I don't think we have too much of a hazmat issue here, with the air moving through the station. Most of the smoke has already dissipated."

Kincaid realized that even in the heated lower concourse, the station was bitterly cold.

"I would recommend that the crime scene techs and the pathologist wear protective gear since they are going to have prolonged exposure to the victim. And you three as well if you intend to get up close and personal."

"That smell," Kincaid said. "Was there an explosion in the café as well?"

"You mean the garlic odor? No, that's a component of the white phosphorus. But I don't think you'll want to get too close to the victim without a respirator, contamination or no."

Now Kincaid detected a hint of nauseating oiliness beneath the phosphorus.

"I've got the DS who contained the scene into a suit," Stacey continued. "Is she one of yours?"

"She?" Kincaid shook his head. "No, I don't think so."

"Good job, anyway. Look, I'll get you some suits. You can gear-up by the cash point, just this side of the temporary stage."

The square center of Searcys champagne bar spanned the upper concourse just ahead, and beneath it Kincaid saw the freestanding vertical oblong of one of the station's cash machines. The stage must have been really close to the incident, then, but he held his concerns about Andy and Poppy until he could see for himself.

Stacy spoke into his radio and another firefighter brought them three Tyvek suits.

When they had done the always-awkward dance of slipping into the suits and booties, Stacey handed them the respirators and led them forward.

Beyond the stairs leading up to the upper concourse, he could see firefighters and ambulance service medics assisting the injured and setting up stretchers. Then he saw what lay behind the temporary barrier and all other thoughts fled.

"Jesus."

Beside him, Sidana gave a little gasp, audible even through the respirator, but this time it was not because she was offended by his language. They both stared at the thing on the floor.

"Told you," said Callery, but without satisfaction.

It was not the first time Kincaid had seen a body consumed by fire—the blaze in the Southwark warehouse flashed through his mind, as well the horrible events in Henley the previous autumn. But there seemed something particularly obscene in the contrast between the charred corpse and the gleaming perfection of the station.

Callery had referred to the victim as male, but Kincaid wasn't sure anyone but the pathologist could be certain of the gender.

A smaller, suited figure moved away from the body and came towards them. "Here's your sergeant," said Callery.

Beneath the suit hood and the respirator, Kincaid glimpsed dark hair and familiar blue eyes. He shook his head in disbelief. "Melody?" His voice was muffled by the respirator.

Grasping his arm, she squeezed it, relief visible even beneath the mask. She motioned back the way they'd come and the others followed.

When they reached the cash point, Melody yanked off her respirator and pulled back her hood. Her face was smudged, her eyes red rimmed. "Duncan! I'm so glad it's you. Somehow I hadn't realized—"

"I take it you two know each other," broke in Nick Callery, as they all removed their masks.

"Mel— DS Talbot works on a South London team with my wife." Kincaid turned to Sidana. "Melody, this is my DI, Jasmine Sidana."

Melody started to extend a gloved hand, thought better of it, and gave Sidana a shaky smile instead.

"You were here for the concert," Kincaid said, light dawning.

"I saw it happen." Melody's eyes were wide. "I mean, I saw him burn. I tried to help but it was too late."

"You're sure it was a man?" asked Kincaid.

Melody hesitated, frowning. "I think so, yes. I saw his outline in the flames. It never occurred to me to think otherwise."

Checking a text on her phone, Sidana said, "We'll know soon enough. The pathologist and the SOCOs are here. Sweeney's bringing them in."

"Melody," Kincaid said. "Andy and Poppy, they're all right?"

"They're fine. They were great—they helped clear the crowd. But, Duncan—" She swallowed and went on. "Tam and Caleb were here. Standing outside the café, not twenty feet from him. People got splashed with phosphorus. Tam got burned. The medics are getting him ready for transport now. I think it's pretty bad."

As Gemma drove down St. John's Gardens, she saw their friend Wesley Howard's white van parked across from their house. He'd left her the empty parking space nearest the front door, bless him. And she had to admit, as she pulled up and got out of the car, that the weather was too miserably cold for humans and animals alike. Even in her puffer coat, she shivered and pulled the collar up to her chin. It was already dark, and the lights gleaming from the front windows of the house radiated welcoming cheer.

But when she unlocked the front door and stepped in, the house was remarkably quiet. No dogs barked or came to greet her, nor were there any of the expected childish shrieks. Usually—especially when Wes was there—everyone would be gathered in the kitchen and something good would be cooking. Were they all still out in the garden, in the dark, trying to rescue the cat?

Then she heard a sound, and Toby came round the corner from the central hallway in an exaggerated tiptoe, finger to his lips.

"Shhh, Mummy. Bryony says we have to be really quiet, and only one person at a time can go in to see Xena or she'll be scared."

"Xena? Who's Xena?"

"The mummy cat. I named her," he added proudly. As Toby neared his seventh birthday, his fascination with pirates had mutated into an obsession with old episodes of *Xena: Warrior Princess*.

Gemma sighed. "Where's Charlotte?"

Just then their foster daughter came running from the hall and wrapped her arms round Gemma's legs in her usual greeting hug. Gemma picked her up and kissed her cheek.

"How's my favorite girl?" Gemma whispered into her curly hair.

"Mummy, there are kittens!" Charlotte squirmed down and grabbed Gemma's hand. "Come and see."

"Shhh," said Toby, scowling.

"Wes says Toby is bossy."

"If they gave medals for bossy, Toby would get one," Gemma agreed, but she kept her voice to a whisper. "Okay, where's Xena?"

"In the study with Bryony," said Kit, coming into the room with Wesley. Gemma had yet to get used to the fact that in the last few months, Kit had grown almost as tall as Wesley, who was now in his mid-twenties.

"I'll take you, Mummy," whispered Toby.

"Gemma's perfectly capable of finding her own way to the study," said Kit.

"Kit, don't snipe," she scolded, but gently. He still looked pale and strained about the eyes. "Why don't you all go into the kitchen and make a pot of tea?" she suggested, thinking that what she would really like was a nice glass of wine, feet up, and the telly on.

She let Toby and Charlotte lead her to the study, then very gently nudged them back and eased herself in the door.

"Hey," Bryony said softly, smiling up at Gemma from where she knelt on the study floor. Her deep auburn hair gleamed in the light from the shaded desk lamp. Beside her, tucked partway under the desk, was a large pasteboard box.

"Hey, yourself." Gemma knelt beside her. Bryony was not only their veterinarian but a good friend. "What have I got myself into?" She looked into the box, then breathed, "Oh. My."

The cat was a brown tabby. A white blaze ran down one

side of her nose and splashed onto her chest and belly. All four paws were white as well. She lay on her side, looking content-edly up at Gemma and Bryony with gold eyes. Four tiny kittens were lined up to her belly, nursing, like a row of little mice.

"She's so thin," Gemma whispered. "And the kittens are so young."

"I'd say they're not more than a couple of days old. And that mum here was close to starving. The boys did a good thing. I'm not sure she'd have lasted the night."

"She just let you pick her up?"

Bryony nodded. "I took a carrier and put the kittens in first. She's very tame. She must have been someone's pet."

"Well, she got around a bit, didn't she?" said Gemma, ex-amining the kittens more closely. One was a tabby, like its mother. One was black and white, one as black as Sid, and the fourth was calico. "Maybe Toby wasn't too far off with the name. Warrior princess, indeed."

Gemma contemplated the logistics of making sure the smaller children didn't let Sid or the dogs into the room. "We need an airlock."

There was a scratching noise at the door. "Mummy," came Toby's plaintive voice. "Mummy, when are you coming out? Your tea's ready. I want to see the kittens."

"Tea?" said Bryony, stretching and standing.

"Not much repayment for this," Gemma told her. With a last brush of a fingertip on the first kitten's head, she stood as well.

"Not at all." Bryony grinned. "It got me out of giving in-jections to Mrs. Scherzer's bulldog, which looks like Winston Churchill and has the disposition—and the gas—to match. Oh, Gemma, one more thing," Bryony added as they reached the door. "As I said, she's very tame. Before the children get too attached to her, we'll need to make sure she's not micro-chipped."

Gemma stopped with her hand on the doorknob. "Chipped? Oh, damn, I hadn't thought of that."

"If she is someone's pet, they may be looking for her. You'll have to reunite her with her owners."

In that instant, Gemma went from wondering how she was going to manage a stray cat, with kittens, to contemplating the horrifying prospect of telling the children the cat belonged to someone else. "Bugger. That's a good thing, I suppose," she said, but without conviction.

Bryony clapped her on the shoulder. "All's well that ends well. In the meantime, your boys have saved her and her kittens from freezing to death."

In the kitchen, Gemma gathered Kit and Toby to her in one-armed hugs, all they would tolerate. "You two are very kind and very resourceful. Bryony says you probably saved the kitties' lives."

Toby puffed up like a little blond penguin. "But," Gemma went on before Toby had a chance to brag. "Don't make a habit of breaking and entering, all right? I might have to arrest you. Next time you hear something crying, you call me first. And as it is, I'll have to have a word with the communal garden committee about the damage to the shed." She gave them another squeeze and let them go. "What smells so heavenly?"

Wesley was stirring something in a pot on the Aga. His ready grin lit his dark face. "I brought you some of Otto's famous Russian stroganoff from the café. And Kit has the makings of a salad, I think." Since they had met Wesley in the course of a murder investigation two years previously, he had worked part-time at Otto's café in Elgin Crescent, just off Portobello Road. The youngest of five children, he still lived at home with his mother, Betty, while attending business college.

Wes and Bryony had been friends when Gemma met them,

but in the past few months their relationship seemed to have developed into something more intimate.

"Tea," Bryony said, pulling mugs from the rack and lifting the steaming pot. "I could murder a bloke, me matey, for a good cuppa." She flourished a mug at Toby, who giggled and danced away.

Bryony added milk to the mugs and poured for herself and Gemma.

"I want tea," said Charlotte. She sat at the kitchen table, her legs swinging, drawing a pink blob that Gemma suspected was a cat. She coughed a little, but it wasn't the hacking of last night. She looked better, too, her blue-green eyes bright, her café-au-lait skin almost rosy.

Bryony poured her a mug of milk and added a splash of tea. "There you go, sweetie. Good for what ails you." She picked up the remote for the kitchen television. "Let's just see how cold it's going to get tonight, if you don't mind."

Glancing at the clock, Gemma saw that they'd just catch the end of the six o'clock news.

"Gemma." It was Kit, his voice hesitant. "Look." He pointed at the breaking-news banner scrolling across the television screen.

Focusing on the screen, Gemma caught "Explosion" and "St. Pancras International." She grabbed the remote from Bryony's hand and turned up the sound. The perfectly groomed news presenter looked seriously into the camera as she said, ". . . an incident at St. Pancras International railway station has closed all traffic through the station at this time. There are reports of an unidentified explosion and injuries, but we have yet to ascertain the extent of the damage." The camera cut to the Gothic front of the station and the St. Pancras Renaissance Hotel, eerily illuminated by the flashing lights of emergency vehicles.

Only when Gemma felt the kitchen chair beneath her did she

realize Bryony had guided her into it. The broadcast switched to the weather, but no one was paying attention.

"Andy was playing," whispered Gemma. "Andy and Poppy. Melody was going to the concert. And St. Pancras—that's Duncan's patch."

CHAPTER FOUR

Mary Shelley, the author of *Frankenstein,* used to rendezvous with Shelley next to her mother's tomb to plan their elopement, Dickens recalls wandering through the churchyard, and Blake placed the site on his mystical map of London.
—*Matt Shaw, kentishtowner.co.uk,*
"Why It Matters—Saving
St. Pancras Old Church"

Melody had never been so glad to see anyone. She almost gave in to the urge to hug Kincaid, although she was not a hugging person. But her relief lasted only until she had to tell him about Tam.

"Where is he?" Kincaid asked.

She gestured towards the triage area. "Andy and Poppy are with him."

"I'll be right back," Kincaid said to DCI Callery and, pulling his respirator back on, headed towards the triage area.

Callery glanced at Kincaid's back, then gave Melody an assessing stare. "Who the hell are Andy and Poppy? And Tam when he's at home?"

Melody noticed that Callery's eyes were the same silvery

gray as his hair and his suit. She wondered if the clothing co-
ordination was vanity or happenstance, then chided herself because she didn't seem able to discipline her random thoughts.
"Andy and Poppy are the band," she answered, trying to collect
herself. "They were playing when the . . . device . . . went off.
Tam is Andy's—the guitarist's—manager. They're—we're—
family friends."

"What were you doing here?"

She was tempted to say that she had just as much right to
walk through the station as anyone else, then wondered what it
was about the man that made her feel so stroppy. "I'd come for
the concert. I'd just got here when it happened."

"You ran towards the fire."

Melody wasn't sure if it was a criticism or a commendation.
"I did my job."

"Did you see anything—or anyone—else?"

"I—"

Sidana, Kincaid's new DI, interrupted her. "Sorry. But the
SOCOs are here."

Turning, Melody saw two crime scene techs, already suited,
and a plainclothes officer she didn't recognize. He wore a long
camel-hair overcoat that looked too snug on his overly muscu-
lar frame.

Behind him, wearing a familiar black leather jacket and carrying a bag, was Rashid Kaleem, the Home Office pathologist.
Kaleem was one of a dozen pathologists on the rota for Greater
London, but Melody had worked with him often enough to
consider him a friend. They'd met during the case in East London that had brought Charlotte to Kincaid and Gemma.

Rashid flashed her his brilliant smile. "Melody, what are
you doing here?" he asked as he pulled a sealed Tyvek suit
from his kit. "Surely this isn't South London's case?"

"I just happened to be here. But what are you—"

"Duncan rang me." He slipped on the blue crinkly suit with

practiced ease, then the shoe coverings. "Asked if I was on call. So what have we got?"

"Crispy critter," said one of the crime scene techs. "Better you than me, mate, having to deal with the remains."

Kincaid returned to the group. He wasn't wearing his respirator, and his face was grim. He nodded to the pathologist. "Rashid, thanks for coming." To the others, he added, "The brigade crew manager says he thinks we can do without the respirators now. This concourse is a wind tunnel. And I've had the station manager on the phone. We need to get this scene cleared. ASAP."

As they walked back towards the corpse, Kincaid said to Melody, "Can you tell me exactly what happened?"

"I was late. Andy and Poppy were already playing. I stood at the back. Then, there was a whooshing sound—no, wait." Melody frowned. "No, that's not all." The scene came back to her jerkily, like rewound film. She coughed and cleared her raw throat. "I saw some protesters. Half a dozen, maybe. Over there." She pointed towards the Marks & Spencer. "They had placards but I couldn't read them. I remember thinking what a nuisance. I didn't want them to spoil Andy and Poppy's show, and I didn't want to have to deal with them. Officially, you know. Then I saw a British Transport officer, a woman, and I thought, okay, her job. I remember feeling relieved. I looked away and that's when I heard it. The sound. A whoosh like the gas burner on a hot-air balloon. Then the screaming started." She realized she was shivering as she finished. Rashid gave her a concerned look.

Nick Callery picked up the questioning. "You didn't see the victim before the fire?"

"I looked that way. I saw Tam and Caleb, standing in front of the café. They had coffees. I could tell they'd been sitting, but they'd stood up to see the band, pushing back their chairs. They didn't see me." Melody rubbed her face. "No, wait. That was before I saw the protesters. The sequence is all jumbled. But I don't remember anyone standing out when I looked in that direction . . . Maybe the cameras picked him up."

"I've already got someone running through the station's feed," said Callery, and Kincaid shot him a look.

Melody wondered just exactly who was in charge here.

The techs marked a perimeter and began taking photos. The flashes made Melody feel a bit dizzy. "I don't know how much we'll get here, considering there have been thousands of feet tromping through the space since it was cleaned last night," said the talkative tech to Rashid, who had taken out his own camera. "But let us have a pass at it before you get up close and personal." The tech turned to Melody. "Did you touch him?"

"No." She shook her head. "No. He was still burning in places. And he was—it was obvious it was too late to help him . . ."

"How close did you get?"

She tried to think, but it was such a blur. Five feet? Ten? Where had they been standing, she and her helper, when they'd broken through the throng and seen the body? "About there, I think." She pointed to a spot.

"Did anyone else go close to him?"

Melody shook her head again, suddenly reluctant to describe her companion. Had he been real? She wanted to see the CCTV footage for herself before she said anything. Nick Callery had stepped away and was speaking urgently into a radio.

"We'd better take some trace samples from you, just for elimination," said the tech. He had a round face, the shape emphasized by the suit's hood and his stylishly shaved red-blond stubble. "I'm Scott, by the way." He gave her a friendly grin and she smiled back, a little shakily.

"DS Talbot."

"Sit tight, DS Talbot, and I'll get back to you," Scott told her, with another quick smile.

Melody wondered where he thought she should sit and almost laughed. She really was feeling odd.

"Tell me more about these protesters," said Kincaid as Scott and his colleague continued to mark and photograph, while Rashid prowled the perimeter with his own camera.

"They were facing the band, so their backs were to me. I got the impression that they were all Caucasian, except for one girl, who might have been Asian." Melody paused, trying to recreate the scene. "They were all wearing winter gear, hats and jackets. One bloke was tall—he stood out above the others. I remember thinking that their placards looked homemade, and that they were hoping to get the attention of any media cameras here for the band."

"We'll need any media footage," Kincaid said to Nick Callery. "And we'll hope we got bystanders out before they uploaded the entire scene to Twitter or Instagram. Were any of the press held with the evacuees?"

"I'll check." Callery got on his radio again.

To Melody, Kincaid said, "Did you see any of them after you saw the victim burning?"

"No. No, I never looked back that way. It was chaos, and then the smoke . . ." The memory seemed to trigger her cough.

"Dr. Kaleem," called Scott. "You can have a go now."

They all moved in a little closer as Rashid approached the corpse. "DS Talbot," said Scott, "can you tell us how far the phosphorus splattered? The radius will help us determine exactly what was used."

"Far enough to burn the people sitting outside the café, obviously. But everyone else was moving. Rolling or running away. I'm sorry not to be more helpful."

Scott nodded. "The range of a white phosphorus grenade is about twenty-five feet. We're going to need a bigger team," he added, glancing at Callery and Kincaid. "There's no way we can process this scene without more manpower."

"On it." Kincaid turned to Jasmine Sidana and murmured instructions.

Rashid was crouching now over the corpse, his blue Tyvek suit made bulky by the leather jacket underneath.

"Is the victim male?" Kincaid asked, impatience evident.

"Judging from the facial bones, probably," said Rashid. "Parts of the shoes are left . . . hiking boots, I'd guess, a fairly large size. But the hands are gone. And the center of the torso . . ." He used a probe, carefully. "The body contracted, of course, but I'd say he was holding the device at waist level, more or less."

"Any ID?"

Rashid glanced back at Kincaid. "Bloody hell, Duncan. This guy is toast. I'll be lucky to get teeth. Although"—he prodded again with the probe—"there does seem to be some fabric remaining underneath him. It might have been somewhat protected by his torso. A backpack, maybe? There's not going to be much more I can tell you until I get him on the table. We'll need a gurney to get him into the van." He stood and rejoined them, pulling back his hood.

"If you're finished with me for the time being, I need to check on Tam," said Melody. "And, oh, God, someone has to ring Michael and Lou—" She tried to draw a breath and began to cough. Michael was Tam's partner, Louise their next-door neighbor and closest friend.

Rashid peered at her, then stripped off his glove and took her wrist, pressing his fingers on the pulse point. "Melody, you look like hell. You're white as a sheet, and your heart rate is sky high." He gave her hand a pat and let it go, but gently. "How much of that smoke did you breathe?"

"I covered my face." *It's bloody phosphorus,* she heard in her head, and the blue handkerchief flashed in her memory. "I tried to cover my face," she said aloud. It came out almost as an apology. "I didn't have a bandanna."

"You're going to hospital."

She'd never heard Rashid use that tone of command.

"What? But I— Tam—"

"No buts." Rashid turned to Kincaid. "It's toxic, the smoke from white phosphorus. She needs to be monitored. And she needs oxygen. Now."

"But—" Melody tried again to protest, but she felt woozy.

A firm hand grasped her elbow. "I'll take her to the medics." It was the officer Kincaid had introduced as DI Sidana. "Steady," said Sidana. Then, more softly, "It's Hindi, the word *bandanna*. Did you know that? The root of the word means tie-dyeing."

Melody knew when she was being managed and she wasn't having it. "I'm fine, really. I—"

A squawk came from Nick Callery's handheld radio and they all turned.

Callery listened, murmured something Melody didn't catch, then clicked off.

"That was British Transport," he told them. "One of their officers has a witness who says she can identify the victim."

"Where is she, this witness?" Kincaid asked Callery.

"Down at the market concourse. They've got some coffee going, and a warm place to sit."

"Sidana, I want you to stay here," said Kincaid. "Make sure DS Talbot gets the medical care she needs, and oversee the scene."

"But, sir. I should be in on the interview. I'm second in command—"

Kincaid stepped away from the others and jerked his head for Sidana to follow. "It's precisely because you are my second in command. I need someone here that I can depend on. Sweeney's perfectly capable of taking notes on the interview and I'll fill you in afterwards." More softly, he added, "Look, Sidana, I'm not sure what's going on here with SO15. I want someone from our team on the scene until I know who has jurisdiction. Clear?"

"Sir." Sidana nodded. She didn't look happy, but she didn't seem inclined to argue further, which was an improvement.

"Rashid," Kincaid added, "you'll let me know as soon as you have anything?"

"Of course. But right now I'm going to deal with the living." He put an arm round Melody's shoulders and steered her towards the triage unit.

Kincaid motioned to Sweeney and they both followed Callery, who had already started back along the concourse. Taking advantage of the brief chance for privacy, Kincaid made two phone calls.

The first was to Gemma. "I'm fine," he said when she answered. "Andy and Poppy are fine. Melody needs some observation in hospital for smoke inhalation. But Tam was pretty badly injured. I don't know if Andy will have called Michael and Louise. Can you do it?"

"Which hospital?"

He hadn't thought to ask. "I don't know. UCL is the closest A-and-E. But Tam, at least, may need to go to the burn unit at Chelsea and Westminster."

"Don't worry. I'll find out," said Gemma. He could hear the kids in the background, the little ones clamoring to speak to him. Gemma shushed them. "What about Doug?" she asked. "He should know about Melody."

"I'll ring him. More soon," he said as he caught up to Callery. "Love you," he added softly, then rang off.

Callery raised an eyebrow. "Girlfriend?"

"Wife."

"Ah. The long-suffering little woman. Keep your supper warm, will she?"

"I doubt it." Kincaid felt a wave of irritation. "She's a DI. Brixton. Look, I've got to make one more—"

His own phone interrupted him. It was Doug Cullen. "What the bloody hell is going on?" Doug said before Kincaid could speak. "I saw it on the news. Where's Melody? I know she was going to be there. She's not answering her bloody phone and I—"

"Slow down, Doug. I was just going to ring you. She's okay, but she's going to need to be checked out. Probably at UCL A-and-E. She'll fill you in. Got to go." He clicked off.

They'd reached the market concourse.

"The manager of the Starbucks opened up for us," said Callery. "He's serving up coffees to the officers. And the witnesses."

Two women sat at a table inside the curved glass wall of the Starbucks. One was in British Transport Police uniform. Her cap lay on the table, and her brown hair, which must have been loosely pinned up beneath the cap, was falling in strands about her face.

Seeing them, she jumped up, said a quick reassuring word to the other woman at the table, and came out to meet them. Her expression was intelligent, her manner competent. "I'm PC Rynski. Colleen."

Kincaid introduced himself and Sweeney. "And this is DCI Callery, from SO15. That our witness?" He nodded at the woman in the shop, who had put her face in her hands.

"Yes, sir. Her name is Iris. She hasn't given me a last name."

"Can you give us a little background?"

Rynski took a breath and brushed hair from her eyes. "I was on duty in the concourse. The band was playing. I saw a group with placards. I thought they might be disruptive. I'd just begun to move them towards the exit when the grenade went off."

"You're sure it was a grenade?" asked Callery, his tone sharp.

Rynski looked at him, face expressionless. "I was in the military. Two tours in Afghanistan. I know a WP grenade when I see one. Sir."

"Then what happened?" Kincaid urged, not wanting to lose this officer's cooperation.

"It was my job to get people out. It's toxic, white phosphorus, and I didn't know what else might happen. It was bloody chaos in the concourse, people running every which way and shouting. This group bolted for the street, signs and all. I didn't think about them again until I saw her"—she nodded towards the girl in the shop—"crying outside. She'd better tell you the rest."

PC Rynski led them inside. "Iris, these are the policemen who need to speak to you."

The young woman looked up. Her face was so swollen and splotched from weeping that Kincaid couldn't tell if she might be pretty. Her blond hair showed two inches of dark roots and wasn't particularly clean, and he could see, even with her bulky coat, that she was a bit overweight.

"Hi, Iris." Kincaid pulled out a chair and sat down. Callery followed suit, and at a glance from Kincaid, Sweeney sat down behind and to one side of the witness, just out of her line of sight.

When Rynski started to excuse herself, Iris gave a hiccupping sob. "Don't leave me," she pleaded.

After a questioning look at Kincaid, Rynski pulled up a chair as well.

"Iris," Kincaid began, "it sounds like you had a really bad day. Would you like some more coffee? Something else hot to drink?"

"Could I—could I have some hot chocolate?" The girl's teeth were chattering.

The manager, who had been unobtrusively wiping down the serving counter, came over. He had a goatee, and despite the cold, was wearing a short-sleeved T-shirt that showed off the colorful tattoos on his forearms. "Can I, you know, get you anything?"

"Hot chocolate for the lady." When Sweeney started to open his mouth, Kincaid shot him a quelling glance. "Thanks."

"What's your last name, Iris?" he asked as they waited for the hot chocolate. A machine behind the counter hissed loudly in the now-quiet station.

"Bark— Barker. Iris Barker. I know it's old-fashioned, but with all those shows on the telly these days—the historical ones—it doesn't seem so bad."

The manager brought the steaming hot chocolate in a paper cup. Kincaid pulled a few banknotes from his wallet.

"Oh, it's on the hou—," the manager began, but Kincaid was already shaking his head. "For your trouble," he said, handing over the notes.

"It's a pretty name," he told Iris, although at the moment he couldn't imagine anything less flowerlike than this girl, cupping the hot chocolate with pudgy, cold-reddened fingers, oblivious to the new tears streaking her mascara-stained cheeks.

"I was bullied at school." Iris hiccupped again and gingerly held the cup to her lips. "Barking pansy, they called me. Might have been funny if I'd been a boy."

"Can you tell us what happened today? You were protesting something?" Kincaid asked as she took another sip of the chocolate.

" 'Save London's History.' That's our slogan. Do you know how much damage is being done by the Crossrail project? Why do we need another rail route running right through Central London? There are twenty-six miles of new tunnels. That means ruins dug up without proper archeological supervision. Pre-Roman artifacts, even. All so that people can get somewhere faster. And can you imagine what else could be done with the sixteen *billion* pounds it's costing?" Iris's voice vibrated with indignation. "Things that might really help people? We thought we might get some media coverage, you know, because of the band. People need to know."

"Who's we, Iris?"

The girl's brief animation flickered out. "We're just . . . a group. We're not anything official. We care about London's history, that's all," she added, jutting her chin out with a bit of attitude.

Left-wing radical fringe? Kincaid wondered. "Save London's History" could translate into antiprogress, anticapitalist, even antipolice. "How many of you are in this group?"

"It depends." Iris shifted in her chair. "People, sort of, you know, drift in and out."

"You had placards, right?" Kincaid noticed that while Sweeney was looking bored as he took notes, Nick Callery was listening with quiet interest. "Is that how you meant to get attention?" he went on.

Iris nodded, then bit her lip. "Yeah. And—we—uh—"

"You what, Iris?" he prompted when she didn't go on.

Her eyes welled with tears again and she looked at PC Rynski. "It was—it was supposed to be a little smoke bomb. To get people to listen to us. It was Matthew's idea. Everything is always Matthew's idea." The words were spilling out now. "But Ryan said he'd do it. He said he'd been arrested before, so it didn't matter if he got into trouble. The rest of us would still have clean records."

"Arrested for what?" asked Nick Callery.

"Protesting. Things like the nuclear power stations, you know. Real stuff."

"And Ryan had the smoke bomb?"

Iris gulped and nodded.

"Who gave it to him?" There was something in Callery's tone that made her look away from him, back to Kincaid, as if she might find more understanding there.

"Matt— Matthew." Iris pushed her half-drunk chocolate away and folded her arms across her chest, rocking a little bit. "We—we never meant for anyone to get hurt. And I can't think how something could have gone wrong . . . I still can't believe it. Ryan's . . . dead? Are you sure it was Ryan?"

"We're not sure of anything," said Kincaid. "Where was Ryan supposed to set off the smoke bomb?"

"Across the concourse from us. By the entrance to the taxi rank. We ran when people starting screaming. Everyone was pushing and shoving. We didn't expect such a panic. I got separated from the others. Then, when I got outside, I heard someone say a man was on fire, and I couldn't leave without knowing . . . And then people were saying he—that he—that the man—was dead—burned—and I couldn't—" Iris was crying again. PC Rynski patted her arm, a little awkwardly.

"What's Ryan's last name?" Kincaid asked.

"Marsh. Ryan Marsh."

"And you say Ryan's been in some big protests? Is he about your age?"

Iris shook her head. "No. He might even be, I don't know, thirty." The emphasis on the last word made it sound as if thirty were ancient. "But he's cool. Cooler than anyone. And he's—he was—nice to me."

Kincaid glanced at Sweeney, making sure he'd gotten the last name. Nick Callery was already typing it into his phone.

"What di—does Ryan look like?"

"Sort of—ordinary, I guess," Iris said, but she smiled. "About as tall as you"—she nodded at Callery—"with hair about the color of yours, maybe lighter." Another nod, towards Kincaid. "Blue eyes. Not too thin like Matthew the scarecrow. He keeps his hair short. Sometimes he grows a little stubble but I've never seen him with a real beard."

Kincaid translated all this as average height, average weight, light brown hair, blue eyes. Not entirely helpful.

"What was he wearing today? Do you remember?"

"Oh, the usual. Jeans. Boots. A heavy dark hoodie. Blue, I think. I told him he'd be cold, but he never seemed to feel it." Iris frowned. "And he must have had his backpack, because he never goes anywhere without it."

"Any distinguishing marks?" asked Callery.

When Iris didn't answer, Kincaid added, "You know, like tattoos? Or birthmarks?"

She shook her vehemently. "Ryan hates tattoos. He's always warning us we might get infected or something."

"Birthmarks, then?"

Flushing, Iris said, "Not that I ever saw."

"Did Ryan have any family we could contact?" Kincaid asked.

"No. There was—no, he never said."

"Do you know where he lived?"

Iris looked at him blankly. "With us. I thought I said."

Glancing at Callery, Kincaid said, "You mean with your group?"

"Yeah." She wiped her sleeve across her nose and sniffed.

"Where?"

"Oh, just up the Caledonian Road." She jerked her head towards King's Cross. "Not half a mile from here."

CHAPTER FIVE

St. Pancras Old Church is one of the oldest sites of Christian worship in Northern Europe. The churchyard is the resting place for the remains that were exhumed when the Midland Railway was built in 1866. The railway ran through an extensive graveyard, and the Vicar of St. Pancras insisted that the remains be respectfully removed and re-interred. The job fell to a junior architect—Thomas Hardy. 8,000 remains were relocated in all, many to the churchyard at St. Pancras Old Church. You can see the relocated headstones which were placed around an ash tree, which has become known as the Hardy Tree.

—*camden.gov.uk/parks*

Kincaid hadn't realized that he'd grown accustomed to the relative warmth of the railway station until he stepped outside. The bitter March wind hurled itself down Pancras Road, snatching the breath from his mouth in passing and seeking every slight gap in his clothing.

Callery had ordered a car to take them to the address in the Caledonian Road. And an armed response team as backup.

An unmarked silver Vauxhall nosed past the police cordon

and pulled in at the curb. Nick Callery got in front with the driver, leaving Kincaid to take the backseat with a shivering Iris Barker.

"I shouldn't have told you," she said as the driver began to inch the car through the crowd gathered outside the cordon. Reporters shouted questions, then held their mics towards the car, but Kincaid doubted they could see much through the tinted glass. "Matthew and the others, they're going to kill—," Iris began, then stopped, perhaps realizing that was not the best metaphor. Then she shook her head. "But—Ryan—someone had to say. We couldn't just leave him, not knowing . . ." Iris fell silent again, chewing her lip.

The driver turned north on Pancras Road, away from their destination, and Kincaid knew he would have to snake through the backstreets in order to work his way round the one-way system. It would, under more clement circumstances, have been much quicker to walk.

Before leaving the station, Kincaid had sent a sullen Sweeney to help DI Sidana with the witness statements. Then he and Nick Callery had Iris stay with PC Rynski while they stepped outside Starbucks's glass-walled enclosure and argued over the use of the response team.

"We're going in with an armed unit to tell these people their friend is more than likely dead?" Kincaid said. He wasn't averse to calling in armed response when the circumstances dictated it, but he wasn't convinced they did. "Surely just uniformed backup would be sufficient. It might have been suicide. Or at worst, accidental death."

"Aren't you the Pollyanna. These people," Callery said pointedly, "may have meant to blow up a good part of St. Pancras station. As it is, mystery man managed to injure a good number of people, including your friends, and disrupted the whole bloody rail system during rush hour, for God's sake."

Kincaid dug in his heels, even though he knew that Callery

was right, and that he was skating on jurisdictional thin ice. "We're not even certain that the victim really is a member of this group. Or that Iris is telling the truth about who they are or where they live. Or, if she is, that any of the rest of her group will be there."

After a moment, Callery shrugged. "We'll go in, then, the two of us, with Weeping Myrtle here." He nodded towards the café.

"It's Moaning Myrtle," Kincaid corrected, feeling a flicker of surprise at Callery's Harry Potter reference. He didn't seem the fantasy type. And somehow he couldn't imagine that this man had kids.

"Whatever." Callery shrugged. "But I want the armed unit on hand. Agreed?"

"Agreed. And I'll set up uniformed backup to arrive a few minutes behind us. We're going to want to take the protesters in to Holborn station for interviews, but I want to get a feel for the group on their own patch first."

Once in the car, they'd crossed and recrossed the Regent's Canal and were now heading south again on the Caledonian Road, back towards King's Cross/St. Pancras. As close as they were to the railway stations, the gentrification that had been promised to the area more than a decade ago had not reached this little stretch of road. Kincaid saw a sad shop advertising ADULT DVDS and wondered what delights the videos could possibly hold that couldn't be found on the Internet for free in five minutes.

There was a wine shop, a hostel, a Thai takeaway, and an Internet café—the last a sure sign that the area catered to the disenfranchised.

"There," said Iris as they reached another small strip of shops. "It's this terrace. Above the chicken takeaway."

As the driver pulled into the curb, Kincaid saw a ratty shop selling gym equipment, its windows dark and covered with iron grating. Next to it was a radio car service, and then a bright red sign proclaiming HALAL CHICKEN AND CHIPS.

They exited just as a number 10 bus roared by, sending up an arc of dirty, slushy water. Kincaid shielded Iris, then took her arm, steadying her. He looked up at the building. A three-story terrace, it was the most derelict of any Kincaid had seen in the road so far. With its dark gray-brown brick and windows trimmed in peeling white paint, it looked as if it might be Georgian. Kincaid whistled under his breath. This would undoubtedly be, at some point, prime real estate.

An unmarked van pulled up behind them and sat, lights off, engine idling. Kincaid turned Iris away. There was no point in alerting her to the presence of the armed unit, and he'd just as soon she didn't see the panda cars arrive, either.

Light shone from the second-floor flat. "Is it the second floor, your place?" Kincaid asked Iris.

She nodded and shrank deeper into her coat.

"All of you live here?"

"Well, it's really Matthew's. He knows someone who lets him live here. It's that door," added Iris, pointing to a peeling entrance on one side of the chicken takeaway. Light came from the transom as well.

Nick Callery had stepped away and spoken quietly into his radio, but now he rejoined them and said, "Let's have a word with your friends, then, shall we?"

The door was sturdier than it had looked from a distance, and the lock was both new and expensive. "Who lives on the first floor?" Kincaid asked as Iris fumbled in her pocket for her key.

"Some university blokes. Matthew doesn't like it because they smoke in their flat and the stairwell." Her key clicked and the door swung open.

The entry and the stairwell did smell of smoke, with a faint undertone of mildew and urine. But both were, if slightly shabby, surprisingly clean.

Kincaid deliberately left the door off the latch for uniformed backup, or, God forbid, the armed response team.

They climbed silently, Iris leading the way. The first-floor flat was dark and quiet, and Kincaid thought he could hear his own heart pounding.

When they reached the second-floor landing, Iris stopped, holding another key from her key ring in her hand. Kincaid sensed her indecision—she would, he guessed, normally unlock the door and walk in. But how could she walk in unannounced with two policemen?

Voices came from inside the flat, one indistinct, one louder, nearer the door.

"What the hell happened in there? Can someone tell me that?" The louder speaker was definitely male, and agitated. "And where the hell is Iris, the silly cow?"

Iris flushed, unbecomingly.

"I think that's our cue," said Kincaid, and he knocked, solving Iris's dilemma.

The door swung open, revealing a very tall, thin young man with a head of curly dark hair. "Iris, what the hell—," he began. Then he stopped, staring, as he took in Kincaid and Callery. "Who the—"

"Matthew, they're policemen. It's about Ryan." Iris's voice shook on the name and Kincaid gave her a gentle nudge forward so that they all stepped into the room, making the young man called Matthew move back. Kincaid was scanning the room as he entered, and he could sense the tension in Callery's body as he did the same. They left the door standing open behind them.

Kincaid was sure Matthew's voice was the louder one they'd heard from outside on the upper landing. There were four other people in the room—a young bearded man, standing, who Kincaid guessed had been the more muffled speaker. Another young man and two girls sat on a sofa, startled expressions on their faces. None of them looked potentially threatening.

Nor did the flat fit his definition of the squat he had expected. There were some mattresses and folded bedrolls on the floor, but there was also the sofa, a charity-shop dining table with mismatched chairs, and against the back wall, a large flat-screen television.

And the flat was clean. Scrupulously so. There wasn't a fast-food wrapper or even a dirty coffee mug to be seen. A few clean dishes sat in a rack in the kitchen alcove at the far end of the room.

A doorway beside the kitchen alcove led into what looked like a small bedroom.

The television was on with the sound muted, footage of the crowds and the emergency vehicles outside St. Pancras station scrolling across the screen.

"What about Ryan?" said the man called Matthew, eyeing them warily. Although Kincaid put him in his early twenties, he already had the slight rounding of the shoulders that Kincaid sometimes saw in very tall men. His long face seemed all planes and angles, his expression intense.

Kincaid introduced himself and Callery, then said, "We understand you were demonstrating in the St. Pancras arcade this afternoon." There was no sign of the placards and Kincaid wondered where they had been ditched.

"We had a protest. So what?" There was worry behind the belligerence in Matthew's tone.

"We understand from Iris here that one of you set off what was meant to be a smoke bomb as part of the protest."

If looks could kill, Matthew's glare would have slain Iris on the spot. Still, he hesitated before admitting it. "Yeah. Ryan. It was Ryan's idea. He thought we'd get some attention from the media."

Kincaid nodded towards the television screen. "I'd say you got considerably more than that."

One of the girls on the sofa stood and came towards them. She was painfully thin, with dyed black hair and black-painted fingernails, but there was a sweetness to her face that belied the halfhearted attempt at Goth. "They said someone was—that there was a—a fatality. And Ryan hasn't— We don't know where he—" A look from Matthew stopped her. She shoved her hands into the opposite sleeves of the droopy black sweater that hung on her thin frame like a shroud.

"What's your name?" Kincaid asked, ignoring Matthew for the moment.

"Trish."

"Do you have a last name, Trish?"

"It's—Hollingsworth." Her accent, like Iris's, was decidedly middle class.

Matthew, on the other hand, had the unmistakable drawl of a prep school boy. Doug Cullen, who had done his best to disguise the fact that he had gone to Eton, would have recognized it instantly. What were they playing at, these privileged kids? Kincaid wondered.

"Iris," said Trish Hollingsworth, "where were you? Where's Ryan? What happened?"

"They—they think it might be Ryan that's dead." Iris's words ended on a wail.

"That's bullshit," said Matthew. "Nobody was supposed to get hurt. Ryan knew what he was doing." He scowled at Kincaid and Callery. "Unless you lot did something to him."

Callery spoke for the first time. "What's your name, sonny? And don't mess me about."

"What is this? Good cop/bad cop?" Matthew sneered.

"You haven't begun to see bad cop, so don't tempt me, son." There was a menace in Callery's voice that made Matthew step back.

"Quinn," he said grudgingly. "Matthew Quinn. But I don't see what business it is of yours—"

"Matthew!" It was the other girl, a delicate young woman with Asian features. She came off the sofa with her hands balled into fists, the force of her voice at odds with her small stature. "Just shut the fuck up, will you?"

She crossed the room to Iris. "Is it true?" she asked, her voice shaking.

Iris nodded. "I didn't see. But something terrible happened, and he's not here. Ryan's not here." She looked beseechingly at the others, as if someone might tell her differently, but no one spoke.

The girl's face twisted in grief. "Oh, God. No. Please, no." She put a hand to her mouth and swayed.

Just as Kincaid reached for her, fearing she might collapse, they heard the bang of the downstairs door and the stomp of police-issue boots on the stairs.

"I think," said Kincaid, "that it might be a good idea if we all had a talk down at the station."

They had not got the group into the waiting panda cars without considerable protest from Matthew Quinn.

He was the last to be escorted down the stairs, once he'd locked the door. Turning back, he'd said to Kincaid, "You'll see about this, you and your jackbooted thugs. I'll call my—" Then he'd stopped, clamping his mouth shut.

"Your lawyer?" Kincaid asked. "You have a lawyer, do you? Now that's interesting. Why do you need a lawyer?"

But Quinn had refused to say anything else, and Kincaid decided that he would interview the rest of the group, and separately, before he spoke to Quinn again.

But before he talked to anyone, he wanted to see what had been pulled from the CCTV footage at St. Pancras station.

And all assuming, of course, that SO15 didn't hijack the protesters.

Nick Callery walked away from the idling cars, phone pressed to his ear. After a brief phone conversation, he returned to Kincaid and said, "Your place it is, then, at least for now. My guv'nor's not convinced it's SO15's party. We'll wait and see." He did not sound pleased.

Kincaid had already put in the request for a search warrant for the flat. "We'll see what we turn up once we can get a team in there. Let's hope there wasn't a bomb factory in the bedroom."

"Bunch of bloody amateurs if you ask me," Callery grumbled as they got back in the silver Vauxhall and the driver pulled out into traffic ahead of the panda cars.

"Better than professionals," Kincaid said with feeling, and they made the rest of the trip in silence.

The concrete fortress of Holborn Police Station seemed much more welcoming than it had when Kincaid had left it late that afternoon. It promised warmth, and smelled of stale coffee rather than burned flesh.

Once inside, he had a word with the custody sergeant first thing. "I've got six witnesses coming in, three male, three female. Put them all in one room, but keep an officer in with them. I don't want them comparing stories or using their phones. I'll pull them out one by one."

Then he and Callery went up to the CID suite. There was a hum of activity he hadn't felt before today. The case manager for major incidents, Simon Gikas, had already started a whiteboard with a time line and some of the SOCO photos.

"Sidana and Sweeney not back yet?" Kincaid asked.

"On their way in," answered Gikas. "They've left the rest of the statements for uniform."

Gikas and the rest of the team were eyeing Callery with interest.

"This is DCI Callery from SO15," Kincaid said. "We'll be coordinating until we see what sort of incident we have here."

"Do you think we've got some sort of nutter, boss?" Gikas had dark, wavy hair, and his olive skin was indicative of his

Greek heritage. The name, of course, afforded the team much amusement, and even though Gikas had explained innumerable times that the "g" was pronounced as an English "y," to most he was simply known as Geek. It was perfect for a case manager, who needed to be logical, technical, and organized.

Kincaid sensed a sudden wariness in the room. Homicide considered SO15 the cowboys, the coppers who didn't have to play by the rules. Nor would his team want to invest too much in a case that might be taken away from them if SO15 decided it was their turf. "Too early to say." Kincaid's noncommittal shrug was as much for Callery's benefit as the team's.

He walked over to the whiteboard and examined the photos with as much dispassion as possible, trying to shut out his sensory memory, which was distorted by shock, as well as his worry over his friends. What hadn't he seen?

The charred corpse gave him nothing back but the rictus of a grin.

"Boss." Gikas motioned to one of the monitors. "We've pulled some CCTV footage from right around the time of the incident."

As Gikas hit Play, Kincaid was very aware of Nick Callery moving in beside him, watching the screen with frowning concentration.

It took Kincaid a moment to orient himself to the first camera angle. It was south facing, covering the arcade between the Marks & Spencer and the south entrance to the terminal. The time stamp started at five minutes before Melody had made the call to Control.

The crowd swelled and thinned, swelled and thinned, making Kincaid think of deep sea plants moving in unseen currents. Then some of the passersby slowed and stopped, all turning to face towards the center of the arcade, and Kincaid realized they must be watching Andy and Poppy. A few seconds later, Melody appeared at the edge of the camera view.

She just as quickly vanished offscreen, and he assumed she'd moved closer to the band.

Then he saw Matthew Quinn come out of the Marks & Spencer and join the stream of shoppers and commuters. Even with a woolly hat covering most of his hair, his height made him unmistakable. In gaps in the crowd, Kincaid recognized the others he'd met at the flat.

The group coalesced in front of the Marks & Sparks, causing the crowd to part around them. There was Iris, and with her were the Asian girl and the bearded young man. Trish Hollingsworth stood beside the ordinary-looking bloke with the glasses and the goatee who had been sitting on the sofa with the girl who'd challenged Quinn. He was carrying a flat case that might have been an artist's portfolio. The group huddled around him as he opened it, and a moment later they all raised placards.

The camera caught several of the signs full on. They were printed in clear block lettering, but were obviously not professionally made. SAVE LONDON'S TREASURES said one, NO CROSSRAIL said another, and a third had CROSSRAIL marked with the universal NO symbol.

The protesters looked alert and rather full of themselves, not as if they knew one of their members was about to burn himself to a crisp not more than a few dozen yards away.

Just as they started to pump the placards up and down and chant what looked like "No Crossrail," Colleen Rynski appeared. She gestured towards the exit. Matthew argued with her, waving his free hand. Rynski spoke into her shoulder mic and put her hand on the baton at her belt. She jerked her head towards the exit.

After glancing at Matthew, the group began moving in the direction she'd indicated, still halfheartedly holding up their signs. They disappeared from the camera view.

The time counter on the tape ticked onwards. Twenty seconds. Thirty seconds. Then, suddenly, all the heads in the crowd swiveled as one, mouths opening in shock or horror. People began running, shoving, dropping parcels and shopping bags. Within a few seconds, smoke as thick as pea-soup fog obscured the view.

"It's five minutes before the smoke begins to clear," said Gikas. "Do you want to see more?"

Kincaid realized that everyone in the room had gathered round, watching in silence. "Not now," he answered. "Have we got a view of the victim?"

Gikas tapped keys and another camera angle appeared on the screen. "It's not great. He must have known where the cameras were."

Now Kincaid saw the other side of the arcade. There were Tam and Caleb, standing by one of the café tables, looking towards the temporary stage. He saw Tam smile, and Caleb lift a mug to his lips.

"There." Simon Gikas pointed a pencil at a figure who appeared just at the edge of the screen, a man carrying a lightweight backpack and wearing a hoodie. At least Kincaid assumed the figure was male. The clothing was dark and slightly bulky; the hood was pulled forward so that it shadowed the face and covered any visible hair. The figure appeared to be of medium height compared to the other passersby.

The figure stopped, but did not look towards the band. His head moved—might he have been searching for the group on the other side of the arcade?—but he didn't turn his face to the camera. Then he stood for a long moment as the crowd ebbed and flowed around him. His right hand was in his pocket. Kincaid felt a jolt of dread and an urge to reach out, to stop the action from unfolding.

The crowd around the figure thinned, cleared. The figure took his hand from his pocket but his grasp obscured the object he held. He looked up then, but the hood still shadowed his face.

Then he brought his hands together, and a moment later, fire blossomed between them.

"Sweet Jesus," muttered one of the detective constables. Kincaid heard an intake of breath from someone else behind him as the flames billowed up in a great ball, engulfing the figure.

For an instant, it looked as if the man's arms rose up in the flames. He might have been a conjurer, casting a spell, or a great bird about to take flight. Then the cloud of smoke obscured all.

CHAPTER SIX

The graves, like the corpses they bear, are jumbled; a frantic mass of jagged stones that break the earth as fractured concentric circles, imposing the macabre on an otherwise peaceful area of the churchyard. Bodies lay upon bodies, graves upon graves.

—*Jamesthurgill.com,*
The Hardy Tree, St. Pancras
Old Church, London

Sidana and Sweeney came in as the video finished. "Absolutely bonkers," said Sweeney, shaking his head. "A bloody human candle. Do you think he felt anything?"

Kincaid was glad enough to have Sweeney break the mood in the room. "I hope not. But there's no way he's going to tell us, is there? Did you come up with anything?" he asked, including Sidana in the question.

Sidana flipped open her notepad. "One woman reported a giant invisible flying saucer appearing in the arcade, then blasting off in a heavenly cloud," she reported, straight-faced.

"Meds?" Kincaid asked with equal gravity.

"Um, Valium, and some kind of antipsychotic. She couldn't remember what it was called."

"Well, that's not surprising." Kincaid wondered what it would take to get his DI to crack a smile. "You can watch the tapes, but if it was an invisible alien ship, I doubt you'll be able to see it."

There was a titter in the room, but Sidana didn't join in. He hadn't meant to make her the butt of a joke, only to relieve a little of the tension in the atmosphere. "You'll need to enter your notes for Simon to process, but in the meantime I want you with me on the interviews."

"Sir?"

He explained about the six protesters. "You'll need to watch the CCTV tapes first, spaceship or not. You can do that while I get the interviews set up." Frowning, he thought for a moment, then said, "I want the girls first." He glanced at Nick Callery, who hadn't said a word since they'd viewed the CCTV footage. Callery looked a little green. "Are you going to sit in?" Kincaid asked.

Callery shrugged. "I think I'll watch from the viewing room. I can let you know if something pops up for me."

"What about me, Guv?" said Sweeney.

"You can keep DCI Callery company. Call down to the Custody Suite and have the sergeant set up Interview Room One. Let's start with the Asian girl."

Other than Iris, she was the only one in the group who had shown immediate and obvious grief.

Kincaid took the opportunity to shut himself in his office and ring Gemma. "Any news on Melody or Tam?" he asked when she answered.

"Doug rang. He was on his way to UCL A-and-E to see Melody. And I talked to Michael. Andy and Caleb both had already rung. He and Louise were on their way to Chelsea and Westminster. Hang on a sec, can you?" she said. He heard the sound of a door closing softly. "I couldn't really ask before, with the kids in the room. Tam—how bad is it?"

"I don't know." Kincaid rubbed at the now-well-past-five-o'clock shadow along his jaw. "All I can say for certain is that he was burned and that the medics were working him over pretty thoroughly. They'd given him morphine and had him on oxygen." Thinking back, he realized he'd have to watch the video again to see if he could work out exactly what had happened to Tam—the victim had been between him and the camera.

"Was he conscious?"

"Yeah. He recognized me. Squeezed my hand." Kincaid cleared his throat.

"I feel useless," said Gemma. "I'd at least go and check on Melody, but I can't leave the kids."

"Wes—"

"He's working at the café tonight, although he did bring us dinner first." She sighed. "I just keep thinking—if Melody had been any closer . . ."

"Don't. And it's a good thing she was there. More people might have been badly hurt if she hadn't had her wits about her. Bloody brave, what she did. But don't tell her I said so."

Gemma chuckled, which had been his intent. He imagined her smiling, brushing a stray strand of hair from her face, and suddenly wished very much that he was home. "I'll need to interview Melody formally," he said, "but it will probably be tomorrow. I don't hear the sounds of chaos," he added. "What did you do, shut yourself in the loo?"

"How did you guess?"

"I know them too well. How's the littlest angel?"

"Better. Angelic."

"Give her a kiss for me. I'll be—"

"Late. I know," Gemma said with resigned affection. "You'll be careful?"

"I'm back at the station." It was a nonanswer. He knew she would know it, and that she was asking about more than his safety. "Don't worry, love. I think this was a one-off. I should know more soon. But don't wait up."

"Duncan." Gemma stopped him as he was about to ring off. "Um, when you do get home, the children have a little surprise."

"What? Toby set the house on fire?"

"Not quite as bad as that." There was laughter in her voice now. "Don't let the dogs in the study. Toby and Kit brought home a cat. With kittens."

While Jasmine Sidana started the interview recorder and identified the two of them for the tape, Kincaid studied the girl across the table. She wore an oversize sweatshirt and a down vest that she'd refused to take off even though the interview room was warm. In the utilitarian surroundings, she looked even more fragile than she had in the flat.

"Why don't you tell us your name for the tape," he asked.

Her dark, arched brows drew together in a frown. "Cam Chen. It's not short for Camilla, so don't ever call me that." She ruined the effect of her statement a bit by sniffing.

Kincaid nodded. "Point taken." He'd meant to wind her up, wondering if her reaction to Matthew Quinn at the flat was a normal response for her. Apparently, she was inclined to be pugnacious.

"Right, then, Cam. Can I call you Cam?"

She nodded. "I suppose."

"Where are you from?"

The brows drew closer together. "Wimbledon. But I live here, in London."

"In the Caledonian Road?"

Cam shrugged. "I have a room at uni—UCL—but I don't like it. The flat's better."

"What are you studying?"

After a moment, Cam said grudgingly, "Social anthropology."

"Lots of job opportunities, are there?"

"Fuck you." She glared at him. "My parents are dentists. Both of them. They get up and go to the same boring office and do the same boring thing. Every single day. Why would I sign up for that?"

Kincaid could think of a number of reasons. A nice home. Financial security. The ability to send their kids to university. And maybe they liked what they did. But he didn't say any of those things. Instead, he asked, "So, are you studying the social dynamics of a protest group?"

It had been a shot in the dark. To his surprise, Cam Chen flushed and looked away. He waited, watching her pick up her cup of canteen tea and set it down again.

"It's my graduate thesis," she whispered.

"Do they know?" Kincaid asked.

Cam's flush deepened. "God, no. Matthew would throw me out in a heartbeat."

"Does anyone else know?"

Cam shook her head.

"How did you get involved with the group, then, if you're not a believer in the cause?"

"I didn't say I didn't believe. I do. Crossrail sucks. Why spend all that money to move more people through London? And all that green stuff Crossrail says they're doing? Bullshit. A cover-up for corporate greed. That's who benefits from projects like this—the contractors and the developers. They add on little things like 'creating nature preserves' just to fool the public." Cam was sitting forward now, grasping her cup tightly. "They say they're only going to destroy one listed building. Do they really expect us to believe that?"

"How do you know all this?" Kincaid asked.

"Matthew knows people." Cam sounded less sure of herself.

"People in other groups?"

"Well, yeah."

"You didn't tell us how you got involved with all this. Which came first, the thesis idea or the group?" Kincaid could sense Sidana's impatience.

Cam hesitated, then said, "The group. I was in a class with Matthew. When he talked about his agenda, he was so . . . intense."

"You fancied him?"

"No way." Cam made a face. "I was just . . . bored."

"Matthew's a student?"

She shook her head. "He was. Structural engineering. He dropped out."

"No job?"

"No. He seems to manage okay."

Kincaid wondered if Matthew Quinn was selling drugs. From the look of the flat, he doubted that any of them were users, but that didn't rule out dealing.

"Is that how the rest of the group came together—from university?"

"Some. Trish lost her job when Crossrail tore down the shop she worked in. We were picketing and she talked to us. Matthew felt sorry for her. Or he said he did. Ryan said Matthew likes people to think he's kind. Ryan—" Her face crumpled. "Why are we talking about Matthew when Ryan—when you think Ryan's dead?"

"Tell me about Ryan," Kincaid said. "How did he come into the group?"

Cam rubbed the back of her hand across her eyes, then took a sip of her now surely cold and scummy tea. "It was in the summer," she said, her voice shaky. "Matthew was at an anti-nuclear protest at Islington station, handing out leaflets. You know trains carrying highly radioactive spent fuel rods use the North London line?"

Kincaid didn't, actually, but he nodded.

"Someone introduced him to Matthew. Matthew told him all about Crossrail and he was interested. He started coming round the flat. He—knew stuff."

"What sort of stuff?" Kincaid said when she hesitated.

"About protesting. How to organize things. Properly. You know." Cam shrugged. "After a while, he started staying over."

"He wasn't a student, then?"

"No way. He'd been around, Ryan had. Protested against Hinkley Point on the anniversary of Fukushima. Lots of other important things." Frowning, she added slowly, "I did wonder, sometimes, why he bothered with a small group like us, but he said it could be big, what we were doing."

"Do you know anything else about him? Where he came from? Any family?"

"No. Ryan didn't talk about things like that. And you didn't ask him."

"Can you give us a description? Age? Height? Coloring?"

"Why? Can't you just—" Cam went pale. "Oh, God."

"Just tell us," Kincaid said gently. "The first things that come to mind."

"He's"—Cam swallowed and sipped again at the tea—"he's, I don't know, thirtyish. Medium height. Fit—more than the rest of that lot, except maybe Matthew. Brown hair—light brown, like he might have been blond as a child. He kept it short. A stubbly beard, you know? Just a shadow, most days. Blue eyes, really blue. And—he doesn't—didn't—smile very often, but when he does it's like the sun coming out." Tears began to run down her cheeks. "I feel sick. Who's going to— won't someone have to identify—I still don't believe it. Ryan would never do something so—so stupid."

"Tell me about today," Kincaid said. "The smoke bomb— was it Ryan's idea?"

"No. It was Matthew. Matthew thought we hadn't been

getting enough media attention. They argued. We all argued. But Ryan convinced Matthew that if we were going to do it, he should be the one, because if anyone got arrested, he already had a record."

Iris had said the same. When he glanced over at Sidana, he saw that she was scribbling a note.

"But it was Matthew who had the smoke bomb?"

"Yeah. He showed it to us. It was a canister, about this big." Cam held her hands a little more than a fist's length apart. "It was a sort of camo green and had SMOKE stenciled on it."

"Did Matthew say where he got it?"

"From somebody he met at a protest. There's all kind of stuff that floats around, you know?"

Kincaid did, unfortunately. Talking to Matthew Quinn was going to be interesting.

"What was the plan, then?" he asked.

"We timed it with the band playing. Some new duo. It was the opening event of the music festival, and we knew there'd be cameras. Ryan went early, so he could be in place. Then, when he saw us get out the placards, he was going to set off the smoke."

"And what did you think would happen then?" Kincaid had to make an effort to keep the disbelief from his voice.

"We thought—Matthew thought—that it would be bonkers. That Ryan would slip away in the smoke. And that we would get on the news. We wouldn't claim any connection or anything, but we'd get some press."

Kincaid wondered if Cam Chen had given any thought to what her suburban dentist parents would think when they saw her on the news. He said, "Did you see Matthew give Ryan the smoke bomb?"

"I—no." Cam suddenly looked frightened and more child-like than ever. "They were in the bedroom. In the flat."

"So Matthew could have given Ryan anything."

"No!" Cam pushed her chair back so fast it squeaked on the

tile floor. "You can't think Matthew meant to hurt Ryan. Matthew may be a wanker, but he would never do that."

"Do you have any reason to think that Ryan might have meant to hurt himself?"

"I— No. Of course not. It had to have been an accident."

But Kincaid had seen the hesitation. He waited, willing Jasmine Sidana not to speak or even breathe.

"He—no, he wouldn't." There was a plea in Cam's statement. "Surely he wouldn't."

Kincaid leaned across the table, just far enough to invite a confidence. "But you think it's just possible he might have. Why?"

"He— He hadn't been the same since Wren left."

"Who was Wren?"

"A . . . Just a girl. Another one of Matthew's charity cases. She wasn't part of the group, although she went along with the protests and things. She was homeless, and Matthew gave her someplace to live. She was grateful."

Again, Kincaid waited.

"Ryan liked her," Cam said, reluctantly. "He was different with her."

"Were they lovers?"

"I—I don't know. Not in front of the group. But I always thought . . ." There was a wistful note in her voice.

"Did you fancy him? Ryan?" asked Sidana, with such sympathy that Cam gave her a startled glance.

"We all fancied Ryan. All the girls. And all the blokes wanted to *be* him. But we couldn't . . . reach him, somehow. And Wren did."

"What happened to Wren?" Kincaid asked.

Cam shifted in her chair. Her hand jerked, her cup tipped, and the scummy tea spread across the table like a brown amoeba. "Oh, God. Sorry." She looked round wildly for something to mop the spill.

There was a box of cheap tissues beside the recorder—

handy for weeping witnesses. Sidana pulled out a wad, blotting the tea while Cam made an effort to help.

"Cam." The command in Kincaid's tone made the girl sit back, dropping her hands into her lap. "What happened to Wren? Tell me." He couldn't read her dark eyes.

Kincaid thought she wasn't going to answer. But she said at last, "It was at the New Year. She left. She didn't come back."

CHAPTER SEVEN

Hardy's biographers speculate how far this gruesome experience may have deepened the writer's tendency to see the skull beneath the skin of life.

—*Simon Bradley,*
St. Pancras Station, 2007

Doug Cullen hated hospitals. He'd never really given them much thought until a broken ankle in January had precipitated his first—and so far only—overnight visit, although continued complications had made him overly familiar with the outpatient clinic. His ankle's refusal to heal had kept him, almost two months later, confined to desk duty.

And he was still in a boot cast, which made getting round on the tube not as easy as he would have liked. He'd walked from his house in Putney to Putney Bridge tube station, then changed trains twice, so his ankle was aching when he reached street level at Euston Square tube station. Stepping out of the glass vestibule, he flinched at the bitter blast of the wind.

When he looked east down Euston Road, he could see the traffic still backed up between Euston and St. Pancras station. What a mess. And for Melody to have been in it—

Shuddering, he turned the other way, gazed up at the glass-and-steel hulk of University College Hospital, and limped across Gower Street.

The emergency entrance was easy enough to find. Gaining admittance turned out to be a different matter. It took showing his warrant card to the dragon on reception to get him through the door into the A&E's inner sanctum. A harried but more helpful nurse at the charge desk directed him to a curtained cubicle.

He hesitated, but there was no place to knock, so he pulled the edge of the curtain aside and peered in. Melody was propped up on a gurney, still, he was relieved to see, in her street clothes. A gaping hospital gown would have sent him into a paroxysm of embarrassment.

She had an oxygen cannula in her nose. Her face was soot smudged and her eyes red rimmed, but otherwise, she looked alert. And irritated.

But her face lit up in a smile when she saw him. "Doug. What are you doing here? How did you—"

"Duncan told me. I wanted to make sure you were all right. No sad flowers, though," he added with an apologetic shrug.

Melody grinned at the reminder of the rather pathetic bouquet she'd brought him when he'd broken his ankle. "Sit." She pointed imperiously at the one plastic chair in the cubicle and he saw that she had an oxygen sensor on her index finger.

He sat gingerly, not wanting to jostle any of the intimidating bank of equipment behind the gurney. "I thought you might be able to use some help getting home. Or at least moral support," he added, gesturing at his ankle, "since I'm not so great on the physical support. I spoke to Gemma, too. She'd have come except she has the kids."

"I'm not going home." Melody's voice was tight. "They say I have to stay overnight. They'll move me to a room as soon as one's free."

"But you seem fine." He glanced at the oxygen machine, bubbling gently in the background.

"They're concerned about damage from the smoke inhalation. White phosphorus is highly toxic, apparently, and they have to test my blood levels. They haven't said what they'll do if the results aren't good." Melody blinked and reached for the cup of water on the cart beside the gurney.

Doug tried to remember when he'd seen Melody look frightened. She was the one who seemed to charge into everything head-on, and always left him envying her confidence.

"I'm sure you'll be fine," he said a little too heartily.

"Yeah. Me, too." Her smile this time was uncertain. "We're neither one of us very good at this, are we? The hospital reassurance thing."

They were an odd couple as far as friends went. Thrown together by their respective bosses, Kincaid and Gemma, during a case, they had disliked each other instantly. He had thought her cavalier and arrogant, she had thought him—as she'd told him more than once—a self-righteous prick. Gradually, they had come to an uneasy détente, and then, to their mutual surprise, had begun to develop something more complicated, a sort of friendship that neither of them, loners by nature, had expected.

"I'd say that was a good thing," Doug responded now. "The lack of practice. Um, can I get you anything?"

"I suspect they'll supply a toothbrush, and I don't intend to be here any longer than necessary."

"Shall I ring your parents?"

"Oh, God, no." Melody looked more distressed than she had at the prospect of her possible medical complications. "The last thing I need is my father barging in and expecting everyone here to jump to his command. And God forbid he sees me on the news feeds."

Kincaid had told him only that Melody needed to be checked out at the A&E. "What? Why would you be on the news—"

The cubicle curtain swung open. Doug turned, expecting a nurse or a doctor, but it was Andy Monahan. Pale and disheveled, he looked worse than Melody. "Doug." Andy held out a hand.

Doug stood and shook it. "Andy."

Now there was an awkward thing. Doug hadn't been sure his friendship with Melody would survive her relationship with Andy Monahan. Not that he didn't like Andy—he just couldn't quite get his head round the fact that they were—no, he didn't even want to go there. He could feel himself flushing, and he hated the little nagging spark of jealousy.

But if he'd had any doubts about the couple's feelings for each other, he only had to see the way they looked at each other across the sterile cubicle.

"You want to know why she's worried she'll be on the news?" Andy asked. He shook his head at Doug's offer of the chair and moved to the side of the gurney, where he rubbed at a smudge on Melody's forehead. The gesture seemed more intimate than a kiss. "Did she tell you what she did? She ran *into* the fire. She tried to help the nutter who set himself alight. She could have been—"

"Andy. It's my—"

"Job," Andy finished for her. "I know. But somehow I never thought . . ."

Reaching for Andy's hand, Melody gave it a squeeze. "How's Tam?"

Andy sank into the chair he'd refused as if his knees had suddenly given way, but he didn't let go of Melody's hand. "The burn is painful, but it can be treated. But they say white phosphorus burns can cause serious organ damage. And that they won't know, maybe for days, how bad it is."

The look Melody shot Doug made it clear she didn't mean to tell Andy that they were keeping her overnight to check more than the effects of smoke inhalation. "Michael and Louise?" she asked.

"There. But Tam's in ICU, so they're taking turns with the allowed visits. Louise refuses to go home, so I've said I'll pop in to look after the dogs."

Tam and his partner, Michael, a landscape designer, lived in the flat adjoining that of Louise Phillips, the solicitor who had been Charlotte Malik's late father's partner. The three had formed an odd little family, stronger than most Doug had seen that were related by blood.

"If anything happens to Tam . . ." Andy didn't finish the sentence. He looked from Melody to Doug, then said, his voice shaking with anger, "How could someone do something like that? *Why* would someone do something like that?"

Kincaid had had Jasmine Sidana and Sweeney interview everyone else except Matthew Quinn, while he watched with Nick Callery from the viewing room. Sidana had done a good job. They had all told the same story as Iris, that Matthew had bought the grenade at a protest.

Their stories had been consistent in other respects as well— they all thought it was a smoke bomb; Ryan had offered to set it off; they had only meant to attract some attention for their cause; and they had never meant to hurt anyone, least of all Ryan.

All, except for Trish Hollingsworth, were former or current university students. Dean Gilbert, the young man with the glasses and the goatee who had carried the placards, had been studying advertising. Lee Sutton, the bearded boy, computer science. They all lived in Matthew's flat, apparently on his generosity, as none of them seemed to have regular jobs.

Nor, apparently, did Matthew. When Kincaid and Sidana had settled across the table from him in the interview room, Kincaid asked, "How did you manage to get the flat in the Caledonian Road? It's not exactly a squat."

Quinn shrugged his bony shoulders. "I don't have to tell you."

Kincaid kept his tone conversational. "You feed that lot, too? Must be pretty expensive."

"I have some money," Quinn said grudgingly after a moment. "And they get a bit here and there from their families, most of them. Not that it's any of your business."

Kincaid noticed that, contrary to his earlier belligerence, Quinn hadn't asked for a solicitor. He wondered why.

"So, tell me about the smoke bomb," he said. "Whose idea was it?"

"Mine." There was a hint of pride there, even after the day's consequences.

"But you must have got the idea from somewhere."

Quinn shrugged again. "Lots of protests use smoke bombs."

"So somebody suggested it to you."

"No."

"Was it Ryan Marsh?"

"No. I told you." Quinn shifted, as if trying to adjust his large frame to the ordinary-size chair. His knees bumped the underside of the table. "We might have talked about it. I don't remember. Ryan's done lots of cool stuff."

"Were you trying to impress him, then?"

"No," Quinn barked at him. "He thought it was stupid. But I was—I thought—" For the first time, Matthew Quinn looked near tears. "I said we should do it anyway. I don't understand how this could have happened."

"You were absolutely sure the grenade was just smoke?"

"Of course I was sure," he spat at them. "Why would I have thought otherwise? It was labeled, and I'd seen videos . . ."

Sidana leaned forward, managing, with the slightest twitch of her mouth, to convey utter disbelief. "How could you be certain that what you saw on a video was what you bought?"

Quinn didn't answer.

"Where did you get it?" Kincaid asked.

Quinn looked like he might balk again, then he muttered, "Just from some bloke."

Kincaid raised an eyebrow. "Name?"

"Man, I don't remember. It was just some guy I met at a demo. I had no idea what I was going to do with it at the time."

"It was just something to keep around the house, like a blender?" Sidana's sarcasm was cutting.

"No. No— It was— I'd seen them used in protests. I just wasn't sure when would be the right time."

Happy enough to let Sidana play bad cop for the moment, Kincaid made an effort to keep his tone neutral. "What made you decide that today was the right time?"

"The band. It was the band. We knew there would be media there."

"Christ," Kincaid muttered under his breath, earning him a surprised glance from Sidana. If Andy ever heard this, he'd take the responsibility for Tam's injury on himself.

"I read something online about how to deploy a smoke bomb," Quinn added, sounding pleased with himself.

"So that will be in your browser history?"

Quinn looked at Kincaid as if he'd said something incomprehensible. "But you can't look at my computer—"

"Oh, yes, we can." Kincaid couldn't help feeling satisfaction at Quinn's obvious dismay. "It's part of the search warrant. Every computer in that flat will go to forensics, and nothing is ever really erased. You know that, don't you?"

"But you never said anything about a search warrant," Quinn said stubbornly.

Kincaid glanced at Sidana, saw her looking just as perplexed. "Matthew." He leaned forward, making certain he had eye contact with Quinn. "Can I call you Matthew? There has been a death. A very painful and unpleasant death, whether accidental, suicide, or homicide, and injuries, some of them severe, to other people. You admittedly acquired the device responsible. Of course we will be searching your flat. And we will be holding you—all of you—here until we have some answers."

"Could anyone really be so clueless?" Kincaid asked as he and Sidana entered the CID room, followed by Nick Callery and DC Sweeney.

Sidana frowned. "He's like a little boy playing at terrorist."

"Doesn't make him any less dangerous," said Callery. "And I think he's not nearly as gormless as he makes himself out to be."

"He still didn't ask for a lawyer," Kincaid added. "Is it because he's decided to go with the 'little boy lost' act?"

Nor had any of the others, even when informed they were being held overnight. They simply might not have the resources or be aware that they could ask for a public defender, but he wasn't convinced either of those things was true of Matthew Quinn.

"We have twenty-four hours," Kincaid told the team as Simon Gikas joined them. "Less than twenty-four hours," he added, glancing at his watch, "to come up with something that will allow us to hold them longer. I want to know everything there is to know about Matthew Quinn. And the others.

"We won't get the search warrant until first thing in the morning. I want everyone to be fresh, so do the best you can tonight, but get some rest." He turned to Callery. "Do you have an update on St. Pancras?"

"The trains are running again. But that area of the arcade is still cordoned off and will be guarded until forensics has been over every molecule." Callery sketched them a salute. "I'm off. Things to do, people to see." He sauntered out.

Kincaid raised an eyebrow but didn't comment. It was after ten o'clock. The station had been closed for almost five hours.

It could take days to sort out the train delays that would affect not only all of Britain but spill over into Europe.

To Simon, he said, "I want someone going over the CCTV footage as far back as necessary. The victim didn't appear from out of nowhere. He has got to be on camera at some point, and I want to see his face. Simon, can you organize—"

"Boss," Gikas interrupted. "I've come across something very odd. They all claimed this Ryan Marsh was a well-known protester who'd been arrested at demonstrations, right? Well, there are no arrests recorded for any Ryan Marsh. Nor am I seeing a Ryan Marsh in the public databases that looks like a good match for the description of our victim."

Having assigned everyone a task, Kincaid walked out of Holborn Police Station and stood, shivering against the wind, irresolute. This was turning into such a bizarre case, and he really wanted someone to chew it over with. By the time he got home, Gemma would—at least he hoped she would—be asleep, the children tucked in their beds.

He supposed he could have requisitioned a car, which would, this time of night, have got him home faster than the tube. Or he could take a taxi, but that idea didn't suit him, either. He wanted time to think.

His phone rang. An irritation, unless it was Gemma or news of Tam.

But when he checked the caller ID, he saw that it was Doug Cullen, and then he knew exactly what he needed.

"Where are you?" he asked before Doug could speak.

"Euston Road. I've left the hospital."

Kincaid checked his watch again. "Look. There's just time and you're not far. Grab a taxi and meet me at a pub in Lamb's Conduit Street. It's called the Perseverance." He hung up without giving Doug a chance to argue.

It was a short distance, even walking, and Kincaid was

there first. The triangular frontage of the pub rounded the corner of Lamb's Conduit and Great Ormond Streets. Warm and unpretentious, during the day the pub was often filled with doctors and staff from Great Ormond Street Hospital, but this late on a Wednesday night it was quiet.

Kincaid had come to like it in the weeks he'd been working at Holborn, although he'd discovered that most of the coppers preferred the pub a bit farther along the street, the Lamb.

Having also acquired a fondness for the American Sierra Nevada beer the pub kept on tap, he ordered a pint at the bar while he waited for Doug. A glance at the chalkboard menu made him realize, suddenly, that it was hours since he'd eaten and that he was starving.

"Anything left to eat?" he asked the barmaid, a pretty young woman whose name he hadn't learned.

"Sorry. The food's off at ten. Kitchen's closed." He must have looked desolate, because after a moment she added, "Look. There's some steak pie left. I can pop it in the microwave for you, but there won't be any chips."

"Pie is just fine. More than fine." He grinned at her and she smiled back.

"Right, then. Back in a tick."

There was a blast of cold air as the door opened, and Doug Cullen said, "Charming the girls, as usual," as he came up to the bar beside him.

"Well, I managed food." Unabashed, Kincaid clapped him on the shoulder hard enough to make Doug wince.

"What are you drinking?"

"Ale from the Wild West of Colorado. Have one on me when the barmaid comes back." He took a good long swallow.

Doug looked at Duncan as if he might already be a bit tipsy. "American beer? Are you all right?"

"I'm fine." Kincaid waved a dismissive hand. "How's Melody? You did see her?"

"She's— I hope she's going to be okay." The glint off the

lenses of Doug's gold-rimmed glasses hid his eyes. "They're keeping her overnight to monitor her blood and oxygen. She might have breathed enough of the damned stuff for it to have poisoned her."

"Shit." Kincaid's little burst of good humor vanished as quickly as it had come. "And Tam?"

"Andy showed up to see Melody, straight from sitting with Tam at the Chelsea and Westminster ICU. It sounds bad. It's not the burn itself. It's the poison from the white phosphorus getting into his organs."

The barmaid came through from the kitchen, bearing a steaming portion of steak pie surrounded by some carefully arranged greens. "No chips, but I managed to put together some salad for you." She put the plate in front of him with a flourish.

"Lovely. You're a star." Kincaid managed another smile and gestured at his drink. "How about one of the same for my friend here?" While she filled the pint, he paid for their drinks and his meal, then nodded towards a nearby table.

They sat on opposite sides, a guttering candle between them. Kincaid had lost his appetite, but he knew eating was a necessity. He studied his friend as he waited for the pie to cool a bit. "You're limping."

"Lots of walking in the cold. Aggravates the damned ankle."

Kincaid knew they were both thinking about where Doug would be transferred when his ankle finally healed.

Doug confirmed it by saying, "So, how's the new sergeant?"

"You know she'd kill you with a glance if she heard you refer to her as a sergeant."

"Sorry. Your new *DI*, then."

Kincaid tasted the pie. It was still hot enough to burn his tongue. He sighed and put his fork down again, frowning. "She's an odd duck, Jasmine Sidana. Good in the interviews tonight—sharp as a tack. And she was kind to Melody. But me, she doesn't care for at all."

"So your charm's failed you for once."

"Apparently. And if I ever needed a good right hand, this would be it."

Picking up his fork again, Kincaid ate, slowly, while he told Doug everything they had learned about the case, including the liaison with SO15, represented by DCI Nick Callery. He ended with the fact that the alleged victim, Ryan Marsh, did not, in fact, have a police record, the rumor of which had given him such credibility with the group. And that his case manager had not found a likely match in the public databases.

"Assumed name?" said Doug, draining the last third of his pint. "Not bad, this stuff," he added, tilting his empty glass.

The barmaid came over. "Last call, gentlemen. One more?"

Kincaid considered the fact that he was not driving, and that if he had to take a taxi all the way back to Notting Hill, it was a worthwhile expense. "Why not?" he said. "Make it two." When Doug started to protest, he cut him off. "You can have another. You're not hobbling your way home on the tube or the night bus. You can take a taxi on the Met. I'll put it down as a consultant's fee." He was, he realized, only half joking.

He missed talking to Doug. He missed Doug, full stop, and he wondered if his friend was really all right. Doug looked thinner, his face drawn beneath the boyish blond hair and Harry Potter glasses, but perhaps it was the worry over Melody.

"So," he went on, when they had their second pints. "Assumed name, that's one possibility. But what I keep wondering is why this supposedly experienced protester would attach himself to this piddling protest group. From all the accounts, he was a good few years older than the rest of them, and the group has never done anything noteworthy."

"Maybe there's more to them than meets the eye, although they don't sound a very organized bunch," said Doug. The candle gave one last flicker and went out, leaving a pall of smoke between them. "Or maybe this Ryan Marsh needed to lie low and the group gave him the opportunity." Doug drank a little more beer, giving it an approving nod before getting back to the matter at hand. "But it's the lack of records that really bothers me. I've spent the last month and a half entering data, and I can tell you how rare it is for a person to not show up, anywhere, in any sort of public record. Even assumed names tend to creep into the system."

Kincaid frowned. "So how is it possible that this guy is invisible?"

The pub was empty now except for the barmaid, who was putting up clean glasses at the far end of the bar. Still, Doug lowered his voice and glanced round the room before he said, "What if he's been scrubbed?"

CHAPTER EIGHT

"We late-lamented, resting here,
Are mixed to human jam,
And each to each exclaims in fear,
'I know not which I am!' "

—*Thomas Hardy,*
"The Levelled Churchyard," 1882

Jasmine Sidana ground the gears on her Honda sedan as she pulled away from a traffic light on the Westway. When she reached Shepherd's Bush, she turned south, then west again, towards Hounslow, where she lived in a large detached house with her parents and her grandmother.

"Go home, get some rest," Superintendent Kincaid had said, then strolled out of the CID room as if he hadn't a care in the world. She'd wondered, when he'd come in that morning, late and bleary-eyed, if he drank. Then, tonight, as she was leaving the station, she'd seen him walking up the street towards the pub. She knew they all sneered at her because she didn't drink alcohol, but she at least did her job.

Another light. This time she tried to keep the grinding to her teeth. "Go home, get some rest." What was he thinking? If she'd been in charge, they'd have worked all night. She'd have executed the search warrant as soon as it came through, no matter the time, no matter how tired they were.

"Condescending bastard," she said aloud, the swearword feeling alien on her tongue. "Bastard," she said again, with more force, then added, "Bloody bastard," for good measure. It was strangely satisfying, but it didn't temper her righteous indignation.

He'd taken all the important interviews for himself and thrown her the others like a bone.

And the way he'd manipulated the other woman. Jasmine could tell he was sneering at Cam Chen, with her suburban upbringing and striving professional parents.

What must he think of her, then, with her doctor parents, and the fact that at thirty-five she still lived at home? But good Punjabi girls did not get flats on their own, even if they could afford them. Good Punjabi girls finished their career training, then married someone suitable. But Jasmine had never found anyone that seemed worth taking the focus away from her job. Men only wanted to talk about themselves and their accomplishments, and Detective Superintendent Kincaid was obviously no different.

What had he done, she wondered, to get himself demoted from heading an elite Scotland Yard liaison unit to commanding a borough major incident team?

And if he cocked up this case, she'd make sure it was clear where the blame lay. By the time she reached Hounslow, she was humming.

He had disappeared.

What was one more average bloke in a dark hoodie, wearing a backpack, on a bitter London night?

Head down, hood pulled well up, careful not to hurry,

he walked out of St. Pancras International before the police started cordoning off the evacuees.

And then he kept walking. Through Bloomsbury, Covent Garden, Soho, staying in the crowds whenever possible. No way he was getting on the bus or the tube—bloody cameras, bloody cameras everywhere.

He'd hesitated once, in Holborn, contemplating the flat he'd kept in Hackney under a different name. It was an ordinary flat in an ordinary estate, a bolt-hole he'd thought safe. But now he knew he couldn't depend on it, couldn't depend on anything.

What the hell had happened back there?

He shivered, from shock as much as cold. The images kept replaying in his brain and he couldn't shut them off.

If they'd wanted to take him out, why choose that way? Unless they'd used fire deliberately, a twisted sort of revenge for the thing he hadn't done. A wave of nausea swept over him. He staggered, and a passerby stepped away from him, probably thinking he was drunk. Jesus, the last thing he needed was to call attention to himself.

He had to get himself in hand, had to think.

So he couldn't go to Hackney.

God knew he couldn't go home. His eyes teared at the thought. When he wiped at them, his fist came away smudged with soot. Fumbling for his blue handkerchief, he spit on it and scrubbed his face. A dirty face was something people remembered.

He kept walking. Leicester Square. Piccadilly. The backstreets of Westminster. He lost sensation in his feet and hands. Finally, when he judged it late enough, he crossed the river at the Vauxhall Bridge. He kept a car in a lockup on the south side of the river. Its taxes were paid, it was insured and up-to-date on its MOT, all under another assumed name. He'd been very, very careful, and this one, he hoped, Uncle knew nothing about.

When he reached the lockup, he stood for five minutes, watching and listening, alert. There was the scurry of a rat, and the dank smell drifting up from the river, but nothing else. With a little breath of relief, he took the minitorch from his pocket and held it in his teeth while he unlocked the roll-up door.

No Aston Martin DB5 greeted him. The car was a ten-year-old Ford Mondeo, dark blue, nothing flashy about it but not a clapped-out banger, either. Ordinary. It was covered with a light coating of dust, and in this weather it would soon be sleet spattered, adding to the camouflage.

First he checked the emergency supplies in the boot. Tinned and dehydrated food. Water. Survival gear. A Walther 9-millimeter pistol and ammunition. And in a small zip bag, cash. Untraceable cash. It would have to do.

The Mondeo started first time—he'd put in the best battery he could buy. The petrol tank was full, the tires aired.

There were no more excuses for delay. But still, when he'd pulled the car out and relocked the storage door, he sat for a moment, letting the engine idle.

He had to have time to think, to figure out exactly what had happened and who was responsible. Only then would he have any hope of protecting himself and of protecting his family. And there was only one place he could go where he might be safe long enough to do it.

He put the car into gear and drove west.

Gemma woke, unsure if she'd been jarred by a dream or a sound. There was weight and warmth nestled against her side, and it took her an instant to realize that it was not Duncan, but Geordie. The cocker spaniel had taken advantage of Duncan's absence to creep his way up from his accustomed place at the foot of the bed and snuggle beside her.

The lamp in the adjoining bathroom cast a dim glow, just enough to reveal the familiar outlines of the furniture. The digital clock on Duncan's side of the bed read 1:15.

That brought her fully awake. She sat up, listening carefully. Had it been Duncan coming home she'd heard? Or Charlotte coughing?

Easing out of bed, she slipped into her dressing gown. Geordie snored, undisturbed, as Gemma left the room and tiptoed down to the first-floor landing. The children's rooms were dark. Gemma could hear Charlotte's slightly raspy breathing through her open door, but at least she wasn't coughing, poor love.

Tess would be sleeping with the boys, and hopefully as soundly as Geordie. Barking dogs in the middle of the night would rouse everyone.

Gemma knew that some of the kids at Kit's school were starting to tease him about sharing a room with his little brother. But Gemma had shared with her sister until she left home, and the middle-class assumption that every child was entitled to his or her own room irritated her. Fortunately, Kit didn't seem to mind, as long as Toby adhered to Kit's strict "Don't Touch" protocols.

She supposed that on both hers and Duncan's salaries they could afford a nice four-bedroom semidetached somewhere out in the suburbs, but she was not giving up this house for the sake of an extra bedroom. That was assuming she had the option.

The worry that had been nagging her for weeks flooded back. Duncan had heard nothing from Denis Childs, nor had there been any message from Denis's sister, Liz, in Singapore, and they still hadn't learned if Liz had been involved in an accident. They were less than halfway through the five-year lease they'd signed with Liz and her husband, but if something had happened to Liz . . .

Gemma couldn't bear the thought of losing this house. She felt as though her heart was woven into it. The house was a tapestry of all that had changed in their lives since they'd come to live here. A baby lost. A child gained. A marriage she hadn't intended and now couldn't imagine life without. New jobs for her and Duncan, and a future that felt uncertain. Unexpected illnesses—her mum, then Louise, and now Tam seriously hurt. The house had become her fortress, her safety net.

Gemma shook her head and went quietly down the last flight of stairs. No use in borrowing trouble, as her mum would say, and they had enough to worry about now with Tam and Melody both in hospital.

The ground floor was silent as well. But in the light of the hall lamp, she saw Duncan's overcoat thrown over the coat hook by the front door. So he was home, then. Why hadn't he come to bed?

She peeked into the sitting room, in case he'd stretched out on the sofa to keep from waking her. But the sofa was unoccupied except for Sid, who blinked sleepy green eyes at her and curled into a tighter ball.

She tried the French doors and found them locked, although why Duncan would have gone out into the garden at this time of night, she couldn't imagine.

Then, as she went to check the kitchen, she saw the crack of light at the bottom of the study door. She'd left on the green-shaded banker's lamp on the desk, in case she needed to check on the rescued cat. Easing open the door, she stepped inside and closed it behind her.

Her husband lay on his side on the floor, still in his good gray suit and lace-up shoes, beside the box with the mother cat and kittens. The lamplight highlighted the stubble on his chin, and the rise and fall of his chest. He was sound asleep.

But the sound that filled the room was not his breathing, but the deep and regular purring of the cat.

CHAPTER NINE

In mid-19th century London, it would be fair to say that St. Pancras was not the most obvious spot to build a new railway station.

—*Bbc.co.uk/London/St. Pancras*

Gemma woke him with a gentle touch on his shoulder. As he sat up, startled, she said, trying not to laugh, "I think I could make you a bit more comfortable."

"I didn't mean to fall asleep." Kincaid seemed disoriented and smelled faintly of beer. He gestured towards the cat. "It's just that she seemed so glad of my company."

Kneeling beside him, Gemma stroked the mother cat on the snowy white patch under her chin. "She is a love, isn't she?" The kittens were sleeping in an indistinguishable heap. "I hate to think what would have happened if the boys hadn't found her."

"But the shed's kept locked— Oh, I see." He rubbed a hand through his hair and looked a little more alert. "They've added breaking and entering to their list of accomplishments, have they?"

"And very good at it, too," Gemma agreed. "Punishment

deferred, this time, although they will have to apologize to the gardener and help him repair the padlock."

"What on earth are we going to do with the little beasts? The cats, I mean, not the boys," Kincaid added with a smile.

"Bryony said she'd help find homes for them."

"I can see that going over well with the little ones."

"They are besotted," Gemma admitted. "But I'm not becoming the crazy cat lady with six cats in the house." Why, she wondered, was it always "crazy cat ladies" and not "crazy cat men"? Were men immune to the too-many-cats syndrome?

"I rather think it would suit you."

Gemma gave his shoulder a punch. "No. Way." Then, hesitating, she said, "But maybe we could—" She shook her head. That way lay madness. "No," she went on firmly, "it's too early to think about it. But for the present, at least, we seem to have become adoptive parents. Bryony said she'd stop by again tomorrow and scan mum here for a chip."

"Bryony was here?" Kincaid asked.

"Bryony and Wes participated in the Great Rescue. And Wes brought us some of Otto's stroganoff. Are you hungry?"

"I had something at the pub near the station. Doug met me for a drink—he'd just come from seeing Melody. They were keeping her in hospital overnight."

"I know." Gemma shivered. "She rang me. She told me what Andy said about Tam, too. How terrible that it should be Tam who was injured. And I don't even want to think what could have happened to Melody or Andy. Do you have any idea who it was or why he did it?"

"Too soon to say." From his tone, she could tell he wasn't ready to talk about the case.

"Come to bed, then."

"That is an invitation even more tempting than kittens." He stood and stretched, then grasped her hand to pull her up. "But I just want to have a look-in on the kids first."

She knew then that what he'd seen had been very bad indeed.

In spite of his late night, Kincaid was at the station before eight the next morning. Simon Gikas was early as well, and had the search warrant in hand.

"I've arranged for a locksmith, boss," he said. "How do you want to handle this? How is the search team going to know what belongs to whom, unless they've been kind enough to leave big name tags on their stuff?"

Jasmine Sidana came into the CID room, looking a bit harried, and Kincaid could have sworn she was not happy to see him already there.

Kincaid had been thinking about Gikas's question on the way into work. He'd driven this morning, not wanting to be dependent on the tube for the day's commitments. "DI Sidana, good morning." He gave Sidana his best smile. "While the search is in progress, I'd like you to have one of the group members in an interview room. Cam would be the best choice, I think. I'll have the SOCOs send you and Simon digital photos. You can have Cam identify items as they go through the flat."

"But—"

"I know it won't be foolproof, but I don't want any of them at the scene until we've processed it."

"I meant I expected to conduct the search." Her jaw was set and she rocked on the balls of her feet. He wondered if she was about to punch him in the middle of the CID room. Had she been as recalcitrant with his predecessor? And if so, had she got away with it?

That was not going to happen on his watch. Keeping his expression pleasant, he said, "And I think you can be more useful interviewing a witness." He turned back to Gikas. "Any word from DCI Callery?"

"He'll meet you at the search site," Gikas answered, casting a wary glance at Sidana.

"What about the CCTV?"

"We've found a dozen possible matches to Ryan Marsh's description. But I expect that by the time we get through all the footage, we'll have at least a dozen more that fit 'male, short brown hair, blue eyes, medium height, medium build, jeans, backpack, and dark hooded sweatshirt.' And we don't have a photo of Marsh to use for facial recognition."

"Show them to Cam," Kincaid said to Sidana. "If we don't get a match, run them by the others. If we get a confirmation, send it to me. Sweeney can help you." He turned back to Gikas. "Any better luck finding records on the elusive Mr. Marsh?"

Gikas shook his head. "We've found a few more Ryan Marshes. But they are all present and accounted for, don't match his physical description, and are not likely to be moonlighting as protesters."

Before he and Doug Cullen had left the pub last night, Kincaid had asked Doug to do a little digging on the side. Maybe he was paranoid after the events of last autumn in Henley, and then his yet-to-be-explained job transfer, but this whole business of the victim who couldn't be found in any records made him itchily uncomfortable and he wasn't ready to make suppositions to Gikas and the rest of the team.

"Right, then," he said to Gikas. "Simon, can you set up a monitor in Interview Room A? And Jasmine, if you could run Cam through the CCTV images first. Then we'll send photos over of the flat as soon as we've got them."

He'd used her given name without thinking, but she was very deliberately organizing her desk and did not respond.

That was bollocks, he thought. But he wasn't going to treat her like a child even though she was acting like one. He had to assume she would do her job and he would get on with his. He grabbed his overcoat off the coatrack and headed for the door.

• • •

The building in the Caledonian Road looked even less appealing in the cold gray morning light. It had stopped sleeting, for which Kincaid was thankful, but the wind was still blowing down from Siberia as if Britain had become its designated funnel.

Nick Callery was waiting, stomping his feet and drinking coffee from a polystyrene cup. Beside him stood the uniformed PC who had been posted on the flat overnight, and a balding man wearing a heavy parka and carrying a metal case.

"The chicken shop's already open," said Callery by way of greeting. He held up his cup. "The coffee won't kill you, and at least it's hot. This is Mel." He nodded towards the other man.

"Locksmith," said Mel. "Good to meet you."

Kincaid took off his gloves to shake his hand. "Can I get you a cup? I take it we're waiting for the SOCOs."

"On their way, apparently," answered Callery.

When Mel accepted the offer of coffee, Kincaid went into the chicken shop. Even at this early hour, the odor of hot grease made his throat tighten. How did anyone eat fried chicken for breakfast?

But when he looked at the menu board, he saw that the place did bacon and egg sandwiches. With chips. The thought of bacon reminded him that he had skipped breakfast, leaving Gemma to get the children fed and off to school.

The man behind the counter was Middle Eastern, middle-aged, with a paunch hinting that he indulged in his own fare. But the apron over his expansive middle was clean, as was the serving counter and what Kincaid could see of the kitchen. "I'll have the bacon and egg sandwich, no chips. And two cups of coffee."

"I cook the bacon and egg fresh," said the man. "Mind waiting a minute?"

Kincaid saw that there was a griddle in the back. "That's fine."

The man, who Kincaid guessed was the proprietor, put two slices of bacon on the griddle, cracked an egg onto the hot surface, then sliced a soft roll in half and added it. He then poured two cups of coffee into polystyrene cups and added snap-on lids. "Cream and sugar are over there." He nodded towards a side counter as he handed Kincaid the cups.

Kincaid took his as it was. He hadn't asked Mel, but the locksmith could come in and add whatever he liked. "Cheers," he said, accepting the cups. "Back in a tick."

He walked outside and handed Mel his coffee. The locksmith took a cautious sip, then raised his eyebrows in surprise. "Not bad stuff."

"There's cream and sugar inside."

Mel shook his head. "I like mine black as black."

"Anyone else for a bacon and egg sandwich?"

When Mel and Callery both refused, Kincaid went back inside. There was no sign yet of the SOCOs, and he was glad of the respite from the cold.

"Good coffee," he told the proprietor.

"We know coffee where I come from," the man said as he deftly turned the eggs and bacon.

"Where's that?"

"Morocco. But I've been in London for thirty years, and in this place for a decade."

"Know anything about the group that lives upstairs?" Kincaid asked.

The man gave him a sharp look. "Cop?"

Kincaid nodded. "Detective."

"I wondered what all the commotion was about last night, and then a copper on the outer door when I got here first thing this morning. I gave him a cup of coffee on the sly when I opened up," he added with a wink, then said, "They're a quiet enough bunch. What have they been up to?"

"We're not sure yet. Do you own this building?" Kincaid added as he took the wrapped sandwich.

"Me? No. Corporate landlord. KCD, Inc. Stands for King's Cross Development, which means that when this building goes under the wrecking ball, I'll have to find a new place. Or maybe retire."

A corporate owner? Interesting. Kincaid typed a note into his phone before he opened the wrapping around his sandwich. Then, taking a bite, he said, "Um, delicious," through a mouthful of perfectly cooked egg and bacon.

"Ta." The proprietor wiped his hands on his apron and held one out over the counter to Kincaid. "I'm Medhi. Medhi Atias."

Kincaid set down his coffee and shook Atias's hand. "Duncan Kincaid. So, is this place slated for redevelopment?"

"Has been for years. But things haven't progressed in King's Cross as fast as the planners thought they would. Good for me, as there's not much competition and I get business from the corporate offices that have gone into the area. There's the Driver for upmarket meals, but not many places that serve decent ordinary fare."

"I'd say it's more than decent." Having eaten as if he were starving, Kincaid popped the last bite of sandwich into his mouth and fished a card from his wallet. "I expect we'll be coming and going from the upstairs flat for a bit." Through the window, he saw the SOCO van pull up. "Hopefully we won't disturb your business. If you do think of anything unusual going on upstairs, you can always give me a ring."

Atias took the card, his eyes widening as he read it. "You didn't say you were a detective superintendent." His tone was suddenly wary. "I hope something bad hasn't happened upstairs."

"Not upstairs," Kincaid said noncommittally. "As far as we know."

• • •

As the SOCOs climbed out of the van, Kincaid recognized the techs from last night's crime scene at the railway station. "Did you work all night?" he asked as the men joined them.

"We've just finished," said the one with the red-blond beard. Scott, he had said he was called. "But as we were here and there wasn't another team available in the area, we said we'd take this one, too." He looked tired, as did his partner, who was taller, thinner, and clean shaven.

"Scott—is that first or last name?" asked Kincaid.

"Last. I'm called Arthur, so you can see why I prefer it. This is Chad Mills." Scott indicated his partner. "What have you got for us here? Is there a connection with the poor bugger in the station?"

Kincaid explained what they'd learned and how he wanted to process the scene, as Mel the locksmith started on the street-level door.

Mel made quick work of it, shaking his head. "Some people's idea of security," he muttered. Kincaid, Callery, and the two techs followed him up the stairs, waiting on the first-floor landing while he tackled the door to the flat itself. His tsk of disapproval was audible from the flight below as he opened the interior lock. "There you are, then," he said as they climbed up to the second floor. "The door will lock itself, so be careful you don't shut yourselves out." He handed Kincaid a card. "Just give me a ring if you need anything else."

The flat was bone-chillingly cold, and looked considerably less appealing in the gray light filtering through the dirty front windows than it had the previous night.

Kincaid and Callery put on latex gloves and slipped paper booties over their shoes while the techs got into full gear. "We were in the flat last night," Kincaid explained. He and Callery stood just inside the doorway, studying the place, as Scott and Chad Mills opened their collection kits and prepped their digital SLR cameras.

There were the sleeping bags he'd noticed the previous night, stuffed under the sofa, and a few more were folded in another corner of the sitting room. There were several duffel bags and sturdy cloth shopping bags against the wall as well. A laptop sat open on the coffee table, and beside it a stack of newspapers and magazines, but none of the publications looked out of the ordinary. Various items of outerwear hung on coat hooks he hadn't noticed before. There was a threadbare rug under the sofa and coffee table, but the flooring in the rest of the room was bare boards, much worn and scuffed.

There were no cupboards except for those in the kitchen area. A breeze for the forensics team, then, except for trying to figure out what belonged to whom.

"I can take your ID shots with my phone camera," said Scott, "so you won't have to wait for a digital transfer. You won't need the level of detail we get with the SLRs. How many people live here?"

"Six, we think," Kincaid answered. "Plus the victim. Since we haven't made a positive identification we're hoping we can find something here that will give us a lead."

He wondered how the occupants of the flat decided on sleeping arrangements, if any of them slept together, if anyone shared the bedroom with Matthew, and how they shared a bathroom. The thought of the bickering he and his sister Juliet had done over the bathroom when they were in their teens made him smile, earning an odd glance from Callery.

"Something funny?" asked Callery.

Kincaid shook his head. "Just wondering how so many people managed to live in this small space without killing each other."

"Who says they didn't?" Going to the coffee table, Callery touched the laptop with a gloved fingertip and a lock screen popped up. "Here's one for the boffins." He shrugged. They hadn't expected access. "Let's just make certain there's no bomb-making factory in the back room, shall we?"

• • •

Jasmine Sidana sat in Interview Room A across from Cam Chen, who was definitely the worse for wear after her night in the custody suite.

Jasmine brushed a stray hair from her crisp white blouse and straightened her skirt, then concentrated on the computer monitor that had been set up where they both could view it.

Turning on the room recorder, she identified them both and gave the time and date, then said, "Cam, do you understand what we're going to do here? We've got some digital photos, and I need you to tell me about the things in the room. We need to identify Ryan Marsh's possessions."

Cam stared at her. "I can tell you anything you want. None of us have much—Matthew won't allow it. But I can't show you which things are Ryan's."

"Why not?" asked Jasmine, wondering if the girl was acting out of some stubborn and misguided sense of loyalty.

"Because Ryan never left anything in the flat," said Cam. "Not even his toothbrush."

They had not found anything in the flat's bedroom. Not unless you counted the double bed—upon which Kincaid imagined Matthew Quinn must sleep diagonally in order to fit—a wardrobe, a battered chest of drawers, and various items of clothing that were labeled TALL and obviously belonged to Quinn. The adjoining bathroom yielded much the same—one bottle of shampoo, one bottle of shower gel on the rim of the clean tub. The medicine cabinet held toothbrush, toothpaste, and shaving things that again obviously belonged to one person, presumably Quinn, and various over-the-counter medications, plasters, and tweezers.

If there was a trace of white phosphorus or any other explosive, it would be up to the forensic techs to find it.

"If he's making bombs or harboring terrorists, I doubt it's here," Callery had said, and shortly thereafter took himself off, talking on his mobile as he left.

Kincaid took a phone call from Simon Gikas, who relayed what Cam had told Sidana. When he'd rung off, Kincaid stood for a while, watching and thinking, as the SOCOs methodically took photos and collected trace evidence.

Matthew Quinn was looking more and more like a little despot who let the others literally camp in the flat, dependent upon his charity. Why? And why had Ryan Marsh tolerated it? And who had introduced a white phosphorus grenade into this seemingly innocuous group who seemed capable of little more than amateur protests?

When his phone rang again, he answered quickly, expecting Gikas. But it was Rashid Kaleem, calling from the morgue at the Royal London Hospital.

"I think you'd better come and have a look at our victim," said Rashid.

Having spent the morning being poked and prodded, having blood drawn and oxygen levels checked, by a little before ten o'clock Melody had been told she was discharged from hospital. She'd just got out of the horrid hospital gown they'd given her in the room and back into her own clothes when there was a tap at the door.

Andy put his head in, then came into the room with a look of relief. "Oh, good, you're decent."

"You would mind if I weren't?" she asked, giving him a quizzical look as she brushed at a smudge on her sweater. Did she just imagine that her clothes bore the odor of fire and singed flesh?

"Of course not. It's just—" He gestured at the hospital paraphernalia surrounding the bed. "I didn't want to—"

"I know." Melody studied him. He, too, wore the same clothes as yesterday, including the sky-blue cardigan under his peacoat. His face looked drawn, the skin under his eyes blue tinged. "Have you slept at all?" she asked.

"A bit of a kip on the sofa at Tam and Michael's. The dogs were glad to see me."

Melody sank down on the edge of the hospital bed, her legs suddenly weak. "Have you seen Tam this morning? How is he?"

"I've just come from the Chelsea and Westminster. There's no change, really. He's still in critical care, and they're still monitoring his organ function. They say it's too early to tell how bad the damage is."

"What about Michael and Louise?"

"Michael's finally convinced Louise to go home and get some rest. He's gone home, too, for a bit, to look after the dogs. And to make sure Louise does as she's told," he added with a ghost of a smile.

"I don't envy him that," Melody said, and earned another smile. She reached for her boots.

"They've released you, then?" asked Andy.

"I have to come back tonight for more blood work, but yes, I can go."

"Let me take you home." He straightened, as if a renewed sense of purpose had given him a much-needed boost.

Hating to disappoint him, Melody said, "I'm not going home. Duncan's going to want to debrief me." She had a thought. "Can I shower and change at your place? I can go to Holborn from there."

Tucked away behind the intersection of Oxford Street and Tottenham Court Road, Andy's building would surely fall victim to the Crossrail redevelopment scheme at some point. In fact, it surprised Melody that it hadn't already been condemned. Of the two rooms in his first-floor flat, the alleged bedroom served as a guitar workshop. The sitting room held a futon that Andy folded out into a bed at night. Most of the rest of the space seemed to be taken up by more guitars and amplifiers and Andy's large orange cat, Bert.

But in spite of the grubby building and cramped quarters, Melody had quickly come to prefer it to her own much nicer flat in Notting Hill. She slept there more often than she did at her own place, stocked a few things in the fridge, and had found space for enough odds and ends of clothing that she thought she could make herself presentable.

And she found that today, especially, she didn't want to go home alone.

"You don't seriously mean to go into work today, after what you've been through?" Andy said, frowning.

"It's my job," Melody answered, as she had last night.

"But it's not your case."

She thought of the smoke and the smell and the panicked faces of the mob she'd pushed her way through. She thought of the man burning before her eyes in what must have been unimaginable pain, of the cries of the injured, of the Good Samaritan who had helped her, of Tam.

"It is now."

"Poor bugger." Rashid Kaleem sat behind his desk in his tiny office at the back of the basement in the Royal London Hospital. Beneath his white lab coat, he wore one of his usual pathologist-humor T-shirts, this one more unsettling than most. Against a black background, the white bones of a rib cage were split down the middle. A stylized heart hung suspended outside the ribs, with the slogan DON'T LOSE YOUR HEART beneath it.

"Rashid, you really should reconsider your sartorial choices," Kincaid said, looking, as usual, for someplace to sit.

Every surface in the room was covered with papers, books, or computer monitors. He settled for the edge of an overflowing filing cabinet.

"Really?" Rashid pulled out the front of the T-shirt and studied it. "I rather like this one. At any rate, your bloke in there would wish his ribs looked half as good." He glanced up and nodded towards the postmortem lab down the hall.

Kincaid could smell it, always, as soon as he came into the basement—the pinch of chemicals at the back of the nose, and beneath that, the slightest sweet taint of death. He supposed Rashid was used to it.

"Want to see your bomber?" Rashid stood and shrugged out of the lab coat. Hanging it on a hook that protruded from one of his heavy-metal posters, he added, "Bloody cold down here. The coat adds an extra layer. And it makes me look important."

"I suppose I can't say no, can I?"

"My description wouldn't do him justice. But you'll need full gear. And a respirator. Believe me, you don't want to smell him. And what's left of him is saturated in white phosphorus, so you don't want to risk contamination, either."

They changed in the lab's anteroom, after which Kincaid followed Rashid into the lab proper. When he saw what lay on the table, he was very glad of the respirator.

The corpse looked worse than he remembered, perhaps because the removal of remnants of clothing had left exposed bone, perhaps because Rashid had bisected the chest and the fragments of rib looked much more obscene than the pristine white slivers on Rashid's T-shirt.

And because, in the aftermath of the chaos in the railway station, he hadn't realized that the corpse's hands were gone.

"I take it you are sure this is a male?" Kincaid asked. His voice sounded odd through the respirator.

"From the shape of the skull and what's left of the pelvic

girdle, the height, and what was left of the shoes, yes. Ninety-nine percent, anyway." Rashid's enunciation was perfect, even with the distortion from the respirator's mouthpiece. "My rough estimate is that he was a bit less than six feet tall, and was probably between twenty and thirty."

"Helpful." Kincaid didn't curb the sarcasm. "No distinguishing marks?"

The roll of Rashid's eyes was visible through his protective goggles. "Not bloody likely. And no fingerprints. Obviously."

"Dental?"

Rashid shook his head. Moving closer to the body, he pointed with a gloved finger. "You can see he was holding the grenade at just about waist level when it went off. Maybe he had it in his pocket and took it out at the last minute. The blast traveled upwards, taking his hands, his chest, and most of his face. I doubt even a forensic odontologist could put much together from what's left of his teeth."

"Was he Caucasian?" Kincaid asked.

"Again, not much left of the facial structure to go by. But I'd say it's likely, unless you have reason to think otherwise. The good news, however"—Rashid pointed again with a gloved finger—"is that because the force of the grenade traveled upwards, and our boy was wearing fairly heavy boots, there was enough tissue left on the bottoms of his feet for a good DNA sample."

Glancing at the items on the evidence table that had looked like nothing more than burned bits of rubbish, Kincaid saw that some of the scraps might indeed be pieces of boot.

"Forensics should be able to tell you more about the boots," Rashid said, following his gaze. "The other good news is that he was wearing a backpack. Because the blast was generated on the front of the body, the pack provided some protection to the skin on his back when the fire engulfed him. I was able to get a DNA sample there, and I'll go over what's left of the skin again."

DNA might be helpful eventually, Kincaid thought—assuming they had something with which to match it. But the tests took time, so for the moment DNA samples did him no good at all.

"Could you tell what was in the pack?" he asked, thinking of Cam Chen's statement that Ryan Marsh had carried all his belongings with him whenever he left the flat.

"Not much. I've collected as many samples of nonorganic goo as I could manage. Forensics may be able to tell you more on that, too."

"Nothing that might have been a sleeping bag? Or extra clothing?"

Rashid shook his head again. "Not likely, no."

"Any grenade fragments?"

"Not that I could find. The SOCOs may have better luck."

Kincaid stood, staring at the mess that had been a human being less than twenty-four hours ago. If this was Ryan Marsh, and he had taken his belongings from the flat, they had apparently not been in his pack when the grenade went off.

In which case, what the hell had happened to Ryan Marsh's things?

CHAPTER TEN

The Midland Railway had been running services into London since 1840 and expanded services had led to chronic congestion and delays. In 1846 when Parliament approved the proposal of another route into London, the Great Northern Line, Midland Railway paid £20,000 for the rights to operate the service. Minds could now be concentrated on building the new station.

—*Bbc.co.uk/London/St. Pancras*

When Gemma went to wake Charlotte, she found her warm and slightly flushed. Sitting down on the bed, she felt the child's forehead, then put her hand flat on Charlotte's chest beneath her white cotton nightdress, feeling for the telltale rattle of congestion.

Charlotte's breathing seemed unlabored, but when she opened her eyes she reached out to Gemma, her face puckered. "Mummy," she whispered, "I had a bad dream. I dreamed something happened to the kitties."

"The kitties are just fine." Gemma smoothed Charlotte's tousled hair back from her forehead. Her hand looked pale against Charlotte's golden skin. "I've just checked on them."

"Promise?"

"Promise."

"I want to see them," said Charlotte, but instead of bouncing out of bed, she snuggled against Gemma and closed her eyes drowsily again.

"Oh, dear," Gemma murmured. Although the child's cough seemed better, she'd obviously overdone things yesterday with all the excitement over the cat and kittens. And she was obviously not going to school.

"Want to stay in your jammies awhile longer?" Gemma said now, kissing the top of Charlotte's curly hair. "I'll bring you some toast, and then you can see the kitties. Bryony is coming by to have a look at them, too."

"What about school?" Charlotte asked.

"I think you can stay with Betty today, lovey."

Charlotte's forehead creased. "Oliver will miss me."

"I'm sure he will. But you need to get better so that you can see him tomorrow. Now, you just cuddle up for a bit while I get things organized."

And organizing she would have to do, Gemma thought, not just for Charlotte, but for herself. She had rung her guv'nor, Detective Superintendent Krueger, last night to tell her what had happened to Melody and that she intended to check on her this morning. But first she had another visit to make.

Caleb Hart was sitting alone in the waiting area of the burns unit at Chelsea and Westminster Hospital, head bowed. Gemma said, "Caleb? Mr. Hart?" a little tentatively, as the last time she'd seen Caleb Hart she'd been interviewing him as a murder suspect.

Unlike Tam, who tended to look as though he'd put on whatever tumbled out of his cupboard—not that anything would clash with his faded tartan wool cap—Caleb Hart looked the part of a musician's manager. Slender and fit, with neatly trimmed hair and goatee, he wore designer clothes and trendy eyeglasses. This morning, however, his clothes were rumpled and stained and his eyes red rimmed.

He looked up at her, his expression puzzled. "It's Inspector Ja— Gemma, isn't it? Tam talks about you and little Charlotte all the time."

She perched on the edge of the chair next to him. "How is he this morning?"

"They have him pretty well sedated for the pain from the burn. But it's the poisoning from the chemical that they're really worried about," Caleb answered, his voice hoarse.

"Have you been here all night?" she asked.

Nodding, Caleb said, "I promised Michael I'd stay while he went home to clean up."

Caleb, Gemma remembered, for all his hip appearance, was an AA sponsor, and was accustomed to pitching in when help was needed. He sighed. "I've been fielding texts all morning from a producer who saw them last night and wants to put them in a demo session slot—at Abbey Road Studios, no less. But Andy won't agree to it under the circumstances, and I don't think Poppy will, either."

Gemma had yet to meet Poppy, although she'd seen the duo's viral video so many times she felt she knew her. "Would you want them to do it?" she asked Caleb.

He gave a tired shrug. "I understand how they feel. But it's their career, and there's nothing Tam would want more than to see them have this sort of chance."

"Can I see him, do you think?"

Caleb glanced at his watch. "It's about the time they'll let someone visit for a few minutes. How alert he is will depend on his pain medication."

Gemma stood, and Caleb stood with her, holding out his hand. "It was good of you to come."

She hesitated, then said, "I'm sorry. About what happened before. I was—"

"Doing your job," Caleb finished for her.

Tam looked better than Gemma had expected. He was propped up a little in the hospital bed, and although there were some small burns and scrapes on his face, his color was good. The oddest thing was seeing him without his tartan cap. He looked, with his shorn and thinning hair, naked.

The charge nurse had given her ten minutes, so she sat beside the bed in the only available chair, trying not to think about the times she'd visited her mum in hospital. Her mum's leukemia had been in remission since the autumn, but Gemma worried about her constantly nonetheless.

After a moment, Tam's breathing changed and his eyes fluttered open. "Gemma?"

"Hello, Tam. I just came by to see how you were doing." She patted the hand that lay outside the sheet that was draped lightly over his midriff.

"Not looking my best, am I, lass?" he whispered, then grimaced. "Hate being a bloody nuisance. And no one will tell me anything. Is Melody—"

"Melody's fine," Gemma assured him.

"Was anyone else—" His face creased with distress.

She shook her head. "No. No one was killed except the man with the grenade."

"Man?" Tam blinked at her.

"It wasn't a man?" Gemma asked, puzzled.

"No. 'Twas just a lad."

Gemma stared, startled. "You saw him? Before the fire?"

Tam nodded. "I looked away from the stage. Just for an instant, I don't know why. A movement in the crowd, maybe. And I saw him, a boy wearing a backpack. I remember

I thought he looked like one of the lads in the band about to play a prank."

"Not frightened?"

"No. A bit nervous, maybe, but excited with it. And then— it was so bright—" Tam winced and lifted a hand to pick at the sheet over his stomach. "And I was burning. Who the bloody hell would have thought something could hurt so much?" He had paled, and there was a sheen of sweat on his brow.

Gemma patted his hand gently. "You rest, Tam. I'm going to get the nurse. When you're feeling a bit better, I'm sure Duncan will be in to see you, too."

He closed his eyes and settled back into the pillow. She thought he'd drifted off again, but when she stood, he turned his head to look at her and said, "You'll do something for me, won't you, lass?"

"Of course, Tam. Anything."

"You'll make certain Michael and Louise look after themselves."

Caleb was asleep in his chair, head lolling to one side, when she came back through the waiting area. She didn't disturb him, but hurried to the hospital exit and out into the bustle of Fulham Road.

She intended to call Duncan and tell him what Tam had said about the victim, reliable or not. But before she could dial, her phone rang. It was Shara MacNichols, the detective constable on her team in South London who was working leads on Mercy Johnson's murder.

"Guv," said Shara, "we need you. I've been talking to Mercy's friends again. One of the girls has admitted she has a photo on her phone of Mercy talking to Dillon Underwood. I'm bringing her in. You'd better get to the station as soon as you can."

• • •

Kincaid left the Royal London Hospital with more questions than he'd had before. He considered Rashid's findings as he drove west on Whitechapel Road towards Holborn, but as he passed by Brick Lane his thoughts were drawn, as always when he visited this part of the East End, to Charlotte and to the events that had brought her to them. It was the sale of Charlotte's parents' Georgian house in Fournier Street that had allowed them to put her in a school where she felt comfortable.

And that led him to Tam. He hadn't had a chance to get an update on Tam's condition that morning. He'd made a mental note to check on him as soon as he reached the station, when his phone rang. When he saw that it was his borough commander, he put the phone on and answered.

"Sir."

"Where are you?" asked Chief Superintendent Faith without preamble.

"Just leaving the postmortem at the Royal London, on the way to the station."

"Anything definitive on our victim from the pathologist?"

Definitive was the last word Kincaid would choose. "No, sir. And no ID."

"Well, you'd better hope you can come up with something palatable for the media, because you have a press conference at noon."

"Sir?" Kincaid frowned. "What about SO15?"

"The assistant commissioner Crime just rang. Orders handed down straight from the top. The deputy commissioner doesn't feel the case warrants SO15's involvement. He wants it treated as a suspicious death, so it's our bailiwick. Or yours, I should say. Although I don't think the AC Special Operations was terribly chuffed with the decision." These two divisions of the Met, Crime and Special Operations, were infamous for territorial scuffles.

Kincaid wondered what Nick Callery had reported to his superiors.

"DCI Callery will be joining you in the press conference," Faith continued, as if reading his mind. "It's important we reassure the public that we don't feel there is a likelihood of further incidents."

While Kincaid was beginning to think it likely that the intent of the poor bugger on the postmortem table had been only to burn himself to a crisp, he felt far from comfortable assuring the public of anything. Especially when he couldn't ID the victim.

As Chief Superintendent Faith rang off, the traffic slowed to a creep at Aldgate, and then to a complete stop. Kincaid looked anxiously at the dashboard clock, drummed his fingers on the wheel, then decided to make good use of the holdup. He rang Doug Cullen.

"Can you talk?" he asked when Doug picked up.

"You're asking the man locked in the dungeon with the computer?" Doug was not one to take the drudgery of being assigned to data entry at Scotland Yard with good humor.

"Seriously."

"Yeah." Doug sounded suddenly alert. "There's no one else in the room just now. What's up? Is it Melody?"

"No. I mean, I haven't heard anything." Kincaid nosed the car forward another inch. "Do you remember what we talked about last night?"

"You mean your mystery man?"

"Invisible would be more like it." Kincaid told him about the search of the squat and Rashid's findings—or lack of findings—at the postmortem. "This bloke left nothing behind him and kept nothing on his person. No phone, no credit cards, no toothbrush. Who lives like that? What have we got here?"

After a moment's hesitation, he voiced the fear that had begun to nag him. "A spook?"

There was silence on the other end of the line. Then Doug said quietly, even though he'd told Kincaid he was alone, "Or an undercover cop."

That was a supposition Kincaid certainly didn't intend to make public, or to share with anyone else on the team for the time being.

What on earth would an undercover cop have been doing in a group like Matthew Quinn's?

As soon as he reached Holborn, he checked in with Simon Gikas, the case manager.

"Anything new from the SOCOs at the flat?"

"They're still matching possessions to the group. But no bombs or bomb-making paraphernalia, or grenades."

"Drugs?"

"One of the blokes—Lee, I think—had a tiny bit of grass. Maybe a quarter ounce. Obviously personal use, and no evidence of dealing. Did you get an ID from the postmortem?" Gikas added.

Kincaid shook his head. "Not enough left of him. Dr. Kaleem thinks he can get a decent DNA sample, but we have to have something to compare it to." He glanced round the CID room. "Where's Sidana?"

"She and Sweeney are prepping for the press conference." Gikas looked at his watch. "And you have ten minutes."

"Bugger," Kincaid muttered, then dashed for the men's loo. He washed his hands, combed his hair, and straightened his tie, glad he'd worn his best suit. But when he took a moment to study his reflection in the mirror, he saw that his eyes were shadowed. He looked, in fact, like he'd spent part of a short night sleeping on the floor with cats.

Shrugging, he made his way to the conference room. Sidana and Sweeney had set up a table with two chairs and mics, reporters were trickling in, and Nick Callery was there before him, looking as well turned out as he had yesterday.

"It's your show, apparently," Callery murmured as Kincaid sat. "I'm just here for decoration." He seemed unperturbed, but Kincaid remembered his quick exit from the Caledonian Road flat. What, he wondered, was Callery's stake in this, and had he wanted in or out?

When the room had gone quiet, Kincaid began taking questions.

No, they had not identified the victim. No, they had not found evidence of a terrorist plot or other terrorist activity. They were treating the incident as a suspicious death and it would be handled by Homicide. He had been named senior investigating officer.

Yes, he would be liaising with Detective Chief Inspector Callery from Special Operations in the event that any information regarding terrorist activities came to light in the course of the investigation. Yes, all rail services had been returned to normal operations, thanks to the efficiency of the British Transport Police.

"Are you considering the victim a suicide?" asked a reporter from a major newspaper.

"We cannot make that determination at this point," Kincaid answered. "More information will be forthcoming after the inquest." He hated police-speak, but it beat saying, "We're bloody clueless, mate."

A female reporter in the back of the room raised her hand. She was, God forbid, from Melody's father's newspaper. "We understand you've arrested suspects in connection with the bombing."

"Let's be clear," he said sharply. "First, there was no bomb. The victim was apparently carrying an incendiary device, not an explosive. Second, we have not arrested anyone. There are, however, several witnesses to the event who are helping us with our inquiries."

How, he wondered, had that got out? One thing he could guarantee—Melody hadn't been the leak. The last thing she'd want was her father knowing she'd been anywhere near the damned grenade.

Sidana stood at the back of the room, behind the seated reporters. She gave him a slight nod and mimed a throat cut.

"All right, ladies and gentlemen. Thank you for your time." Kincaid stood and Callery followed suit. They exited the conference room with reporters still calling questions behind them.

"Your borough commander didn't make an appearance," said Callery when they'd left the public access area of the station. "I thought the uniform was meant to reassure the public."

"Maybe it was the *absence* of the uniform that was meant to reassure the public." Kincaid glanced at him. "Any idea why Special Operations signed off on this one?"

"A waste of time and resources, according to the deputy commissioner," Callery said with a shrug, but for the first time, Kincaid thought he saw a flicker of emotion in his gray eyes.

Callery clapped him on the shoulder. "Keep me updated, will you?" He smiled. "At least if this thing goes to hell, it will be on your head, not mine."

Back in CID, Kincaid spent an hour with Simon Gikas, Sidana, and Sweeney, going over the information that had been gathered that morning.

"What's your impression of the group after taking Cam through their belongings this morning?" he asked Sidana.

She seemed to hesitate, then said, "They seem a bit pathetic, really. They have almost no possessions. No regular income.

They all seem dependent on Matthew Quinn's charity and that seems a bit . . . creepy."

"Did he choose them because they were vulnerable?" Kincaid mused.

"Or was it the other way round?" said Sidana. "Maybe they're all habitual spongers and they saw him as a target."

It was an interesting perspective, and Kincaid reminded himself that just because she resented him didn't mean she didn't have valuable insight to contribute. She hadn't got to be a DI without being good at her job.

"I can tell you a couple of interesting things." Gikas tapped the computer screen on the worktable. In spite of the nickname, Simon Gikas was a very good-looking bloke. His dark hair and deep blue eyes had female staff scurrying to do his bidding, and he certainly got results. "There were two laptops. The warrants were a bit iffy, but because we had SO15 in the game, we were able to get forensics on them. A two-year-old could have got into them." He shook his head in disgust. "One of them belongs to Lee Sutton, and one of them to Matthew Quinn, although I expect that most of the group used them. Sutton is big into social networks, and has about as much sense as you'd expect."

"Drugs?" Kincaid asked.

"References, yeah. A few joint-smoking selfies. Photos from pop-up raves. Some mild porn. Pretty much typical university drop-out material. But Mr. Quinn, now, that is interesting."

"Go on," said Sweeney when Gikas paused. "We're bloody dying of suspense here."

"His browser history is stacked with visits to wacko Web sites. End-of-the-world preppers. 'True Britain will rise again from the ashes—but only for the chosen few.' "

"Of course," Sidana said under her breath.

"And when you get into the preppers, you don't just have the wannabe Druids," Gikas went on. "You have the paramilitary dafties."

"Guns?" Kincaid asked. "Munitions?"

"Name your poison. It's mostly fantasy, but it's ugly stuff."

"So is there a record of Quinn buying—or shopping for— the grenade?"

Gikas shook his head. "No. But"—he paused again, obviously enjoying himself—"he did buy bitcoins. And what he did with them, there's no way to tell."

Kincaid swore. "But surely you can trace—"

"No. That's the whole idea. You can gamble. You can buy drugs. Or diamonds. You can buy guns. Or rocket launchers, for that matter. And no one can trace the transaction. It's virtual cash, in unmarked bills."

"What about personal stuff on his computer, then?" Sweeney asked.

"Unlike Sutton, Mr. Quinn stays away from social networks. His photos were all of London historical sites and ongoing construction. Of course they won't have got to the things he deleted, but at least on the surface he seems to have been quite careful."

Kincaid was liking this less and less. "You said you found a couple of interesting things."

"Ah. He did his banking online. It took forensics all of fifteen minutes to crack his password. Matthew Quinn doesn't pay rent, unless he pays it in cash—or bitcoins. But every month money is drafted *into* his account. The same amount, from the same source, and it's enough to keep him and his playmates quite comfortably."

"Do you know where it comes from?"

"According to the wire transfer records, something called KCD, Inc."

It took Kincaid a moment to realize why the name sounded familiar. It had been Medhi Atias, the owner of the chicken shop, who'd told him that KCD, Inc., owned the building.

"King's Cross Development," he said. The others looked at him blankly.

"The corporation owns the building. The chicken shop owner told me this morning." More blank looks. "The chicken shop is on the ground floor," Kincaid explained. "Matthew Quinn's flat is on the second floor. So why is the landlord paying Matthew Quinn every month, instead of the other way round?"

"You can ask Quinn," said Sidana.

Kincaid thought for a moment. "He doesn't have to tell us. And why his landlord pays his rent is not necessarily germane to our inquiry, at least legally. But I'd like to know the answer, and I suspect there are better ways of finding out." The disappointment was obvious in the team's expressions. Forestalling them, he said, "I'm going to let them go. All of them. I don't like it that the media got wind of the fact that we were holding them for questioning, and I don't want bully-tactic allegations when we have no bloody idea what's going on here. Simon, find me everything you can on KCD, Inc."

Once settled in his office, Kincaid rang down to the custody suite and told the sergeant to release all six of the detainees.

"You want to speak to them first, Guv?" asked the sergeant.

Kincaid considered a moment, then said, "No. Just check them out." He wanted them unsettled, and the less explanation they were given, the better.

And he wanted to be better prepared before he questioned them again.

He'd started through the transcripts of last night's interviews when his office phone rang. It was the front-desk sergeant, telling him she'd buzzed up Melody Talbot.

As he stood, he saw Melody crossing the CID suite. Jasmine Sidana looked up and gave her a friendly nod, which Melody returned with a smile. Opening his office door, he wrapped an arm round Melody in a hug of relief. When he realized his team was watching with unabashed interest through the glass walls of his office, he let her go, ushered her into a chair, and closed the door.

Melody wore, rather than her customary scarlet wool coat, a too-large navy peacoat that he recognized as Andy's. He had a sudden flash of memory from the night before—Tam lying on the concourse floor at St. Pancras, covered in something red. Melody's coat, splotched in the darker red of blood and splashed with phosphorus. She would not be wearing that again.

"Should you be out of hospital?" he asked. And belatedly, "Can I get you something? A cup of tea?"

"No, I'm fine," said Melody, although she didn't look it. She wore no makeup, and her usually sleekly styled dark hair waved loosely around her face, as if she'd showered and forgotten to comb it. "I have to go back to hospital for more tests later this afternoon, but there was no point in my just sitting there."

"Have you heard anything about Tam?"

She shook her head. "Not since Andy checked on him this morning. They say the burn should heal, but it's too soon to tell how much damage the phosphorus has done." Before he could ask another question, she went on, "I saw the press conference from Andy's flat. Are you really holding suspects?"

"Not anymore." At her inquiring look, he explained why he'd let the group go.

Melody listened intently. When he showed her the photos of the Caledonian Road protesters, she frowned. "I just had a glimpse in the crowd. I was more focused on the placards, and I was worried they were going to disrupt the show. But I recognize this one, because of his height and the curly hair even though he was wearing a watch cap." She tapped a photo, then glanced up at Kincaid for confirmation. "Matthew Quinn?"

He nodded and she shuffled through the photos again. "And

this one." She tapped Cam Chen. "But the rest . . . I can't be certain."

"Can you tell me exactly what happened, from the time you arrived at the station?" he asked. She'd given him a brief account when he'd arrived at the scene last night, but she'd been shocked and frantic about Tam. "Every detail."

Melody seemed to marshal her thoughts. "I was late, because there was a jumper—I think—on one of the tube lines, so the trains were delayed. I'd promised Andy I'd be there and I didn't want to disappoint him. Andy and Poppy were already playing—I could hear them as soon as I came into the concourse. I may have pushed a bit, getting through the commuters. I'd just reached the edge of the crowd gathered round the band when I saw them"—she glanced at the photos again—"pulling out placards. I was bloody pissed off. I looked round and there was a British Transport officer heading for them."

Kincaid nodded. "Colleen Rynski."

"So I thought she could deal with them—the last thing I wanted was to make a police-officer scene in the middle of Andy and Poppy's gig." Melody sank back in her chair, looking exhausted. "Seems pretty stupid now, considering."

"Go on," Kincaid encouraged her.

"I saw Tam and Caleb standing outside the café. They looked pleased as punch. Wait." Melody rubbed her hands on the knees of her jeans. "Was that before or after the placards? I can't remember." She sounded distressed.

"Just give it time. I'm sure it will come back to you. Go back to Tam and Caleb. When you saw them, was there anything—or anyone—that caught your attention, even for an instant?"

Melody shook her head in distress. "No. I wasn't expecting—I wasn't thinking . . . I turned back to watch the band, and I remember I was hoping that Andy could see me at the back of the crowd. And then—" She stopped, swallowing. "The music was loud. But I heard it. A . . . sound. I realized that everyone's heads were turning in the same direction. Then I heard the screams start. I turned, too—and there he was. Burning." She frowned. "No. That's not right. At first I wasn't even sure what it was, the light was so bright. And then I saw the outline of a man, inside the fire."

"Why were you certain it was a man? You're sure you didn't see his face?"

"No, I—I don't know. That was just what flashed through my head. And then he collapsed, right before my eyes, and I started trying to get to him while people were pushing and shoving to get away. I shouted at people to get out, but the smoke was billowing and there was feedback screeching from the sound system and I'm not sure anyone heard me.

"I bumped into a man and he grabbed me by the shoulder, hard, and told me to get back. He was holding a handkerchief over his face and I realized that he was going towards the victim, too. I identified myself and then he shouted at me to cover my face and we . . . we pushed forward together."

Watching Melody, Kincaid realized he'd never seen her seem so unsure of herself. It was partly the clothes, he thought—usually she was as smartly turned out as any senior detective. But even off duty, more casually dressed, she'd always presented a breezy confidence made even more noticeable by her hint of reserve.

Melody Talbot had passed the test. She had run into the chaos, as all police officers were trained to do—but one never knew until faced with a crisis whether one had the bottle to meet it. But this experience seemed to have left her shaken and looking . . . ill. With a little clutch of fear, he wondered if the doctors were giving her false reassurance about her exposure to the phosphorus, but he shook it off with a mental admonition not to be daft. Of course they knew what they were about . . .

"Duncan?"

He focused on Melody with a start. "Sorry. Tell me what happened next."

"We— We got to him. And"—she shrugged—"you saw. There was nothing we could do. He—the man with me, said something . . ." She rubbed at her face. "I can't remember. 'Too late,' maybe? Something like that. But he sounded so . . . so . . . despairing, and for a moment I felt like I might pass out from the shock. And the smell. It was—horrible. Then I realized people were still screaming. And then I saw that Tam was on fire." Melody cleared her throat. "You know most of the rest.

"I tried to secure the scene and help Tam and the other victims at the same time. There was a girl, one of the waitresses in the café. She got a fire extinguisher and helped people who were still burning. I'd like to thank her." Melody sat up a bit straighter.

"And I'll want to interview her," said Duncan. "She might have seen something beforehand. Did you get a name?"

"No. But she was pretty, with short dark hair. I'd know her again anywhere. I could go with you to talk to—"

Kincaid was already shaking his head. "It's not your case, Melody. You know I can't take you with me on an interview."

Her shoulders slumping, Melody glanced through the glass at the CID room. "Your new team, of course. Your DI was good at the scene last night. Very competent." She added, with a rueful smile, "But not Doug."

"No." Kincaid was glad that someone liked Sidana.

"He would never say it," Melody went on. "It would be very un-blokey—but he misses you."

"You mean he misses all the excitement," Kincaid said, making a joke, because it was one thing to miss your sergeant but entirely another to admit it.

He considered a moment. He'd told Melody only what he'd told the rest of the team. But who could he trust if not her?

"I saw Doug last night," he said. "He came to the station after he left you at A-and-E." Lowering his voice, he went on to tell her about the digging Doug had done for him on the victim, Ryan Marsh, and the suspicion they'd begun to form, especially after today's postmortem.

Melody stared at him, eyes wide. "Undercov—" She clamped her mouth shut for a moment, then said succinctly, "Shit."

"Yeah. My thoughts exactly. Matthew Quinn meets mysterious stranger at a protest. The stranger gives his name as Ryan Marsh, and apparently has street—or group—cred for having been involved in protests. After a few more casual interactions, Ryan Marsh insinuates himself into Matthew Quinn's little group, eventually sleeping in the flat at least part-time. When Quinn acquires a smoke bomb—or what is supposedly a smoke bomb—and wants to use it in a protest, Marsh says he'll do it, although there is some disagreement in their stories about whether the smoke bomb was Quinn's idea or Marsh's. If he gets arrested, Marsh tells them, he already has a record from previous protests. The others can stay clean.

"Except there is no record. There are no arrests. No phone, no driving license, no national insurance, no credit cards."

"The name isn't uncommon."

"No. But Doug is thorough and he ruled out other possible matches, as did my case manager, Simon Gikas. And why would Ryan Marsh go to the trouble to make certain he never left anything of himself behind? Not just yesterday—that might make sense if he meant to commit suicide—but every time he left the flat?"

Melody shrugged Andy's big coat a little tighter, even though it was warm in Kincaid's office. "Why would anyone bother with Quinn's little group? Who would bother? If it was Counter Terrorism, SO15 wouldn't have turned it over. Vice?"

"With no evidence of drugs, other than a little personal use?

Or gambling. Or prostitution. Even if Matthew Quinn was pimping the girls—or the boys—it would be small potatoes."

"It doesn't make sense," Melody agreed, frowning. "But . . ." She sat forward, a little more color in her cheeks. "I have an idea. Can you send me the photos of the group?"

"Yes, but—"

"Let me do a little digging in the *Chronicle* photo files. Not for Ryan Marsh specifically, but for anything Matthew Quinn or his group might have been involved in. You say they were protesting Crossrail tunneling and damage to London's historical sites. If they got themselves into any photos, I'll bet I can find them, and it's possible Marsh might have been photographed with the rest of the group."

Kincaid pushed the prints on his desk into a neat stack, thinking about the individuals he'd interviewed. "They may not be willing to identify him. No one picked him out from the CCTV shots we showed them this morning. There's something going on in the group dynamic that I don't understand."

"Is there someone else who could?"

He looked up at her, an idea dawning. Medhi Atias, the chicken shop proprietor, who saw them all come and go. "Yes. Yes, I think there might be."

"Great." Melody started to stand. "I'll—"

"Can you do this without anyone at the paper knowing what you're up to?"

She nodded. "I'm sure I can. I can access the files from my laptop."

"And don't talk to anyone about it except Doug. Not even Andy."

"But— You don't mean I shouldn't speak to Gemma—"

"No, of course I didn't mean Gemma. Although I haven't had a chance to talk to her since last night, so I'll need to fill her in." And, he thought, given that Melody was Gemma's officer, as well as her friend, Gemma might not be too happy at his pulling Melody away from her duties and into the fray of this case. But he needed help, and he didn't want to go through official channels until he had some idea of what he was dealing with.

"All right," he said. "Just be careful. And look after yourself, will you?"

He had just seen Melody out when his office line rang again. "Bloody hell," he muttered as he hurried back to his desk to pick it up, thinking it was his chief superintendent—if not the AC Crime himself—ringing to tell him he'd made a balls-up of the press conference and demanding a progress report.

But it was the desk sergeant again, sounding apologetic.

"Sorry, sir, but there's a young woman here. She's that upset. She says she saw you on the telly—on the midday news—and she insists it's you she wants to speak to. She says her boyfriend's been missing since that protest yesterday and she's worried something's happened to him."

CHAPTER ELEVEN

If the Directors and officers of the Midland Company had pooled their collective experience with a view to securing a site for their London station that would combine the greatest possible number of difficulties, they could hardly have fixed on anything better than the one they chose at St. Pancras.
—*Jack Simmons and Robert Thorne,*
St. Pancras Station, 2012

He left the dark blue Ford in the car park at Didcot Parkway railway station sometime before dawn. You weren't likely to be noticed coming or going from a railway station car park at odd hours, nor was the car likely to be thought abandoned if left for a few days.

A few days . . . Who was he kidding, after what had happened at St. Pancras? Maybe forever. But he couldn't think about that, not yet, and at least in a railway station car park it would be some time before the car was tagged and towed, and even then nothing in it should link it to him.

After a quick check to assure there was no one else about, he stowed the supplies from the boot in his big pack. Then he wiped down everything he'd touched with a clean cloth, locked the car, and pocketed the key.

He stood for a moment, adjusting the weight of his heavy pack on his shoulders, gazing at the deserted station platform. Even in the dark he could see the towers of nearby Didcot power station. Ironic, that, as he'd participated in the protests that had got Didcot A shut down. And what had it mattered, in the end?

A train horn hooted in the distance, the sound carried on the bitter wind. He shuddered. He couldn't bear trains now.

He turned east, towards the Thames, and began to walk.

When Gemma reached the police station, she found that DC Shara MacNichols had placed the two girls, Izzy Lamar and Deja Harriott, along with Izzy's mother, in the family suite used for sensitive interviews or when dealing with the grieving families of victims.

In the initial round of interviews after Mercy's death, it had been these two girls who had reported that Dillon Underwood had paid special attention to Mercy, and that they thought Mercy had fancied him. Glancing through the room's glass door, Gemma refreshed her memory. Izzy was white, a little chubby, with breasts already developing and clothes a bit tighter than Gemma thought appropriate. Her shoulder-length hair was dirty blond and she wore just a suspicion of makeup—the sort Gemma remembered wearing and thinking her mother wouldn't notice. Her mother, of course, had made her go and scrub her face as soon as she caught sight of her. Later, her younger sister, Cyn, had somehow managed to get away with her experiments.

Izzy's mother, also blond, but with the help of professional highlights, wore a dark olive-colored suit that did nothing for her coloring. She looked tired and distressed, and as if the last thing on her mind was Izzy's amateur attempt at blusher and lipstick.

The other girl, Deja Harriott, was black, thin, and gawky,

with hair scraped back into a tight knot and clothes that looked as if she'd outgrown them. She sat opposite the mother and daughter, her hands held awkwardly between her knees.

"The mother, what's her name?" Gemma asked Shara Mac-Nichols.

"Emily," said Shara, without consulting notes. "She's a loan officer in a bank. She came forward when Izzy admitted to having a photo on her phone."

"And you saw the photo? You're sure it's him?"

"Clear as day. But Mercy is partly turned away from the camera."

Gemma frowned. "Right. Well, let's see what we've got."

Opening the door, she went in with what she hoped was a reassuring smile. "Mrs. Lamar, thank you for coming. And you as well, girls." She pulled up a slightly battered conference chair, positioning it so that she would see both girls' faces. Izzy shifted on the sofa, moving almost imperceptibly away from her mother and closer to her friend. On closer inspection, Gemma saw that Izzy's eyes were puffy and red—she'd been crying.

Gemma turned to the other girl. "Deja, where's your mother today?"

"Teaching," Deja whispered. "She teaches year nine English at our school. She gave me permission to leave as long as I was with Izzy's mum."

"You two and Mercy were all in the same year at school, is that right?"

Both girls nodded, and Izzy said, "Year seven. It's bl"—she glanced at her mother, coughed, then substituted—"awful."

"I appreciated you coming, Deja," said Gemma, "but I can't interview you without your mum present." Glancing up at Shara, she added, "DC MacNichol, could you have someone get Deja a cup of hot chocolate from the vending machine? She can wait in the vestibule."

"Can I—" began Izzy, then trailed off when her mother frowned.

"Of course you can have some chocolate, too. Mrs. Lamar, some coffee?"

"Oh. But I have to get back to wor—" Emily Lamar sank back in her chair and sighed. "Okay. With sugar, please."

When Gemma saw the look that passed between the girls as Deja followed Shara out, she was glad she had an excuse to interview them separately. There was something going on here and she suspected she was more likely to get at the truth if she questioned them one at a time. She wished she could interview Izzy without her mother present, but then anything the girl told her would be inadmissible.

Gemma made small talk while waiting for Shara's return, asking Izzy what subjects she liked best at school, hoping to relax both Izzy and her mother.

When Shara came in with their hot drinks and settled with her notebook, Gemma leaned towards the girl. "Izzy, why didn't you tell us about the photo when we talked to you before?"

"It was from a couple of weeks before—" Izzy broke off, her eyes filling.

"Before Mercy died?" asked Gemma.

Izzy nodded. "I didn't remember I'd taken it." Gemma must have looked skeptical, because she added defensively, "I have a ton of photos on my phone. And we were doing an art class project, so I'd been taking more pictures than usual."

Gemma didn't believe for an instant that Izzy had forgot she had the photo, but she didn't press her. "Can I see it?" she asked.

Reluctantly, Izzy pulled an iPhone from her jeans pocket, woke it up, and scrolled down the screen. "Here."

When Gemma took the phone, she saw that the screen was slightly cracked. Even though the phone was obviously not new, she had to wonder at parents buying such an expensive gadget for a twelve-year-old. Just this year, they'd bought Kit a cheap phone with a limited number of texts, and he was fourteen.

She focused on the photo. It had been taken from a distance and was slightly out of focus, but she recognized the location immediately—it was outside the Starbucks next to Brixton tube station. And the man in the photo was definitely Dillon Underwood. The date stamp was indeed two weeks before Mercy's murder.

Enlarging the image, she saw the other figure more clearly. Mercy.

Dillon seemed to be talking to her, urgently, and reaching towards her. Mercy was looking down, her face half hidden by the cloud of her hair. Even at twelve, Mercy Johnson had been beautiful—mixed race, Gemma guessed from the lightness of her skin, with delicate features and dark, curling hair that fell just to her shoulders.

She enlarged the image again, then looked up at Izzy. "He's handing her something. What was it?"

"We think it was a phone. She wouldn't tell us."

Gemma waited.

After a moment, Izzy went on, sounding aggrieved now. "She said it was none of our business. We were her best friends! And she said if we told her mum she'd kill us."

"You didn't think it was strange that she wanted to keep it a secret?"

"Well, sort of. But she was already in trouble . . ." Izzy swallowed, and went on. "See, she'd lost her phone. It wasn't an iPhone, but it was pretty nice, and she was supposed to be responsible. She had a limit on her texts, and her mum checked them." She gave a quick glance at her own mother, as if hoping she wouldn't get any ideas. "So there was no way Mercy was getting a new phone anytime soon, and she was afraid her mum wouldn't buy her the computer she wanted because she'd lost the phone."

Gemma considered this. "Okay. But that still doesn't explain why she didn't want you and Deja to know about the phone."

"She'd been—I don't know—funny, for a couple of weeks. Ever since she started looking at computers."

"And talking to Dillon Underwood?"

Izzy nodded.

"Did Dillon ever talk to you?"

"Nah. Not really," said Izzy, mouth turned down in a pout. "He had this way of, I don't know, sort of singling Mercy out. But then she was the one wanting the computer. Deja and me—we've had them forever." She shrugged—the disdain of the haves for the have-nots.

"Did Dillon know that Mercy had lost her phone?"

Izzy frowned. "I should think so. She thought she might have dropped it in the store. She went back in there all upset and crying."

"How long after that was this photo taken?" Gemma tapped the phone.

"I don't know. Maybe a week."

Gemma looked at the photo again, checking the date tag. Six days before Mercy's death. "Tell me about the day you took this picture."

"It was Mercy's idea. She said we needed to study for our history exam and we should meet up at Starbucks. But she was all, like, distracted. She even spilled her chai latte all over my papers. We thought maybe she'd had another fight with her mum. Then she wanted to leave and told us to go on, she'd see us at school. But when we looked back, she was talking to him."

"What did she do then?" asked Gemma.

"She glared at us for a minute, and we were like, we're not

going anywhere. So she just walked away from him. But she wouldn't talk to us, and she wouldn't tell us about the phone."

Shara spoke up for the first time. "So how did Dillon Underwood know Mercy would be at Starbucks that afternoon? You think she meant to meet him, and that's why she was so fidgety?"

"Yeah. She must have," Izzy answered, nodding.

"There were no calls to his mobile or to the store's phone from Mercy's mum's landline. And no calls to unidentified numbers." Shara tapped her pen on her notebook. "Did she use your phone at any time before that meeting, Izzy? Or Deja's?"

Izzy shifted in her seat. "Well, yeah. After school that day. She sent a text."

"Izzy!" Emily Lamar had gone paler and paler as she listened to her daughter's recital. "Why on earth didn't you tell anyone?"

" 'Cause she deleted the text, see? I didn't think—we didn't think it would make any difference."

"But why didn't you tell us you'd seen Mercy talk to that man outside the electronics shop?"

"Because . . . because she didn't go back to the shop after that. And then, after she was . . . we were afraid . . ." Izzy's voice faltered.

"Go on," said her mother more gently.

Izzy's words came out in a rush, as if the thought behind them had been too long dammed up. "We—we thought that if we'd told someone, that maybe—maybe Mercy wouldn't have been killed. We were afraid that it was our fault." She began to cry, knuckling her eyes like the child she was.

"Oh, love." Emily Lamar gathered her daughter into a hug and patted her back. "You couldn't have known."

Exchanging a glance with Shara, Gemma gave them a moment, then said, as calmly as she could, "Izzy, we're going to need your phone. Our forensics people should be able to retrieve that number. And we're going to need you—and Deja when one of her parents can accompany her—to make a formal statement."

"But—"

"Don't worry. It's not hard. Detective Constable MacNichol here will type up what you've told us from her notes. Then you and your mum can read it, and if you feel comfortable with it, you can both sign it."

She stood, signaling the end of the interview, but Emily Lamar stopped her with a touch. "Detective, can I have a word?"

"Of course."

"Come on, Izzy," said Shara. "Let's find your friend." She shepherded Izzy from the room.

Emily Lamar looked at Gemma, her gaze unflinching. "Detective, is my girl in danger from this . . . monster? And Deja? Tell me the truth."

The last thing Gemma wanted was to start a panic among the parents in the area. As diverse as Brixton was, it was a tight community. If Dillon Underwood was harassed or hurt by frightened citizens, it could cost the police a case against him. But she was a parent, too, and she had a duty to protect these girls. If Dillon Underwood was indeed Mercy's killer, he could not be sure that Mercy hadn't told them something damning.

"Detective?" said Emily again.

"Mrs. Lamar, you understand I can't tell you anything officially. We have no proof that Underwood did anything other than show Mercy computers. But if Izzy and Deja were my daughters, I'd see that they were supervised outside of school hours. But please don't discuss this. Rumors could be damaging to our investigation."

Emily Lamar nodded. "You will catch him?"

"Yes. We will," Gemma assured her with more confidence than she felt.

When Gemma had seen Emily out, she met Shara in the corridor. "He groomed her," said Gemma. "Separated her from her friends. Gained her trust."

"And her missing phone—"

"The phone she thought she dropped in the shop—"

"What do you want to bet he picked it up when she was distracted," Shara finished. "If he is what we suspect, it would have been irresistible. Pictures, texts—"

"And then, when she was so upset about the loss, maybe an unforeseen opportunity. Give her a phone, probably a cheap pay-as-you-go, tell her she could only use it to communicate with him or he would get into trouble," agreed Gemma. "We couldn't figure out how he could have set up a meeting with her the night she was killed. Now I think we can guess."

"So what happened to the phone?" asked Shara. "There was no phone on the body or in her belongings at home."

"He took it." In that instant, Gemma knew it with a certainty that went bone deep. "After he'd killed her."

They looked at each other. Shara shook her head. The red beads on the ends of the dozens of tiny plaits in her hair bounced with emphasis. "He wouldn't have been so stupid as to keep it."

"Probably not. But we can hope," said Gemma. "And at the very least the photo on Izzy's phone will get us a search warrant."

By the time the glow that presaged dawn had begun to light the eastern sky, he'd left the main road.

He smelled the river before he saw it, a deeper, earthier dampness carried by the cold wind. His canoe was where he'd left it, camouflaged by carefully arranged brush in an overgrown area near the river's edge. Stowing his gear, he dragged the boat to the bank and slid it gently into the water. He pulled the canoe against the bank, stepped in, then turned the canoe as he pushed off. He rested the paddle across the bow as the little boat nosed through the rushes towards open water.

The sky in the east showed pink now, through tatters of cloud. It was only then that he realized the wind had died with the dawn. There was nothing, not the chirp of a bird or the rustle of reeds in the breeze. The silver surface of the river spread before him, polished as glass.

The silence enveloped him. He felt he might have slipped into a vacuum in time. For that moment, he forgot that his hands and feet burned with the cold. He forgot everything that had happened, and everything that he knew was to come.

The sky bloomed rose, then morphed almost imperceptibly to gold.

Then the reeds swayed, dark clouds blotted the sky, and the current took the boat.

The first word that came to Duncan's mind when he saw the girl was *ethereal*.

Her skin was alabaster pale, with a translucent quality to it. Her hair, which cascaded over her shoulders like candy floss, was so fair it was almost white. She was slight, even in a padded jacket, and looked younger than the age on the ID she'd given the desk sergeant—twenty.

The desk sergeant had put her in the conference room with a cup of tea—in a china cup and saucer, no less—but the drink sat untouched. When she looked up at him, he saw that she wore no makeup, and that her eyes were a blue so light they were almost colorless.

"I'm Detective Superintendent Kincaid," he said, taking the chair across the table. "And you're"—he glanced at the notes the sergeant had scribbled for him, although he didn't need to—"Ariel. Is that right? That's very Shakespearian."

"My dad's a history professor at UCL." Her voice was soft, almost a whisper. "But he loves Shakespeare."

"Mine, too. I'm Duncan, by the way."

"Oh." She smiled, visibly relaxing. "The Scottish play."

"For my sins. Do you mind if I call you Ariel?" Her last name, he saw from the notes, was Ellis.

"No, that's fine." She touched the cup, but didn't lift it. "I'm afraid I don't drink tea. I didn't want to say."

"That's okay, Ariel. I had no idea the sergeant knew how to make a decent cup of tea. So, how can I help you?" Kincaid wanted to hear what she had to say without any lead-in from him.

She shifted a little in her chair but met his eyes. "Now that I'm here I feel a bit of an idiot. It's probably nothing, and I don't want to be the hysterical female."

"Why don't you tell me anyway. I promise I won't think you're hysterical."

Ariel Ellis bit her bottom lip, then sighed. "It's my boyfriend. His name is Paul Cole. We had a bit of a . . . row . . . yesterday morning. I knew he meant to go to that demonstration at the railway station, and I haven't seen him or had a text or anything from him since. When I saw on the news last night that someone was . . . killed, I guess I started to get a little panicked. Then this morning, I went to Matthew's flat, and there was a policeman on the door. I didn't know what to do. Then I saw you on the news. So I thought you were the person I should talk to."

"So you know Matthew Quinn?" Kincaid asked.

Ariel shrugged. "Matthew was one of my father's students. He got his 'save historic London' ideas from my dad's walking tours. Dad's a bit of a fanatic about it." Ariel drew together brows that were as pale as her hair, and Kincaid noticed she did nothing to define them. It gave her face a slightly unfinished look. "I mean in a good way," she went on. "It's Dad's passion, but he'd never do anything destructive."

"So your dad wouldn't condone demonstrations?"

"Not if someone might get hurt. The demonstrations were Matthew's idea. He and my dad pretty much parted ways after that."

"What about your boyfriend, Paul? Is he one of your father's students, too?"

"He was. That's how he knew Matthew and some of the others. And me, of course. Paul's still officially enrolled at uni, but he hasn't been going to classes lately."

"That's UCL?" Kincaid asked.

Ariel nodded. "That's one reason I was worried about him. I think Paul's dad is a bit of a bully, and Paul was worried about what he would do when he found out Paul was failing his courses."

"Did Paul stay at Matthew's flat?"

"I don't know. Sometimes, I think. But he still has his student accommodation."

"What about you? Do you stay at Matthew's?"

Making a face, Ariel said, "Sleep on the floor and be bossed about by Matthew? I don't think so. I live with my dad. We're not far from here, actually. Cartwright Gardens."

Kincaid made a note. "You're still at university, then?"

"Finishing my degree in graphic arts."

"So tell me about this row."

Ariel Ellis flushed a becoming rose. "It wasn't—we hadn't been getting on too well lately. I thought he was letting Matthew make a mess of his life. And then I—" Her color grew deeper. "I got—pregnant. It was so stupid. My dad doesn't even know. Paul thought we should get married. I told him he was daft. I wasn't ready to get married, and what would we live on? He was furious. And then—" Her eyes filled with tears, but she made no effort to wipe them away, even when they began to trickle down her cheeks. "I—I had a miscarriage. It was a baby I didn't even want, and I never imagined I could feel so awful about anything."

Kincaid thought about how Gemma had felt—how he and Gemma had both felt—losing a child that way, even though the pregnancy had been unplanned.

"I'm so sorry," he said, with such sincerity that Ariel looked startled.

"You understand, don't you?"

"I do." He stood and fetched her the box of tissues from the conference room's corner table.

"Thanks." Ariel gave him a tremulous smile as she took a tissue and dabbed at her eyes. He wasn't sure if she meant for the tissues or the condolences.

"What about Paul?" he asked. "How did he feel about the miscarriage?"

"He—" Ariel balled the tissue up in her fist. "He—he said it was my fault. That I must have done something. I told him he was crazy, and he said he'd show me crazy. He was being so childish. That's why—" She swallowed. "Oh, God. Surely he wouldn't have . . ."

"Did you know that Matthew's group meant to deploy a smoke bomb at St. Pancras?"

"I'm not really privy to the group's insider stuff. But I went to see Paul yesterday morning at Matthew's to try to make him see reason, and I heard them arguing."

"Who was arguing?"

"Paul and Matthew. Paul wanted to be the one to set off the smoke bomb. But Matthew said Ryan was going to do it. Then Paul stormed out."

"So you know Ryan Marsh?"

Ariel nodded. "He stays there, at least some of the time. Even Matthew thinks Ryan is God, but Ryan never acts like it. You know?"

Kincaid thought he heard a hint of hero worship. "Was Paul jealous of Ryan?"

"He didn't like everyone looking up to Ryan, if that's what

you mean." Ariel twisted the now-shredded tissue. "You don't think—you don't think Paul could have done something to hurt Ryan? Was it—was Ryan—" She stopped, shaking her head.

If this Paul Cole had been the one to give an incendiary device to Ryan Marsh, where was he now? Or— Kincaid considered the other possibility, equally dire. What if Paul Cole had *taken* the incendiary from Ryan Marsh? He had to rule it out, if he could.

"Ariel, you and Paul were close."

"Obviously." A hint of sarcasm, tinged with embarrassment.

"Is there anything . . . unique . . . about Paul? A tattoo, for instance? Or maybe you know if he broke a bone at some point?"

"Oh, God." Ariel pressed a hand to her mouth. "You mean like a—what do they call it on the telly—a distinguishing mark?"

"Yes. Is there something?" Kincaid pressed.

Ariel just stared at him, her blue eyes wide.

"What is it, Ariel? If you want to help, you need to tell me."

"I don't—I can't think—oh." She went still, as if suddenly facing the terror she had been dancing around. "Yes. He does. Just inside his left shoulder. Paul has a birthmark."

CHAPTER TWELVE

It was occupied by a canal, a gas-works, an ancient church with a large and crowded graveyard, and some of the most atrocious slums in London, and through it all ran the River Fleet.
—*Jack Simmons and Robert Thorne,*
St. Pancras Station, *2012*

Kincaid had escorted Ariel Ellis out after getting her contact information, telling her to go home and promising that he would be in touch.

As he opened the station front door for her, she'd pulled a woolly hat over her hair and smiled at him. "Thank you. I do feel better now, just having got things off my chest. I'm sure Paul's fine and I've just made an idiot of myself."

He hoped she was right. But now they had another avenue to explore, and he wondered why no one in the group had mentioned Paul Cole or Ariel Ellis. Before talking to the team, he shut himself in his office and rang Rashid. He could hear traffic noise in the background when Rashid picked up.

"Rashid, it's Duncan," he said. "I need you to check something for me on our victim. Did you see anything that might have been a birthmark inside his left shoulder blade?"

There was a muffled murmur of voices, then Rashid again. "Sorry. Just reached the scene of a suspicious death in Dalton. It will be a while before I can get back to the London and pull him out of storage."

"You don't remember seeing anything like that?" He explained about Ariel Ellis and her missing boyfriend.

"It's possible," said Rashid after a moment. "The skin there was somewhat protected by the backpack. I may be able to see some differentiation in the tissue under a microscope."

"Could he have been twenty rather than thirty?"

"It's possible. I'll ring you as soon as I get back to the lab."

And with that Kincaid had to be content.

When he walked back into the CID room, he was met by curious faces.

"Is there news, Guv?" asked Simon Gikas.

"Who was that girl downstairs?" put in Sweeney. "The one with the fairy hair. I'd call her a looker."

Kincaid suspected that Sweeney would call anything with two legs and breasts a looker, but that didn't mean he was wrong about Ariel Ellis.

Ignoring Sweeney, Kincaid said, "We may have another possible identity for our victim." He repeated Ariel's story, although he left out what she'd told him about having had a miscarriage. Unless they had some concrete evidence that her boyfriend was the victim, it seemed an unnecessary disclosure. "I've already rung Dr. Kaleem. While we wait for him to check on the birthmark, let's see what we can learn about Paul Cole."

Kincaid paused for a moment, reminding himself that it was no longer his job to do all the legwork. "Jasmine, George," he said, making an effort to use his detectives' first names, "I'd like you to go to UCL. I've got an address for Paul Cole's student accommodation, a residence hall called Ramsay House near Gower Street, but"—he glanced at his watch—"first, you'd better get on to the admin office before they close and get a contact address for Cole's parents."

"Right, Guv." Sweeney unplugged his phone from its charger and reached for his overcoat. Sidana just nodded and gathered her things.

"Check in after that, will you? We'll see where we are. In the meantime, maybe Simon can come up with more information on Paul Cole than we've found on the elusive Mr. Marsh. It may be that we've been looking for the wrong victim all along."

Melody rummaged in Andy's small kitchen cupboard for something that would soothe her aching throat. In the very back, behind an old jar of Marmite and an empty bottle of olive oil, she found a box of lemon-ginger tea bags.

She opened the box and sniffed. A little stale, but she'd found a shriveled lemon in the fridge that would help. Not that she could criticize—there was nothing in her own fridge at all. She found a clean mug emblazoned with the Gibson logo and put the kettle on to boil.

Even that made her woozy. Slicing up the lemon, she dropped it in the mug with the tea bag. When the kettle boiled, she filled the mug and took it back into the sitting room to steep.

She'd felt so exhausted after her interview with Duncan that she'd come back to Andy's flat, curling up on the futon in the sitting room with her laptop and Bert, Andy's cat. Although Andy hadn't returned from visiting Tam, Melody hadn't been able to talk herself into going back to her own place in Notting Hill.

Bert had resettled himself in the warm spot she'd vacated, and now gave her a disgruntled look as she said, "Shove over, Bert," and shifted him. She set the tea on the amp that served Andy as a coffee table. Then, on impulse, she picked up the blue cardigan he'd tossed on the end of the futon and wrapped it round herself. It was warm and oddly comforting, considering the circumstances in which Andy had worn it yesterday. And it smelled faintly of him—that indefinable combination of his soap, shampoo, skin, and the faint mustiness imparted by the flat itself.

Pulling her computer into her lap again, Melody sipped at her tea and found it not as bad as she'd expected. But her throat felt no less raw, and within a few minutes she was coughing again. Her head hurt, and no matter how hard she tried to concentrate on the computer screen, her brain seemed sluggish and foggy.

She had accessed the *Chronicle*'s photo files, setting "environmental protests" as the search term and the past ten years as the parameter. But the photos blurred and her head throbbed. She sighed, closing her eyes and scratching Bert under his chin. He obliged by upping the volume of his purr and kneading his paws against her leg. Melody found to her surprise that she didn't mind the pricking of his claws.

She must have dozed, because she woke with a start when the flat door opened, and almost dumped her laptop onto the floor.

"Melody?" said Andy. "Are you all right?"

She closed the laptop and sat up, groggily, rubbing at her eyes. "Fine."

"You don't look fine." He sat beside her, studying her with a frown.

"Thanks a lot. You don't look so hot yourself," she said. There were dark smudges under his eyes, his face was drawn, and his blond hair looked uncombed. "How's Tam?"

Andy reached across her to give Bert a rub on the head. "Sedated. They say there's not much change in his test results today, but the pain from the burn is worse."

"And Michael and Louise? How are they holding up?"

"I stayed so they could both get some rest. And then Caleb and Poppy came." Andy shifted away from her and Bert, folding his arms across his chest.

"What?" Melody asked, sensing something wrong. "Shouldn't Caleb and Poppy have come to hospital?"

"No, it's not that. It's just . . . You know the producer who was coming to the concert?"

Melody nodded, waiting.

"In spite of everything that happened yesterday, he still wants us to do a demo for him. And he wants us to do it tonight. He has a slot open at Abbey Road."

"Abbey Road?" Melody sat up, now completely awake. "Abbey Road Studios? But that's fabulous."

"Not without Tam."

She stared at him. "You're not seriously telling me you don't mean to go ahead with this?" When he didn't answer, she said, "Andy?"

He shook his head, and when he met her gaze, she saw that he was close to tears. "How can I do something like this without him there? After everything he's done for me?"

"How could you *not* do it? How do you think Tam will feel if he finds out you'd passed up something like this? And what about Poppy and Caleb and what this would mean for them? You can't possibly be so selfish as to deprive them of this chance."

Andy stared at her, wide-eyed, and Melody realized she was shaking with anger. "Oh, God, I'm sorry," she whispered, appalled. "I didn't mean to lash out at you like that. I don't know what's wrong with me. I just want you to look after yourself." She started to cough.

"Maybe you're right. But what about *you* looking after yourself?" Andy countered. "Isn't there someone you should be talking to about what you saw yesterday? No wonder you're a bit . . . testy."

"Thanks. Not that it's not deserved." Melody managed a smile.

"And if I do this demo," Andy went on, "I can't go to hospital with you for your tests tonight. I have a responsibility to you, too. Or at least I thought I did."

"Of course you do." Melody stroked his arm. "But I'm used to doing things on my own. I'll be fine."

"What about your parents? Couldn't you call them?"

"No." It came out more forcefully than she'd meant. "It's just . . . my parents are a bit overwhelming sometimes. My dad's a . . . a journalist . . . and once he gets his teeth into something, he won't let go. If I didn't set boundaries, I'd never have a life of my own."

"Is that so bad?" he asked, and she knew he was thinking of growing up without a father, and with a mother who was neither physically nor emotionally capable of caring for him.

"No, of course not. But I've fought my whole life to be independent. It's . . . important to me. You have to understand that." There was so much she wasn't telling him—couldn't tell him, not just now. But at least what she *had* said was the truth.

"Is that why you haven't introduced me to them? I thought it was because you were ashamed of me."

"Oh, no. Not in a million years." She turned to him, putting her head on his shoulder, and after a moment he put his arms round her in a hug. "I promise I'll take you to meet them," she said. "Let's just get this behind us. And you promise me you'll do that demo tonight." She coughed again and Andy stroked her hair.

"What about your tests at hospital, then?"

As much as she hated to admit it, Melody realized that she didn't want to go alone. And that she was frightened, not only for Tam but for herself.

"I'll call Gemma," she said.

• • •

Kincaid was normally neither impatient nor fidgety, but he hated waiting for people to get back to him—especially when those people were doing tasks he might have done himself. That was one of the reasons he'd loved the special homicide liaison team at the Yard—he'd been able to do more legwork than his rank normally allowed. Nor had he been accustomed to having an entire team under his command. Now he wasn't sure if that had been a blessing or a curse.

He hung over Simon Gikas's shoulder until Simon told him to go away, that he'd let him know if he found anything.

Pouring another cup of coffee from the CID room pot—and making a mental note to buy a decent machine for his own office—he settled back at his desk, rescanning the reports on the case while checking for messages from either Rashid or Jasmine Sidana, and all the while keeping an eye on the wall clock as it ticked round towards half past six.

He'd just thought he should check in with Gemma when his phone rang and her face flashed up on the screen.

"Hello, love," he said. "I was about to—"

"Can you meet me somewhere for a drink?" she said. "Near your office. I'm at UCL Hospital."

Kincaid's heart thumped. "Is everything okay?"

"I went with Melody for her tests."

"Is she all right?"

"They're not seeing any systemic damage as yet, but the doctor insists that she not come back to work for a few more days." A taxi horn honked in the background and the wind rumbled across the phone's mic, cutting off part of Gemma's sentence. ". . . and I could really use some moral support," she finished. "Didn't you say there was a good wine bar near your station?"

"There's Vat. But that will be bonkers this time of day." He thought for a moment. "There's another small place a bit closer to the station. It's called, um, La Gourmandina, I think. Next to Persephone Books."

"Okay, see you in a— There's a taxi!"

The connection went dead.

Kincaid grabbed his coat from the rack and went out through the CID room, telling Simon where he was going and to ring him if anything came through.

If there was any light left in the sky, it was blotted out by the lowering clouds, and the wind had not died with the dusk. But, at least, he thought as he yanked his coat collar up around his ears, it wasn't raining, and he hadn't far to go.

He'd only glanced in the small deli/wine bar as he'd walked by on the way to the Perseverance, but when he entered the place he was glad he'd chosen it. It was small, quiet, and warm. A couple drinking wine occupied one of the high tables by the front window, and at another a woman sipped coffee while writing in a notebook.

He chose a table nearer the back of the small shop and ordered, a crisp white wine for Gemma and a decent coffee for himself. The waiter had just brought the drinks when Gemma came through the door.

She smiled and kissed him as she shrugged out of her coat, her cheek cold against his, then pulled off her hat and ran her fingers through her coppery hair.

"Lucky taxi," she said as she slid onto the stool. "And you"—she picked up her glass—"are an angel." Raising her glass to him, she took a sip, then sighed and closed her eyes for a moment. "Perfect."

"You do look a bit frazzled. What's up? Are the kids okay?"

"The kids are fine. Charlotte's still at Betty's and I've put Kit and Toby to work making posters for the cat—not that they're happy about that."

"Posters? Why?"

"Bryony brought her little scanner when she checked on

mum and babies this morning. She didn't detect a chip. But she said as the cat was so tame, she might belong to someone in the neighborhood, and we should put up posters in the vet clinics and the coffee shops."

"And the boys don't want to give her back to her owner. *Potential* owner."

Gemma rolled her eyes. "Yes. I'm beginning to think Kit has a future as a barrister rather than a biologist. I've heard every argument in the book, including the most telling one— that if the owner had taken proper care of her, she wouldn't have been pregnant or lost. But that still doesn't make it right to keep her if someone claims her."

"You don't sound too thrilled with the idea of giving her up, either."

Her expression rueful, Gemma said, "Call me a sucker."

Kincaid grinned. "I'm thinking Hazel Cavendish needs a kitten."

"And your friend MacKenzie," Gemma countered.

"But which two are you going to give up?"

Gemma gave him a little punch on the arm. "Don't even start with the crazy cat lady thing again. We're not keeping four kittens. No way."

"That means you're open to the possibility of keeping fewer than four kittens."

She laughed. "I can see that Kit's been taking lessons from you." Gemma drank a little more wine, then admitted, "I am a bit partial to the black-and-white one."

"Their eyes aren't even open, and you don't know what sex they are."

"I know. It's stupid." Her face fell, and now that her cheeks weren't pink from the cold, he saw that she looked pale and strained. He remembered that she'd said something about needing moral support.

"You can keep whichever and however many kittens you

like, love," he said gently. "But I don't think you came to talk about cats. Is it Melody you're worried about?"

"Partly. She looks terrible. And she seemed very . . . I don't know. Withdrawn, maybe. How bad was it, really, what she saw?"

He thought for a moment. "I'm trying to remember if I've seen worse. I can't say I have. And I was only there for the aftermath. I didn't witness it. She did."

"I suppose we've both been lucky not to have worked a bombing." Gemma drank a little more of her wine. The threat was something that all London coppers lived with, but anticipating was not the same as actually dealing with it. "And she's not only worried about herself, but about Tam. We all are.

"But the thing is"—Gemma slid her almost empty glass forward on the table—"it's horribly selfish of me, but I've never needed her help more." She told him about the girls she'd interviewed that day, and the developments regarding the suspect in Mercy Johnson's murder. "But now that we have something concrete," she went on, "we can't find the bastard."

"He's done a bunk?"

"Not necessarily. It was his day off work, and he wasn't at his flat. But now I'm worried that when he hears we've been looking for him, he *will* do a bunk." She frowned. "Although he's arrogant enough that it may not faze him. I suppose I'm just missing having Melody's input, but of course I couldn't even talk to her about it at hospital."

"You've got DC MacNichol, right?"

"Yes. And she's done a bloody good job with this. But—" Gemma's face went still. "Oh. The hospital. I know what I meant to tell you. I went to see Tam this morning. He was awake. I think I caught him just as the painkillers were wearing off. I'm not sure how lucid he was, but he said that he saw the victim. Before he pulled the grenade. Tam said he didn't look frightened, only a little nervous and excited. And he said that he was young."

"Young?" Ryan Marsh had been described as being close to thirty. "What did Tam mean by young?"

" 'A lad,' " he said. " 'Just a lad.' "

Kincaid's phone vibrated in his pocket. Pulling it out, he saw that it was Rashid.

When he answered, Rashid said without preliminary, "Duncan, you had better get the missing boyfriend's blood type."

CHAPTER THIRTEEN

First, the site needed to be cleared. It was a brutal process. The landlords sold up and the dwellers were displaced for no compensation.

—Bbc.co.uk/London/St. Pancras

He awakened to a surprising sensation of warmth and an all-enveloping darkness. Shifting a little, he felt the slippery confines of his sleeping bag. Unlike the cheap bag and bedroll he had left behind with his friend Medhi in London, the bag he'd stashed in the boot of the Ford was rated for subfreezing temperatures, protection against even this bitter unseasonable cold.

As his eyes adjusted, he began to make out shapes. The solid darkness above him was the camouflage-printed tarp he'd fixed in place with stakes made from birch branches, angled to protect him from both wind and rain. Now, to either side of the tarp, he could see the lacy fingers of the bare trees and the dim outline of clouds against the night sky. And there, in a gap between the clouds, a star.

When he turned his head, he saw the tiniest glimmer from the embers of the fire he'd built in his fire pit earlier in the day. They flickered, like fairy sparks.

He moved and couldn't stop a groan. His back hurt. His shoulders hurt. When he tried wiggling his toes, pain shot through his feet. How many miles had he walked? Too many, even for his good boots. And his feet had been so cold by the time he'd crawled into the sleeping bag that he'd been afraid sensation wouldn't return. Now he wished it hadn't.

His fingers, when he flexed them, were swollen and raw. Once he had reached the hidden island, he'd beached the canoe and covered it with bracken and branches, then found his lightly buried spade and begun to dig. First, the fire pit. When it was deep enough, he'd used damp logs to barricade three sides as protection against the wind.

Then he'd uncovered the five-gallon plastic jug of fresh water, enough to keep him going until he could set up the filter for the river water, and the first section of sealed eight-inch PVC pipe, filled with dehydrated rations and tinder for the fire.

Dryer lint and Vaseline. His wife had caught him once, saving the lint from the dryer filter, and asked him what in hell he was doing. "It's for starting fires," he'd said. "Sometime you might need to start a fire."

She'd looked at him as if he was speaking Greek, shrugged, and shaken her head. "You and your self-sufficiency thing. You're just like a kid." The disdain had been clear. He supposed it was then he'd realized, at some subconscious level, that they had reached an unbridgeable gap.

But it had been play at first, really, the river hideout. A reminder of the time he'd spent scouting as a boy and camping with his dad. And a need for a rare day or two when he had to be no one but himself.

The events of last autumn, and his failure to perform the task he'd been set, had changed that. He'd begun to come to the island in the Thames whenever he could get away, and he'd begun to take provisioning more seriously. Thus the cache tubes, one filled with food, another with ropes and stakes and

*silver emergency blankets modified to make wind barriers,
another with a compact fishing rod and tackle. All legal, all
easily obtainable. Except for the last two. The larger tube held
an Armalite AR-7.22 rifle, all the components broken down
and fitted into the stock. It was good for killing small game
and would float.*

*The last tube, a smaller one, held a false passport and sev-
eral thousand pounds in cash. It was his desperation cache, the
one he'd hoped he'd never have to use.*

*Anxiety clutched at him, making him begin to sweat in
the warmth of the sleeping bag. His stomach cramped. He
realized he was hungry. And thirsty. And he had to pee. The
fire needed tending. He would have to get up, no matter how
much it hurt, and no matter how hopeless his plight seemed.*

Kincaid found Gemma a taxi on Theobald's Road, then went
into the station and up to the CID room. There was no sign of
Sidana or Sweeney, but Simon Gikas was still huddled over his
computer.

"News, Guv?" Simon asked when he looked up and saw
Kincaid's face.

"Rashid rang. He thinks there may very well be a birthmark on the victim's left shoulder. And he says the blood type
is fairly rare—A negative—so if we can find out Paul Cole's
blood type, it will help make an identification. And there's
another thing leaning in Cole's favor." He told Simon about
Gemma's visit to Tam. "I need to show Cole's photo to Tam."

He rang Michael, Tam's partner. "Michael, Duncan here.
Are you with Tam?"

There was the sound of movement and a door closing before Michael said, "Yes. They've moved him into a room. I've
sent Louise home, but I'm staying the night."

"He's better, then?" Kincaid felt a rush of relief.

"So far his organs seem to be holding their own. The pain from the burn is worse, though."

"Gemma says he told her this morning that he saw the victim before he pulled the grenade. We have a possible ID. I was hoping Tam could look at a photo to confirm it."

"I don't think he could tell you if it was Father Christmas at the moment. They've changed his pain meds. It's given him some relief, but he's out. Doped to the eyeballs, poor love." There was great tenderness in Michael's voice—a glimpse behind the partners' usual matter-of-fact facade.

Kincaid couldn't imagine how he would feel if it were Gemma in that hospital bed. "Michael, let me know if there's anything I can do."

"I'd say catch the bastard who did this, but he's dead, isn't he?"

Kincaid didn't say that it could be a bit more complicated than that. "Could you ring me just as soon as you think Tam might be up to looking at a photo?" he asked. "Oh, and, Michael, tell Louise to take care of herself."

Ringing off, Kincaid thought for a moment. What about the waitress in the café? The one Melody had said was so helpful. Could she have seen something?

He glanced at the clock. It was after eight already and he didn't know how late the café stayed open. Or if the waitress would be working the evening shift.

His phone rang, and this time it was Jasmine Sidana.

"Sir," she said. No casual "Guv" from her. "No one at Paul Cole's residence hall has seen him since yesterday morning. The boy in the next room—they have single rooms"—Sidana sounded disapproving—"said he'd seemed a little off lately."

"Off, how?"

"Apparently he was never particularly outgoing, but the last few weeks he hadn't been talking to anyone."

"Did he mention seeing him with the girlfriend, Ariel?"

"No."

Ariel had told him she and Paul had had a big row yesterday morning. Where had they argued, he wondered, if not in Paul's room?

"I spoke to administration," Sidana continued. "Paul Cole was failing his courses."

A serious row with his girlfriend, failing at uni—both possible indicators of suicide with a boy of Paul's age and apparent temperament. But Tam had told Gemma that he looked excited, not frightened, and surely someone about to commit suicide would look frightened. And in any case, it didn't explain how Paul Cole had got hold of a white phosphorus grenade. Or why he and not Ryan Marsh had been carrying it.

And that was still a bloody big assumption.

"Did you get the parents' information?" he asked Sidana.

"They live in Battersea. Father's a bank manager."

"You and Sweeney had better go and see them. Ask about the birthmark. Rashid says it's a possibility. If they say yes, you'd better prepare them for the worst."

For once, he was glad to let someone else do the job.

Kincaid took a taxi from Holborn to St. Pancras International. If he couldn't see Tam, he wanted confirmation from someone who might have seen Paul Cole. He thought of the waitress Melody had described. If she had been serving tables in the arcade, it was possible she'd caught a glimpse of him.

He had the cabbie let him out at the first Pancras Road entrance, the Eurostar taxi drop-off. There were no longer uniformed officers on duty. He entered with a little jolt of apprehension, but the scene that met him bore no relation to the previous day's chaos.

The concourse positively sparkled. The Marks & Spencer food store was filled with shoppers buying last-minute things for supper or bouquets of flowers. It was late enough in the evening—almost nine o'clock now—that the pedestrian traffic was light. But the travelers and commuters passing through the concourse were chatting or listening to iPods and showed no signs of discomfort.

The temporary stage was gone, and someone was playing the station piano. Bach, Kincaid thought, stopping for a moment to listen. The speaker chimed with regular rail service announcements.

He crossed the arcade. Where yesterday there had been a crime scene, he thought he saw only the faintest shadows of scorch marks on the polished floor. At the café's arcade tables, one man sat reading a newspaper, and a woman at another table was engrossed in texting on her mobile phone.

It was as if all yesterday's terror and anguish had been magically erased, and he found it a little surreal.

Entering the café, he looked round for a waitress that fit the description Melody had given him. There was no one at the WAIT TO BE SEATED sign by the front door, so he had a moment to scan.

He recognized her the instant he saw her, not waiting tables, but sitting in the back with what looked like a large cup of coffee or chocolate. She was slight, with dark hair cut boy short, but there was nothing masculine about her. It was a pretty face and a memorable one.

When a young man wearing the café staff's black shirt and trousers came to greet him, he asked to see the manager, deciding it was best not to barge in on the waitress without an introduction. The manager came from the kitchen and Kincaid explained his business quietly, complimenting the staff and the waitress in particular.

"That's Natalie," the manager, a middle-aged woman, said. "She's a bit cut up today. We're all feeling some reaction"—she shook her head—"I still can't believe what happened. But what

Natalie did was exceptional. I told her she should take the day off but she insisted on coming in."

"Do you mind if I speak to her?"

"No, of course not. I'll just introduce you. Can I get you something while you're talking?"

"Coffee would be great," he said, looking longingly at the customers drinking glasses of wine and eating delicious-looking sandwiches and salads. He realized that he was starving and that he didn't remember lunch. But he needed his wits about him, and he couldn't very well chomp on a sandwich while interviewing a witness.

The girl looked up as the manager brought Kincaid to her table. When the manager introduced him, she looked slightly alarmed.

"Natalie, do you mind if I sit down?" Kincaid asked.

When Natalie shook her head, Kincaid pulled out a chair.

"I think I saw you yesterday," she said, frowning.

"I was here, yes. I'm the senior investigating officer. I have a couple of questions for you, but before that, I just want to say what a great job you did helping the people who were injured. The detective who was on the scene said you were brilliant."

"She wasn't so bad herself." Natalie smiled, then sobered. "The man who was so badly burned—do you know if he's going to be all right?"

"He's doing well, but just now he's pretty heavily sedated for the pain. But this morning, when he was awake, he told another detective that he saw the victim just before the grenade went off."

"The medics said it was phosphorus. That's why they checked us over and told us to wash up so thoroughly."

"Exactly."

The manager brought Kincaid's coffee, a steaming cup that smelled heavenly. When he'd thanked her and taken a grateful sip, he turned back to Natalie.

"Why would someone do something so horrible?" she asked, with such gravity that he hated not being able to give her an answer.

"We don't know. But we'll have a better idea when we know his identity. Can I show you a photo? This young man has been reported missing, and we can't ask the man in the hospital to look at it until he's feeling better."

Natalie gripped her cup, looking tense but determined. "Okay."

Taking out his phone, Kincaid pulled up the photo of Paul Cole and handed the phone across.

Natalie studied it, frowning. "No, I didn't see him before the fire. I was working the tables in the back, and the first thing I knew was that people were screaming and the customers in the front of the café were ducking under the tables."

"Why didn't you?" Kincaid asked, curious about this girl. "Duck under the tables."

She looked at him as if the question were unfathomable. "People were *burning*. How could I just hide under a table?" Shaking her head, she went back to gazing at the photo. "But I do recognize him. He comes into the café sometimes, sits in the back writing in a notebook."

"What sort of notebook?" Kincaid asked, interest quickening.

"Oh, a journal, I think. A plain black one. I always notice when people write in notebooks rather than on laptops because I like journals, too."

"Did you ever see him with a girl? Very blond. You'd remember her."

Natalie shook her head. "No, he always comes in by himself. And keeps himself to himself, if you know what I mean. Not unfriendly, really, just very focused on what he's doing." Her eyes widened as she met Kincaid's gaze. "You don't think . . . it was *him*? I never imagined that it was someone I knew." She put a hand to her mouth and swallowed. "That's horrible."

"We're not certain of anything, but we have to follow up leads. Did you know his name?"

"No. He only ever got coffee, and he always paid cash. Oh," she added suddenly, "I did see him a couple of times with a book about the station. I wondered if he was a history or an architecture student. Or just a train spotter. An anorak."

Kincaid didn't tell her that at least her first guess was a good one. He wondered if the train spotter observation was valid as well. If the victim was Paul Cole, and if his death was a suicide, might an obsession with trains have driven his choice of location, rather than his association with Matthew Quinn's eco-protesters? That was far too many ifs for his liking. He needed more information.

Finishing his coffee, he thanked Natalie. "Are you a student at UCL?" he asked on impulse.

She smiled. "English. My parents told me I should learn something useful, so I wait tables."

"Very wise," he said, grinning. He gave her his card. "If you think of anything about the incident, you can always reach me." Standing, he paused for a moment, wondering if he should give unsolicited advice, then thought, why not? "Natalie, what you did yesterday—you have the makings of a good police officer. And university grads get fast-tracked. If you should ever decide you're interested, let me know and I'll point you in the right direction."

Light shone green-gold through the stained glass panels of Doug Cullen's front door.

After having had her evening tests at UCL hospital, Melody hadn't wanted to stay at Andy's alone, and she hadn't wanted to go home. Having assured Gemma that she'd be fine on her own, she'd dithered at Andy's, feeding Bert the cat, tidying up Andy's small kitchen. Then she'd put on Andy's coat, grabbed her bag, and taken the tube to Notting Hill Gate. She'd walked down the hill to the mansion block that contained her flat and picked up her car without going inside. Then she drove to Putney.

By the time she crossed the Thames and turned into Doug's street, she'd realized she was starving. She stopped at their favorite pub and picked up an assortment of sandwiches. It was only now, having parked and locked her car, that she wondered if coming here had been a good idea.

She should have rung first. What if Doug had company? She knew he'd been seeing Maura Bell, the detective from Southwark, occasionally, but she didn't know how serious it was. She'd taken out her phone to ring him when Doug opened the door.

Not looking the least bit surprised, he said, "Whatever it is that you're doing, you had better come inside. It's bloody freezing out here."

"How did you know I was here?" Melody asked as she walked up to the door.

"I recognized the sound of your car. Why were you standing gawping on the pavement?"

"I wasn't gawping," Melody said, incensed, as Doug opened the door. "It just occurred to me that I should have rung first— that I might be intruding."

"Don't be an arse." Doug led her into the warmth of the hall and shut the door firmly. "Are you all right?" he asked, pushing his glasses up on his nose and frowning at her. He wore an old raveling woolly jumper and jeans, and his fair hair stuck up in unintentional spikes. "What about your tests?"

"Everything seems okay so far. Gemma went with me. I've just come from hospital." She walked into the sitting room and gave a little gasp of pleasure. "Oh, thank goodness. You've got the fireplaces going."

The sitting room and dining room in Doug's little house

had been opened up to form one big room, with a small kitchen area in the back. When he'd bought the house, the beautiful fireplaces in each room had been boarded over. Melody had insisted that he restore them, and had helped him find the gas fires and the antique mirrors over the mantels. Now the fires blazed merrily and she could feel the warmth.

Since she'd been here last, he had, she saw, finished painting the two rooms, a lovely green-gold color that she'd suggested would pick up the colors in the front door's stained glass. The ceiling was finished as well. A fall while trying to paint the center rosette himself had been the cause of Doug's broken ankle. "You didn't—"

"No. I had someone in." He gestured at the boot cast. "Not climbing ladders these days."

The cream ceiling paint had splashed all over the old carpet when Doug fell, but now the carpet had been pulled up and the polished wood floors gleamed.

"It looks . . . lovely," said Melody with a pang, knowing it had been too long since she'd visited.

"Maybe you should come more often." Doug's voice had an edge of sarcasm, and he seemed, as usual, to read her mind.

"Did you do this all on your own?" Melody asked, thinking of Maura Bell and feeling a sudden and uncomfortable stab of jealousy.

"Yes. As per your advice. Take off your coat, unless you're intending to run out again." He took it from her and put it on the end of the sofa. If he noticed that it wasn't hers, he didn't say. "What have you got in the bag?"

"Oh." She'd forgotten she was holding it. "Sandwiches from the pub. I thought if you hadn't eaten . . ." She sniffed, then spotted the cardboard container on the coffee table. "Don't tell me. Ramen noodles."

"I was hungry. And I was busy." Doug's laptop was open on the ottoman next to his favorite armchair. "But I certainly won't turn down a sandwich. And I have wine *and* beer. The larder is at least well stocked in the liquids department."

"I'd love tea, actually," said Melody, sinking gratefully onto the sofa. "Lashings and lashings of tea."

"Suits me. And that I *can* do."

As Doug put the kettle on in the kitchen, Melody pulled out the sandwiches. "Smoked Scottish salmon with cucumber and horseradish chive cream," she called out. "Handmade fish fingers in a roll, and chicken and smoked bacon club."

Frowning, Doug said, "They don't serve sandwiches after five."

"I used my wiles on the chef. Desperately hungry police officers on a stakeout. Works every time."

Doug brought mugs and the steeping pot of tea on a tray, as well as plates for the sandwiches. As Melody shared them out, Doug poured her tea with a little milk, just the way she liked it. "Where's Andy?" he asked, not looking up at her.

She told him about the recording demo at Abbey Road Studios.

Doug whistled. "Big-time."

"We sort of had a row," Melody admitted. "He didn't want to do it because of Tam. I told him Tam would kill him if he found out he'd passed up something like that."

"You must have been convincing." Doug took a bite of the salmon sandwich and gave her a searching look. "You know what this means, don't you? If Andy and Poppy really do take off—and they deserve to—he'll be gigging all the time. You'll never see him."

"So I should tell him to pass it up?" She shook her head. "You know I wouldn't do that."

"No," said Doug. "You wouldn't." She thought there was approval in his voice.

Melody chewed a bit of the chicken club, finding that for the first time since yesterday, food tasted delicious. "That wasn't the only thing," she added hesitantly. "He thinks I'm ashamed of him because I haven't introduced him to my parents."

Doug took half a fish finger sandwich and looked up at her, considering. "You haven't told him, have you?"

"No."

"You're going to have to, you know."

Melody sighed. "I know."

"And the longer you wait, the worse it will be."

"I know that, too. But I don't want to think about it just now." Melody tried the other half of the fish finger bap, then blew across the top of her tea. To change the subject, she nodded at Doug's laptop. "What are you doing?"

He hesitated. "Just a project. I can't really say."

"You're working on something for Duncan, aren't you? He told me."

"He did? Oh, well, then." Doug's relief was obvious, and it occurred to Melody that that was one of the things she liked about him. He was utterly transparent, and God forbid he should ever have to tell a lie.

Doug continued, eagerly now. "I've been trying to get a lead on Ryan Marsh. Duncan told you we thought he might have been an undercover cop?" When Melody nodded, he went on. "He was described as being around thirty, and we have a rough physical description, so I've been searching police cadet classes, starting a dozen years back, to see if I could find a possible match. Undercover cops often keep their first names, and choose a last name similar to their real one, or associated in some way. So far I've been through three years of classes for the Met, with no luck."

"Sounds like a needle in a haystack. But no worse than what I'm doing." Melody pulled her own laptop from the large handbag she'd brought in with her. "I'm looking for photos of Matthew Quinn's group in the paper's photo archives. There might be one with someone that fits Marsh's description."

Doug raised an eyebrow, a gesture that reminded her of Kincaid. "Your idea?" She nodded. "Good one," he said. "We should keep at it."

So they did, drinking tea and nibbling sandwiches in companionable silence. Melody took off her boots and curled up on the sofa, scanning through photo after photo. Her eyelids had begun to get heavy from the food, warmth, and comfort when she saw something that made her sit up. The photo was a year old. Archeologists from the Crossrail project had dug up bones at the site of the infamous Bedlam hospital, including a skeleton of a male who appeared to have had crude brain surgery. A few protesters stood at the edge of the safety fencing, holding placards that said DESTROYING LONDON'S HISTORY.

She recognized lanky Matthew Quinn from the photos that Kincaid had sent her, even though he was wearing a cap. There was an older man beside him, perhaps in his fifties but silver-haired. There was no one else she recognized from the group, or anyone that fit the description of Ryan Marsh.

"I've found something," she said, "but I don't think it's much—"

"Shit." Doug was looking at his computer screen, not her. "*I've* bloody found something. It wasn't the Met. It was Thames Valley." He got up, still awkward with his boot cast, and sat beside her with his laptop. As Melody looked at the class photo on the screen, Doug enlarged it. "There. Second from the left, front row. Ten years ago. He was nineteen. His name is Ryan Marlowe. He fits the description."

Melody stared at the face. Young. Serious beneath light brown hair. She couldn't tell the color of his eyes.

His eyes . . . "Oh, my God," she whispered. She knew those eyes. They were very blue, and she had last seen them in a haggard and smoke-smudged face, above a blue bandanna.

CHAPTER FOURTEEN

William Henry Barlow was born near Woolwich, the son of
an eminent mathematician and physicist. At sixteen he began work with his father before serving an apprenticeship in
mechanical and civil engineering at both the Woolwich and
London Dockyards.

—networkrail.co.uk
/VirtualArchive/WH-Barlow

Melody woke from a restless sleep on Andy's futon to the
touch of cold flesh against her back.

"Ow," she said. "You're freezing." But instead of flinching
away, she tucked herself closer, into the curve of his body.

"Tell me about it." Andy put a bare arm round her, and it
was cold, too. "I had to walk all the way to Baker Street before
I could find a cab."

Melody took his hand and brushed her lips against it. His
fingers smelled faintly metallic, the way they did when he'd
been playing the guitar for hours. "What about Poppy?"

"Caleb drove her back to Twyford. She missed the last train
ages ago."

"What time is it?" She tried to squint at the clock, but Andy
pulled the duvet up over her head.

"You don't want to know," he said, his breath in her ear, the stubble on his chin scraping the side of her cheek.

She pushed the duvet down again and turned onto her back, so that she could see the outline of his face in the dim light of the flat. "So how was it?"

He sat up a little, tucking her head against his shoulder. "It was . . . it was absolutely brilliant," he said slowly. "I've done some session work at Abbey Road, but I never imagined I'd be there doing my own recording. *Our* recording," he amended. "Poppy was amazing, and everything just flowed like—like magic. We even roughed out a couple of new songs."

Melody realized she'd never heard him sound like this. Whenever he'd talked about his music, there had been a reserve, as if he didn't dare believe that things would—or could—actually go right.

She also realized that as much as she'd wanted him to be happy, it frightened her a bit. Was Doug right? Would she lose him to this?

No, she thought, chastising herself. She couldn't go there. She wouldn't go there. And she wouldn't do or say anything to spoil this moment for him. "What about the producer?" she asked. "Was he impressed?"

"He's set up a meeting with Caleb tomorrow. And I'm going to think that Tam will be better by then and that we'll be able to tell him all about it. I'm going to hospital first thing in the morning." And that was the first time since the accident that she'd heard anything but panic in his voice when he talked about Tam. She bloody well hoped he was right.

"Then you'd better get some sleep, hadn't you?" She didn't want him to ask her where she had been or what she'd been doing. Or what she would be doing in the morning while he was visiting Tam.

"I can think of better things to do than sleep." He snuggled back down under the duvet and ran his hand across her belly. "What are you doing with all these clothes on, anyway?"

Melody had worn a T-shirt and yoga bottoms to bed. "I was cold."

"Well, you're not anymore, are you?" he said.

Jasmine Sidana drove straight to the London on Friday morning. She'd arranged to meet Paul Cole's parents there at half past eight.

As she parked her Honda in the hospital car park, she wondered which she had dreaded more—the visit to their home last night or this morning's interview. She didn't do grief well. It made her cross and uncomfortable because she felt awkward. She never knew what to say or do that would offer any solace to the bereaved.

Not, she thought, that it would have made any difference last night. She'd put on her best manner, told Sweeney to keep his mouth shut, and rung the bell of the big Victorian semidetached house in Vardens Road in Battersea. Jasmine liked to look at houses and kept up with real estate values, so she'd whistled to herself as she got out of the car. Even at night she could see that the cream trim on the brown brick was freshly painted, and the tiny front garden perfectly manicured. If the house had had any modernization, it could go for between two and three million pounds. Paul Cole was not a struggling student, it seemed.

The wife had answered. Her expression had been one of instant distaste, and Jasmine had thought the woman might shut the door on them before they had a chance to identify themselves as police officers.

"There's no soliciting," said Mrs. Cole, her frown deepening as, Jasmine felt certain, she took in the color of Jasmine's skin. "Look. There's a sign."

There *was* a sign beside the ornate brass bell, in delicate script on a ceramic plaque.

"Mrs. Cole?" Jasmine said. "We're police officers. We'd like to speak to you about your son."

The distaste turned to dismay, and Jasmine, her face burning, was almost glad of it.

Mrs. Cole's husband came up behind her. If the wife was one of those women who seemed stretched too thin in a desperate fight against aging, the husband was a bit paunchy and sleek. And like Sweeney, he wore too much cologne, although Jasmine guessed his was more expensive. She didn't like it. It made her nose itch.

"What is it, Lisa?" he snapped, and Jasmine couldn't tell if his irritation was directed at them or at his wife.

"We're police officers," Jasmine repeated. "I'm Detective Inspector Sidana and this is Detective Constable Sweeney."

"It's about Paul," whispered Mrs. Cole.

"What's he done now?" There was no fear in the husband's voice, only annoyance.

"May we come in?" said Jasmine. She held out her warrant card and stepped forward so that they had little choice but to step back. She wasn't going to stand freezing on their front step while she questioned them about their son.

With obvious reluctance, Mrs. Cole led them into a formal sitting room that overlooked the street. It was ornate and overfurnished. Every object seemed to be gilded, and Jasmine couldn't imagine that they actually used it for anything other than impressing guests. She sat, uninvited, on a hard, brocaded sofa, and Sweeney gingerly followed suit. The room was cold and Jasmine thought it just as well the Coles hadn't offered to take their coats.

"Mr. and Mrs. Cole, please, I'd like you to sit down," she said.

Mrs. Cole sank onto a settee opposite. She looked pinched and frightened now, and Jasmine regretted her earlier uncharitable thought.

"Robert, please," Mrs. Cole said. "She said she's a *detective inspector*." The wife, it seemed, was brighter than the husband, and had grasped the import. Senior detectives didn't come calling for misdemeanors.

Mr. Cole shook his head and remained with his back to the cold fireplace. "I'll stand. And I'll ask you again, Detective whatever-you-said-your-name-was, what's Paul done this time?"

"We don't know that your son has done anything, Mr. Cole," answered Sidana, ignoring the deliberate insult with an effort. She hoped Sweeney wouldn't be sniggering over it at his gym. "But some of his friends have reported him missing," she went on, collecting herself. "Have you seen or heard from him in the last two days?"

"No," said Mrs. Cole. "I rang him yesterday but it went to voice mail. But sometimes he doesn't ring back for a day or—"

"If these friends you're referring to are those hippie protesters, you can't believe anything they say," broke in her husband.

"They're ecowarriors, Robert. That's what Paul says."

"They're dropouts and troublemakers. Paul needs to focus on his degree and do something useful with himself."

Although Jasmine was inclined to agree with Robert Cole about the protesters, she wasn't going to let this disintegrate into an obviously well-worn family argument. It was apparent that the father neither liked nor knew his son, and that the mother babied him. For the first time, Jasmine felt a twinge of pity for Paul Cole.

"Mr. Cole, you asked me if Paul was in trouble *again*. Has he been in some sort of trouble before?"

"He was warned off for protesting against one of the Crossrail projects. I told him he was lucky he wasn't arrested. Wasting people's time and money. Don't they understand what happens when they put the contractors behind schedule?"

That, thought Jasmine, they understood very well, and was exactly the point.

And now she had to get to hers, as much as she disliked doing it. "Mr. and Mrs. Cole, there was an incident yesterday at St. Pancras International. Do you know if Paul had any plans to attend a demonstration there?"

"I saw it on the news." Lisa Cole clenched her manicured hands together in her lap. "A man was killed. Surely you don't think Paul had something to do with that?"

Jasmine felt Sweeney stir beside her and shot him a look. "Mrs. Cole," Jasmine said with unaccustomed gentleness, "we are still attempting to identify the victim. Can you tell me if your son has any distinguishing marks?"

Mrs. Cole's answer had brought them here this morning.

Jasmine had hoped for a chance to speak to the pathologist, Dr. Kaleem, before the Coles arrived. But they were even earlier than she, and were already pacing in the mortuary's family room. Mrs. Cole, although still dressed in designer clothing and perfectly made up, looked as if she hadn't slept. Mr. Cole was red-faced and seemed to be working himself into a temper. "I'll want to speak to your superior about your wasting our time and causing my wife distress," he said before Jasmine had even got out a "Good morning."

She'd insisted on coming alone, and was now glad Sweeney wasn't there to see her flush. "Thank you both for coming," she'd managed to say with a grimace of a smile, when Dr. Kaleem came in and introduced himself to the couple.

He gave Jasmine a courteous nod. "Detective Sidana."

Jasmine had been prepared to dislike him, first because he'd been called in by Kincaid, and second because he was too good-looking by half and she didn't trust handsome men. But at the scene he had seemed both competent and kind, and now she discovered she was willing to give him the benefit of the doubt.

"What is it you want us to see?" said Robert Cole, ignoring Dr. Kaleem's outstretched hand. "I want this nonsense over with."

What an insufferable bully, Jasmine thought, and then she saw that his hands were shaking. The man was terrified, she realized, and his only defense was to bluster.

Dr. Kaleem seemed unperturbed. He sat in one of the family room chairs. "First, I'd like to ask you a few questions." He leaned forward, elbows on his knees, in a posture that invited confidences. "Do you by any chance know your son's blood type?"

Lisa Cole shook her head. "I'm not sure. But I know I'm AB negative. When I was pregnant, I had to have RhoGAM injections. For the antibodies. To make sure Paul would be all right."

"Ah. That makes it quite possible that your son was A negative, Mrs. Cole. It's fairly rare."

Jasmine saw the confirmation in Kaleem's expression, although she wasn't sure that the parents realized the importance of what Lisa had just told him.

Dr. Kaleem went on. "Will there be hospital records anywhere that we could access? Did Paul have any medical problems or surgeries?"

"He had his appendix out when he was nine," said Lisa Cole.

"That's very good," Kaleem told her. "Do you remember the name of his pediatrician or his surgeon?"

She shook her head. "But I'm sure I have the records somewhere."

Dr. Kaleem smiled at her. "No matter. It's doubtful they would have typed his blood anyway."

"Look," said Robert Cole, "what does all this matter? Why did you bring us here?"

"I'd just like you to look at a couple of photos." Kaleem pulled printed sheets from a folder that he had casually set down by his chair when he came into the room. "Now, this first one. Last night, you told Detective Inspector Sidana that your son has a birthmark. Does it bear any resemblance to this?" He handed a sheet to both parents.

Robert Cole took one glance and crumpled the paper in his hand. "That's ridiculous. How do you expect us to tell anything from that? That could be the moon or one of those Rorschach things."

Glancing over Lisa Cole's shoulder, Jasmine saw a blown-up photo of what looked like a dark comma, partly covered by the red blisters of burns. A ruler on one side gave the scale. She estimated the dark patch as about three centimeters.

Kaleem handed another sheet to Lisa, this time focusing on her. It was a boot, Jasmine saw. Or what was left of a boot. The laces had melted into a tangled mass, but a little brown leather or fabric was still visible around them and the sole seemed intact. "Do you recognize this hiking boot, Mrs. Cole?"

Lisa Cole stared at the photo. Her carefully applied blusher now stood out in clown patches against her blanched skin. "It— It looks like one of the boots I gave Paul for Christmas." Her voice was a thread of sound. "They were expensive but he really wanted them."

"That's enough," broke in Robert Cole, snatching the page from his wife. "You're needlessly harassing my wife and me over some juvenile prank. We're going home. If you want to speak to us again, you can contact our solic—"

"Robert!" Lisa Cole stood and turned on her husband. She was shaking. "That's enough! Can you not see anything other than yourself and your own importance? Don't you understand what they're telling us? Paul is dead. Our son is dead."

Kincaid had chosen a little café just a few doors up Lamb's Conduit Street from the station. It was a tiny place with cheerful red trim on the windows, an illy coffee sign and a newspaper rack out front, and benches inside the windows. He hoped it wasn't a regular morning-coffee stop for the detectives at Holborn station, but there was no one else inside.

He ordered coffee and a bacon sandwich, as he'd again skipped breakfast. When the sandwich came, it was good, but not as good as Medhi Atias's bacon butty. He'd taken the last bite when Doug and Melody came in.

Melody wore the same clothes as the day before, jeans and Andy's navy peacoat over a jumper. He wondered if she had been home at all. When Doug had rung him late last night to say that he and Melody had information for him, he'd arranged to meet them here. Looking at them now, both their faces tense with excitement, he realized he should have known they'd team up. He also saw that they'd both brought laptops.

"I'll get coffee while you get set up," he said.

When he came back with cups for them both, they had their laptops open on a bench.

Doug began by explaining his search through police cadet classes for a graduate the right age with a name similar to Ryan Marsh. "I found this," he said, turning the screen to Kincaid and lowering his voice, even though the shop proprietor was busy cleaning the espresso machine. "A Thames Valley class from ten years ago. Ryan Marlowe. He worked for Thames Valley for two years, was promoted into CID, then he disappeared. But during that time, he gave blood to an injured officer, and there's a record of his blood type. He was O positive."

"Then he's not our victim," Kincaid said.

Melody looked as if she were about to burst.

Doug nodded to her. "No. But Melody can tell you more."

"If Ryan Marlowe is Ryan Marsh, he's not dead, either," she said. "Or at least he wasn't dead on Wednesday, after the grenade went off."

"What? How can you be certain?" Kincaid asked.

"Because I *saw* him. He was the man who helped me. The Good Samaritan."

"You're sure?"

Melody nodded. "As sure as I'm looking at you. Ten years older than the photo, but it's him. Remember I said I thought he was a cop? He ran towards the fire, not away. He was trying to help."

"You can't know that," Kincaid told her. "Maybe he was checking his handiwork."

"No." Melody's head shake was vehement. "You didn't see his face. When he saw the body. He—he was . . . distraught."

"Do you think he knew who it was?"

Melody thought for a moment. "I'm trying to remember exactly what he said. Something like, 'There's nothing we can do for him now.' "

"Not conclusive," Kincaid said, frowning.

"No, but . . ." Melody chewed on a fingernail, something Kincaid had never seen her do. "I would swear he knew," she finished. "There was just such despair in his voice. I can't explain it any better."

"Okay, let's go with that for now," Kincaid conceded. "According to his girlfriend, Paul Cole wanted to set off the smoke bomb and he argued with Matthew over it. What if, having been rejected by Matthew, Cole talked Ryan Marsh into letting him take it?"

Doug and Melody stared at Kincaid. Then Doug said slowly, "If Marsh thought it was a smoke bomb and then saw that it was white phosphorus, he'd have been frantic."

"Because he felt responsible," Melody agreed.

Kincaid studied the photo on Doug's laptop screen for a long moment. "There is another possibility. What if he thought the grenade was meant for him?"

"Shit." Doug's eyes were wide behind his wire-framed glasses.

"That would explain why he vanished," said Melody, so softly she might have been talking to herself. "I couldn't understand. I thought he was still beside me. And then he was gone . . ."

"It's a possibility." Kincaid tapped the laptop screen with his forefinger. "Doug, can you send me a cropped version of this photo? We need someone to give us a definitive ID."

"Someone in the group?" asked Doug.

"I'm not sure I want to share that with them just yet. But I know someone else I can ask." He explained about Medhi Atias, the chicken shop owner.

"I can do better than that photo." Melody scooted her chair closer to Kincaid and turned her laptop so that Kincaid could see the screen. "Once I knew what—and who—I was looking for, I hit the jackpot in the newspaper archives." She scrolled through half a dozen photos, most slightly grainy. But in each one, Kincaid recognized Ryan Marsh. In some he had a short beard, in others, longer hair, or a colored bandanna tied round his head, but Melody was right. Once you knew what you were looking for, his face jumped out in every one. Although by description he had sounded ordinary, there was something about him that stood out, that drew the eye back.

"These are from the Fukushima protests. This one is Didcot. The usual nuclear power stuff," Melody went on, going through the photos again, more slowly. "And then I found this." She froze one on the screen. "It's from early autumn last year. I'd been looking for photos of Matthew's group protesting Crossrail."

"This is Crossrail?" Kincaid asked, studying the image. He didn't see any digging going on.

"No. But it's a protest against the destruction of a listed building."

The group carried the now-familiar SAVE HISTORIC LONDON placards. Kincaid picked out Matthew Quinn first, towering over the others. Beside him were Iris and Dean.

There was Ryan, on the edge of the frame, wearing a blue bandanna rather jauntily round his neck. A girl stood next to him. She had wispy brown hair cut just to her shoulders, and was looking into the camera with a slight smile. She was not one of the girls he'd met.

He enlarged the image. She was wearing a necklace, a pendant that looked like a small brown bird.

And there, behind Iris, was Paul Cole, looking straight at the camera. Had Ariel Ellis been the one taking the photo?

His phone dinged with a text. It was from Sidana, and it was timely. "Paul Cole's blood type likely match for victim," it said. The phone dinged again with a second text. "Mother confirms ID. Organizing collection of DNA."

Instead of replying to Sidana, Kincaid looked up at Doug and Melody. "We've got a probable confirmation on Paul Cole. Unless DNA rules him out. Now we have to decide what to do about Ryan Marsh." He scrolled back through Melody's protest photos, thinking furiously. "Why does Ryan Marlowe disappear from view?" he asked. "If he went undercover as Ryan Marsh, was it with Thames Valley? Or with the Met? Is he still undercover, or did he go native?" Kincaid drummed his fingers on the café tabletop. "He was too careful. He left nothing behind with the group, ever. Who—or what—was he afraid of?"

"If he was still undercover," put in Doug, "who was running him? And why? I don't believe the government any longer sees homegrown protest groups as a serious terrorist threat."

Kincaid felt an itch between his shoulder blades. He looked round, suddenly acutely aware of their visibility through the café's glass windows. Except for them, all of the café's custom had been takeaway, and no one had lingered after picking up their coffee or breakfast rolls.

"I don't like this," he said quietly. "We don't know enough.

For now, I think this stays between the three of us, and Gemma. Doug, start with Ryan Marlowe. Birth, school records, marriage, anything you can dig up. Ryan Marsh can't have simply vanished, and his past may give us a clue as to where he is. And I want to find him before anyone else does."

CHAPTER FIFTEEN

In 1857 Barlow . . . was retained by the Midland Railway as its new consulting engineer after the retirement of George Stephenson. His major commission from the Midland came with the company's extension from Bedford into London. Starting in 1862, the extension gave them independent access to London for the first time. Barlow was responsible for the arrangement of St Pancras station, the company's own terminus on Euston Road. This included the station's magnificent train shed roof; at 240ft, it was at the time of construction the largest in the world.

networkrail.co.uk
/VirtualArchive/WH-Barlow

With the judicious use of a few tablets of his stash of over-the-counter codeine and ibuprofen—he'd never link himself to a prescription—he'd managed to get moving, build up the fire, and make himself a hot meal and a hot drink. When he'd cleaned his cooking gear, he organized his campsite a bit better, setting up another windbreak. Thank God the rain had stopped for the moment. In the morning, he could begin filtering water from the river, and if he was lucky, perhaps catch some fish for breakfast. One task at a time. He couldn't think past that. Not yet.

When he'd finished chores and banked the fire, he'd settled himself on his camp stool and dug another treasure from one of the cache tubes—a glass-lined flask filled with very good whisky. It was the last of a bottle of Balvenie, his favorite handcrafted, single-barrel Speyside Scotch. Wren had given it to him as a surprise, bought with money she'd saved up from doing odd jobs. He'd protested—she never bought anything for herself, wearing the other girls' castoffs, but she'd looked so crushed that he'd relented, but only on the condition that she share it.

Wren shied away from both drink and drugs, but she had enjoyed the whisky in very small nips.

They had, in fact, drunk it here. She was the only person he'd ever brought to the island, and only once, when he'd dared to take the Ford out of the lockup for a few days. He'd made an excuse to the group—protest business—and had picked Wren up well away from the flat. The others were used to her coming and going, and he'd hoped that their simultaneous absence wouldn't attract attention.

It had been autumn, when the trees were just beginning to show their brilliant color and the nights were turning crisp. She had been enchanted with everything—the canoe, the river, the woods, the little shelter, the fire, the brilliance of the stars. That night he had taken fresh food, steaks, and jacket potatoes, to roast in the embers. Everything had been as new to her as if she were a child.

He sipped again at the whisky, lost in memory.

Wren. The girl from nowhere. Too thin, although they didn't suffer lack in the flat in the Caledonian Road. With her wispy brown hair that never stayed in place and eyes the color of dark honey, she did make him think of a small brown bird. Her movements were quick, too, and often eerily quiet. When *he'd asked her, early on, if that was her real name, she'd just smiled and said, "I was given it," leaving him to wonder what she meant.*

She never talked about herself. Not that everyone in the Caledonian Road gave out a potted history—and even if they did, it didn't mean it was true—but Wren said less than anyone else. But the rest shed clues just as they shed skin and hair, unconsciously. A word here, a word there, a reference to a mother or a father or a sister or something that had happened at school. But not Wren.

He started to watch her, first with a copper's curiosity, because she was a challenge, a puzzle to be solved. She was a Londoner, he was sure of that from her accent, and he guessed south rather than north. Middle class. But then they were mostly a middle-class bunch, living in pseudosqualor, and he thought that any of them could have gone home to beds more comfortable than sleeping bags on the flat's old board floors. Except Wren.

And then he began to watch not just out of idle curiosity, but because he realized he liked her. They all had motives, this bunch, they always did. Rebellion, idealism, a need to be different, a need to be noticed. But Wren, Wren simply was. He'd never known anyone who lived in the moment the way she did, and with such innocent delight.

By that autumn, he'd realized that he more than liked her. He loved his wife, of course he loved his wife, they'd been together since just out of school. But this, this was something he'd never felt for anyone. And he'd known that the line, once crossed, could never be erased, but he hadn't been able to help himself.

The night he'd brought her here had been the first time they'd slept together. He'd trembled with terror and desire, afraid to touch her, afraid she would reject him. And then, when she'd welcomed him as though it was the most natural thing in the world, he'd been so afraid he would hurt her. She seemed so fragile—and yet he knew she'd survived life on the streets, and better than he might have done.

Yet he had broken her in the end, hadn't he? Why else would she have done what she did at New Year's? Had she sensed that he'd compromised himself to protect her and to protect his family?

And in the end he had broken himself.

Having seen Doug and Melody off in different directions, Kincaid hesitated outside the café. Melody had sent him the most recent photo of Ryan Marlowe, the one that showed the girl with the wispy hair.

Should he check in at the station, follow up on Sidana's probable confirmation of the victim?

No, he would let Sidana do her job without his interference. He had other fish to fry, and he needed time to think before he spoke to any of the Holborn team. Turning away from the station, he turned up his coat collar and hoped the rain would hold off for half an hour.

At the top of Lamb's Conduit Street, he turned right and cut over to Gray's Inn Road, continuing northwards. The wind stung his cheeks and whipped at his hair—he hoped it might clear his mind. Was he being an ass by not sharing what he suspected about Ryan Marsh with his team and with Nick Callery at SO15? He'd never been one for paranoia, but ever since the end of the case in Henley last autumn, nothing had seemed right. Not Gemma's promotion. Not his transfer. And especially not the absence and continued silence of his former boss, Chief Superintendent Denis Childs.

Denis Childs had never been an easy man to read, but Kincaid had always liked and trusted him. He still trusted him, even though he knew Childs had manipulated him in the business over former Deputy Assistant Commissioner Angus Craig. He also knew that Childs had known more about what was going on in the Met than he had told Kincaid, but who had he been protecting? Himself? Kincaid? Or someone else?

And now Childs had quite literally dropped off the map, so Kincaid couldn't attempt to get at the truth, and he was worried that there was more to Childs's absence than his sister's having been injured in Singapore.

Nor was he sure how much he could tell Gemma about his misgivings, because he hadn't told her he suspected her promotion was meant as a sweetener to keep *him* from making trouble.

There was no reason any of that should influence his actions in this case. Except that he had the same sense of unseen things moving beneath dark waters, and it gave him that same itch between the shoulder blades.

Turning into the Caledonian Road, he dodged slush thrown up by a passing car and concentrated on paying attention to his surroundings. Going northeast from King's Cross, the road seemed drearier than ever beneath the mass of dark clouds building to the north. It couldn't last, wouldn't last— the high-rises and hotels and office blocks would go in, and people like Medhi Atias would be forced out. He hoped that at least the best of the Georgian buildings would be saved, even if no one except the very rich could afford to live in them. In fact, he realized he felt considerable sympathy with at least some of Matthew Quinn's agenda.

He'd reached Quinn's flat. There was no sign of activity to be seen in the windows, and as he gazed up at the peeling window frames, he found himself thinking that a little money, at least, wouldn't be amiss.

The chicken shop beckoned. He pushed open the door and stepped into warmth, steam, and the smell of cooking bacon.

Medhi Atias looked up from his counter and smiled. "Mr. Kincaid. Have you come for another bacon butty?"

"Unfortunately, no. I've already eaten, and I'm afraid it wasn't up to your standards."

Atias clicked his tongue in disapproval. "You should have come here first. But never mind. What can I do for you now?"

"Some of your wonderful coffee for starters."

Kincaid waited until Atias had given him a steaming cup, then handed across his phone with the photo Melody had sent him up on the screen. "The man—do you know him?" he asked.

All the jovial expression drained from Atias's round face. He stared at the screen a moment longer, then handed the phone back to Kincaid. "That is Ryan. Is he—have you—" Atias shook his head.

"We don't think it was Ryan who died at St. Pancras. But we can't find him. Do you have any idea where he might be?"

"Who, then? Who was it who died?" asked Atias, without answering Kincaid's question.

"We're still working on identification. But we think it may have been a young man named Paul Cole."

Atias looked at him blankly. "That name means nothing to me."

Kincaid pulled up the photo of Paul Cole on his phone and handed it across again.

"That one?" said Atias, frowning as he returned the phone. "Why would he do such a thing?"

"You know him, then?"

"He came in here, sometimes with the others, sometimes on his own. Never a polite word. And complained. This, that, the next thing. Coffee too hot, coffee not hot enough. Chicken too cooked, not enough chips. Pah," he added on a breath of disgust. "Not that I would have wished him ill, you understand."

"No, of course not. One more thing." Kincaid scrolled back to the photo of Ryan. "The girl beside Ryan. Do you know her?"

Atias looked again, squinting as if he might be a bit nearsighted. "I saw her sometimes, coming and going from the flat. A few times she came in with Ryan."

"You don't know her name?"

"No. She was very quiet. But she smiled." Atias paused and gave his counter another wipe with his ever-present tea towel. "As if she really meant it. Really saw you. Do you know what I mean, Mr. Kincaid?"

"I think I do, yes." Kincaid finished his coffee. "Thank you, Mr. Atias."

"Medhi, please."

"Medhi, then. You've been very helpful. You will keep this in confidence?"

"Of course. I know how to keep a secret, Mr. Kincaid."

When Kincaid pushed the bell for the top flat, the street door buzzed open before he could identify himself. He climbed the stairs and found Iris waiting at the open door to the flat.

"We saw you," she said, and he couldn't tell if her tone was accusatory or frightened. "I helped you. And then you put us all in jail."

Accusatory, then. "I'm sorry, Iris." He went for conciliatory. "You know what happened was very serious. We had no choice."

She stepped back to let him in, but her expression didn't soften.

They were all there. The television was turned on—one of the morning shows on ITV—the sound muted. Trish and Dean stood in the kitchenette, and as Kincaid glanced at them, toast popped up in the toaster. The smell of warm toast filled the room.

Matthew Quinn sat next to Lee on the sofa, a laptop open on the table between them. The computer must be new, Kincaid thought, or one that had not been in the flat at the time of the search.

The sofa was low and Quinn looked slightly spiderlike, his long legs folded so that his knees were almost on a level with his ears, his hands dangling between them. Kincaid had to remind himself that there was nothing absurd about him.

Cam Chen stood in the bedroom doorway, toweling her damp black hair. She wore jeans and a jumper, but her feet were bare. Kincaid thought he caught the scent of bath salts.

What did they do all day? he wondered. The six of them, in this small, Spartan space, if they didn't go to jobs or classes? He thought it was an environment in which small slights could fester into very large grudges. Grievances large enough, perhaps, to precipitate a murder?

Quinn reached out and snapped the laptop shut. "What do you want with us now?" he asked. "We've told you everything we know."

No one asked Kincaid to sit, and the toast stood in the toaster, growing cold. "I'm afraid I have some bad news for you," Kincaid said, watching them.

It was Cam who spoke first. She'd put one hand on the doorjamb and clutched the towel to her chest with the other. "You're sure it's Ryan?" Her voice shook. "Ryan's really dead?"

Instead of answering, Kincaid said, "Why did none of you tell me about Paul Cole?"

Six blank faces looked back at him.

Dean recovered first. "Why should we have? He's a wanker."

"Because he was here. Because he knew about the protest and the smoke bomb. Because he argued with Matthew over being allowed to set off the smoke bomb."

"I'd never have let him do that," protested Matthew. "He didn't really care about the cause. He just wanted to make himself seem important. He'd probably have—" His mouth dropped open as realization sunk in. "You're freaking kidding me."

"I'm afraid not. We believe we've identified the victim as Paul Cole."

"Oh, dear God," whispered Cam. "You're telling us it was *Paul*? Paul is dead? Not Ryan?"

Iris sank down on the floor beside the sofa, put a hand to her mouth, and sobbed. Whether it was with relief or grief, Kincaid couldn't tell.

Matthew shook his head. "That's just not bloody possible. I gave the smoke bomb to Ryan."

"Would Ryan have given it to Paul?"

"No way."

"He might have," said Cam, frowning. She came all the way into the room and sat on the arm of the sofa beside Lee, still hugging the towel to her. "Paul idolized Ryan. He followed him around like a puppy. I think Ryan felt sorry for—"

"So what if Ryan did give it to him?" broke in Matthew. "I keep telling you. It was a smoke bomb. Not a bloody grenade."

"So you say," Kincaid said "Let's agree for the moment that Matthew gave Ryan a smoke bomb. And that Ryan told Paul he could set it off. But what if Ryan gave Paul the grenade instead of the smoke bomb?"

They all stared at him as if he'd lost his mind.

"Why?" said Matthew. "Why would Ryan do that?"

"I can think of lots of reasons. Maybe Paul knew something about Ryan that Ryan wanted kept secret, for starters." Kincaid propped himself against the radiator and folded his arms. "Why don't you begin by telling me what you know about Ryan Marsh." He wanted to see if the others agreed with what Cam had told him.

"We just started seeing him around," volunteered Iris, still sniffing. "It was in the summer, I think. He was interested in what we were doing," she added with a note of pride. "After a while, he stayed."

"Do you know anything else about him? Where he came from? Where he might be now?"

They shook their heads in unison. Trish spoke up. "He never talked about himself. He just . . . listened. He made everyone feel . . . important. Special."

Kincaid saw Matthew flinch. He suspected Matthew didn't like the idea that he needed anyone else to make him feel important.

"Then tell me about Wren," he said.

This time the blank looks held apprehension. Cam started to speak, then looked away.

"Why do you want to know about Wren?" Matthew asked. "She was just a homeless girl. She stayed with us for a while. I used to see her outside King's Cross. I'd give her food sometimes. And then one day I could see she was really ill. A bad cough. She needed a place to stay while she got well."

"So you took her in. And then she just left? Sounds a bit ungrateful," Kincaid prompted.

Again, the covert glances. "Yeah," said Matthew. "Maybe she found greener pastures."

"Meaning?"

Matthew shrugged. "We gave her food and a place to stay. Maybe she found something better."

"When did she leave?"

"I don't remember. Somewhere around the New Year."

"Without telling you goodbye or where she was going?"

Matthew shrugged. "We're a free community."

Right, Kincaid thought, a free community where Matthew Quinn paid the bills and set the rules. "Could Ryan have had something to do with Wren leaving?" he asked.

"No," said Cam. "He was gutted." Matthew shot her a glance that could have curdled milk. "I mean, we were all gutted," Cam amended. "We liked her."

"Why are you asking about *her* when Paul is dead?" Iris pulled herself up by the arm of the sofa. "Why isn't anyone talking about Paul?" Her face was tear streaked, but her voice was ferocious. "You are bastards, all of you. Doesn't he deserve something?"

"Tell me about Paul," Kincaid said. "Why was he so determined to carry the smoke bomb?"

There were more glances, then Cam spoke. "Maybe Ariel had been paying a little too much attention to Ryan."

"Was there something going on between Ariel and Ryan?"

"No." Cam scowled at him. "No way. Not on Ryan's part, anyway."

"Why didn't any of you tell us that Paul and Ariel had been here that morning? You didn't notice they didn't come to the protest?" Kincaid shifted his position slightly, partly to unsettle them, partly because he kept hoping he'd see something in the flat that seemed out of place or catch an unschooled expression.

It was Lee Sutton who shrugged and answered. "We just figured Paul had gone off in a sulk because he didn't get his way. And that Ariel didn't come because Paul didn't. After all, it's not like they lived here."

Matthew added, with another shrug, "They weren't really part of the group."

"Even though most of you came together through a connection with Ariel's father?"

"Professor Ellis may have opened our eyes, but he has nothing to do with who we are now." Matthew would not cede credit gracefully.

"Does Ariel know?" asked Cam. "About Paul?"

"We haven't informed her that we believe we have a positive ID, no. But it was Ariel who came to us and reported Paul missing. She said they'd had a row the morning of the protest and that she was worried about him."

"They did have a row," Cam said slowly. "They were arguing when they left the flat. Ariel said he was making an arse of himself over the smoke thing."

"And they left before anyone else?"

"Ages earlier," put in Iris. "Paul was in a right huff."

"What about Ryan? When did he leave?"

Cam frowned. "Midday, maybe. We'd agreed that everyone except Ryan would meet up outside the Marks and Spencer food store in the St. Pancras arcade. Ryan would already be in place."

"So you have no idea where Ryan was between the time he left the flat and the demonstration?" Kincaid didn't tell them that he knew Ryan *had* been in the station when the grenade went off.

"No," said Cam. "We never knew where Ryan went when he left here."

"Did anyone see him at the demonstration?" Kincaid looked at each of them in turn. They all shook their heads.

"What about Paul?" That question got the same response. "So Paul and Ryan could have met up anytime later that morning, or that afternoon?"

"Well, I suppose they could," put in Dean from his spot by the toaster. "But . . . if they did, they didn't plan it here."

"They both had phones," said Cam. "They could have texted and met up anywhere."

"Matthew, when exactly did you give Ryan the smoke bomb?" Kincaid asked.

"Just before he left. Like Cam said, it was before midday. I started to explain to him how it worked, but he just clapped me on the back and told me not to worry, he bloody well knew how to do it." Matthew sounded aggrieved.

"So he didn't seem worried or upset?"

"No."

"What about Paul? Had he been behaving oddly recently?"

"Other than being pissed off at Ariel, no," said Cam.

"Do you know why they weren't getting along?"

"No. They didn't live here, like Lee said. It wasn't our business." Cam's answer was a little too vehement.

"Do you think Paul was so upset that morning that he would have harmed himself?"

Cam stared at him. "You're suggesting that Paul committed *suicide*? Like that? That's horrible. And Paul would have run home to Mummy if he stubbed his toe. I can't believe he would ever have deliberately hurt himself."

"Give me another explanation, then." Kincaid moved closer to the group, crowding their space. "Did Ryan agree to let him have the smoke bomb and give him a grenade instead? Or did someone who thought Ryan was going to set off the smoke bomb switch it with a grenade?"

There was a stunned silence while they took this in.

Cam was the one to break it. "You're saying that either Ryan meant to kill Paul or someone meant to kill Ryan?" She stood up and started to pace, her damp towel forgotten on the floor. "I don't believe it. That's just mad."

"But Paul is dead," Kincaid said.

"And Ryan is missing." Iris's voice was barely a whisper. "If Ryan is alive, why didn't he come back?"

Jasmine Sidana had sent Kincaid the most definitive news of the case so far, and his response had been a text that said merely, "Carry on."

Well, she had done that. She'd arranged for the crime scene techs to search both Paul Cole's room at university and his bedroom in his parents' house. They would be looking for any evidence that tied him to the grenade, anything that intimated he'd been contemplating suicide, and they would, of course, be gathering DNA samples from his personal belongings so that the lab could get a definitive match with the DNA recovered from the corpse.

She had also made arrangements for a family liaison officer to meet with Paul Cole's parents at their home. Unable to decide whether a male or a female officer would suit them better, she'd left it to the rota. She didn't think a motherly touch would be appreciated by either of the Coles, but she thought Mrs. Cole could use some support, as it was unlikely she'd be getting any from her husband.

When she arrived back at Holborn Police Station, there was no sign of Kincaid.

"Has he been in at all today?" she asked Simon Gikas.

Simon looked up from his computer. "He stuck his nose in for about five minutes first thing this morning."

"Did he say where he was going?"

"Not a word."

What the hell was he up to? Jasmine thought, slamming her bag down on her desk. "He's not a bloody cowboy," she muttered, then gaped, shocked by her own profanity. Detective Superintendent Duncan Kincaid was driving her to distraction.

Melody left the clinic at University College Hospital feeling much lighter than when she'd gone in. They had poked, prodded, and pricked her, checked her blood oxygen level and her breathing. Then, although they wanted her to come in for one more blood test, they had pronounced her fit for work as long as she didn't overdo things. She'd smothered a grin, wondering if very enthusiastic sex in the middle of the night counted as overdoing things, but didn't ask.

"You're very lucky," the doctor had told her as she signed her release form. "If you'd breathed enough of the phosphorus, your lungs and your organ function could have been permanently compromised."

The comment was meant to be kind, but it sent Melody right back to worrying about Tam. And to worrying about the man they now thought was Ryan Marsh.

How much smoke had he breathed in the railway station?

Had he touched the victim? She couldn't remember now. Everything was such a blur. She kept replaying it in her head, trying to see him more clearly through the smoke and her own panic.

What had happened to him? Was he getting any treatment for smoke inhalation or injuries?

Standing outside the hospital, she breathed in the windborne petrol fumes from Euston Road, and hesitated. She'd left her car at Andy's. From here, she could take the tube home, shower, change, and take the tube to work at Brixton.

That was what she should do. But she couldn't stop wondering if there was something else she could do to help Duncan, something she'd missed. Or if she could help Doug trace Ryan Marlowe/Marsh.

Every time she closed her eyes she saw the anguish on his face as he looked down at Paul Cole's charred body. Where had he gone? Why had he run? Why did she feel such a connection to this man?

Her phone rang, making her jump. She fished it from the pocket of Andy's peacoat, expecting it to be him.

But it was Gemma, who said without preamble, "Can you come in? I arrested Dillon Underwood when he showed up for work this morning. I've put him in a holding cell while we execute the search warrant for his flat. I'd like you to be there, if you're up to it."

CHAPTER SIXTEEN

It is fairly common knowledge that the undercroft at St. Pancras Station, which now houses ticket offices, cafés and smart shops, was once used to store beer. It is, however, largely forgotten that St Pancras was once the hub of an industry which transported, matured, packaged and marketed beer in a completely different way to any that exists today.

—*meantimebrewing.com*
/stpancras-station

Kincaid's phone rang as he reached the street. When he saw that it was Michael, he felt a pang of worry. He should have checked on Tam before now.

But when he answered, Michael said, "I wanted to let you know he was awake. Still not very coherent, though. He keeps talking about 'the flash.' "

"I'm not surprised." Phone to his ear, Kincaid kept walking towards King's Cross. "He must have been looking right at the grenade when it went off. He's lucky his sight wasn't damaged. What are the doctors saying?"

"That he's doing as well as can be expected. Maybe better. His organs seem to be coping, but the burn is still very painful. Of course, he wants to go home, the stubborn bastard," Michael added, his voice softening. "Says he misses the dogs."

"Well, don't worry him about talking to me. We're pretty certain we've identified the young man without Tam's help. But when he does feel better, I'll pay him a social visit."

Michael seemed to hesitate, then said, "Duncan, I think it might help him to speak to you. His state of mind, I mean."

"Of course. Just let me know when you think he's up to it, and I'll come either to hospital or to the flat. How's Louise coping?"

"I've made her stay home. And told her she'd better not use worry as an excuse to start smoking again."

Kincaid laughed. "Good man. Tell her I'll bring Charlotte for a visit when Tam is home and comfortable." He rang off just as he reached King's Cross station.

He stood for a moment, gazing at the station's new facade and thinking about the fire that had ravaged King's Cross Underground station in 1987. Started by a match or a cigarette thrown carelessly into the gap in one of the old wooden escalators, the fire had smoldered, then flashed over into the ticketing hall, killing thirty-one people and injuring many more. Survivors and witnesses had never forgotten it. He shuddered to think what might have happened at St. Pancras if the fire from the incendiary grenade had spread. Even with modern fire safety regulations, it could have been disastrous.

This time they had been lucky that the injuries hadn't been worse, and that the only fatality had been the person responsible. But that still left him with an unsolved death, a missing person, and more bad news to deliver.

He contemplated going back to the station, but he was nearer Cartwright Gardens where he was. Instead, he texted Jasmine Sidana and asked her to meet him in a half hour's time at the address Ariel Ellis had given him.

• • •

The sun came out briefly as he walked, giving a lie to the day. By the time he reached his destination, the sky had darkened once more, and a splatter of rain made him realize he'd left his brolly at the station when he'd gone to meet Doug and Melody that morning at the café.

Cartwright Gardens was a crescent of houses, the buildings white arched below, then typical Bloomsbury brown brick on the upper, less desirable floors of the houses. The crescent faced a garden with a playground at one end, and Kincaid imagined that on a nice day, the garden would be filled with mums and shrieking toddlers.

Today, however, the street looked deserted except for Jasmine Sidana's black Honda sedan idling at the curb near the Ellises' address. He wondered how Sidana managed to keep her car looking spotless even in this miserable weather, and imagined her out giving it a polish after every shower.

He wiped the smile from his face as Sidana got out of the car. She did not look as though she would appreciate his amusement.

"Where have you been?" she challenged him. "You've hardly been in the station at all."

"I was never very good at paperwork."

"Obviously. But you can't run a murder team like some sort of maverick."

Kincaid knew Sidana's anger was justified, and that he had to find some way to mend things with her if they were going to work together effectively—without telling her what he suspected about Ryan Marsh.

He went back to her question. "I walked from the Caledonian Road. I wanted to have a word with Matthew Quinn's group about Paul Cole before I gave Ariel the news. And I wanted to do it on a less formal basis. Sometimes you get better results that way."

"And did you?" Sidana sounded at least somewhat mollified.

"I'm not certain. They were shocked, but I think they were more relieved that it wasn't Ryan that was dead. No one seemed to have liked Paul much. They didn't, however, think it likely that he was suicidal. They confirmed that he did have an argument with Ariel that morning, but said that both Paul and Ariel left the flat before Ryan, who had the smoke bomb."

"And they still insist it was a smoke bomb?"

"Yes. But they wouldn't tell us otherwise, would they?" When Sidana nodded reluctant agreement, he went on. "They did say they thought it was possible that Ryan might have given in to Paul's pleas to let him carry the smoke bomb, because he felt sorry for him."

"And they haven't seen Ryan Marsh since?"

"So they say."

"Do you believe them? About any of it?"

Kincaid felt in his overcoat pocket for a handkerchief. His nose was starting to run from the cold. "I believe they thought Ryan was dead. Which means they don't know where he is now."

"Then if there was an intended victim, it was Ryan Marsh. Unless Ryan Marsh meant to kill Paul Cole."

Kincaid wasn't ready to tell her that Melody had identified Ryan Marsh as the man on the scene, and that they now believed he was—or had been—an undercover copper. Neither of those things ruled out Marsh as a murderer—or that he was going strictly on Melody's instinct.

Nor could he tell Sidana he thought that if Marsh had killed Paul Cole, the most likely motive was that Cole had somehow discovered his true identity. But when undercover cops were blown, they usually had a carefully planned exit strategy in place. There was no need to resort to murder.

Instead, he said, "Let's get this over with, shall we?"

Sidana glanced at him in surprise. "You don't like doing death notifications?"

"Despise them. Never gets easier."

"So that's why you sent *me* to the Coles last night."

Kincaid thought he detected the tiniest hint of humor in Sidana's tone. Could the Ice Maiden possibly be thawing? "Exactly," he replied, straight-faced, as he started for the Ellises' front door.

Then he stopped so suddenly that Jasmine bumped into him.

"What?" she said, frowning. "You're going to run off again and leave me to it?"

"No, nothing like that. It's just that I meant to ask you to have the tech teams look for a black notebook or journal in Paul Cole's things. I should have asked the group as well. The waitress in the café at St. Pancras recognized Cole from the photo. She says she didn't see him the day of the incident, but he came in the café fairly regularly and wrote in a journal. I'd very much like to know what happened to it."

"When did you interview the waitress? Playing maverick again?"

"No, not exactly," he temporized. "It was last night. I just wanted to see the scene again. I'd wanted to show the photo of Paul Cole to Tam—Tam Moran, the man who was injured— but he wasn't up to it. Then I remembered Melody telling me the waitress had been so helpful, and I wondered if she might have seen something."

"You think he might have written something useful in this notebook?" Jasmine sounded genuinely interested. She took out her phone and sent a quick text, then followed him to the door.

ELLIS was written beside the bell for Flat 1. So it was the ground-floor flat, which Kincaid imagined was the best in the building.

He pushed the bell and identified himself when the intercom clicked on, then opened the door when it buzzed.

A man stood at the open front door to the ground-floor flat.

The resemblance to Ariel Ellis was immediate in the fair, wispy hair and delicate features. But the fair hair was fading to gray, and he wore silver-rimmed reading glasses perched on the end of his nose. Kincaid guessed he was in his early fifties, but fit, slender, and attractive in a way that probably made female undergraduates fancy him.

He peered at them. "Can I help you?"

"Mr. Ellis? I'm Detective Superintendent Kincaid and this is Detective Inspector Sidana. We're from Camden CID. May we come in?"

"Of course, of course." Ellis led them through a small entry and into a sitting room that made Kincaid look round with pleasure.

Light flowed into the room from the three tall, arched windows facing the street. A gas fire blazed in the fireplace, and except for a mirror over the mantel, every other bit of wall space seemed to be taken up by bookcases and artwork. An obviously well-used desk sat in front of the windows. Two squashy leather sofas flanked the fire. A cup and a stack of what looked like student essays filled a small end table beneath a reading lamp. The flat smelled of coffee and old books, with a hint of something that might have been cherry pipe tobacco. Radio 3 played softly from a small radio on the mantel.

This, Kincaid thought, is how he would like their Notting Hill house to look if it was theirs to do with as they liked. And then he realized that it was very much like his parents' sitting room in Cheshire.

"Let me take your coats," said Mr. Ellis.

Sidana declined, but Kincaid, suddenly roasting after his long walk in the cold, handed over his coat. Ellis hung it on a hook in the entry, then joined them in the sitting room.

"We've come to see Ariel, Mr. Ellis," said Kincaid. "Is she at home?"

"No. No, she's at class at the moment, but she should be back shortly. Please, sit down."

Kincaid and Sidana took seats on the sofa opposite the one where Ellis had been marking papers.

Seeing Kincaid's glance, Ellis said, "They want to turn everything in digitally now, but I make them print their essays. I may be a dinosaur, but I don't feel I can mark an essay properly unless it's on paper. Can I get you some tea or coffee while you're waiting?" he added.

Kincaid shook his head without waiting for a response from Jasmine. He wanted to take advantage of this time with Ellis, both to prepare him for what was coming and to see what he knew. "No, thank you, Mr. Ellis."

"If you're certain . . ." Ellis sat down facing them. "It's Dr. Ellis, actually. But I prefer to have my students call me Stephen."

Of course he did, thought Kincaid. It was just the chummy sort of thing he would expect from a professor who took favorite students on tours of London's vanishing historic sites, and probably had them over for tea or sherry afterwards. And who wore cashmere cardigans. Kincaid felt quite sure that the man's soft gray sweater was cashmere.

"Dr. Ellis, I'm afraid we have some distressing news for Ariel. She told you that her friend, Paul Cole, was missing?"

"Paul, yes." Ellis frowned. "Always a bit emotional, that boy. I told her I thought he'd probably gone off in a sulk."

"They hadn't been getting on?"

"I try to mind my own business in these things," Ellis said after a moment's hesitation. "But I could see that Paul was becoming clingy. My daughter is a bit of a rescuer, but enough is enough."

"Did you ever fear that Paul might become violent or suicidal?"

Ellis paled. "No! Are you telling me— For God's sake, what's happened?"

"We believe we've identified Paul Cole as the victim in Wednesday's incident at St. Pancras International."

"You don't mean—" Ellis pulled his glasses off and pinched the bridge of his nose. "The person who . . . burned?"

"I'm afraid so," said Jasmine, in a gentler voice than Kincaid had heard her use before. "Can I get you something? A glass of water?"

Ellis nodded and Jasmine went to the kitchen, returning with a glass of tap water. Kincaid wondered, not for the first time, why a glass of water was considered a remedy for shock or grief. But Ellis drank it obediently, like a child told to take medicine, and set the almost empty glass on the end table.

"I just can't believe it," he murmured, shaking his head. "Paul . . . whatever little tiff he and Ariel might have had . . . Why would he do something like that?"

"That's what we have to find out," said Kincaid, "and we're hoping Ariel can help us."

"Oh, Ariel!" Ellis looked round wildly, as if his daughter had suddenly appeared. "I'll have to—"

"Don't worry, Mr. Ellis," broke in Kincaid. "We'll break the news."

"You don't understand." Ellis picked up the glass again but didn't drink. "Ariel . . . she's had too much loss already in her life. Her mother died when Ariel was fourteen. A terrible accident. Ariel was impossibly lucky, but it's been difficult for her." He gestured towards some of the paintings Kincaid had noticed over the bookcases. "That's when she started painting. The therapist recommended it."

Kincaid looked more closely at the paintings. "These are hers? No wonder she's going for an art degree." The canvases were large, with bold colors and photo-realistic images that faded suddenly into abstract. Some had letters and words stenciled across them. They were very striking, and not at all what he would have expected from such an ethereal girl. "She's very talented."

Ellis nodded agreement. "Yes. I couldn't see why she would waste her time with this boy or with that group."

"But you knew them. Many of them were your students, I believe."

Ellis drew himself up. "I'm an historian, Mr. Kincaid. I care about the irrevocable damage being done to historical sites by rampant development. Especially by the Crossrail digging, even though they have excellent archeologists on their projects. Who knows what they may miss that may never be recovered? But I don't condone violence of any kind."

"So do I take it you parted ways with Matthew Quinn?"

"Ah, Matthew . . . He was a brilliant structural engineering student. Did you know that? I never understood why he gave it up. The two things were not at odds that I could see. But something seemed to go wrong with him, and I could sense it spreading in the group of followers." Ellis frowned. "Maybe I was being fanciful, but I'd encouraged Ariel to distance herself."

"Did you have any sense that Matthew might become violent?" Kincaid asked.

Ellis frowned. "It wasn't that so much as controlling. And the beginnings, perhaps, of some sort of an obsessive-compulsive disorder. I never thought—"

The front door of the building slammed, then, a moment later, there was a rattle of keys and the front door of the flat opened.

They all froze, as if caught in some unseemly act. From the entry came Ariel's light voice. "Daddy, there's a strange car—"

Coming into the sitting room, she saw Kincaid and Jasmine, and stopped.

Just as her father said, "Darling—" Kincaid stood and interrupted him.

"Ariel, I'm very sorry. I'm afraid we have bad news about Paul."

Her eyes widened. The bag full of books she carried dropped to the floor with a thump.

"Oh, no." Ariel looked from Kincaid to her father, as if seeking confirmation. Then she whispered, "Please . . ." as her knees buckled and she fell with as little sound as a feather.

"You're certain you're cleared to be back at work?" Gemma asked, studying Melody, who sat on the other side of Gemma's desk in the South London Police Station CID suite. Melody appeared to be wearing the same clothes she'd worn when Gemma had met her for her tests at UCL hospital last night. "If you don't mind my saying so, you look a right mess."

Melody smiled. "Thanks, boss. I didn't want to take the time to go home and change. I thought you'd rather have me as I am."

"Oh, I'm not complaining, believe me," said Gemma with a smile. "But have you been home at all? Since it happened?" she asked. Her partner looked not only wan and a bit unkempt, but as if she'd dropped half a dozen pounds in three days.

Melody shook her head. "No. Well, yes, actually, I picked up my car, but I didn't go in. I was in a rush. I went to Doug's for a bit last night."

"A rush to see Doug?" asked Gemma. "Are you sure you're all right?" She was beginning to wonder if Melody was as well as the doctors had said.

"Oh, long story." Melody brushed back a stray strand of dark hair and sat forward. "Tell me about the search. Did you find anything? Why didn't you interview Underwood first?"

"I thought it might unsettle him a bit if I left him to stew while we searched the flat. And that I might find something to use as ammunition."

"Did you?"

Gemma sighed. "Nothing. I wish my kids were half as neat. What twenty-two-year-old makes his bed and does the washing up? It's a one-bedroom flat—not bad for someone his age with a job as a salesclerk."

"Do you think he dabbles in something else?"

"If he does, there was no sign of it. All cheap IKEA furnishings. Gigantic TV. Expensive sound system. Pretty much what you'd expect for someone who works in an electronics shop. But"—Gemma tilted back in her chair and rolled a pen between her fingers—"no computer. He said his died and he just hasn't replaced it yet. He uses his phone and the computers in the shop. But my guess is that the hard drive's smashed in a bin somewhere and the computer's smashed in another."

"Did we get a warrant for the phone?" Melody asked.

Gemma shook her head. "No. But I doubt there's anything useful on it. He's too clever by half, is Dillon Underwood." She stood up. "Let's go see what he has to say for himself."

Dillon Underwood was as clean as his flat. He sat across from Gemma and Melody in the interview room, looking as unconcerned as if he'd been invited for tea. He wore pressed tan trousers and a polo shirt with his shop's logo embroidered on the breast. His brown hair was buzzed short, his nails manicured. His eyes were a light brown, and Gemma found them oddly flat, unreadable. When he smiled, Gemma felt sure he whitened his teeth. There was a small nick from a shaving cut under his chin.

"Hello, Dillon," she said, and nodded for Melody to turn on the recorder. "For the record, I'm Detective Inspector Gemma James, and this is Detective Sergeant Melody Talbot." When he didn't speak, she went on. "You remember we talked before, Dillon."

Melody had brought in a pen and notepad, which she placed on the table. They had agreed beforehand that good cop/bad cop was not likely to be effective with Underwood, and that Melody making a show of silent note taking might be more likely to make him edgy.

Now he leaned back in his chair and crossed his legs. "Of course I remember. You interrupted my work, just like today. I'm needed at the shop."

Gemma silently thanked him for giving her the perfect opening. She leaned forward, elbows on the table. "You're very good at your job, aren't you, Dillon?"

"Yeah. You could say that." His mouth curved in a smirk.

"Popular with the customers?"

"They ask for me. They know I'll steer them right."

"All the customers like you, the men and the women?"

"Well, yeah. I know my stuff."

"I would think you'd remember them."

Underwood shrugged. "Do you know how many people come in our shop every day?"

"But you remember the special ones. The ones that come back."

He uncrossed his legs, and it seemed to Gemma that his eyes grew flatter. "If this is about that girl, I told you before. I don't remember her."

"The *girl*'s name was Mercy Johnson. She was twelve years old. She came to see you regularly because she wanted her mother to buy her a computer for her thirteenth birthday. Unfortunately, Mercy didn't see her thirteenth birthday. She was raped, strangled, and left on Clapham Common like a piece of rubbish."

Most people, on hearing such a description, couldn't help a grimace of shock or distaste, or a blink. Dillon Underwood's face remained completely blank. "That's too bad," he said. "But it's nothing to do with me."

"Oh, I think it is, Dillon. And I'm surprised you don't remember her, because you gave her a phone."

This time he did blink. "I don't know what you're on about." His accent was South London, his voice slightly nasal and a little too high pitched.

Gemma had brought in a file folder. Now she opened it and pulled out a print. It was the photo from Izzy Lamar's phone, blown up. It was clearly Dillon Underwood, and there was no doubt he was handing Mercy Johnson a phone. "Tell us about this, then."

He stared at the photo. Gemma saw his hand twitch with the desire to touch it, but he controlled it, rocking back in his chair and crossing his arms. "Who took that?"

"I don't think that's any of your concern. But it is you, and it is Mercy, and you are handing her a phone."

"It was those little sneaks, wasn't it? Those girls, always watching and whispering, the cows."

It was the first crack, the first hint of venom, and Gemma had to stop herself casting a jubilant glance at Melody. "So you admit you gave Mercy a phone."

Underwood didn't answer. Melody was scribbling something on the notepad, shielding it with her hand just enough to make certain he couldn't read it, even upside down and across the table.

"Dillon," said Gemma, "we have a photo, and we have witnesses. We can prove you knew Mercy and that you gave her a phone. Now tell us why."

"All right, then." He tore his eyes away from Melody. "I felt sorry for her. She came in the shop all crying and carrying on. She'd lost her phone and her mum was that pissed off, she wouldn't get her another one. A kid that age, they live for their phones, don't they? So I gave her a cheap burner phone. Put ten pounds on it. There's no law against it."

"Why give it to her in front of the tube station? You must have arranged to meet her."

"I couldn't give it to her in the shop, could I?"

"Why not?"

Gemma saw him struggle with that one for a moment. Then he shrugged. "I only thought of it as she was leaving. She had to get home to her mum or something. I told her I'd look out for a phone and see what I could do. I had it with me when I saw her outside the tube."

"That's a good story, Dillon. But Mercy's friends said it was her suggestion to meet for coffee at the Starbucks. And that the entire time she was fidgety, watching for someone, then she tried to get them to leave her on her own. It was you she was watching for, wasn't it, Dillon? And you couldn't give her the phone inside the shop because you didn't want anyone there to see you do it. Did you pay for the phone or did you just take it out of stock so it couldn't be traced?"

He crossed his legs again. "It was some old phone lying round in the stockroom. Sometimes people just leave the old ones when they get a new phone."

Gemma didn't believe that for a minute. She guessed he'd taken a new phone from stock, but theft of stock was common in electronics shops, and going over the inventory wouldn't do them much good if they didn't know what kind of phone he'd given her. They'd not been able to tell the brand from the photo. "And you paid cash for the top-up?" she asked with a little smile, as if she thought he'd been a Good Samaritan.

"I don't use credit cards. Big Brother and all that. No law against that, either."

"And you told Mercy the phone was hers to do with as she wanted?"

"Well, yeah, why wouldn't I?"

"If she'd told her mum, you could have been in trouble with the shop."

"Yeah, and her mum would have taken it off her. Fat chance

she'd have told her." He was getting cocky again as he got comfortable with his story.

Melody handed Gemma a note. It read, "What if Mercy didn't lose her phone? What if she set it down in the shop when he was showing her the computers, and he took it?"

Gemma glanced at her, nodding, and wrote back, "Perfect opportunity to set up untraceable contact."

"What are you doing?" asked Underwood. "You're like two stupid girls in school passing notes."

How he must have hated that, thought Gemma, because he would always have thought the notes and the giggles were about him.

She ignored the question and the comment. "Can you explain to me why Mercy didn't tell her friends about the phone?" she asked. "Her best friends? Or call or text them from it?"

"How should I know? Maybe she lost that one, too."

"I'll tell you what I think, Dillon." Gemma leaned closer to him, and as she did she caught an odd smell. It wasn't fear—she could recognize the acrid stink of fear in an instant. The odor coming from Dillon Underwood was slightly soapy and somehow chemical. Unpleasant. She wrinkled her nose and went on. "I think you told her not to. That the phone was a secret, and that it was only to be used to communicate with you. And I'll bet you stole another cheap phone for yourself so there'd be no record of the contact."

"I never. And I didn't steal anything," he shot back.

"What happened to the phone, Dillon? It wasn't in her flat or on her body. Did you take it after you murdered her?"

"I told you before. I was at a club with my mates that night."

"You also told us you didn't remember Mercy Johnson. You lied. I think you're lying about being at the club that night, too. I think you texted Mercy and told her to meet you on Clapham Common. What did you tell her? That you had something for her? Or did she think you fancied her?"

"I never saw her outside the shop but that one time, and you can't prove that I did." There was a spark of anger in the flat eyes now.

"Oh, but we have your DNA now, Dillon. We took samples from your flat. Your toothbrush. Your razor. We'll be able to match it to evidence collected from Mercy's body."

He smiled at her. "No, you won't. Because I wasn't there, and I never touched her. Now, I want to go back to work. And I'm not talking to you anymore unless I have a lawyer."

"You could have kept him the remainder of the twenty-four hours," said Melody when Gemma had authorized the custody sergeant to sign Dillon Underwood out.

"I don't think it would have accomplished anything, especially since he finally got round to demanding a solicitor. I'd rather he think he's convinced us."

"And did he?" asked Melody, sounding skeptical.

"I think he's guilty as sin. I think he murdered Mercy Johnson, and I'm going to prove it. I just can't see why he's so sure of himself."

"Now that he's admitted to the phone, defense could argue that any trace DNA found on her body was cross-contamination from the phone."

Gemma frowned. "Would he know that?"

"I suspect he would."

"Maybe," Gemma answered slowly. "Unless it's under her fingernails or somewhere ordinary transfer would have been unlikely. I'm going to put a rush on the tests," she said with decision. "And I'm going to tell Izzy's and Deja's parents to keep them under lock and key. He knows now that they saw him give Mercy the phone. He may think they saw something else."

"Would he be that stupid?" asked Melody. "He's a calculating bastard, and he'd know that if anything happened to either of those girls, we'd be on him like a shot."

"He's also vicious," said Gemma with utter conviction. "And he thinks he can get away with anything. I'm going to make those calls, and then we're going to pick his alibi to pieces."

CHAPTER SEVENTEEN

W. H. Barlow, the engineer behind the design of the stores, used iron beams and pillars to maximise the utilisation of space. He said, "The length of a barrel of beer became the unit of measurement upon which all the arrangements of this floor were made."

—*meantimebrewing.com*
/stpancras-station

Stephen Ellis had put his daughter to bed. She'd revived within a minute or two but had seemed unfocused, uncoordinated, and a little confused. Ellis had lifted her and helped her into the bedroom, refusing help from Kincaid or Sidana.

He'd come back apologetic. "I'm so sorry," he'd said. "It's the shock. She's had these episodes under severe stress, ever since the accident. She should be all right when she's had a little sleep."

Kincaid and Sidana had taken their leave and driven back to Holborn station in Sidana's Honda.

"I'm not sure what's worse," Kincaid said as they walked into the station, "delivering unexpected bad news or bad news that's been dreaded."

"I suppose fainting is better than hysterics," Jasmine answered. "Woman gave me a black eye once when I told her that her husband had been killed in a pub fight."

"You were lucky she wasn't holding a frying pan, then." This merited a sideways glance and what he thought might have been a smile.

The CID room was empty except for Simon Gikas.

"Where's Sweeney?" Sidana asked, not sounding a bit pleased.

"He left an hour ago. Said something about pulling a tendon in the gym this morning."

"He's a slacker." Sidana's lips were pinched in disapproval.

Although Kincaid hadn't seen anything about George Sweeney so far that impressed him, he didn't envy the man being on the sharp end of Jasmine Sidana's tongue.

"Well, I'm not," Gikas said with a grin, "and I've found something interesting for you." He swiveled in his chair to face them. Kincaid leaned against one of the worktables, listening attentively. Sidana, having dropped her bag and coat at her desk, came to join him.

"You remember I found that Matthew Quinn gets a check every month from the corporation that owns his building?" asked Gikas.

"The mysterious KCD," agreed Kincaid. "King's Cross Development."

"Right. Well, I did some digging into the corporate records, and guess what I discovered?"

"Don't kill us with the suspense."

"One of the corporation's owners—in fact, the major shareholder—is Lindsay Quinn. He's one of the movers and shakers in the revitalization of the King's Cross area. And he is also Matthew Quinn's father."

Kincaid raised an eyebrow. "Do you suppose Quinn senior knows what Quinn junior is up to? A viper in the nest?"

"I thought you'd want to talk to him. I managed to get his PA on the phone. He was tied up this afternoon, but can see you tomorrow at the Booking Office Bar at the St. Pancras Renaissance Hotel. That seems to be his favorite place to hold meetings."

"Nice. Thanks, Simon." Kincaid thought for a moment. "I think I'll hold off talking to Matthew Quinn again until after I've spoken to his father." He turned to Sidana. "Have you heard anything back from the family liaison officer at the Coles'?"

Sidana checked her phone. "He says no on the journal, but that Paul's bedroom was full of books on trains. His mother says he'd been a train anorak since he was a kid, but there were timetables in his room that looked as if they'd been used fairly recently."

"I don't know what that tells us." Kincaid said. "That he picked St. Pancras to burn himself to a crisp because he loved trains?" He shook his head. "Seems a bit daft. And I'm still not at all convinced that he did intend to burn himself up, poor bugger."

After talking to Simon, Kincaid had gone through the day's reports at the station. Finding nothing that seemed particularly helpful, he'd decided to brave Friday rush-hour traffic and try to make it home on time. Until he could talk to Lindsay Quinn, or got DNA results back, or heard from Doug, or came up with a new line of inquiry, he was in a holding pattern on Paul Cole's death.

Friday night was pizza and games night at the Kincaid/ James household. But the ritual had rules, and those were that the pizza had to be homemade, and no electronics were allowed. The idea had at first been met with protest from the boys—Toby wanted takeaway pizza *and* television *and* electronic games, while Kit didn't object to the homemade pizza but did not want to be separated from his phone. Charlotte was perfectly happy with anything that they all did together.

Arriving unscathed and only a bit late, Kincaid parked the Astra behind Gemma's Escort. He got out and locked the car, but then he stood for a moment, looking up at the house. The blinds had not yet been drawn, and light shone from the front windows. He could see Gemma and Kit in the cheerful blue and yellow kitchen.

They had all come to love this house. It was a haven for the children, and the first home he and Gemma had made together. If anything had happened to Denis Childs, or to Denis's sister, would they lose it?

He told himself to stop worrying. He was not doing himself or anyone else any good. But he hated the feeling of not having control over his own life, and that had been plaguing him since his transfer.

Gemma glanced out the kitchen window, then turned away. She wouldn't have seen him standing out here in the dark and cold. He gave himself a mental shake, strode up the walk to the cherry-red front door, and put his key in the lock.

He was met by the heady smell of baking dough, the barking of dogs, and a shriek of welcome from Charlotte as she ran to hug him.

"Daddy, I was watching for you," she said as he picked her up for a hug.

"Were you? You're a good watchdog, then."

Charlotte giggled. "I'm not a dog."

"Oh. I thought you were Geordie. Let's see, a curly coat"—he stroked her hair—"a long snout—" He pinched her nose.

"I'm *Char*lotte," she announced, putting the emphasis on the first syllable. She wriggled out of his arms. "Come and see. Toby's dancing!"

Gemma came out of the kitchen.

"Darling, I'm home," he said, grinning.

"So I see." When she kissed him he saw that she had tomato sauce on her cheek. He wiped it off with his finger and gave her another kiss. "Yum." Taking off his coat and hanging it on the peg over the bench by the door, he asked, "What's this about dancing?"

"We went to ballet," said Charlotte, bouncing up and down on her toes. "MacKenzie took Toby and me to Oliver's ballet class."

"Oliver's taking ballet?" Kincaid looked a question at Gemma. Oliver Williams was Charlotte's best friend. Kincaid had met Oliver and his mum, MacKenzie, at one of the local cafés when he was home on paternity leave. MacKenzie had managed to get Charlotte a place in Oliver's very prestigious school, after their attempt to settle Charlotte in Toby's old preschool had proved a complete failure.

When Kincaid had learned that his practical and down-to-earth friend MacKenzie was co-owner with her husband, Bill, of the enormously successful online and catalog clothing retailer Ollie, *and* that MacKenzie was the top model for the catalog, he had been horribly embarrassed. MacKenzie and Gemma, who had since become friends, still snickered about his cluelessness.

"It seems it's the in thing for little boys in Notting Hill at the moment," said Gemma. "MacKenzie took Charlotte and Toby along after school today. Charlotte couldn't be bothered," she added quietly as Charlotte ran off, "but Toby is besotted."

Toby came leaping in from the sitting room, arms held out at right angles, shouting, "See what I can do? It's a . . . a . . . I can't remember what it is. But I can do it."

"Are pirates over, then?" Kincaid whispered in Gemma's ear.

"I think so." She sighed. "But I suspect this is going to be considerably more expensive. Come on. Pizza's in the oven and I've put the kettle on."

• • •

While they were waiting for the pizza to finish, Kit went with Kincaid to see the kittens. Having greeted Kincaid, Geordie was now lying in front of the study door, head on paws.

"What's this, then?" Kincaid asked, leaning down to rub the spaniel's ears.

"He got in the room this afternoon, when Toby didn't close the door all the way," Kit said. "Xena came out of her box like a shot, hissed at him, and smacked him on the nose. Since then he's been guarding the room like he's taken charge. Do you think he got close enough to realize they were babies?"

"Quite possibly. He's a smart dog."

Kit opened the door, but rather than trying to go in, Geordie continued to keep watch, settling back into the same position.

When they entered the room, Xena gave them a little chirp of greeting. She stood up, stretching, and when Kincaid knelt by the box, she butted her head against his hand and he rubbed her behind the ears.

The kittens were sleeping. Their bellies had rounded, and now they looked more like little sausages than rats.

"They're starting to move around in the box," said Kit, kneeling beside Kincaid. "They're so funny. They're blind, and they bumble into each other. Bryony says their eyes should open in a few days."

"Bryony came today?"

"This afternoon, while Toby and Charlotte were out with MacKenzie. She taught me how to tell the sex," Kit added proudly. "She says it's easier now than it will be when they're older." He touched the calico. "This one's female, of course— I've been reading up on cat genetics—and so is the tabby. The black one and the black-and-white one are male."

"I'm impressed." Kincaid could tell that the mother cat was improving as well. She looked less thin, her coat was shiny, her eyes bright. "Amazing what a few days of food can do. She is very tame," he said to Kit. "Have you had any luck with your posters?"

It was the wrong thing to say. Kit sat back, scowling. "No. And if someone is missing her, shouldn't they have called by now? I want to take the posters down."

"We can't keep the mum and all the kittens," Kincaid said gently.

"MacKenzie says they'll take one. Oliver loves them. Gemma said she'd talk to Hazel. And I'm going to talk to Erika. We're supposed to have lunch with her on Sunday. I think it would be good for her to have a cat."

"Possibly. But that leaves a kitten unaccounted for."

"Surely we could keep Xena and one of the kittens?" Kit didn't quite manage to keep the pleading note from his voice.

Kincaid stroked the black kitten, which was beginning to stir and root around towards its mother. "I suppose it would depend on how they get along with Sid." He felt completely at sea with all of this, but he was quite taken with the cats himself. "Which kitten would you want to keep?" he asked.

Leaning over the box again, Kit frowned and gave each kitten a little stroke in turn. "I don't know. I like the calico. I think it's cool that only females can be calico. And I like the black-and-white one. He looks like James Bond in a tuxedo."

Kincaid heard Gemma calling them. "Well, I think we have lots of time to decide. And you can ask Bryony tomorrow, but I should think it would be okay to take the posters down."

"Really?" Kit bounced up with almost as much enthusiasm as Toby.

Kincaid stood and put a restraining hand on his shoulder. "But let's not say anything until you've spoken to Bryony again, okay?"

"Deal," said Kit.

• • •

"You spoil him dreadfully, you know," Gemma said to Kincaid as they finished the washing-up together a few hours later.

"Who, Kit?" Kincaid looked his most innocent.

They had eaten their pizza, played a quick game of Snakes and Ladders—with much cheating on Toby's part—for Charlotte's benefit, then settled in for a game of Beatles Monopoly. Charlotte was allowed to play with the extra tokens, and after a bit had settled sleepily in Gemma's lap. When Charlotte was dozing and Toby had begun to get cranky, they'd put the younger children to bed and released Kit to reunite with his phone and his iPod.

As he left the room, he'd tossed back at them, "You know I can't tell my mates why I can't go out on Friday nights. They'd think I was a total wa—"

Gemma gave him the *watch your language* evil eye.

"They'd think I was totally wet," Kit amended. Then he'd grinned at them and a moment later they heard him running up the stairs.

"Yes, Kit," Gemma said now. "I don't know what you told him in the study, but the rest of the night he looked like the cat that got into the cream. And I suppose it was something to do with the cats."

"He only wants to keep the mum and one kitten."

"That's what he says *now*. And imagine the arguments with Toby and Charlotte over which one."

"Well then, they'll have to learn to negotiate, won't they? And don't tell me you're not tempted to keep at least one of the little blighters. You said the other night that you fancied the black-and-white one."

Gemma sank into one of the kitchen chairs and he thought that she looked tired . . . and . . . something more.

"I suppose we *should* give them what they want—within reason—when we can," she said slowly.

Kincaid glanced at her, then took a rather expensive bottle

of Sancerre he'd been saving for the weekend from the fridge, pulled the cork, and poured them both a glass. He handed one to Gemma, who smiled her thanks, and sat down across from her.

"What's up, love?" he asked quietly. "I don't think it's kittens."

"No." Gemma told him about her interview with Dillon Underwood. "And now I keep thinking," she added, "what if Mercy's mum had gone with her to pick out that computer she wanted so badly? Or what if her mum hadn't been so harsh with her over the lost phone? Which Melody and I suspect Dillon may have pinched as a way to manipulate her."

"Gemma." He took her hand across the table. "Mercy's mother didn't do anything wrong. Neither did Mercy. You know that."

But he felt the same chill. There was no guarantee that Friday-night games or any of the other ways they cared for and loved their children would keep them safe from monsters like Dillon Underwood. They knew that better than anyone else.

"You need to take the weekend off," he said, pouring her a little more wine. Her expression had softened, her cheeks had gained a bit of color, but he didn't miss the guilty look that flashed across her face. "You're not going in? You said you were pretty well stuck until the DNA results come back."

"No. No, I'm not going in. But . . ." Gemma glanced at him and took another sip of her wine. "I did bring her case report home. I keep thinking there's something I've missed. And don't come the copper with me," she added before he could speak. "Because you *are* going in."

Kincaid grimaced. "Honestly, I don't know whether I'm coming or going with this case. The more I find out, the less I know."

Frowning, Gemma said, "Melody told me she'd gone to see Doug last night in a rush. Have you pulled them into this?"

"Doug, yes," he admitted. "But I think you could say that Melody pulled herself in, under the circumstances."

"What are they doing that your team can't do?"

"Ah. There's the rub. It seems Tam was right. We've got an ID on the victim. He was young. Just twenty." He went on to tell her all the things he hadn't had a chance to share with her—that he and Doug had suspected the initial supposed victim, Ryan Marsh, might be an undercover police officer, and that Doug had subsequently proved that Ryan Marsh had at least *once* been a cop. That Melody, looking for photos of the protest group, had identified Ryan Marsh as the man who had helped her on the scene. That Ryan Marsh was now missing, and that a girl in the group had disappeared suddenly at the New Year.

And about Ariel Ellis, who had come to him to report her boyfriend missing, after they'd had a row about her miscarriage.

He hesitated a bit over this, hating to remind Gemma of the baby they'd lost, but he knew she'd be furious with him if he didn't tell her.

"Do you think it was suicide?"

Kincaid shrugged. "Paul Cole has been described as moody and attention seeking, but no one thinks he was suicidal. And apparently he kept a regular journal, which has not turned up in his belongings."

"And you haven't told your team what you've found out about Ryan Marsh? Why?"

"If he was still undercover, who was he working for?" Kincaid leaned forward, elbows on the scrubbed pine table, wineglass between his hands. "Why did he infiltrate this group unless they were a serious threat? Why has no one in the force claimed him? Why did he disappear?"

"You think he thought the grenade was meant for him?"

"Melody said he reacted to the incident the way any trained

copper would, but that when he saw the body, he was distraught. It was personal. I think he was more than shocked. I think he was frightened, and I'm not letting anyone else know that I know who he is *or* that he's still alive until I know why."

Gemma sipped and thought. "You're assuming that Ryan Marsh agreed to let Paul Cole set off the smoke bomb, and that someone switched the smoke bomb with a grenade without Marsh's knowledge. Who could have done that?"

"Matthew Quinn seems the obvious choice. I've found out that Quinn's father is a big player in the area redevelopment scheme, and that he's been supporting Matthew. Maybe Matthew was planning more serious stuff, and Marsh threatened to tell his father. Or the police. Or Matthew found out Marsh was an undercover cop."

"But," said Gemma, "would Matthew Quinn have made himself such an obvious suspect?"

Kincaid topped up both their glasses. "It doesn't seem very likely, does it? He may be a bit compulsive, but I don't think he's stupid."

"Unless he thought he could convince people that Marsh was suicidal," Gemma suggested.

"Several people in the group said that Ryan hadn't been the same since the girl—Wren—disappeared," Kincaid said, trying to recollect the statements exactly. "But I don't think Matthew was one of them."

"And no one has said what happened to the girl?"

"No. Just that she walked out and didn't come back."

"Well," said Gemma, raising her glass to him. "There's your missing piece, love. Find out what happened to the girl. And why it mattered to Ryan Marsh."

CHAPTER EIGHTEEN

Each arm [of Barlow's arches at St. Pancras] is composed of sturdy parallel members made up of riveted iron plates, conjoined by fifteen main braces and a lattice of fifty cross-braces . . . There are twenty-five arches in all, set in intervals of 29 feet 4 inches, double the spacing of the basement columns—the . . . beer-barrels controlling influence again—to form an enclosure 689 feet (210 meters) long. Much of the visual power of this huge interior comes from the way in which these soaring arches allow the eye to calibrate the space immediately.

—*Simon Bradley,*
St. Pancras Station, *2007*

"Do you mind if I take the Astra today?" Gemma asked Kincaid as he was eating a piece of toast and gulping down a cup of tea on Saturday morning. "I've promised to take the kids to Leyton to see Mum and Dad this afternoon, and the kids want to take the dogs. I can't jam them all in the Escort."

Kincaid nodded, mouth full of toast and marmalade.

"You can take the Escort," Gemma added kindly.

"I'm not taking a purple car to work," Kincaid said, swallowing. "I'd be the laughingstock of Holborn." When Gemma looked affronted, he laughed and kissed her. "Just teasing, love. But it is a bit hard to fit my long legs in your little orchid. I'll just take the tube. I can use the walk either end."

The sky was the color of pearl this morning, rather than gunmetal, and—at least so far—the wind had not come up. A walk would give him an opportunity to enjoy the break in the weather.

He'd dressed with some thought that morning. Not wanting to wear a suit into work on Saturday, he settled on a crisp pale blue shirt, a sports coat, and jeans. Hopefully he would be presentable for the Booking Office Bar.

Now he pulled on his overcoat, added an umbrella, kissed Gemma, and shouted goodbye to the kids, who were all upstairs.

It was a straight shot up Lansdowne Road to the tube station. As he walked, he noticed that the tips of the tree branches were swelling with buds, and that a few daffodils were lifting brave heads in the gardens he passed. The weather would break, and spring would arrive with a bang. In the meantime, however, he buttoned the top of his coat and wished he'd thought to grab a scarf.

Before he reached Holland Park tube station, he rang Doug from his mobile.

"Are you at home?" he asked when Doug answered.

"No, I'm out rowing." Doug's voice dripped sarcasm. "Of course I'm home. It's Saturday, and I'm doing Internet searches for you."

"Any luck on Ryan Marlowe-slash-Marsh?"

"Not as of yet."

"Bugger." Kincaid thought a moment, then said, "Can you add something else? I want to know what happened to the girl who disappeared, the one they called Wren. I think that might be her in the photo next to Ryan Marsh. Nothing anyone has told me about her makes it seem likely that she just walked out of the group of her own accord."

"Maybe Ryan Marsh killed her and Paul Cole found out. That would give Marsh a motive for agreeing to the switch and giving Cole a grenade instead of a smoke bomb."

"I might buy that except for two things," Kincaid said. "The first is Melody's evidence that Marsh was shocked to the core when he saw Cole's body. The second is statements from some of the other group members that Ryan Marsh changed after Wren's disappearance."

"Maybe Paul Cole killed her and Marsh found out?" suggested Doug. "That would have given him a very good motive for killing Paul Cole. But," he went on before Kincaid could argue, "again, that discounts Melody's observation, and even under duress I don't think she would mistake what she saw. And why would Paul Cole have killed this missing girl, unless he was some kind of a nutter?"

Kincaid was coming up to Holland Park. "Can you check the records for the death of a young female, perhaps around twenty, probably unidentified, right around the New Year? No one's given me the exact date she disappeared, so I'd check New Year's Eve and New Year's Day. I can ask, but I don't want to interview Matthew Quinn or his disciples again until I've spoken to Quinn's father."

"Not asking much, are you?"

"I have every confidence in you," Kincaid said, grinning, and rang off.

Kincaid's new boss, Detective Chief Superintendent Faith, was not so pleased with him.

Both Jasmine Sidana and Simon Gikas had come in. As soon as Kincaid entered the CID suite, Gikas jerked his head towards the building's upper floors. "Boss wants to see you."

"Anything new to tell him?"

Gikas shook his head. "Sod all, Guv. Still trying to find some trace of this Ryan Marsh, but he seems to have vanished."

"Where's Sweeney?"

"Still complaining about a pulled tendon, sir," answered Sidana.

"Right." Kincaid went out again and took the lift up to Faith's office.

The chief super's receptionist was out. When Faith saw Kincaid, he got up and ushered him into his office himself.

"Tell me you've made some progress on this," Faith said without preamble when Kincaid had taken a chair. "We've had to release the victim's name to the press as a potential identification now that his family has been informed. Do you think the stupid boy meant to burn himself up?" He shook his head. "I've got university-age sons. I can't imagine what his parents must be going through."

"No, sir." Kincaid shifted uncomfortably in the chair. It was too short for him, so that his legs stuck out awkwardly, and he wondered if Faith had chosen it on purpose. But unlike Chief Superintendent Denis Childs, Faith seemed a straightforward man, although perhaps one without an eye for decor or ergonomic furniture. "Nothing we've learned so far leads us to believe that Paul Cole was suicidal," he said, "or that he saw himself as a martyr for any sort of cause.

"The member of the group who was meant to be setting off the smoke bomb, Ryan Marsh, seems to have disappeared, but we've found no background on him, and no reason to think he would have deliberately killed Cole."

"What about this leader? Quinn? Any reason he might have had for killing either Marsh or Cole?"

"That looks a bit more promising. We've learned that Matthew Quinn's father is the primary investor in King's Cross Development, the company that not only owns the building in which Quinn and his group have been living, but whose corporation is involved in just the sort of project that Quinn was so vocally protesting. Quinn's father was also supporting him. It could be that Marsh found that out and threatened to tell Quinn's father what Matthew was up to."

"You think Quinn's father didn't know?" Faith asked, raising an eyebrow.

"I have an interview with him after lunch, so I'll go from there."

Faith leaned back in his chair and sighed. "It would certainly be easier all round if it turned out the boy was a suicide."

The hair rose on the back of Kincaid's neck. He'd heard, "It would certainly be easier . . ." before. He hadn't liked the suggestion then, and he liked it even less now.

He'd taken Thomas Faith for a straight-ahead copper, but he no longer trusted his own judgment. He could only hope that Faith had meant it in the most literal sense, and not as a veiled instruction.

"Well," said Faith, "tread delicately with Mr. Quinn, but do what you must. Have you checked in with SO15?"

"Not since they signed off, no."

"See that you do. There is a possibility worse than murder here."

Kincaid waited for Faith to go on.

"What if Matthew Quinn really bought what he thought was a smoke bomb? And this Ryan Marsh gave what *he* thought was a smoke bomb to Paul Cole. All in good faith."

"So you're suggesting the man Quinn bought the smoke bomb from sold him a white phosphorus grenade"—Kincaid took a moment to process it—"with intent to harm?"

"I am," said Faith. "And who knows what else this bloke has or intends to do. In that case, we have a very big problem. I want you to find out who sold Matthew Quinn that grenade. When you do, I want you to liaise with SO15."

"Sir," Kincaid said.

"You'll let me know what you learn from Quinn senior."

"Yes, sir." Kincaid stood, taking that as a dismissal. He was already running the possibilities through his mind. "I'll get on it."

"Kincaid." Faith stopped him before he reached the door. "I know you were accustomed to running your own show. But this is not Scotland Yard, and I expect regular updates."

"Yes, sir." Kincaid waited.

"How are you settling in with your team, by the way?"

"Fine," Kincaid said, and was surprised to find that, with one exception, he meant it. But he wasn't ready to drop Detective Constable George Sweeney in the shit.

Yet.

He had just left Faith's office when his mobile rang. It was Gemma.

"Hello, love," he said, taking the stairs down to the CID suite. "Everything all right?"

"The Astra won't start. We tried jumping it from the Escort, but it wouldn't even turn over."

Kincaid groaned. It never rained but it poured. "We'll have to get it looked at, then, but no one will do it before Monday." The old estate car had been a little sluggish the last few days, he realized, but he'd put it down to the cold.

"Kit had a peek but he's a bit out of his depth, poor love."

By the time Kincaid was Kit's age, he'd been able to do most basic maintenance on a car, but his skills had been driven by necessity. They'd lived in the country, his father was famously unmechanical, and if the family car didn't start it meant a five-mile walk to town. "I'll have to give him some lessons," he said, "but in the meantime, will you take the Escort to your mum and dad's?"

"Actually, since there's not room for the dogs, we thought we'd just take the tube. The children want to see where you work. I know you have an appointment, but is there someplace child friendly you could meet us for an early lunch?"

They would be taking the Central line from Holland Park to Leyton, and it stopped at Holborn. Kincaid looked at his watch. He could manage a quick lunch as long as they were finished in time for him to get to St. Pancras for his meeting with Lindsay Quinn. "There's a little café down at Great Ormond Street. Called Tutti's, or something like that. But come to the station first and I'll give you a little tour."

The break in the weather made him more restless. Dawn had brought watery sun and a cessation of the brutal wind. The island seemed eerily quiet. He was aware, for the first time, of the movement of the birds in the trees, and the faint chirp of birdsong.

He'd caught two perch, just after daybreak, cleaned them, and cooked them over the low coals of the fire for his breakfast. But somehow the smell and taste of fresh food made isolation less bearable rather than more.

His days had run together, but as he tidied up, he realized it was Saturday. That meant there might be people on the river, even though it was still very cold. Rowers, fishermen, maybe wet-suited kayakers. So he let the fire die—he didn't want even a trace of smoke drifting above the trees—and gathered more brush and deadwood to camouflage his little encampment.

Then there was nothing he could do but sit quietly, watching the river through a small gap in the trees, and think. And he felt that for the first time in months, he could think. The last few days had brought an unexpected clarity.

How could he have believed for a moment that Wren had committed suicide? He knew her. He knew her better than he'd ever known anyone. She loved life, every little bit of it. And she had loved him.

Had Uncle had her killed as a punishment of him for his failure at Henley? Or as a warning of what might happen to his family if he didn't cooperate?

Ariel had been there, but she hadn't actually seen Wren jump. Had Wren been pushed? Or—had they somehow convinced Wren that she must make a sacrifice for his sake?

God knew they were good at manipulating.

He poked at the fire with a stick. There were embers still, beneath the ash.

Were Christie and the kids all right? he wondered. He wanted desperately to see them, to hold his daughters and breathe in the clean, sweet scent of their hair and skin, and to see his good old dog.

But how could he? If Uncle was responsible for this, and they had discovered by now that he was not the victim, they'd be watching his house, his family. What in hell's name was he going to do? He could leave the country—he had enough cash and a false passport. But then what? He'd leave Christie with no support, and what would he do with himself? He'd never been anything but a copper, never wanted to be anything but a copper.

And that was how they'd got to him, all those years ago. It had been his first undercover op with Thames Valley. Someone had leaked their identities. His partner, the senior officer, had been stabbed, and no amount of blood transfusions had been able to save him. After that, the looks had begun, then the whispers. His mates turned away from him in the pub. He heard "snitch" and "coward" said behind his back. When he finally confronted one of the whisperers, he'd been so angry he'd punched the other cop in the face. That had been all the justification his bosses needed to suspend him.

It was while he was on leave that the men from London

came to his house one day and said they'd like a word with him. His copybook was blotted, they told him, whether it was his fault or not. No one in his force wanted to work with him. But they had another job for him, one that would give him a new start. And he would still be a copper.

He knew now that he should have walked away, no matter the consequences.

Kincaid met Gemma and the children in the station's reception area. He'd introduced them to the desk sergeant when Toby said, "I want to see where you work. Can we?"

"Afraid not. Special super-secret grown-ups only." The board in the CID room was covered with photos of Paul Cole's charred corpse. Very definitely not a sight for children.

"I want to see in the glass," said Charlotte, pointing to the reception window.

"That you *can* do, love." Kincaid had picked her up when Jasmine Sidana walked through the main door. She'd gone out while Kincaid was with Chief Superintendent Faith, checking on Sweeney, Simon Gikas had told Kincaid.

From the thunderous look on her face, she hadn't liked what she'd found. She stopped short when she saw Kincaid and his family. "Sir? Is everything all right?"

He smiled. "Detective Inspector Sidana, this is my wife, Detective Inspector Gemma James. And this is Kit—" He gestured to his son.

Kit shook her hand. "How do you do?" Erika had obviously been coaching him on his manners.

"And Toby," Kincaid continued.

"I'm six," Toby informed her. "Howja do?" he added, imitating his brother.

Sidana solemnly shook his hand as well.

"And this is Charlotte." Charlotte smiled, then shyly tucked her head into Kincaid's shoulder. "They're kidnapping me for half an hour. When I get back, you can tell me what Sweeney's done."

He glanced back as he led his family out the main doors. Sidana stood in the middle of reception, staring after them and looking utterly perplexed.

Kincaid felt a bit like the Pied Piper as he led his family down the street, periodically encouraging one child or another as they lingered at shop windows.

"That's your DI?" Gemma said in his ear as they walked. "She didn't look a bit pleased. What was that about?"

"Hopefully, not me this time. But I think the DC may be in hot water."

They reached the café, a friendly, order-at-the-counter place on the corner of Lamb's Conduit Street across from Great Ormond Street Hospital. By dint of borrowing a chair and putting the two boys at the window counter, Kincaid managed to seat all of them in the busy place. There were other families with children, and several pushchairs blocking the already crowded space.

"You'll have to make up your minds," he told the children, knowing the younger ones would take forever if not managed. "Charlotte, Toby, how about ham, cheese, and pickle?"

"Can we have Orangina?" asked Toby.

"You can. Kit?"

"I want hot chocolate," piped up Charlotte. Kincaid took her cold hands in his and rubbed them. "Good girl. That will warm you up. Kit?"

Kit was still studying the menu, but he said, "Hummus and feta wrap, with cucumber and mint. And can I have a latte, please?"

Kincaid hid a smile. Kit and his friends had started to meet in coffee shops, and Kit was doing his best to learn to like coffee. Kincaid suspected he'd much rather have had hot chocolate.

"Crayfish and rocket for me," said Gemma. "And I'll have a latte, too." She winked at Kit.

"And tuna for me." Kincaid closed the menu with a snap. "Stay here. I'll order. And don't let anyone steal my chair."

When he returned to the table, Toby pulled at his sleeve. "We're going to the ballet. Tomorrow. MacKenzie's taking us to the . . . matinee." He struggled a bit with the word.

"It's *Sleeping Beauty*," put in Charlotte, who was bouncing with excitement. "I want to be the princess."

"You can't be the princess, silly. You're too little, and you're not in it. And, besides, she sleeps all the time. Boring." Toby rolled his eyes.

"Mind your manners, Toby," said Gemma. "Don't call your sister names."

Kincaid shot a glance at Gemma. "I thought you were going to lunch at Erika's."

"Kit and I will still go. MacKenzie managed to get just enough tickets for the children at the last minute."

As the server delivered their drinks, Kincaid cocked an eyebrow at Gemma. He knew MacKenzie Williams. If she'd decided the children should go to the ballet, tickets would have materialized. He suspected she was hatching a plot, and as Charlotte hadn't particularly enjoyed the ballet class, that whatever MacKenzie was up to had to do with Toby.

Gemma gave a little shrug that let him know she was thinking the same thing. "I told Erika I didn't know if you'd be able to manage lunch," she said.

"It's not looking likely," he answered as their sandwiches arrived.

He needed a break in this case. Doug hadn't rung with any news on Ryan Marlowe or on the missing girl, and his team hadn't turned up anything helpful other than the connection between Matthew and Lindsay Quinn. Once he'd seen Lindsay Quinn, he was going to pin Matthew down about the seller of the grenade.

"Dad, you're not paying attention." It was Kit, sounding aggrieved. "I want to meet some of my mates at Starbucks when we get back from Leyton. Gemma said to ask you."

"I don't see why not. As long as it's the Holland Park—" Kincaid stopped as the café door opened and Ariel Ellis walked in. She stood just inside the door, hesitantly, until Kincaid jumped up and went to greet her.

"Ariel? Are you all right? What are you doing here?"

"I'm so sorry. I didn't mean to intrude." She flushed and pushed her candy floss hair away from her face. "It's just— I was coming to the station to see you, to apologize for yesterday, and I saw you through the window. I'll wait at the station."

"No, come and sit down," he urged, taking her elbow and guiding her to the table. "This is Ariel. She's been . . . helping us with an investigation." He introduced Gemma and the kids, then added, "Can I get you something? A sandwich? Something to drink?"

Ariel smiled shyly at them. "Nothing to eat, thanks. But I'll have a cup of hot chocolate."

"I'll get it," said Kit, jumping up and leaving his half-finished sandwich on the plate. "Any whipped cream?"

She shook her head. "Just plain is fine." Her pale skin seemed stretched over her cheekbones and Kincaid thought she'd lost weight just since yesterday.

He filled the awkward silence by fetching her a chair from another table. By the time she was seated, Kit had returned with her chocolate, which he delivered with as much care as if he'd been serving at the Savoy. She smiled her thanks and Kit managed to get back on his stool without falling over something.

"Please," said Ariel, "don't let me keep you from eating. Is this a special occasion?"

"Our car wouldn't start, so we had to take the tube," volunteered Toby, through a mouthful of ham and cheese.

Kit scowled at him and explained, "Dad left us his car today so we could take the dogs with us to visit our grandparents in Leyton. But it wouldn't start this morning. I think it's the alternator," he added, sounding as if he could take a car apart in his sleep.

"You have dogs?" Ariel asked. "What kind? I love dogs."

"I have a terrier named Tess. We're not sure what sort of terrier she is, though. She was a rescue. And we have a cocker spaniel named Geordie. He's a blue—"

"We have a cat, too," broke in Toby. "Her name is Xena. And she has kittens! We rescued them. They were in a shed in the garden and they were *freezing*. We had to break in."

Kincaid ruffled Toby's hair. "That's the part you're not supposed to tell anyone, mate."

"That was really brave of you," Ariel said to Toby, but she glanced at Kit, who flushed.

"I took the posters down this morning," Kit said a bit defiantly. "Bryony said I could."

"Bryony's our vet," explained Gemma. "The cat wasn't chipped, but Bryony said we should put up posters in the neighborhood for a few days in case someone in the area was looking for her."

Ariel's face fell. "I've never had a cat. My mum was allergic, and we just never . . ."

From Kit's expression, Kincaid could tell he'd caught the past tense. That was a direction in which he didn't want the conversation to go, especially with Charlotte at the table. "I see they have smoothies," he said quickly. "Does anyone want one for a special treat?"

"Me." Toby waved a hand in the air.

"Me," echoed Charlotte.

Kit hesitated, and Kincaid guessed he was torn between refusing in order to seem sophisticated, and getting the drink he really wanted.

Kincaid pulled out his wallet and handed Kit some notes. "How about you get everyone what they want," he said. "Ariel? Would you like one?"

She shook her head. "No, but thank you."

As Kit herded the little ones up to the counter, Ariel turned to Gemma. "You have a lovely family. Thank you for including me."

Smiling, Gemma touched her arm. "Thank *you*. Although they are a handful sometimes." More quietly, she added, "I'm sorry for your loss. Duncan told me."

Ariel's eyes filled with tears. "I still can't believe it," she said, her voice trembling. She took a breath and turned to Kincaid. "I found something. That's the other reason I came. In my mail cubby at uni. A note from Paul. I don't know if it means anything." She started to reach in her bag but Kincaid stopped her with a shake of his head.

"We'll have a look at the station, all right?"

"You go on," Gemma said to Kincaid as he took the last bite of his sandwich. "You two need to talk. I'll settle up here. We should get on our way to Leyton, anyway. I promised I'd help Dad with the Saturday-afternoon rush."

"Right." Kincaid gave her a grateful glance. When the children came back with their smoothies, he stood and said, "Ariel and I need to take care of something at the police station." He picked up Charlotte for a hug and tousled Toby's hair. "I'll see you all tonight." He gave Gemma a quick peck on the cheek and ushered Ariel out.

As they walked towards the station, she said, "You tell your wife about your cases?"

"She's a police officer, too. A detective inspector. Now, let's see this note."

Ariel reached into her handbag and handed him a sheet of paper. It looked as if it had been torn from an inexpensive journal.

The handwriting was barely legible, but Kincaid was able to make out the words scrawled across the page.

You'll all be sorry.

CHAPTER NINETEEN

For two years after the passing of the Act sanctioning the
London extension [of the railway], the Company had concentrated the whole of its efforts on the building of the railway
from Bedford and of the train-shed, which was the first necessity for the reception of passengers at St. Pancras. It had still
to provide for the permanent booking-offices, waiting rooms,
and other amenities that would be required; and for the hotel
that was to supply the station façade on to the Euston Road.
—*Jack Simmons and Roger Thorne,*
St. Pancras Station, *2012*

"Do you have any idea how long the note had been in your
mail cubby?" Kincaid asked Ariel when he had seated her in
the family interview room.

"I hadn't checked it since . . . that day," she said. "I think
I looked the day before, but I'm not certain. It's usually just
junk, college leaflets and things, so I only check if I'm in the
building and happen to think about it."

"But Paul knew where it was."

Ariel nodded. "Of course. He has one as well, and our
names are on them."

Kincaid made a note to check that the search team hadn't missed Paul Cole's mail slot. He looked at the page again, now in a clear evidence sleeve. "And you're certain this is Paul's handwriting?"

"It couldn't be anyone else's. Paul's handwriting is—was—dreadful. I could never understand why he kept a paper journal. He would talk about Samuel Pepys's life being preserved for posterity, and how today's records of daily life—e-mails and texts—will just disappear into the ether. Like disappearing London, I guess."

"So he kept a journal?" Kincaid asked, keeping to himself that he already knew this. He wondered why Paul Cole thought anyone would *want* to read his scribbles in a century or two. But then why had Sam Pepys thought future generations would be interested in his digestive issues and toilet habits?

"Yes," answered Ariel. "A cheap black one."

"Do you have any idea what happened to it?"

"It wasn't in his room? Or his backpa— Oh, God." She put her face in her hands. "I can't—I don't even want to think about—"

"Don't," Kincaid said. "There's no point in torturing yourself by trying to imagine it. Do you think it's possible he put the note in your cubby the day of the . . . incident?"

"I don't know." Ariel sounded near tears again.

"Then tell me exactly what happened that day. You said that you and Paul argued. Where? At Matthew's flat?"

"It started there, yes. But then we went back to his room at uni."

"And?"

Huddling farther into her padded coat, Ariel said, "It went from me telling him to leave it alone—nagging Matthew about the smoke bomb, I mean. That it was stupid, and that his parents and my father would be furious if he went to jail. Then . . ."

Kincaid waited.

"Then . . . then he started telling me it was my fault I'd had the miscarriage. As if there was something I could have done. And I said how would we have supported a baby, and why would I want to have a child with someone who would do something as stupid as set off a smoke bomb in a railway station?" Ariel took a breath. "I didn't mean it. But I was so angry. I was shaking."

"What did you do?" Kincaid asked.

"I left. I think he threw something at the door behind me. I never—I never saw him again." She pressed her lips together in an effort not to cry. "If I had—"

"Don't," Kincaid said firmly. "You are not responsible for Paul's decisions. And we have yet to come to any definite conclusions about what happened." He stood. "Come on. I'll see you out. You go home and get some rest. And eat something. No more fainting, okay?"

"Okay," agreed Ariel, and gave him a smile that trembled a little.

But when they got to the door of the station, she turned back. "I'm so worried about Ryan. No one's seen him. What if he thinks it was his fault?"

"We're looking into it. Now don't worry. We'll let you know when we have any news."

After seeing Ariel out, he studied the note as he went back to the CID suite. He was still not at all certain that Paul Cole had meant to kill himself. "You'll all be sorry" could mean he'd convinced Ryan to let him set off the smoke bomb. It could mean that he was going to leave the group because he felt unappreciated. No one seemed to have liked him much, the poor git. And everyone had liked Ryan.

So where the hell was Ryan? he asked himself for the hundredth time.

When he reached the CID suite, he asked Simon to enter the

note into evidence, then he went to Sidana's desk. He explained about the note and asked her to track down a sample of Cole's handwriting and get a comparison done. Then he said quietly, "Tell me what DC Sweeney has been up to."

She seemed to hesitate, and he guessed she felt that Sweeney's conduct reflected badly on her. After a moment, she said grudgingly, "I was talking to one of the PCs, asking if he'd seen Sweeney. He said not today, but on Thursday he saw him in the car park, talking to one of the reporters before the press conference."

Kincaid stared at her. "So you think Sweeney leaked the fact that we were holding suspects?"

She nodded. "That would be my guess."

"The little snitch." Kincaid remembered with some shame that he'd thought it might have been Sidana, trying to make him look bad at his first press conference for the unit.

"And I think he lied about why he didn't come in today," Sidana added. "I'm going to make some inquiries at the gym. He wasn't officially requested to come in, but we all assume we're needed if there is a major investigation on."

"Let me know what you find out," said Kincaid. He didn't want to have to take this to Faith, but he didn't want someone on his team that he couldn't trust, even for the most trivial of reasons.

"Sir." Sidana stopped him as he turned away. "Can I have a word? In your office?"

"Of course." He glanced at his watch and saw that he had enough time. "Take a seat," he told her as she followed him into his office.

"No, I—I won't take up more than a moment." It was the first time he'd seen Jasmine Sidana look unsure of herself. "It's personal," she went on, "and I have no business asking."

He was curious now. "Go on."

Sidana shifted from foot to foot and clasped her hands in

front of her. "I didn't realize your wife was a senior police officer," she blurted out. "It seems—you have a very nice family.
But your daughter—your little girl—she's—"

"Charlotte is our foster child. We'll start proceedings for
legal adoption when Social Services give us the green light.
Charlotte lost both her parents last year." That was as much
as he would ever say, except to those who were intimately involved in Charlotte's life.

"But I didn't think Social Services would allow a mixed-
race child to go to a white family."

"Our social worker tells us that their policy has become
more lenient. And there are other factors involved."

"Oh," Sidana said, frowning. "Well, best of luck, sir.
Thank you."

As Kincaid watched her walk back to her desk, he wondered why she had asked, why she was frowning, and what she
was thanking him for.

Kincaid hailed a taxi in Theobald's Road. It had begun to rain
again, a fine, cold drizzle, and besides he had no time to walk
to St. Pancras. He was paying the cab in front of the Renaissance Hotel when his phone rang. He almost ignored it, but
then he saw it was Doug and answered while he sprinted for
the arched entrance to the hotel. It would give him some shelter
from the rain.

"She was a jumper," said Doug.

"What?" Kincaid put his hand over his other ear to block
some of the traffic noise.

"Your girl. She was a jumper."

"A jumper? Good God." Kincaid thought of the girl in the
photo and felt sick. There was nothing worse. "Where? When?"

"New Year's Eve. West of London. One of the lines coming
into Paddington."

"But how did you identify her?" Kincaid asked. There was usually not much left of someone who went under a train.

"Her face wasn't too badly damaged. She was only half on the tracks. Maybe she changed her mind." Doug cleared his throat. "You don't want to see the photos, Guv."

"Could it have been an accident?"

"Not unless she liked to climb railway embankments in the middle of the night for fun."

"And no one claimed or identified her?"

"No. And she didn't match any missing person description."

Why, Kincaid wondered, had no one in the group reported her missing? "Look, I've got to go," he said to Doug. "I'm meeting Matthew Quinn's father. Can you keep digging on Ryan Marsh/Marlowe?"

"I live to serve." With that, Doug rang off, and Kincaid couldn't help grinning.

His smile faded as he thought again of the girl. Wren. Did the group know what had happened to her? They'd all been cagey whenever she was mentioned.

And was there any connection between her death and Paul Cole's fascination with trains?

He glanced at his watch and shook his head. That would have to wait.

Entering the hotel, he nodded at the doorman, then paused for a moment to look round the reception area. It was the first time he'd been in the hotel since the refurbishment. The restoration had done justice to the Victorian architect Gilbert Scott's glazed entrance hall, which mirrored the spectacular Barlow train shed next door in the railway station. Even on such a gloomy day the space was filled with light. It was now a very elegant lounge with groups of comfortable conversation areas. Some of the occupants having tea or cocktails looked extremely well heeled, while some just appeared to be tired tourists.

He asked for the Booking Office Bar at the reception desk and was directed to a doorway on his right.

It took a moment for his eyes to adjust. From light into dark, indeed. But it was a glorious dimness. The room had been the original booking office for St. Pancras station, and the restoration had celebrated George Gilbert Scott at his most Gothic. Shaded lighting and intimate groupings of tables and leather chairs kept the focus on Scott's deep-red brick walls and his soaring windows. Light shone through them from the lobby on one side and the terminus itself on the other.

It was past the lunch rush, but the bar was still busy. The high ceiling and brick walls magnified the sounds of conversation and cutlery. When an attractive blond hostess greeted Kincaid, he told her he was meeting Mr. Lindsay Quinn.

"Oh, Mr. Quinn, of course. He's expecting you." She smiled and led him the length of the room to a table against the very back wall, tucked in beside a decorative screen.

Kincaid would have recognized the man who rose to greet him without any introduction. He had his son's distinctive tall, lanky frame, although without the stoop. His hair, curly like Matthew's, was threaded lightly with gray, but he radiated an easy confidence that was far removed from Matthew's blustering self-importance. Like Kincaid, he wore jeans, but his tweed sports coat had fashionable suede elbow patches, and Kincaid suspected that the jacket was hand tailored.

"Mr. Kincaid, do sit down."

As Kincaid took one of the leather armchairs, he saw that the table held a pot of tea and two cups, as well as a water jug and two distinctively etched water glasses.

As Quinn sat down again, he said, "I like this table because it's quieter back here. You can actually have a conversation. I ordered tea—I prefer Ceylon this time of day—but if you'd care for something else?"

"Tea is fine," Kincaid told him. "A little milk, no sugar, thanks."

Quinn did the honors gracefully, but the glance he gave Kincaid was very sharp.

"Now, Mr. Kincaid," he said as he handed Kincaid his cup, "tell me why a senior Metropolitan Police detective wants to talk to me about my son."

"Have you spoken to Matthew?" Kincaid asked.

"I thought I would wait until I'd met with you. Best to be prepared."

Kincaid stirred his tea, unnecessarily. "I understand that you are a major shareholder in the corporation that owns the building in which Matthew lives."

"The building is slated for refurbishment soon. It's best to have it occupied in the meantime." Quinn frowned. "But why is that police business? Has something happened in the building?"

"Not in the building, no." Tasting his tea, Kincaid was quite sure it hadn't come from a tea bag. "Did you know that your son is involved in antidevelopment protest activities, Mr. Quinn?"

"Antidevelopment? That's putting it a bit strongly, don't you think? Matthew's a bright lad, but he's having trouble finding his footing. I thought it best to give him some time to get it out of his system. Most young men go through a rebellious stage."

True enough, Kincaid thought, sipping his tea, but those rebellious stages were not usually financed by their parents.

"Matthew's studied structural engineering," Quinn went on, topping up his cup, "and he's concerned about the preservation of London's buildings. As am I. I hope that once he's had some time to think about it, he'll decide to study architecture and put his concerns to positive use."

"So Matthew has been living in the building in return for looking after it. That sounds a good arrangement."

"I thought so, yes. Unfortunately necessary these days, with the threat of squatters and vandalism." Quinn looked curious but still relaxed. Kincaid was fairly certain now that Matthew Quinn had *not* run to Daddy with his troubles.

"Are you aware that Matthew has been sharing the flat with half a dozen fellow protesters?" asked Kincaid, pouring himself a glass of water.

Now Quinn looked thoroughly taken aback. "Protesters? *Living* in Matthew's flat? Surely you're mistaken. I assumed he occasionally had friends in, but I can't imagine—"

"There were three other men and three women living there on a regular basis. Matthew was apparently supporting them."

Quinn seemed about to protest again, but after a moment he shrugged. "I give my son an allowance. I don't tell him how he can spend it. And how I manage my building is not really your concern." Then he frowned and studied Kincaid intently. "You said *were*. And *was,* Mr. Kincaid. Now tell me what this is about."

Leaning forward, Kincaid said quietly, "Mr. Quinn, did you know that Matthew's group of antidevelopment activists was involved in Wednesday's incident at St. Pancras?"

"What? Here?" Quinn's eyes widened in shock. "Where the man burned? But that's absurd."

"I'm afraid not." From the expression on Lindsay Quinn's face, Kincaid thought he understood why Matthew Quinn had not demanded a solicitor. He hadn't wanted his father to find out he was in trouble.

But what had he thought would happen if his protest had gone according to plan? Had he assumed Ryan would avoid arrest, and that the group would gain media attention merely by proximity? Even if he had never been connected with the smoke bomb, his father would not have been pleased to see him waving placards on television.

"We've identified the young man who was killed as Paul Cole," Kincaid continued. "He was a university student who was affiliated with Matthew's group, although he didn't actually live in the flat."

"That doesn't mean that my son had anything to do with this chap deciding to burn himself up." Quinn was wary now, on the defensive.

"We're not sure that Cole killed himself intentionally. It was Matthew's idea that another member of the group should set off a smoke bomb while the rest were carrying protest placards."

"Matthew's idea? What a harebrained—" Quinn stopped and ran a hand through his curly hair. "But you said a smoke bomb. That was no smoke bomb. It was a grenade. What happened?"

"We were hoping you might be able to tell us. Do you know how Matthew might have got access to a white phosphorus grenade?"

"White phosphorus? Matthew? Christ. Of course not." Quinn looked really rattled now. "Surely it was someone else—"

"Matthew's admitted buying what he thought was a smoke bomb from someone he met at a protest."

"You've interviewed him? Without a lawyer?"

"He didn't ask for one."

"Bloody hell." Quinn sounded thoroughly disgusted. "My son has a genius IQ. Did he tell you that? But no common sense. I can assure you, however, that he would never deliberately hurt anyone. Especially not in such a horrible way," he added, shaking his head. "I had no idea he was dabbling in anything that radical."

"Did you happen to mention to anyone that your son was involved in antidevelopment protests?"

Quinn thought for a moment. "I might have mentioned something at my club. Men my age get together over a drink or two, they are apt to start complaining about their children's exploits. I'm sure no one took it seriously."

But what if they had? If Ryan Marsh was a cat among the pigeons, someone had taken Matthew Quinn seriously enough to put Marsh there. Unless, of course, Ryan Marsh had gone rogue—but in that case, *Marsh* would have to have taken Matthew seriously as someone he would want as an ally.

Lindsay Quinn sat back with an air of decisiveness. "My son has gone quite far enough with this protest business. I can see I've been too lenient with him, but I never thought he'd get himself involved in something like this. My God . . . If any of my clients had any idea . . . Do you know, Mr. Kincaid, what it costs to shut down a major rail terminus like St. Pancras International for even half an hour? The entire country's rail system will have been disrupted, and there will have been delays and reroutings in Europe due to the Eurostar trains. Hundreds of thousands of pounds, at the very least. Maybe into the millions."

Quinn shook himself like a dog coming out of water, and Kincaid could see that the shocked father had morphed into the businessman.

"I'm sorry not to have been more helpful with your inquiries," Quinn went on, "but I'm certain that Matthew is guilty of no more than stupidity."

"He's admitted to buying the smoke bomb."

"I don't believe that's illegal."

"Setting off a smoke bomb in a public place with intent to cause disruption is certainly illegal," Kincaid countered.

"But Matthew *didn't* set it off, and I think you'd have a hard time proving intent." Quinn pushed his teacup aside with a clink that was audible even over the noise in the bar. "I'm very sorry for the boy who was killed, but I want my son kept out of this, Mr. Kincaid. And if you find it necessary to speak to Matthew again, he'll have a solicitor present." He stood, and Kincaid thought it interesting that he didn't signal for the bill.

It was an obvious dismissal and Kincaid didn't like being

dismissed. But he was willing to let it go for the moment. He stood as well and said courteously, "Thank you for your time, Mr. Quinn. It's been most enlightening. I expect we'll be speaking again soon." He held out his hand for Quinn to shake, turned, and walked away.

CHAPTER TWENTY

The frontage of St. Pancras is Gothic . . . That something
as new and up-to-date as a railway terminus hotel should
speak the architectural equivalent of the language of Dante or
Chaucer is ostensibly bizarre.

—*Simon Bradley,*
St. Pancras Station, 2007

Kincaid left the bar by the exit that led straight into the upper
level of the railway station. He knew he'd better get to Matthew Quinn before his father did. It was obvious that Lindsay
Quinn would do whatever he could to keep any of this from
sticking to Matthew, and that paternal concern might be the
least of his motives. The south exit on this level of the station
led straight out into Euston Road. He could walk to the Caledonian Road flat.

But he paused, for just an instant, to look out at the station. Light flooded in through the single great span of the
train shed roof. He remembered reading that when William
Henry Barlow had designed it, it had been the largest single-
span train shed in the world. Even though it might have been
surpassed since, it was still stunning. How could Paul Cole or

Matthew Quinn or the nameless protester who had sold Quinn the smoke bomb—if that were the case—have wanted to damage something so beautiful?

He suspected now, however, that Matthew Quinn was driven by deep-seated jealousy and resentment towards his father, in which case anything was possible.

The rain had diminished to a cold mist. As Kincaid walked up the Caledonian Road, he passed Housmans, the legendary anarchist bookshop. He wondered how long Housmans would last as the gentrification crept northwards from King's Cross. But for the moment, Matthew Quinn had picked a good neighbor for his defiance of capitalist greed.

When he reached the building, he rang the bell for the top flat and the door clicked open. Cam was waiting for him with the flat door open when he finished the climb.

"You're in pretty good shape," she said by way of greeting. "Not even out of breath."

"Not bad for a middle-aged copper, you mean. It's running with the dogs and playing football with the kids."

She stepped back to let him enter. "It's just me, I'm afraid. I saw you from the window."

"Where is everyone else?"

"The others have scattered like rats, even Trish. They didn't like their night in the nick. Poor Matthew." She gave a little pout of false sympathy. "He's gone looking for the lads, to see if he can at least change their minds. But for once, I suspect his persuasive skills will fail him."

"Why are you still here, then?" Kincaid asked, looking round the bare and unwelcoming room. The television was off, and there was a visible layer of dust on the furniture. He could smell the frying grease from the chicken shop, even with the windows closed.

"Well, it's interesting, isn't it?" Cam said. "I can finish my dissertation. 'The Dissolution of a Radical Group Due to Failure of Agenda.' What do you think of that?" She curled up on one end of the sofa. Kincaid sat on the other end, but didn't take off his coat. The flat was frigid, and Cam was dressed in multiple layers.

"I think 'failure of agenda' doesn't quite describe it. I'd say it was a rousing success if the point was to cause a major disruption and cost the capitalist fat cats a great deal of money—"

"No, it really wasn't," Cam protested. "It was just to get attention for the group's manifesto. A little camera time."

"Well, it didn't exactly work out, did it?" Kincaid leaned towards her. "Cam, even if it *had* only been a smoke bomb, what did you think would happen? There still would have been a massive panic that it was a terrorist threat. The station would have had to suspend service. And a lot of people would have been terrified, perhaps even injured in the crush."

Cam drew her knees up under her baggy jumper and tucked her hands into the opposite sleeves. She had been tough and defiant, and out of all the members of the group, the only one with whom he'd felt a connection. Now she looked tired and disillusioned. "It was stupid. I don't know now what we were thinking. And now everyone is afraid we *will* be connected with what happened. Ironic, isn't it? There we are on video, waving our silly placards, then running like scared rabbits along with everyone else. It was only Iris who was brave enough to stay. I'd never have thought it of her, and I admire her for it. And she stood up to Matthew when he bullied her over it."

"Whose idea was it to stage this at St. Pancras? At the very beginning. Do you remember?" Kincaid asked.

Cam drew her slender brows together as she thought. "It was Matthew's, I'm sure. He saw St. Pancras as the heart of the spreading capitalist takeover that was going to destroy the real London."

"He didn't consider that the restoration of St. Pancras—the hotel as well as the railway station—preserved two priceless examples of Victorian architecture that otherwise would have gone to ruin? They almost did, you know."

"No. Just the opposite. He said St. Pancras was the epitome of capitalist excess when it was built, and that the refurbishment mirrored the same thing in our time." Cam shrugged. "I know it sounds lame now, but he was so vehement that it almost made sense."

"Did it ever occur to you that Matthew might have a very personal motive for targeting St. Pancras, and this area in particular?" Kincaid asked. He was aware of the fact that Matthew might return at any moment. He didn't want to lose his chance to question Cam on her own, but he didn't want to push her too hard, either.

"Other than Crossrail and being close to the university?" Cam looked puzzled. "No, not really."

"Did none of you ever wonder how Matthew paid for this place or where the money came from that he doled out to the group?"

"He said he did some tutoring. Engineering students," Cam added, but there was doubt in her voice even as she said it.

"He never told you that his father is a very successful property developer? And the major shareholder in a corporation that owns, among other properties slated for redevelopment in the King's Cross area, this building?"

Cam just stared at him. "You're fucking joking," she said at last.

"Not only was Matthew's father letting him live in the flat rent-free, he was giving him an allowance to do it."

She started to laugh. "That bloody bastard. So he's been biting the hand that feeds him. And fed us. What a hypocrite. If anyone had found out, he'd have lost all credibility in the protest groups."

"What if someone *did* find out?" Kincaid said. "Ryan Marsh? Or Paul Cole?"

It seemed to take Cam a moment to absorb this. Then she shook her head so violently her dark hair whipped across her face. "No. No. Matthew may be an arse—and an even bigger one than I thought—but to kill someone to keep that secret? I don't believe it. That's—that's unthinkable."

"*Could* someone have found it out?"

Cam thought for a moment. "Ryan, maybe. You never quite knew what Ryan was up to. He planted things"—she anticipated Kincaid's question and cut it off—"I don't mean physical things. I mean ideas. He'd just mention something, very casually, maybe something someone did at a demonstration he'd been in, or a leaflet he'd written, and the next thing you knew it was Matthew's idea and the greatest thing since sliced bread."

"Is that what happened with the smoke bomb?"

Again Cam hesitated. Then she said, "No, I don't think so. It was just some guy Matthew met at a protest. Matthew was going on about how no one paid attention to us and the guy said he had something that would make people sit up and take notice. It was after that when Matthew came up with the idea of St. Pancras."

"Was it the same bloke that sold Matthew the smoke bomb?" Kincaid asked. "If you know, you need to tell me. You're finished here, and the stakes are much higher than you finishing your dissertation."

Cam shifted on the sofa and rubbed a sleeve across her eyes, then sighed. "You're right. I don't like this. I don't like any of this. I can't believe Paul's dead. But I honestly don't know. I didn't actually see anything change hands that day."

"So what happened after Matthew bought the smoke bomb? And said that he wanted to set if off in St. Pancras?"

"At first Matthew wanted to do it himself. He said he'd wear something that would make him unrecognizable on video—although that seems unlikely, considering Matthew," Cam added with a small smile, "and then he'd disappear in the smoke. The rest of us would be demonstrating in a group away from the incident, and of course we would be on video, especially because of the rock band.

"But Ryan said there was always a possibility that something could go wrong, and that he should do it because he'd been arrested before. Everyone else had clean records."

"That seems rather decent of him," Kincaid said a little skeptically.

"Well, that's the thing. Ryan is—was—whatever"—Cam grimaced—"always decent and sensible. He was good at organizing, but he never ranted about stuff, like Matthew. I know he was this seasoned protester, but you always felt that in a way he was looking after us."

"So Ryan talked Matthew into letting him deploy the smoke bomb?"

She nodded. "Not that Matthew argued all that much." Cam's tone was derisive. "Now I can see why. I don't think his dad would have been too thrilled if he'd been arrested for intent to create public disorder."

Having met Lindsay Quinn, Kincaid had to agree. "So where did Paul Cole come into it?"

Cam blew out a frustrated breath. "Oh, Paul . . ." She glanced at Kincaid. "Is it terrible to speak ill of the dead? It was all about attention. He said he didn't care if he got arrested—it would serve his dad right to have to get him out of jail. He was jealous of Ryan, but Ryan seemed to take it good-naturedly enough."

The lumpy sofa kept threatening to suck Kincaid into its depths. He moved to the edge, so that he looked directly at Cam, and said carefully, "Do you think Paul's attention getting would have gone as far as suicide?"

Slowly Cam shook her head. "No. I can't imagine—but then you never do, do you? Unless they threaten, and even then you wonder if it's just for show. And Paul—I know it sounds terrible—but you'd think that if he meant to kill himself, he'd have milked it for every ounce of drama."

"Ariel came to the station today," Kincaid said, watching Cam. "She found a suicide note from Paul in her mail cubby at the university."

Cam's eyes widened. "Today? She found it today? Oh, God, that's terrible."

"Ariel said they had an argument that morning, first about Paul wanting to set off the smoke bomb, then about her miscarriage. Do you think he was that distraught over the loss of the child?"

Cam got up and walked to the window, standing with her back to him. Kincaid waited, and after a moment she turned. "Ariel didn't have a miscarriage. And Paul knew it because I told him. So if he was distraught, it was because he'd found out she'd lied to him. If I hadn't—"

"Just tell me what happened," Kincaid said, cutting her off.

She began to pace. Even in her agitation, she moved like a dancer. "Ariel made no secret of the fact that she was pregnant. But she was not exactly glowing with motherly anticipation. Not that I can blame her. I wouldn't have picked Paul as promising daddy material, either. But Paul was all puffed up. You'd think he'd accomplished something unique.

"And then one day I saw Ariel leaving the abortion clinic—there's one here in the Caledonian Road. I wasn't even quite sure it was her, but I recognized the padded coat. So I went in and said I'd come to be with my friend during her procedure. They said I was too late, she'd just left, so I knew it was true. I didn't say anything to anyone at first—why would I? But then Ariel came to the flat the next day, sobbing, saying she'd had a miscarriage.

"After that, we didn't see her as much, but Paul was here all the time, moaning about how it must have been his fault somehow. So I told him." Cam stopped and stood facing Kincaid, her arms crossed defensively, the gray light from the dirty windows forming a nimbus around her dark hair. "I felt sorry for him."

Kincaid remembered that Ariel had said Paul blamed *her*. If he found out she'd had an abortion rather than a miscarriage, he would have had good reason.

"If Paul killed himself because I told him the truth—," began Cam.

"If—and it's a big if—Paul killed himself, it's no responsibility of yours," Kincaid said firmly. "And that still doesn't account for where—or how—he got the grenade. Or what's happened to Ryan Marsh. Or—"

The front door slammed and there was the sound of feet pounding up the stairs.

Cam whirled towards the door, dropping her hands to her sides. Kincaid stood, absorbing her tension.

The door burst open, slamming against the interior wall. Matthew Quinn stalked into the room, hair even wilder than usual. When he saw Kincaid, his face contorted with fury. For a moment, Kincaid braced himself for an attack.

But Matthew merely raised a shaking finger and pointed at Kincaid. "You! You went to see my father. And now he's cut off my allowance and told me I have to vacate the flat."

"Did you think your father wasn't going to learn about your involvement with this, Matthew?" Kincaid asked, relaxing a little. "You aren't stupid—your father assured me of that. How could you think there wouldn't be consequences?"

"There's no law against demonstrating. I never meant for anyone to get hurt." Matthew's anger seemed to be quickly dissolving into petulance.

"Then tell me about the bloke who sold the smoke bomb, at the demonstration."

Matthew gave Cam a surprised glance, then said, "Bitch."

Cam shrugged. "I'll just be getting my things." She went to the kitchenette and began to pull a few things out of the cupboards.

"Tell me," Kincaid repeated to Matthew.

This time it was Matthew who shrugged. "I don't know. It was just some guy you see sometimes at fairly big demos. Ex-army, I think, because he tells stories about Iraq and Afghanistan. He said it was just a smoke bomb, harmless. He said you never wanted to use a real flash-bang because they could cause a world of hurt. They used them in Iraq, throwing them into civilian compounds."

"That was no flash-bang that Paul set off in St. Pancras," Kincaid said grimly, "although that would have been bad enough. It was a white phosphorus incendiary grenade. It could have been military grade. Do you know this man's name? Where to find him?"

"No." Matthew shook his head. "He never said. I just paid him cash. I offered him bitcoins, but he couldn't be bothered."

"Who else was there when you bought it?"

"Cam, obviously." Matthew gave Cam an evil look. "Most of the group. But people were milling around and I really wasn't paying attention."

Kincaid wondered if Ryan Marsh had been investigating the sale of illegal munitions. But if he'd had any doubt about what the smoke bomb was, would he have let Paul Cole set it off?

Matthew went to the sofa and sank down on it. "What am I going to do now?" he asked, like a little lost boy.

"Go home," Kincaid suggested. "Keep yourself available, because we're not finished with you by any means."

"And what about everyone else, Matthew?" asked Cam, who'd come back into the sitting area and picked up a duffel bag. "I'll be all right, but will Iris? Or Trish? Where do you think Trish will go? We were never any more to you than toys, as disposable as Wren."

Kincaid saw the shock on Cam's face, then Matthew's, saw Cam lift her hand to her mouth as if she could call back the words.

And he realized then that they'd never believed the girl had just disappeared. They had always known exactly what had happened to Wren.

CHAPTER TWENTY-ONE

Sir George Gilbert Scott (1811–78) was the winner of the
Midland Railway's competition to design their London
terminal—and by far the best known of the competitors.
—*Alastair Lansley, Stuart Durant,*
Alan Dyke, Bernard Gambrill,
Roderick Shelton,
The Transformation of
St. Pancras Station, *2008*

"Sit." Kincaid gestured Cam to the sofa, then held up a hand
to keep Matthew where he was. "Both of you." When Cam
complied, hugging the duffel bag to her lap, Kincaid pulled up
a rickety wooden spare chair so that he could face them both.

"Tell me," he said. "What happened to Wren?"

Matthew and Cam glanced at each other, but it was Cam
who began to speak. "It was New Year's Eve. The boys had
brought in some lager and we were going to just kick back.
Ryan was out somewhere, he didn't say. Paul wasn't here, either, and I think Ariel was feeling a bit put out. She said we
should do something radical. She got this idea about tagging
something with our slogan, and she said she knew a place.

Ariel's an artist—she's good with a paint can." Cam hesitated. "I shouldn't even be telling you that—it's illegal . . ." At a look from Kincaid, she swallowed and continued. "Right. None of the lads was up for it—they'd already had a few beers—so Wren said she'd go. Ariel said she had her dad's car. They left." She stopped again, and now she was clutching the duffel bag for dear life. Matthew still hadn't said a word.

"Go on," Kincaid said. "I'm listening."

"Nobody thought any more about it. Ryan came back and asked where Wren was. Then a couple of hours later, Ariel came in by herself. She was hysterical. We couldn't calm her down. It was Ryan finally who made her talk. He slapped her. He was frantic by that time. We all knew something really bad had happened. But we had no idea—" Cam gave a little sob. When she spoke again, her voice shook.

"She said—Ariel said that they went to a railway embankment, a place she'd tagged before. They left the car—Ariel said it was a good walk. But when they got to the top of the embankment, she discovered she'd left one of the paint cans. She went back to get it. Then she—she heard the train. And then a terrible squeal of brakes. She ran back, but when she got there, the train was stopped. And she could see—she could see that Wren had gone under the train." Tears were streaming down Cam's face now. She made no effort to wipe them away.

"What did she do then?" Kincaid asked more gently.

"She said there were lights and shouting and she could hear sirens. She was terrified. She ran back to the car and came straight here. Ryan was—I don't even know how to describe it. He kept asking her over and over exactly what had happened. Ariel said she didn't know if Wren had jumped or fallen. And Ryan kept asking if she was sure she hadn't seen anyone else. If someone had followed them. He was . . . crazy."

"Why didn't you notify the police?" Kincaid asked.

"Ryan said not to. She had no family. There was nothing anyone could do. Not that Matthew was eager to tell anyone"—the look Cam gave Matthew was scathing—"because he didn't want to be connected with it. Ariel was willing, but Ryan said she needn't do it."

"And everyone listened to Ryan?"

"You couldn't *not*. He took charge of everything. But after that . . ." Cam dug a tissue out the duffel and blew her nose. "Ryan was never the same. He was grieving for Wren. We could all see that. But there was something more. He started taking his things with him whenever he left the flat, and he disappeared for days at a time. I think—I think he was frightened of something."

Kincaid left Cam and Matthew after getting their new contact information, and telling them that he had better hear from the rest of the group or he would track them down.

Hailing a passing taxi as he walked back towards King's Cross, he gave the driver Ariel's address in Cartwright Gardens, but when he got there and rang the bell there was no answer. He debated a moment, then hailed another cab to take him back to Holborn station.

Both Simon Gikas and Jasmine Sidana were still in the CID room. He told them what he'd learned about Wren, which he could do now without bringing Doug into it or telling them he'd already known how Wren had died.

"I'll track it down," said Simon, turning to his computer. "Maybe I can get a better idea of whether she jumped or fell."

Or was pushed, Kincaid thought, remembering that Ryan had kept asking Ariel if they had been followed or if she'd seen anyone else, but he didn't say it aloud. He didn't know what—or whom—Ryan was afraid of, but the fear had infected him.

"Any luck on matching the handwriting on the note in Ariel's cubby?" he asked Jasmine.

"The family liaison officer sent over some papers from Paul's room at his home. The lab's handwriting expert hasn't had time to do a detailed analysis, but from a first look, she says she thinks it's the same."

"Right. But that still doesn't convince me it was a suicide note." He glanced at his watch. "You two should go home. It's late, and I don't think we're going to accomplish much more here today. I tried Ariel's house, but no one was home. But it might be better to question her about Wren when you've learned a little more, Simon."

And when he wouldn't be less likely to slip up and mention that he already knew where the accident had happened, Kincaid added to himself.

Kincaid took the Central line home to Notting Hill. When he came out of Holland Park tube station, the rain was coming down in earnest. With a grimace, he turned up his coat collar and unfurled his umbrella. Starting north on Lansdowne Road, he sidestepped puddles and fought to keep the wind from whipping his brolly inside out.

He passed a man in an overcoat walking a buff-colored cocker spaniel. The dog looked as miserable as Kincaid felt. Were Gemma and the kids back from Leyton? he wondered. He hadn't heard from her since he had seen them at lunchtime.

Once he felt that odd twitch between his shoulder blades again, but when he turned back, he saw nothing but a few ordinary-looking, umbrella-wielding pedestrians. He laughed at himself for having had visions of being followed by dark cars with tinted windows, and by the time he reached the house, he was looking forward to dry clothes, a fire, and possibly a finger's worth of his best Scotch before dinner.

Just as he put his key in the door, his mobile rang. "Bugger," he muttered, dropping both umbrella and keys as he fumbled for the phone.

It was Doug. "I think I've found Ryan Marlowe's wife," he said. "She's in a village in Oxfordshire, really a suburb of Reading."

"Christine Marlowe," Doug continued. "Age twenty-nine. Two children. Employed as a bookkeeper to a local builder. She lives in Caversham. We can be there in an hour."

"That's near Henley," Kincaid said, recognizing the name.

"Well, I suppose, yes, but nearer Reading."

"I can pick you up—," Kincaid began, but he saw the Astra sitting at the curb and remembered that it wouldn't start. "Damn and blast. My car's out of commission. I'll have to use Gemma's."

"Melody's here," said Doug. "She's got her Clio. We'll pick you up. Give us half an hour."

"What's Mel—," Kincaid began, but Doug had rung off.

He had enough time to greet Gemma and the kids and to change into dry shoes, at the least.

"Should I keep it hot for you?" Gemma asked as he bent over to sniff the pot she was stirring on the cooker. "It's Turkish ratatouille. Hazel and Holly are coming over to see the kittens, so we're going veggie."

"Already found a mark, eh? Good for you." He kissed her ear. "Better not keep dinner warm for me. I've no idea how long I'll be. Give Hazel my best, will you? Any news on the Tim front?"

"From what I gather, they've reached a comfortable détente. It seems to be working for them for the moment." She turned so that she could look up at him. "Want to tell me about this mysterious interview?"

His phone beeped with a text from Doug saying they were pulling up outside. "When I get back," he promised.

On his way to the door, he gave Sid, who was perched on the kitchen table looking disgruntled, a rub on his furry black head. "Never thought you'd have to share the attention with a girl cat and babies, did you, mate?"

Melody's little bright blue Renault Clio was idling at the end of the walk. As Kincaid climbed in the back, he got a glimpse of her in the dome light. She looked more rested and seemed to be wearing her own clothes for the first time since the incident. He hoped that meant she'd been home.

"Where's Andy tonight?" he asked, buckling up as Melody put the Clio into gear.

"They've let Tam go home. Andy was helping Michael get him settled in. Then he and Poppy are doing a set at the Twelve Bar. Everyone wants their piece of them now."

"Only the beginning, I suspect," Kincaid said; then he told them what he'd learned that day.

"So it's possible Wren wasn't a suicide?" asked Doug. "And Marsh wasn't accounted for during the time she died, nor was Paul Cole. Could either of them have been involved?"

Kincaid thought about it. "From what Cam said, I'd say Marsh was very unlikely. Neither Cam nor Matthew seemed to have had any idea where Cole was that night. But I can't see why he would have killed this girl."

"Maybe he'd had a row with Ariel," Melody suggested. "And that's why she wanted to do something reckless. He could have followed them, been jealous of Wren, and decided to get rid of her. It doesn't seem to have been the most functional of relationships, Paul and Ariel."

"True. But no one's implied that Ariel and Wren were anything more than casual friends. Why should he have been jealous? How did you find Christine Marlowe?" Kincaid asked Doug.

"Amazing what's in public records if you know where to look," Doug answered with such a self-satisfied smirk that Melody spared him a glare.

"Braggart," she said.

Melody was a good driver, and they fell silent as she navigated through the rain-streaked streets of West London and then onto the M4.

Soon they were driving through Reading, and when they reached the outskirts, Melody used her sat nav to guide them to the northern edge of Caversham.

Christine Marlowe lived in a quiet suburban street. The semidetached house was brick and pebble dash. Its garden looked muddy and slightly neglected, and a child's bike lay abandoned on the front walk.

"I suppose I should do the talking," Kincaid said as they got out of the car. "Since you two are not official."

"I don't think any of us are official at this point," Doug reminded him.

"Better my head than yours," Kincaid murmured as he rang the bell, and then he realized that was exactly the stance that Ryan Marsh had taken with the group over the smoke bomb.

He could hear children's voices and the sound of a television. A dog began to bark.

The woman who answered the door was a pretty, slightly faded blonde in her late twenties. She held the door open a body's width, blocking the dog, a Labrador mix going gray at the muzzle. "Get back, Sally," she told the dog, then said, "Yes?" looking them over warily. "If you're Jehovah's Witnesses—"

"We're not," Kincaid assured her. "Are you Christine Marlowe?"

"I'm Christie, yeah. No one calls me Christine. Who are you?"

"Mummy?" said one of the two little girls who'd come to stand beside her. "Who is it? Is it Daddy?" They were blond, like their mum, and Kincaid guessed the younger to be about Toby's age, the elder a year or two older.

"Go to the kitchen," Christie Marlowe told them sharply, then asked Kincaid again, "Who are you? What do you want?"

Kincaid was glad they had Melody with them. Otherwise he sensed the woman might have slammed the door on them. He took out his warrant card. "Detective Superintendent Kincaid, Camden CID. We'd like to—"

"Oh, God." All the color drained from Christie Marlowe's face. Her knees sagged as she grasped the door with both hands. "What's happened?" She gave a frantic look back to make sure her daughters had left the room. "Is he—"

"Mrs. Marlowe, please, can we come in? We just need to ask you a few questions."

She stared at them, taking in their casual clothes and perhaps reassured by their expressions and the tone of Kincaid's voice. "Yes. All right."

When she stepped back, the dog sniffed eagerly at Kincaid, ignoring Melody and Doug. "You smell my pups, don't you, girl?" Kincaid said, giving her a pat.

The television, he saw as Christie Marlowe led them into the sitting room, was playing a repeat of *Doctor Who*—typical Saturday-night children's fare. This was as normal a household as his own—kids, dogs, the smell of something on the cooker—and he realized he had no idea how he was going to ask this woman the things he needed to know.

The sitting room furniture was a matching suite that had seen better days, and they had to move toys to find a place to sit. There was a half-drunk glass of red wine on the end table, but Christie Marlowe didn't offer them anything. She sank unsteadily onto the edge of a chair. "Just tell me that Ryan's all right. That nothing's happened to him."

Grateful for the opening, Kincaid said, "That's what we were hoping you might tell us, Mrs. Marlowe. We'd like to speak to him regarding an incident earlier in the week. He was very helpful in a public emergency, but he seems to have disappeared. Do you know where he is?"

"Oh, God," she said again. "What incident?"

"The fire in St. Pancras station."

"That? Where that poor boy burned?" Her hand went to her throat. "Ryan was there? Was he hurt?"

"No, we don't think so. He assisted a police officer in controlling the crowd and evacuating bystanders."

Some of the tension seemed to drain from Christie Marlowe. She closed her eyes for a moment and leaned back into the chair, then said, "I haven't heard from him. I don't know where he is."

At a slight nod from Kincaid, Melody leaned towards her. "Mrs. Marlowe, I was the police officer that Ryan helped. Together we cleared the crowd away from the fire, and he helped me reach the victim. I couldn't have managed without him. But then he disappeared. We think he knew the victim, and we were hoping he could tell us something about what happened. And we want to make certain that he's all right."

"I don't know where he is," Christie Marlowe repeated, but there were tears in her eyes.

Kincaid said, "What does Ryan do, Mrs. Marlowe?"

"He—he drives lorries. And does landscape gardening, the big sort of jobs."

"So he's gone from home a good bit?"

She nodded. "But he almost always gets home on the weekend, or if not, he calls."

"And this weekend, you haven't heard from him?"

Christie shook her head. "No." It was almost a whisper.

"Your husband used to be a police officer, Mrs. Marlowe?"

"That's right. But he left. Something happened, I don't know what. They took his warrant card. Since then he's done a bit of this and a bit of that."

"Do you know any of the people that Ryan works for now?"

She shook her head. "No. They're just jobs."

"Does he bring you a paycheck?"

"No. Just cash—whatever he's made that week." There had been a subtle shift in her body posture. She had been openly worried, then relieved. But now her answers felt practiced, and she hadn't questioned Kincaid's right to ask such personal questions.

She was lying. And it was a lie she was used to telling.

"Mrs. Marlowe—Christie— Can I call you Christie?" Kincaid asked. He needed a wedge of intimacy.

Christie Marlowe nodded.

Kincaid went on. "Christie, we have reason to think that for the last few years, your husband has been working as an undercover police officer. I think you know this. We're afraid he may be in some sort of trouble and we want to help him."

"No." She pushed herself unsteadily up from the chair. "I'm not talking to you. You'll have to go." She darted a glance towards the kitchen, as if making certain the little girls hadn't heard.

Kincaid raised a hand. "Christie, please. Sit down. We want to help you. We want to help Ryan."

"How do I even know who you are?" Her voice rose and he could see her make an effort to lower it before she spoke again. "You showed me a warrant card—that doesn't mean a damned thing. And you two"—she pointed at Melody and Doug— "didn't even do that. Not that it matters—anyone can make a warrant card. And anyone can lie about anything."

"Look," Kincaid said. "I'm going to be honest with you. Whether you believe me is up to you. This is Doug, and this is Melody. We are all Met CID officers, but we're not here officially. We're friends who work on different teams."

Melody took it up, speaking with an earnestness Kincaid had never seen in her. "Christie, I don't know how to explain this, but those few minutes I spent with Ryan, I felt a . . . a bond. It was something I'd heard about, but it had never happened to me. We ran into the fire together. And then, when he disappeared, I just had a feeling that something was really wrong. It was Duncan's case"—she nodded at Kincaid—"but Doug and I wanted to help. This is all off the record—and anything you tell us is off the record."

"I wish I could believe you," said Christie Marlowe. "But even if I did, I still can't tell you anything. I don't *know* what kind of trouble Ryan is in. He doesn't tell *me*."

The dog, who had been lying beside her mistress's chair, got up and went over to Kincaid and laid her head on his knee. "Hello, girl," he said, and stroked her head.

"Oh, Sally." Christie Marlowe shook her head. There were tears in her eyes. "Don't mind her. Ryan spoils her something terrible. She misses him."

"Christie," Kincaid said gently. "You've been married to Ryan for, what, a decade? Do you have any idea where he is? Where he might go if he was in trouble?"

She wiped her eyes and looked at them. The girls' voices were getting louder in the kitchen, as if there was a squabble brewing.

"I don't know what to do," she said at last. She glanced at the dog, who was now happily drooling on Kincaid's knee. "Ryan always says that dogs are infinitely more trustworthy than people, and that you should pay attention to their instincts." She sniffed, then sighed. "Ryan always had a thing about camping and canoeing. I was a big disappointment to him because I could never see any point in being wet, dirty, and uncomfortable. We—" Christie looked down at her hands. "To be honest, we hadn't been getting on at all well the last year or so. Ryan would come home most weekends, spend time with the girls and the dog, then go off to the river with his canoe.

"Then, last autumn, he didn't bring the canoe back, but he wouldn't say what happened to it."

"Do you know where he liked to go?" asked Doug. It was the first time he'd spoken. "I like the river, too."

"I—" Christie was looking back at her lap again, twisting her hands together. "I'm—ashamed. He—changed. Last autumn. I don't know why. He started to shut me out completely. I was afraid he was having an affair. It happens all the time, I know that, I'd always known that, but somehow I never thought Ryan would . . . So one weekend I—I followed him." She looked up at them. "He was alone. I never admitted to him what I'd done."

"But you can tell us where he went," encouraged Doug.

"It was near Wallingford. The river makes some small marshy lakes there, and there are little islands in them. I saw him dig his canoe out from under some brush and head towards the islands. That's all I know. I never tried to follow him again. I should have trusted him," she added, sounding anguished.

There was no way that Kincaid would tell her that from what they'd learned about Ryan and Wren, she might have been right.

"Thank you," he said simply. "We'll do our best to find him and see that he's all right."

Giving the dog a last pat, he stood. His eye was caught by a photo on the mantel. It was a family group, taken perhaps two or three years earlier judging by the age of the little girls. The man they knew as Ryan Marsh was laughing, an arm thrown round his younger daughter. What had happened to him since that day?

As they took their leave, Kincaid gave Christie a card with

his mobile number on it. "If you hear anything or need any-thing, please ring me. And, Christie—I know you have no reason to trust us, but I think it would be better if you didn't tell anyone else we were here. Or where Ryan might be."

"I know exactly where that is," Doug said when they got in the car. "We'd never find those islands at night, but we can get the River Police launch to take us first thing in the morning."

Kincaid considered it, then shook his head. "No. We still don't know what we're dealing with here. And we sure as hell don't want some sort of a standoff with the Thames River Police involved."

"Okay," said Doug. "Then as soon as the boat-hire places open at Wallingford in the morning, we can rent a skiff. Can you row?"

CHAPTER TWENTY-TWO

For St. Pancras Station, as for so much else in England, the First World War was the herald of change . . . on the night of February 17th, 1918 . . . five bombs were dropped by German aeroplanes on or near the station and hotel. . . . the fifth [bomb], which landed on the glass-roofed carriage approach beside the booking-office, killed twenty people and injured thirty-three. This was the greatest number of casualties suffered in any air-raid on a London station during that war.
—*Jack Simmons and Robert Thorne,*
St. Pancras Station, 2012

Kincaid was awake well before dawn. Edging himself regretfully away from Gemma's warmth, he slipped out from under the duvet and headed for the shower. A half hour later, dressed in jeans, an old fisherman's jumper, and his heaviest anorak, he was on his way to Putney in Gemma's Escort.

When he picked Doug up, he saw that Doug was dressed much the same, and was not wearing his boot cast.

"What about your ankle?" Kincaid asked as they pulled away from Doug's house.

"I can't get in and out of a boat in that thing," Doug answered. "And if I screw up my ankle, I get longer time on the desk job, rather than a stint as Detective Superintendent Slater's bag boy."

"You're malingering," Kincaid said, laughing.

"Wouldn't you?" There was not much humor in Doug's voice.

Kincaid was silent for a while, concentrating on his driving. The sky was just beginning to lighten in the east, and on a Sunday morning hardly a soul was stirring. He loved London in the quiet hours, when the streets were still and the city seemed to have a life independent of its inhabitants.

Soon, however, they were once again heading west on the M4, with the dawn breaking behind them.

"Where exactly are we going?" he asked Doug.

"A little boat-hire place north of Wallingford. They aren't open on a Sunday, but I managed to get the owner on the phone last night. I'll let him know when we're close and he'll meet us there."

"Persuasive, aren't you?"

Doug grinned. "Police business. Top secret."

They left the main road at Didcot and cut across country towards the river, winding down hedge-bordered lanes.

The last tint of rose had faded from the sky when they reached the small marina. There were canoes and kayaks on racks, and tied up to the dock, two small motor launches and a rowing skiff.

"Tell me we're taking one with a motor," Kincaid said as he parked on the grass verge.

"Exactly how much do you want to advertise our approach? You're the one who said no police launch," Doug countered. "Don't worry. I won't make you row."

As good as his word, the owner was there to meet them. He took cash in advance for the use of the skiff, told them to tie it up where they'd found it, locked his office, and left without showing the least bit of curiosity.

Doug proved expert with the ropes and oars, and soon they were on the water.

Although they had driven through a few spatters as they left London, for the moment, at least, the rain was in abeyance. It was cold and still, the only breeze made by their steady passage over the water.

Facing the bow, Kincaid watched Doug row with admiration. "Not bad," he said. "Not bad at all."

"The benefits of a public school education," Doug answered between strokes. "This isn't sculling, by any means, but Eton is a boat-y sort of place."

The river widened, and it seemed to Kincaid that there was nothing before or around them but gray water meeting gray sky. Then, ahead, a dark smudge of trees began to take shape, with water on either side.

"Is that our island?" Kincaid asked.

"You tell me." Doug rested the oars and looked round. "I think so. If I'm anywhere close in my reckoning."

Doug slid the oars into the water once more. The smudge drew closer, until Kincaid could make out individual trees and a tangle of undergrowth. A grey heron flew overhead, its great wingspan casting a faint shadow on the water, the yellow markings visible on its trailing legs, and vanished beyond the treetops.

Again, Doug rested the oars, but now he let the boat drift with the current, towards the island shore.

They sat quietly, and it seemed to Kincaid that they might, after all, be the only humans in this small slice of wilderness. And then he caught the scent of woodsmoke on the still air.

Gemma sat at the kitchen table, drinking a second cup of hot, milky coffee. The house seemed unnaturally quiet for a Sunday. Not only had Duncan left before she'd even awakened, but MacKenzie had picked up Toby and Charlotte early, saying she was going to take them to brunch at Wolseley's café in Piccadilly.

"Are you certain?" Gemma had asked. "You're braver than I am, taking them to such a posh place."

"Not to worry," said MacKenzie with her usual good nature. "I've corralled Bill into going with me, and the sooner the little ruffians learn some manners, the better. No offense meant towards Toby, of course," she added with a grin.

Gemma rolled her eyes. "We already know you're a wonder-worker, so I suppose anything is possible." She'd dressed the children in their best outfits from the Ollie catalog, although she wondered how long Toby would stay clean.

She still marveled at her friend, who most days played down her looks by wearing no makeup and ordinary clothes, and pulling her mass of dark curls back with a clip. But today MacKenzie was dressed to impress, and Gemma recognized the cover outfit from the new spring Ollie catalog. "You look fabulous," she said a little enviously.

"We're a walking advertisement," MacKenzie quipped, but Gemma knew it was true. They would see and be seen at Wolseley's and the ballet. She only hoped her two behaved themselves.

"Enjoy your day," MacKenzie had added, kissing her on the cheek as she herded the children out the door. A whiff of heady, citrusy perfume that Gemma didn't recognize lingered behind her.

She fully intended to do just that, Gemma thought as she sipped her coffee and enjoyed the warmth radiating from the Aga. The kittens were doing well, and two were already spoken for. Last night her friend Hazel's daughter, Holly, who was the same age as Toby and his favorite playmate, had expressed a decided preference for the little black male. And Oliver, MacKenzie's son, had set his heart on the tabby, which was beginning to show white patches like her mum.

The day was her own until she and Kit went to Erika's for lunch. She could even, she thought, practice her much-neglected piano, for which she'd had little time since her transfer.

But first . . . She slipped the file folder from the bag she'd left on the kitchen chair. It held the notes on the Mercy Johnson case, and Gemma was determined to go over them once more. She was halfway through rereading the forensics reports when she heard the clatter of footsteps on the stairs.

Kit came into the kitchen just as Gemma closed the file. "You're working," he said accusingly.

"Just checking a couple of things." She examined him with a smile. "You look nice." He was wearing a new shirt with a Gap pullover, and she could tell he'd just showered and washed his hair.

He ignored the compliment. "Can I have some coffee, please?"

"More milk, less coffee. I don't want a caffeine-addicted teenager. You have enough energy already."

"Bzzzz," Kit teased her as he heated half a mug of milk in the microwave. "Erika rang. She's roasting one chicken instead of two. Still plenty for me. I'm going to help with the veg, though, so she doesn't overcook the broccoli." He retrieved his milk, picked up the coffee carafe, and glanced at her to see if she was watching. "Blast," he said, grinning, and poured only half a cup.

Gemma stood and went to top up her own mug. "What's that on your cheek?" She wiped at a white streak with her finger.

"Geroff!" Kit ducked away from her.

"Shaving cream?" she said, sniffing. "*My* shaving cream? *My* razor?" It couldn't have been Duncan's—he used an electric.

"Well, I—" Kit blushed to the roots of his fair hair. "I thought there was a little fuzz, and I wanted to look nice . . ."

Gemma gave him an affectionate pat. "Rule number one, love. Don't ever use a lady's razor. It'll get you in big trouble. I'll buy you your own the next time we go to the shops."

"Really?"

"Of course," she said, although she didn't like to think about Kit needing to shave—

The thought struck her as she stood with her mug in one hand and the coffee in the other. *Shave . . .*

"Gemma? Are you all right?" Kit was staring at her.

"Yes. I'm fine. I just need to check something."

"Okay." Kit gave her another look. "I'll be upstairs if you need me."

Gemma waited until he'd left the kitchen, then sat down at the table and opened the file folder again. She pulled out the forensics report and reread the chemical names of a substance found on Mercy's skin. It was shaving cream. Traces on her thighs. Mercy was not quite thirteen. Would she have been shaving her legs?

She thought of the shaving and hair removal products they'd found in Dillon Underwood's bathroom. If he had shaved his thighs and pubic area to prevent hair transfer, could it have been *his* shaving cream on Mercy's legs?

She needed to talk to Mercy's mother again, find out if Mercy had been shaving, and if so, what brand of cream she'd used. She needed the lab to give her a brand on the traces they'd found on Mercy. If Mercy didn't shave, and the brand matched that in Dillon Underwood's bathroom, they might at least have a wedge.

Snapping the folder closed, she picked up her phone and called Melody.

Having had the foresight to wear waterproof boots, Doug maneuvered the skiff sideways to the island's edge, hopped out, and pulled it close enough that Kincaid could clamber out without getting soaked. Doug found a low-hanging tree to tie the boat fast. Then, they stood, listening, knowing that if there was anyone else on the island, they had been heard and spotted.

The only sounds were the faint twitter of birds and the gentle lap of water against the hull of the skiff. But the smell of woodsmoke was stronger, and Kincaid sensed another human presence.

He faced inland. "Ryan Marsh," he said quietly. "My name is Duncan Kincaid. I'm a police officer, but this is not official. We know you're here and we need to speak to you."

There was no reply, but he thought he heard a twig snap. He waited, and after a moment tried again. "Ryan, I'm the senior investigating officer on the St. Pancras incident. I need to talk to you about Paul Cole. Your wife told us where to find you, so I can't guarantee she won't tell someone else. I repeat—this is *not* official."

Again he waited. Beside him, he could hear Doug breathing. The silence stretched like beads of water sliding down a string. Kincaid thought he could hear his own heart beating.

Then there was a faint rustle, and a man materialized between two trees a few yards inland. He wore an old anorak. His light brown hair was unkempt, his beard a few days past stubble. Around his neck he wore a blue bandanna, and even from that distance, Kincaid could tell that his eyes were blue.

In his right hand he held, loosely, easily, a small rifle.

"You don't look much like coppers," said Ryan Marsh. His voice was rough, as if he hadn't used it for a few days.

"Nor do you," Kincaid answered.

Marsh's lips twisted in what might have been a smile. "I haven't looked like a copper in a long time. Who's your friend?" He nodded towards Doug.

"Just that. My friend. My former sergeant. Doug Cullen."

"Nice bit of boating," Marsh said to Doug. "So tell me again why you two friends are here."

"Because Paul Cole's death is my case," Kincaid answered. "And because the cop you helped that day is also my friend. We thought you were the one that was dead until she recognized you from an old newspaper photo."

"My reward for being a Good Samaritan," Marsh said, again with that ironic twist. Then, "Is she all right? She was as brave as I've seen."

"She's okay," Doug said. "So far."

Ryan moved a few steps closer. "My wife. You said you talked to her. Is she all right?"

"Fine. Worried about you."

"You didn't tell her about St. Pancras?"

"Only that you had assisted a police officer, and that we were worried about you."

"How did you find Christie?"

"Long story. Look, is there somewhere we can talk?" Kincaid asked.

While Ryan Marsh appeared to think about the request, Kincaid wondered if he and Doug had lost their minds, coming here alone, facing a man with a gun on an island. If Marsh decided to shoot them, would they ever be found?

"As in 'Come into my parlor'?" said Marsh. "I suppose so. I don't think it's likely you two are going to jump me"—the gun shifted slightly in his hand—"and drag me into your skiff. Oh, and by the way, there's no phone reception here. Just in case you were thinking of making a call." He motioned them forward with the gun. "You lead."

When they'd walked past him, he guided them a few more yards. Suddenly a small clearing opened before them. There was a fire pit, several cleverly constructed windbreaks that also served as camouflage, and a small sleeping area under a tarp. There was a single camp stool near the fire.

Marsh had noticed Doug limping. "What's wrong with your ankle?" he asked.

"Bad break."

"Take the stool, then." To Kincaid, he said, "You, there," and nodded towards a log. He squatted on his haunches where he could see them both, the rifle across his thighs.

Kincaid caught the scent of roasted fish. "Nice place you've got here," he said. "Been here since when—Wednesday night? Thursday morning?"

Marsh ignored the question. "I want to know how my wife knew where I was. And if she told anyone else."

"She followed you a few months ago," Kincaid said. "She thought you were having an affair."

"Aw, Christ," Marsh murmured. He lifted one hand off the rifle to pinch the bridge of his nose.

"I don't think she's told anyone else," Kincaid continued. "But now she's really worried about you."

"You said *unofficially*." Marsh fixed his blue eyes on Kincaid. "Why are you here unofficially? No, wait. Start by telling me what you know."

Kincaid thought for a moment, trying to work out how to simplify and how much to tell. "We know you were in Matthew Quinn's protest group," he began, "and that you were living—at least part-time—in his flat. We know that you were the one who was supposed to set off the smoke bomb in the St. Pancras arcade. It was Iris who came to us and told us they thought it was you who had died. She was devastated."

Marsh made a grimace of distress, but didn't speak. Kincaid went on. "We thought it was you, as well, after we'd interviewed the rest of the group. But then we found that 'Ryan Marsh' didn't exist, and things started to smell, very, very fishy.

"Then we discovered that the victim was not you at all, but a young man, a fringe member of the group, named Paul Cole. And Melody—our friend—recognized you as the man who helped her during the fire. She was certain that you were a police officer. And she was absolutely positive that you knew the victim was Paul Cole, but that you hadn't been responsible for his death. We trusted her judgment. You had disappeared. We figured you had good reason. And that's why it's *unofficial*."

"You didn't tell anyone in the security services?"

"No." Kincaid saw Marsh relax a little. "But there are people who know where we are. Just in case you were wondering." He smiled.

"Right," said Marsh. "Point taken."

"We saw three possible reasons why you had vanished," Kincaid continued. "One, you deliberately killed Paul Cole." He raised a hand before Marsh could speak. "If we ruled that out, it left us with the two other most logical options—you thought you would be blamed for his death or you thought someone meant to kill *you*. Or perhaps both. Now, why don't you tell us what happened."

"I gave it to Paul. I gave him the bloody smoke bomb." Ryan rubbed a hand across his stubble. "I felt sorry for him. Matthew had brushed him off like he was a fly."

"You weren't worried he'd be arrested?"

"To be honest, I thought dealing with the consequences might help him grow up a little."

"When exactly did you give it to him?" asked Kincaid.

"That morning. In front of King's Cross. He'd followed me from the flat."

"And you were certain it was a smoke bomb?"

"Jesus, yes. I'd set off a dozen of the things at demonstrations over the years. I'd swear it was an ordinary smoke bomb. When I saw the fire—" Marsh stopped and swallowed, looking ill. "And then when I saw him, I—" He shook his head. Kincaid remembered Melody saying he'd been distraught.

"Did anyone else know that you'd given Paul the smoke bomb?"

Ryan Marsh frowned. "Yeah. His girlfriend. She was the one he most wanted to impress. Ariel. Ariel Ellis."

Kit had just taken the dogs out for their last walk before going down to Erika's when the doorbell rang. It was too early for MacKenzie to be dropping off Charlotte and Toby, and he wasn't expecting Gemma back anytime soon. She'd taken the tube to Brixton, and had told him to tell Erika not to wait lunch.

Hushing the dogs, he went to the door and opened it. He stared in surprise. It was the pretty girl who had come into the café in Lamb's Conduit Street yesterday, the one who said she was on her way to see his dad at the station and had spotted him going in.

"Hi," she said, ducking her head a little shyly. "I don't know if you remember me—"

"Of course I remember you," Kit said, then mentally kicked himself for sounding too eager. "You're . . . Ariel, right?"

She nodded. "I don't mean to barge in or anything. Is your dad in?"

"No, he's gone to—he's out. I'm not sure where. Something to do with work."

"Oh, right. Well, I won't bother you, then. It's just that he'd told me I could come by and see the kittens. I talked to my dad, and he said maybe we could take one. But I can come another time . . . It was nice to see you." She smiled, brushing her white-blond hair away from her face, and started to turn away. Her cheeks were pink from the cold.

"Wait," Kit said. "You want to see the kittens? I can show you."

"Really?" Ariel smiled again. "That would be lovely."

He took her padded coat and woolly hat and put them on the bench in the entry hall. The dogs sniffed round her ankles, but she didn't reach down to pet them.

"Nice house," she said, looking around curiously. "I think you can tell a lot about people by their houses, don't you?"

"I never really thought about it," Kit answered, now wondering rather uncomfortably what their house said about them. There were dog toys on the hall floor, and Toby had left a half-built Lego fortress on the dining room table. The top of Gemma's baby grand piano sported a layer of dust.

"The kittens are this way," he said, remembering as he led her down the hall that he and Gemma had left half-drunk cups of coffee on the kitchen table, and the morning's toast plates were still in the sink. "You go first," he instructed her when they reached the study door. "We have to be careful not to let the dogs in."

Ariel slipped in first and Kit closed the door behind them. The room was dim, lit only by the shaded lamp on the desk and the gray light filtering in from the window.

She went straight to the box beneath the desk and knelt beside it. "Oh, aren't they sweet!" she said, peering in. Kit knelt beside her, suddenly aware of her closeness. He could smell her shampoo, and a hint of spicy perfume. He knew she was at university, but she didn't seem that much older than him.

The kittens were sleeping in a tangle of colors, but Xena blinked at them and began to purr. "Hello, girl," said Kit, and scratched her under her chin.

"How old are they?" asked Ariel. "They're so tiny."

"We're not sure. I only found them on Wednesday. We think maybe a week."

"Oh." Ariel looked up him. "My friend died on Wednesday."

Kit had no idea what to say. He'd been close to death, and nothing anyone had said had made it better. "I—I'm sorry."

Ariel reached out to stroke the bundle of kittens with a finger. "I just thought, maybe it was like an omen or something. That maybe one of them was meant for me."

"The black one's spoken for. And the little tabby."

"Oh, I like the black-and-white one, anyway."

As she said it, Kit realized that he didn't want anyone to have the black-and-white kitten.

"Can I hold him?" asked Ariel, reaching down to the kittens, which were starting to stir.

"Here. Let me." His hand touched Ariel's as he separated the little black-and-white male from the bunch. He felt hot and awkward next to this delicate girl, and uncomfortable in a way he couldn't explain. "See, his eyes are just starting to open," he said as he cradled the kitten. "They're blue. Can you tell?"

"Like mine," she said. "Please, can I hold him?" She took the kitten from him and tucked it under her chin.

"I think we're keeping that one," said Kit, with unexpected urgency. "I'm sure we are."

"Oh, too bad. He'd be perfect for me." Ariel gave a little pout and the kitten mewed, as if she'd squeezed him.

"Here. Let's put him back." Kit reached for the kitten, and for just an instant, he wondered what he would do if the girl refused to hand him back.

Ariel laughed. "I can do it," she said. She lifted the kitten by the scruff of his neck and placed him, none too gently, on top of the others. "Maybe you'll change your mind."

Kit stood. "I'm sorry, but I have to go now. I'm late for lunch with a friend." Just moving away from her was an unexpected relief, but he suddenly wanted her away from the kittens and out of the room.

"Oh, all right. I can tell when I'm not wanted," said Ariel, but she gave the kittens one last pat and stood as well.

"It's not that. It's just that I'm expected. And my mum will be home any minute." Kit didn't know why he'd said that, except that he wished it were true.

"And your dad?" Ariel asked as he held open the study door for her.

"Yeah, him, too." He walked her to the door, waited while she put on her coat, then stepped out onto the porch with her.

"Well, thanks," she said. "Maybe I'll come back someday."

"Okay." Kit managed a smile.

She pulled on the woolly cap that hid her hair and walked away, turning after a few yards to give him a jaunty little wave.

Kit didn't wave back, and he stood and watched until she had turned the corner and disappeared from sight.

CHAPTER TWENTY-THREE

I remember it as a rat-infested dump. Water dripped down walls. Wires hung from ceilings. Pigeons colonised turrets and rafters. Gormenghast could not do justice to the profile of that destitute old lady, slumped at the far end of Euston Road. Poor St. Pancras hotel embodied the contempt of modernism for anything old, stylish, romantic and, above all, Victorian. The place should be left to rot, an example to any who might find beauty in antiquity or economy in restoration.

—*Simon Jenkins,* The Guardian,
Thursday, July 7, 2011,
"Sir George Gilbert Scott,
the Unsung Hero of
British Architecture"

"Could Ariel have told someone else about the switch?" Kincaid asked Ryan Marsh. "Someone who wanted to kill Paul?"

"Someone who just happened to have a WP grenade handy?" Ryan shook his head dismissively. "A WP grenade disguised as a smoke bomb? And why would anyone want to kill Paul, the poor bugger?"

"Was there anyone who saw the smoke bomb and could

have copied it?" Doug grimaced and shifted position as he spoke, and Kincaid guessed that even with the support of the camp stool, his ankle was hurting. It was getting colder as well, and the sky to the west had turned the color of slate.

"Anyone in the group," said Ryan. "Matthew was showing it around. But I'm not buying it." He stood, as if he needed to move in order to think. He no longer seemed focused on the rifle he held, but Kincaid had no intention of trying to take it away from him. "What Matthew gave me must have already been a copy, and I just didn't see it."

"Are you saying Matthew meant to kill you?" Kincaid asked. "Because you knew about his father?"

Ryan stared at him. "What— How did you—"

"Matthew's father is Lindsay Quinn, the developer. He owns that building and was paying Matthew to stay in the flat. If we found that out, I have no doubt you did, too. Unless you knew that from the beginning. That's a secret Matthew might have been willing to protect. Unless, of course, Matthew was swimming deeper in the anarchist pool than anyone knew."

"I don't know what you're talking about." Ryan's expression had turned hard. "And I don't believe Matthew is anything more than a spoiled rich kid. Someone else meant to kill me, and that puts Paul Cole's death entirely on my hands."

A gust of wind rippled through the trees and swirled an eddy of ash from the fire pit into their faces. The sky was growing darker by the minute. "Look," Kincaid said, "I don't know what kind of trouble you're in, but you can't stay here forever. You're afraid to go back to your wife and your kids, and even if you could go back to Matthew's group, they've disbanded. So what *are* you going to do?"

The tension seemed to drain from Ryan. His shoulders drooped. "I don't know. Maybe I've made this all up. Except that Paul is dead, and I don't dare go home. Or go in." He didn't explain what he meant by that.

"Come back with us," Kincaid said. Before Ryan could protest, he went on. "We'll get you sorted, find you a safe place to stay. And we will find out who killed Paul Cole. And why. You can take my word for it."

The wind came through again, stronger this time, rustling the tarps and splattering fat, cold raindrops against their faces. "You can stay at my place in Putney," offered Doug. "But right now, it's bloody freezing, and I'm going to have a swamped boat before long."

"Thanks," said Ryan, with a nod of acknowledgment to Doug for the offer, but he kept his gaze fixed on Kincaid. "But if I was the target, and not Paul, you may not want to know." There was a warning in the words.

"I don't have much choice," Kincaid told him. "And as I see it, neither do you."

They waited, and Kincaid tried not to wonder what he would do if Marsh refused.

Finally Marsh nodded once and said with a quirk of a smile, "I suppose that means I'll be leaving the gun."

If Kit had told his parents that he didn't want his schoolmates to know about their family game and pizza nights, he hadn't been quite honest. Some of them, in fact, did know, and had even asked to be invited. But he'd said no, it was family only, not because he was embarrassed but because he didn't want to share that special time with outsiders.

He did not, however, tell his mates that his best friend in the world was a woman old enough to be his great-grandmother. He had been comfortable with Erika Rosenthal from the moment he had met her. Maybe it was because she, like his mother, was an academic. Maybe it was because she had always talked to him as if he were an adult. Maybe it was because she always seemed to know what would interest him and encouraged him in it.

Or maybe it was because she somehow always seemed to know what he was thinking without him having to tell her.

They ate her roasted chicken and potatoes and his perfectly cooked broccoli at the small table in the kitchen of her flat in Arundel Gardens. The gas fire was lit in the chocolate box of a sitting room, so the flat was toasty warm, even with rain spitting against the kitchen windows. Erika wore a rose-colored cardigan that set off her dark eyes and snowy white hair, and she had been watching him with a slight frown since they'd begun their lunch.

When he placed his cutlery carefully on his plate and sat back, her frown deepened.

"What?" she said, with the trace of German accent she'd never managed to eradicate. "Have you suddenly stopped growing? I seem to remember you telling me you could eat two entire chickens all by yourself."

"Too many Yorkshire puddings," Kit said, which was at least half true. He'd made them himself. Having discovered how easy they were, he'd been practicing, and these had come out just the way he liked them—crispy on the outside but still slightly spongy in the center.

"There is no such beast as too many Yorkshire puddings," Erika said with a twinkle. "In fact, I thought we could have the leftovers with tea, with good German butter and some of my homemade plum jam."

"I'll make the tea." Kit started to stand and clear their plates.

"No. Sit." When Erika used her lecturer's voice, Kit sat. "Why have you not told me anything about these kittens," she asked, "when I have heard nothing but kittens all week? And I thought you had chosen one for me, to keep me company in my old age—not that I'm old quite yet, mind you."

"I thought you might like the little calico," Kit said. "She's going to have the prettiest face."

"Am I not going to be invited to see these wondrous kittens, then?"

"Of course you are," Kit protested, although he thought she was teasing him a bit. "Only, I thought you'd like to come when Gemma and my dad are there. So you can help me convince them that we should keep the mum *and* one of the kittens ourselves. I don't—I don't want anyone else—I mean anyone besides you and Hazel and MacKenzie—to have one."

Erika must have seen something in his face, because all trace of lightness vanished from hers. "Kit, something is worrying you. Tell me what's happened."

"I— It's probably stupid," he began, haltingly. Erika just waited, as he knew she would until she had got it out of him. "There was this girl who came into the café yesterday, when we stopped to see Dad at work on our way to Leyton. She has something to do with Dad's case—I'm not sure what—but she said she was bringing him something to the station and she saw him come into the café. She was . . . nice. Dad bought her a hot chocolate. Toby and Charlotte told her all about the kittens."

"Go on," said Erika when he paused.

"The thing is, after Gemma left this morning, she—this girl—came to our house. She said Dad told her she could see the kittens. But it was—she was—I don't know. It didn't feel right." Kit shifted in his chair. His legs were getting too long to fit under Erika's little table. "And—this is probably really stupid—but just for a minute, I thought she might . . . hurt . . . them. The kittens. And I didn't know what I would do if she did," he finished in a rush.

If he'd been afraid Erika would laugh, she didn't. "Did she leave, this girl?" she asked sharply.

Kit nodded. "I told her I had to go. But I waited until I was certain she wouldn't come back before I left the house."

"Did you tell anyone?"

He shook his head. "No. Gemma's in Brixton, and Dad—he left early this morning. I don't know where he is."

"All right, then." Erika nodded briskly, as if they'd come to an executive decision. "In all likelihood there is nothing to be concerned about. But you must tell your parents, and as soon as possible. Do you promise?"

From Erika's expression, Kit didn't think she was taking it lightly at all. "I promise," he said. "But if Dad gave her our address and said she should come, I'm going to feel like an idiot."

"Kit, I cannot imagine that your father did any such thing." Erika's expression was as grim as he'd ever seen it. "And I do not think I want to consider the alternatives."

Gemma had just got off the phone with the crown prosecutor, who had not been thrilled at being disturbed on a Sunday afternoon, when Melody came into her office.

"Any luck with the CPS?" Melody asked.

Gemma shook her head. "She says that even if we can get an exact match on the shaving cream, it's still circumstantial, and she thinks the defense will blow us out of the water."

They had not been able to interview Mercy Johnson's mother in person, as she was working her shift at a care home, but Gemma had talked to her on the phone. No, she'd said, Mercy had not been allowed to shave, and she herself used a foaming salt scrub rather than an aerosol shaving cream. "Do you mind if we have our forensics team go through Mercy's things again, just in case they missed it?" Gemma had asked.

"Is it important?" said Mercy's mother.

"I don't know," Gemma had answered honestly. "It might be."

"Then do what you must," Mercy's mother had answered tiredly, and rung off.

Gemma had been onto the lab as well, asking if they could narrow the cream on Mercy's skin down to a brand, in hopes that it would match one of the cans in Dillon Underwood's bathroom.

"We'll have to talk to the other girls again, too," Gemma said now. "To rule out Mercy borrowing their creams or razors while visiting. But I don't think we can do any more today."

"Come on." Melody gestured towards the door. "I'll give you a lift home. It's much too miserable out for you to have to walk home from the tube station."

Gathering her things, Gemma protested, "But I've already ruined your Sunday, and most likely for nothing. You must have been planning something nice, too," she added, glancing at Melody's skirt, boots, and turquoise cashmere pullover.

"You saved me from my mum's Sunday lunch, and let me put off telling my parents about Andy a little bit longer."

Gemma stopped what she was doing and gazed at her friend. "Why don't you want to tell your parents about Andy? And vice versa? You're not . . . ashamed of him?"

"Oh, God, no," said Melody. "It's more the opposite. Honestly, I'm afraid they'll gobble him up."

"Gobble him up?"

Melody sighed. "You don't know them. There's nothing my dad would love more than to be the power behind a new and newsworthy sensation—except for that new sensation to be linked to his daughter. I'm not having that, and I won't have Andy feel that his success is down to anything but his and Poppy's talent. So it's not going to be a simple 'I have a new boyfriend' discussion."

"I see," said Gemma, and she did. "Maybe you should prepare Andy to meet the gorgon first. So that you can present a united front."

"Maybe," Melody agreed, but she didn't sound convinced.

"Take me home, then," Gemma told her. "We both missed Sunday lunch, and I'm starving. I'll make us something, even if it's cheese on toast. And"—she glanced at the clock—"as it's Sunday, and the sun is over the yardarm somewhere, I think we could even have a glass of wine."

• • •

Kit came in as Gemma and Melody were finishing their toast and cheese. Gemma had found half a jar of Branston pickle in the fridge, which had perked their snack up considerably, and they had opted for tea instead of wine, at least to start with.

"You're back soon," he said when he'd greeted Melody. Gemma thought he looked surprised and a little uncomfortable.

"The work idea turned out to be a bit of a damp squib," she said, wondering what was up. "You're early, too. I thought you and Erika would be glad of an afternoon to yourselves."

"Oh, yeah, well, we were. But—I'll do that," he said, as Gemma turned on the tap to do the washing up.

"Never refuse a washing-up offer," Melody commented from the table as Gemma laughed and handed him the Marigolds she'd been about to put on.

Kit held the yellow gloves with the tips of his fingers and tucked them back under the sink with an expression of disdain. "No proper bloke would be caught dead using washing-up gloves. You should know that, Gemma." He added a big squirt of Fairy liquid to the basin. "Have you heard from Dad?" he asked, his back to her.

"No. I rang him awhile ago, but it went to voice mail. Why?"

"Oh, nothing. It's just . . . I tried, too. Do you think he'll be back soon?"

Gemma glanced at Melody, who looked as puzzled as she felt.

"Kit." She went over to the sink, reached around him, and turned the water off. "What's this about? Is something wrong?"

He still didn't face her. "Something . . . weird . . . happened. Erika said I should tell you."

Gently Gemma turned him around. His face was flushed. "Okay. Why don't you tell me, then."

"Would you rather I left, Kit?" asked Melody.

"No. You should probably hear this, too." He wiped his dripping hands on the tea towel. To Gemma, he said, "You know that girl who came into the café yesterday? Ariel?" Gemma nodded. "She came to the house. Not long after you left this morning."

"What? She came here?"

Kit nodded. "She said Dad told her she could come see the kittens. She was all apologetic—said she hadn't meant to intrude and she'd come another time. So I—let her in." The last bit came out in a rush.

"What happened?" Gemma asked carefully, fighting a frisson of apprehension and the urge to glance at Melody.

"Nothing. It was just . . . I don't know. It just seemed wrong. I can't explain why. And I feel stupider now than I did when I told Erika."

"She didn't . . . touch you, did she?"

"Oh, God, no." Kit looked mortified, but he didn't meet her eyes and Gemma thought perhaps the girl had done something that he wasn't willing to admit. "But she picked up a kitten and . . ." He shook his head. "It didn't feel . . . I didn't think she really liked it. I just wanted her to leave."

"And did she?"

"Yeah. But—"

Gemma waited, trying not to push him.

"When I told her we found the kittens on Wednesday, she said that was when her friend had died, and that she thought she was *meant* to have one of the kittens. Was she talking about the guy who . . . burned?"

"I don't know," said Gemma, trying to recall everything that Duncan had told her, although a glance at Melody's expression told her that was probably the case.

Shifting from foot to foot, Kit said, "She wanted to know where Dad was."

"You didn't tell her anything?"

"No. Just that he was out somewhere." Kit fidgeted. "Can I go upstairs now? I have a paper to finish for school tomorrow."

"Of course," Gemma told him.

Kit was halfway across the room in one stride. Then he stopped and turned back to Gemma. "Will you tell Dad?"

"Of course," she said again. "As soon as he gets home."

"Thanks." He gave her a fleeting smile, and a moment later they heard him running up the stairs.

"Would Duncan have told the girl that, and given her your address?" Melody asked, coming to stand beside Gemma at the sink.

"I can't imagine that he would." Gemma frowned. "Although he did seem to feel sorry for her. Still . . ." She gazed out the window. The intermittent rain had stopped for the moment, but the sky was heavy, and dark would come early. "I wish they'd get back. Doug hasn't rung you, either?"

"No. I'd just checked in case I'd missed a call or a text when Kit came in." Melody picked up Kit's damp tea towel. "Here, you wash, I'll dry."

Absently, Gemma opened the cupboard and reached under the sink again for her kitchen gloves. Then she stopped, the yellow rubber fingers dangling from her hand.

"What's wrong?" asked Melody, giving her a surprised glance.

"Oh, surely not," whispered Gemma, staring at the gloves. "You heard what Kit said. 'No proper bloke would be caught dead using kitchen gloves.' I've never seen Kit or Duncan use them."

"Doug doesn't own a pair," Melody said. "Nor does Andy. I've bought my own so I wouldn't ruin my hands doing the washing-up."

Gemma held the gloves up between them. "Dillon Underwood had kitchen gloves under his sink. What if—I know it

sounds daft—but what if that's what he used when he strangled Mercy? That's why there were no fingerprints on her skin.
We looked for nitrile gloves, but not ordinary kitchen gloves."

"Yes, but . . . Surely he would have washed them by now, or
even bleached them?" protested Melody.

"But what if he didn't?" said Gemma. "What if those gloves
were the only trophy he dared keep? And he'd have thought
he was so clever, leaving them in plain sight." She dropped the
Marigolds on the work top and grabbed her phone from the
kitchen table. "I'm going to have uniform and the SOCOs pick
them up now. It's worth a try. We've already got the warrant."

Gemma had made the call, and Melody had finished the washing up—sans gloves—when they heard the sound of a car.
They both went to the front window. Gemma's orchid-colored
Ford Escort had pulled up in front of the house. The doors
all opened at once and three men got out. Absurdly, Gemma
thought of clowns emerging from a tiny circus car. But this
was Duncan and Doug, and from the back climbed a scruffy-
looking stranger hoisting a large backpack.

"Oh, my God." Beside her, Melody had raised a hand to her
mouth. "It's him. It's really him. They found Ryan Marsh."

Kincaid had sensed Marsh growing edgy as they drove into the
quiet streets of west Notting Hill. By the time he'd parked the
car in front of his house, Marsh's tension was palpable.

"Nice place you've got here," Marsh said, sitting forward so
that he was breathing down Kincaid's neck. "For a copper," he
added with a sneer.

Kincaid pulled the key from the Escort's ignition and
turned round, deliberately. "Yes. It is a nice place. And
I promise you I am not on the take. But if I am going to invite

you into my home, I expect at least the semblance of respect. Is that clear?"

"Okay. Right." Marsh sat back. "Family money, then?"

"It's a long story, and it's none of your business," Kincaid said, wishing he was as certain now as he had been six months ago that his home was without taint. But this was neither the time nor the place to deal with his worries.

"Let's get you inside," Kincaid said and opened his door.

Doug had spotted Melody's little Renault. "Melody's here." He sounded relieved, and Kincaid suspected his ankle was giving him fits. They were tired and cold as well, although they had stopped at a motorway café and eaten. Marsh had sat with his back to the door and shoveled food in as if he hadn't had a proper meal in weeks, rather than days.

Kincaid led the way to the house, with Doug bringing up the rear. The dogs were already barking, and before he could put his key in the lock, the door swung open.

As Gemma shooed the dogs back, Melody faced them. She looked hollow-eyed and pale, still, and once they were inside, she and Ryan Marsh stared at each other as if they had both seen ghosts. "You're all right," Melody said at last, reaching out as if she might touch him. Then she dropped her hand to her side.

"And you." Marsh seemed to search her face. "I'm glad. I'm sorry I—"

Melody was already shaking her head. "It's all right."

Nodding, Marsh set down his pack, then knelt to pet the dogs. They were sniffing round his ankles as if they'd never smelled anything more enticing. "Who's this, then?" Marsh asked.

"Geordie is the cocker," said Gemma. "And the little terrier is Tess. I'm Gemma, Duncan's wife."

Marsh stood and held out his still slightly grubby hand, but Gemma gave it a firm shake regardless. "You have kids, then?"

Marsh asked, taking in the scattered toys. He seemed, thought Kincaid, reassured.

"Yes," answered Gemma. "Two little ones. And a teenager. But the younger two are out with a friend. Come in the kitchen. I'll put the kettle on. Melody and I have drunk enough tea to sink a battleship already, but we can give you a start at catching up."

It was an awkward gathering. Melody murmured something to Doug, concerned, Kincaid guessed, about his ankle, then pulled out a chair for him. She asked Gemma if they had an ice pack or a bag of frozen peas, and went to dig in their freezer. Ryan Marsh sat, but on the edge of his chair, and looked as if he might bolt any minute.

Kincaid pulled mugs from the cupboard while Gemma filled the kettle. "There's something you should know," she said quietly as he stood beside her. "That girl, Ariel, the one who came in the café yesterday. She showed up here this morning, when Kit was on his own. She said you sent her. That you gave her our address."

"She *what*?" Kincaid's voice sounded overloud, and he realized the room had gone quiet. "Of course I didn't give her our address. What did she want?"

"She said you sent her to see the kittens."

"I never talked to her about the kittens. It was the children who did that." He was still baffled. "Could Toby have told her where we lived? He was rattling on about the cats." They had made both Toby and Charlotte memorize their address, in case they were ever lost.

"No." Gemma shook her head. "He was never alone with her. I'm sure of it."

"Then— How could she— No one at the station would have told her—"

The knowledge hit Kincaid like a blow. "She followed me," he said. "She must have followed me. I took the tube home from the station yesterday. Walking from Holland Park, I thought I felt someone—but I told myself not to be daft—"

"Why?" asked Doug. "Why would she follow you?"

"Kit said she wanted to know where you were," Gemma said.

"He didn't tell her?" Kincaid's heart was pounding with a sudden sickening apprehension.

"He didn't know."

"Bloody hell," Kincaid said. "She followed me! Did she know Kit was home alone?"

Gemma frowned as she thought. "She could have seen me leave. I walked to the tube. But there's no way she could have known you were gone unless she'd been standing in the street since before dawn. I wonder what she'd have said if you *had* been here."

"Maybe that someone at the station gave her your address," suggested Doug. "Or with Gemma gone, she could have said one of the little ones told her."

"She lied about her miscarriage, too," Kincaid said slowly. "I found out yesterday. Cam—one of the other girls," he explained for the benefit of everyone except Ryan, "Cam told me yesterday that she saw Ariel leaving an abortion clinic, and when she checked, the clinic confirmed that Ariel had the procedure. I didn't think it was relevant at the time. But if she lied about that, what else did she lie about?" He turned to Ryan. "You said she knew you'd given Paul the smoke bomb. She told me—and everyone else—that she didn't. Tell me exactly what happened that morning."

Ryan stared at him, openmouthed. He seemed to make an effort to pull himself together, then said, "Okay. Paul was arguing with Matthew. At the flat. Ariel told Paul to just shut up, that Matthew was never going to change his mind. Then she walked out. I left not long after, but Paul followed me to King's Cross." Ryan shook his head. "He just looked so damned defeated. He said Matthew would never give him a chance to prove he was serious about the cause, but that maybe I would. I remember I thought that what he really wanted was to prove himself to Ariel. And I thought"—Ryan hesitated—"I thought maybe it would get her off my back. She'd been coming on to me since—no"—he frowned—"not just since Wren died, but *before* Wren died. She always seemed so fragile—I didn't think I could just tell her to bugger off, so I said Paul was her boyfriend and I didn't want to trespass. Besides, I couldn't afford to alienate anyone in the group. So I thought if Paul was the hero of the day . . ."

"So you gave Paul Cole the smoke bomb, there in front of King's Cross?" Kincaid asked.

"Matthew had given it to me before I left the flat. I don't know where he was keeping it. Somewhere in his things, the stuff that no one else was ever allowed to touch. I had it in my backpack. I gave it to Paul and he put it in his backpack. We went over what he was to do, where he should stand. I said I'd be there but would stay well back, so no one in the group would realize I wasn't in position."

Gemma had gone on making tea while they talked. Now she handed Ryan a cup, which he accepted with a grateful nod. After a sip, Ryan went on, frowning with the recollection. "Then she rang him. It must have been Ariel, because Paul said, 'Yes, I've got it.' Then he listened and said, 'Right. Fifteen minutes,' before he rang off. When I asked him what was up, he gave me a thumbs-up and said, 'Her house. Her dad's not home.' "

"She told me they went to Paul's room at the university," said Kincaid, "and that they had a terrible argument about her miscarriage. So she lied about that, too."

"But—even if you're right, it was a smoke bomb," protested Ryan. "I know what I gave Paul was a smoke bomb. So that doesn't explain anything."

Kincaid began to pace. "Think about it. Was Ariel there when Matthew bought it?"

Ryan nodded. "Yeah. I'm sure she was."

"This bloke, the one who sold Matthew the smoke bomb at the protest, did he sell other things?"

Shrugging, Ryan said, "He's been around demonstrations since he served in Afghanistan. He knows weapons. If he wouldn't sell a WP grenade, he probably knows who would."

"So what if Ariel went back? What if she convinced him to sell her a grenade? Or got the name of someone else? God knows what story she would have come up with, but she'd have been believed."

"But," said Ryan, "how would she have made the swi—"

Doug broke in, excitement in his voice. "She had him come to her house. Say they had sex. He dozed off. She switched the smoke bomb in his backpack with a grenade."

"But Paul would have looked at the damned thing before he pulled the pin," protested Ryan. "Paul was a bit of a wanker, but he wasn't stupid."

"Look." Kincaid stopped his pacing and pulled out a chair, pulling it round so that he was facing Ryan. "She's an art student. I've been in her house. She uses stencils and paints. How hard would it have been to paint over the WP label, then stencil 'smoke' on the canister? You really think Paul would have noticed the difference?"

"No, but . . ." Ryan's blue eyes were dark with shock. "That would mean she *planned* it. Planned it all. Manipulated everyone. Matthew. Paul. Me. Why?" His tea sloshed out of his cup as his hands jerked. "And what if I hadn't agreed? Or Paul hadn't come to her house that morning? Did she intend to kill me if I hadn't agreed to let Paul do it?"

"I think Paul was the target," Kincaid said slowly, "and that if you hadn't agreed to the switch, then Ariel would either have found another opportunity to use the grenade or come up with something else. I believe she's capable of both careful planning and of seizing the moment. As to why . . . You said she was flirting with you even before Wren died—"

"You know about Wren?" broke in Ryan. "About what happened to her?"

Kincaid nodded. "Cam and Matthew told me. Why didn't you come forward? Identify her?"

"I couldn't." Ryan grasped his cup even tighter, his knuckles white. "At first Ariel said she thought Wren had jumped. I couldn't believe it. I was . . . numb. And then she said she thought she'd heard another car, and maybe someone running away. After that, I was afraid. I was afraid she'd been killed because of me. As a message to me."

"But—"

"I couldn't tell anyone. My family's been threatened."

"Your family?" said Gemma, sounding horrified.

"Don't ask me." Ryan looked up at her. "I can't tell you." It was a plea, as well as a warning. Then he said, "But this— if any of this is true, you're saying that both Wren and Paul were killed because Ariel wanted *me*? But that's—that's just— I can't—"

"I wouldn't take it too personally," broke in Doug. He'd propped his ankle up on a spare chair and covered it with the bag of frozen peas, but the peas were now melting. "There's something you don't know. Ariel's father told Duncan that her mother had died when she was a teenager. I looked up the accident report, just out of curiosity. It didn't really mean anything until now. Ariel was fourteen. She and her mum were on their way to see an aunt near Stratford. It was at night, a country lane. The car went off the road and rolled. Ariel was wearing her seat belt. She suffered a broken collarbone. Her mother was not. She was ejected from the car and killed. The thing is"—Doug paused, adjusting his dripping ice pack—"Stephen Ellis, Ariel's father, said his wife was a fanatic about wearing her seat belt. He even threatened to sue the car's manufacturer. But tests done on the car showed that the seat belt latch was functioning normally. They concluded that Mrs. Ellis just hadn't quite pushed the tongue all the way into the latch.

"According to her statement at the time, Ariel said she thought her mother swerved because she saw a rabbit in the road. But what if—what if she unlatched her mum's seat belt and grabbed the wheel?"

"That's worse than crazy." Ryan was looking at them all as if they were bonkers.

"Is it?" asked Kincaid. "Maybe she didn't get on with her mother. Now she has all the attention from a father who dotes on her, gives her anything she wants. If she did what Doug's suggesting she did, she's not averse to risk. And what about Wren?"

"What about Wren?" said Ryan, frowning.

"You said yourself you couldn't believe Wren jumped. But what if she didn't? What if there was no other car? No people running away? And Ariel didn't need to go back to her car for paint?"

"You're saying Ariel *pushed* her?"

"Why should we believe anything she said?"

"But—Jesus Christ." Ryan pushed his chair back and stood up. "But she was hysterical. I felt sorry for her! How could she—"

"There are people who will do anything to get what they want." Gemma had been leaning against the work top, cradling her mug, listening to them. Now she added, with certainty, "And because they can. Dillon Underwood is one. And although her motives may be different, I think Ariel Ellis is another. What we think is reasonable or logical doesn't apply."

"You'll never prove it," said Ryan. "And I can't testify that she knew Paul had the smoke bomb."

"Maybe we can't prove she killed her mother. Or Wren," Kincaid told him. "But she gave me what she said was a suicide note from Paul. I think it was a page from Paul's journal.

Maybe she took it at the same time she switched the smoke bomb with the grenade. And I'll bet you anything that if that's the case, she's kept it."

"That proves nothing," argued Ryan.

"It does if she had good reason to want that journal," Kincaid said. "And a reason to want Paul dead that had nothing to do with you.

"We know that Paul had found out she lied about the miscarriage—Cam told him. What if he'd begun to suspect she lied about Wren's death?"

"Then why go along with her? Why sleep with her, if that's what he did?" Ryan asked. "If he knew, he went to her like a lamb to the slaughter."

Kincaid shrugged. "I'd guess that he didn't want to believe it. And when she gave him any encouragement, he told himself he'd been imagining things. She's very good at what she does, is our Ariel. And why do you suppose," he went on, meeting Ryan's gaze, "that Ariel has been so frantic to find out what I knew? What if she was looking for you? Because you knew that *she* knew Paul had the grenade. I'd guess she hadn't planned on Paul telling you that. Or even if she had, perhaps she thought she could convince you that Paul had always intended to commit suicide. But then you disappeared, and she started to panic."

Ryan stared at him for so long it seemed to Kincaid that everyone in the room had stopped breathing.

Then Ryan said, with an air almost of wonder, "I was the next target. I was the bloody next target."

CHAPTER TWENTY-FOUR

Another sculpture, at platform level, pays tribute to Sir John Betjeman (1906–84). Poet Laureate from 1972 to 1984, Betjeman was . . . a great popular poet. More than anyone else he made people aware of the beauty of Victorian architecture through his colloquial eloquence. . . . It is largely due to him that we owe the survival and subsequent revitalization of St. Pancras.

—*Alastair Lansley, Stuart Durant,*
Alan Dyke, Bernard Gambrill,
Roderick Shelton,
The Transformation of
St. Pancras Station, *2008*

Kincaid had rung a friendly judge who he knew would issue a warrant on a Sunday. He'd then called Jasmine Sidana and Simon Gikas, and asked them, without any explanation, to meet him at Holborn and to have a tech team on standby— preferably the two SOCOs who had worked St. Pancras, because he wanted them to have an investment in the search.

Melody, having promised to meet Andy at Tam's, had left, but not before giving Ryan's hand a quick squeeze and saying, "I'll be seeing you, right?"

"Right." Ryan had grinned, his teeth showing white in the beard. "Like a bad penny."

That left Kincaid to run Doug and Ryan to Putney on his way to Holborn, but first he had one more thing to do.

He went up the stairs and knocked on Kit's partially open door. His son was sprawled on the bed, laptop and open textbook beside him, both dogs curled up by his feet.

"Hey," Kincaid said.

"Hey," Kit answered back a little warily, sitting up.

Kincaid pulled out Kit's desk chair and swung it round to face the bed. "May I?" he asked before he sat.

Nodding, Kit said, "Look, Dad, I'm sorry I—I should never have let her—"

Kincaid was already shaking his head. "You did exactly the right thing. You trusted your instincts, and you acted on what you felt. Don't ever forget that. I'm proud of you."

"Really?" Some of the worried look left Kit's face. "But—that girl, Ariel—did she do something bad?"

"I'm not sure yet. She might have. But that's my job, not yours." Kincaid stood. "But promise me one thing."

"Okay." Kit sounded wary again, and Kincaid knew he wondered what he was agreeing to.

"Let's have a house rule from now on. No one who is not already a good friend is allowed in when Gemma or I aren't home."

"Oh. Okay," Kit said, obviously relieved, and Kincaid hoped it would at least be a while before his son fell for another pretty girl's sob story. He wished his own instincts had been as good as Kit's.

"I'll see you later." Kincaid tousled Kit's hair, and for once Kit let him do it without protesting.

"Dad." Kit stopped him before he reached the door. "About those kittens—"

"Don't start." Kincaid smiled as he left him. There was something to be said for persistence.

• • •

"You'd better go," Gemma said when he came back downstairs. "MacKenzie just rang. They're on their way home. I don't think you want to explain Ryan to MacKenzie and the kids." As they put on their coats and Ryan picked up his pack, she added, "And I'd like my car back someday, by the way."

"Right." Kincaid kissed her. "I'm on it."

"Take care," she added softly.

"I survived Doug and a boat. On the same day," Kincaid answered, grinning.

Gemma turned to Ryan and held his eyes for a moment. "And you. You take care, too."

Ryan nodded. "Thank you." It was clear he meant for more than the farewell.

Kincaid got out of the car with Doug and Ryan Marsh in front of Doug's house in Putney. He and Ryan faced each other beside the idling Escort.

"You know I would help you if I could," said Ryan. "I would do it for Paul. And, oh, God, for Wren." He swayed a little, as if exhaustion and grief were overtaking him. "But I— There are things I can't tell you— There would be . . . consequences . . ."

"Don't worry." Kincaid told him, clasping his shoulder. "I'll manage. It will be all right."

When he reached Holborn, both Sidana and Gikas were waiting for him.

"No Sweeney?" Kincaid asked.

"I had a word at the gym," Sidana answered. "Apparently, there was a triathlon this weekend."

"He could have said."

"But he didn't." A look at Sidana's face told Kincaid that Sweeney had more than likely earned himself a demotion. "It doesn't matter," she added. "We don't need him." And that condemnation, Kincaid knew, was far worse.

"I've got the SOCOs you asked for on standby," said Simon. "As well as a couple of uniformed constables. And your warrant's come through." He swiveled his computer chair to face Kincaid. "So, are you going to tell us what's going on?"

Kincaid had thought it out in the little time he'd had. He gave them an edited version of events, leaving out anything to do with Ryan Marsh. He included a detailed account of Cam and Matthew's statements from the day before, both about Ariel's abortion and Wren's death. He took credit, a little guiltily, for Doug's findings on Ariel's mother's death. He told them what Ariel had done that morning, and his realization that not a single thing she'd told them could be taken as true.

"She came to your home?" Sidana sounded incensed. "And insinuated herself with your son?"

"I think she must have followed me yesterday, when I took the tube."

"But why?" asked Simon.

"Trying to find out how much I knew, I think."

"And power," said Sidana, with unexpected insight. "She was testing—and demonstrating—her power."

"Yes," Kincaid agreed. "I suspect you're right. That, too."

"So what you're telling us," said Simon, "is that you think this girl killed her mother, killed her friend, killed her boyfriend, *and* stalked a senior police officer and his family? If any of that is true, we're dealing with a sociopath. A real nutter."

"I think so, yes." Kincaid didn't add that she scared the hell out of him.

"You'll never prove the first two," argued Sidana. "It's all conjecture. And so is most of what you have against her for Paul Cole's murder."

"And it still doesn't explain what happened to Ryan Marsh," put in Simon. The glance he gave Kincaid was speculative.

Kincaid ignored it. "Nevertheless," he said, "I think we have grounds for a warrant. We may not know how she made the switch, or why Paul and not Ryan had the smoke bomb, but if we can find evidence that she camouflaged the grenade or we find Paul Cole's journal, we'll have a good start."

"I think I'd like to tag along," said Simon Gikas. "This sounds like it might be an interesting evening."

A welcoming light shone through the front window of the house in Cartwright Gardens.

Kincaid had the SOCOs and the uniformed officers—whom he'd had arrive in an unmarked car—wait in their vehicles until he signaled them. He, Sidana, and Simon Gikas went to the door.

Stephen Ellis answered their ring, looking much as he had the first time Kincaid and Sidana had visited. The room looked much the same, too, with a gas fire burning and the lamps lit. This evening, however, a glass of red wine had replaced the tea on the end table, and a stack of Sunday papers littered the coffee table.

"Can I help you?" asked Ellis when he'd let them in.

"It's Ariel we need to speak to, Dr. Ellis. Is she at home?" If Ellis said no, Kincaid had decided they would make their excuses, then watch the house until she arrived. He had no intention of tipping her off and giving her a chance to run.

But Ellis said, "Yes, she's here, but I'm afraid she's not feeling too well. Coming down with a cold, poor thing."

Kincaid bet she was, if she'd stood outside his house for hours in the cold that morning. "I'm sorry, but we really do need to talk to her."

Ellis went to the door that appeared to lead to the flat's bedrooms and called out. "Ariel! There's someone—"

The door swung open and Ariel said, "I told you I didn't want anyone bothering—" Then she saw the detectives, and just for an instant, she didn't manage to mask the shock and the calculation in her expression.

Then she said, "Oh, it's you," and gave Kincaid a wavery smile. "I'm so sorry. I'm afraid I've caught a horrid cold. Could we talk another time?" She held a convincing wad of tissues to her nose, and looked frailer than ever in a baggy sweater and a pair of tartan pajama bottoms.

"No, I'm afraid it can't wait. Can you come into the sitting room, please?"

"What's happened?" she said, coming to stand near her father. "Has someone else been hurt? Don't tell me—You've found Ryan?" She sounded innocently hopeful.

"No. No, we haven't." Kincaid gave a nod to Simon, who stepped outside. "But we've learned some other very interesting things," he went on.

As Simon came back, followed by the uniformed officers and the SOCOs, Kincaid said formally, "Ariel Ellis, I'm arresting you on suspicion of the murder of Paul Cole. You do not have to say anything. But it may harm your defense if you do not mention when questioned something which you later rely on in court. Anything you do say may be given in evidence."

Wide-eyed, Ariel looked from Kincaid to her dad, then at the officers who had entered the room. "You're not serious. You can't just come in here—you can't think—"

Simon handed Kincaid the warrant. "We have a warrant to search the premises," Kincaid continued, passing it to Stephen Ellis. "I think it would be best if you both sat down while the crime scene officers conduct the search."

"But how could you possibly—" Stephen Ellis looked at the constables who had taken up positions on either side of the door, and sank onto the sofa as if his legs had suddenly refused to support him. "There must be some mistake," he whispered.

Ariel sat beside him and took his hand. "Daddy, make them stop." The look she gave her father would have melted a glacier.

"I don't know how, darling." He peered at the warrant he held in his hand. "Let me just—" Reaching for his reading glasses, Ellis sent the glass of red wine toppling. It struck the hearth and shattered, leaving a splatter of red drops on the floor and tile.

Ariel sprang up. "I'll get—"

"No." Kincaid motioned her back to the sofa. "Sit."

"I'll get it," said Simon, and headed for the kitchen.

Kincaid spoke to the now-familiar crime scene tech. "Scott, start with her bedroom. In particular, we're looking for camouflage paint, stencils that might have been used to label a grenade, and a black, handwritten journal."

"Right." Scott and his partner had donned gloves and paper boots, but not their full crime scene suits. As they headed for the door leading to the back of the flat, Kincaid saw Ariel give an involuntary jerk.

Simon returned with a kitchen roll, a whisk broom, and a dustpan. He picked up Ellis's undamaged glasses and handed them to him.

Ariel gave Kincaid another pleading glance. "Can't you just tell me why you're doing this to me?"

"I think we'll save that for the station." Kincaid couldn't help imagining that look turned on Kit, and her in his house. He realized he was clenching his fists, and that Sidana had seen him doing it.

The SOCOs' voices came sporadically from the bedroom as Simon cleaned up the broken glass and spilled wine. Stephen Ellis read and reread the warrant, looking more and more confused. Ariel, after her initial, instinctive reaction, seemed to draw into herself, huddling on the sofa beside her father.

Kincaid was tempted to look into her bedroom, to see if it revealed anything of the girl's true nature or was more artful camouflage, but he felt that if he took his eyes from her for an instant, she might slip from his grasp.

It wasn't long before Scott came back into the room, bearing a decorated shoe box in his gloved hands. It looked to Kincaid as if it was hand painted. There were birds and flowers and swirling vines. It would have looked quite sweet if one hadn't noticed the grotesque little faces half hidden in the foliage.

Scott removed the lid. "Under the bed. Not the best of hiding places. Is this what you were looking for, sir?"

Inside the box was a black journal, and something else that rattled. Kincaid pulled nitrile gloves from his coat pocket and gingerly picked up the journal. The pages were filled with black ink in the crabbed writing he recognized as Paul Cole's, and near the back a page had been ripped out.

Beneath it were two necklaces. One had a broken silver chain, and on it, a small brown enameled bird—a wren. Its clasp was broken.

The other chain was fine gold, and from it hung a green jewel, oval faceted. An emerald, perhaps? The clasp was intact. He held it up to get a better look.

Stephen Ellis came off the sofa like a shot. "Where did you get that?" He reached to take it from Kincaid and the constables stepped forward. Ellis let his hands drop to his sides. "That was my wife's. Where did you get it?"

"I think you should ask your daughter, Dr. Ellis."

"It was Andrea's mother's, handed down from her mother. Andrea was never without it. It wasn't found on her body after the crash. I looked everywhere for it—I even went back and searched the crash site myself. I thought one of the medics, or even one of the police officers, must have taken it." He turned at last to his daughter. "Ariel, how did you—"

Ariel had drawn herself into an even smaller ball. "Daddy, I—I found it. I wanted something to remind me of her. I knew you wouldn't let me keep it."

"Found it where?" Ellis was staring at his daughter as if utterly perplexed. "The chain isn't broken. Nor the clasp."

"I found it in the grass. While they were working on Mum. It was broken, but I—I had it repaired."

"It was dark, Ariel. How did you find it in the grass?" When she didn't answer, Stephen Ellis shook his head in disbelief. "I remember. You argued with your mum that day. You wanted to wear the pendant to a party, and she said no. You were so angry. That was when she decided to take you to your aunt's." He looked back at the pendant. Light caught the emerald, sparking green fire.

His face was pale as chalk as he turned back to his daughter. "You took it. You took it from your mother's body. How could you?"

"I only wanted—"

"You had to have taken it before the medics came." Ellis stared at her in horror. "What else did you do, Ariel? What else?"

For a moment, Kincaid thought Ellis might lunge for her, and Simon and Sidana stepped forward, seeming to sense the violence in the air as well.

Then Ellis staggered a little and Simon reached out to steady him.

Ariel began to cry in ragged sobs. "Daddy, I only wanted something of hers. She loved it more than me."

But Stephen Ellis looked at his daughter as if he'd never seen her before, and he didn't respond as they helped her into her coat and escorted her to the waiting car.

Ariel Ellis continued to weep. But as she was led past Kincaid, she whispered, so low that he had to lean forward to hear, "You'll be sorry." It was an uncanny echo of the words in Paul's journal, but there was a viciousness in Ariel's whisper that made Kincaid's blood run cold.

He stopped her with a hand on her sleeve and said just as quietly, "No. *You'll* be sorry. And don't you ever come near my family again."

CHAPTER TWENTY-FIVE

St. Pancras International today is a new totality. The heroic age of nineteenth-century engineering and twenty-first-century technology have been brought together and coexist happily. There is no station like St. Pancras International.
—*Alastair Lansley, Stuart Durant,*
Alan Dyke, Bernard Gambrill,
Roderick Shelton,
The Transformation of
St. Pancras Station, *2008*

The following Sunday they managed a proper Sunday lunch at Gemma and Duncan's. They'd squeezed nine round the dining room table, by dint of bringing in extra chairs from the kitchen.

Erika had come, as promised, to see the kittens, and Gemma had invited Betty, Wesley, and Bryony as well.

Wesley and Kit had done the Yorkshire puddings, and Gemma was proud as punch that she'd managed a perfect roast in the Aga. The weather had changed yesterday, and for the first time in what seemed like months, they had done their shopping at Portobello Market. There were tulips on the table, and fresh vegetables to go with the roast. Gemma's Clarice Cliff teapot, brought out for the occasion, was waiting in the kitchen, but now Gemma was serving chilled Prosecco to the adults, with half a glass for Kit, and some fizzy apple juice for Toby and Charlotte.

"What are we toasting?" asked Wesley, raising his glass.

"Oh, lots of things," said Gemma, taking her seat again and picking up her own glass. "Spring, at last. Friends."

Only Duncan knew what else she was celebrating, and he raised his glass to her across the table.

On Friday, she and Melody had got the lab report on Dillon Underwood's kitchen gloves. They had been covered in Mercy Johnson's DNA, from both her skin and her saliva. Underwood would go to trial, and with any luck, they would get a conviction.

"Here, here," Duncan said quietly, and drank to her.

Wesley followed with "Cheers," and they all sipped. Gemma managed not to laugh as Kit made a face.

"What about my ballet?" asked Toby, gulping his apple juice. "I'm going to take lessons," he told the company. "We should toast that."

"*Sláinte,*" said Kit. "I learned that from Hazel. To pirate ballet."

"Why is it toast?" asked Charlotte, and they all laughed.

Bryony raised her glass again. "I'm drinking to healthy kittens, and a great job by the foster parents."

All the kittens had their eyes open now, and were tumbling over one another, trying to climb out of their box, and developing personalities as distinctive as their coloring.

Although Toby was still lobbying for keeping all four kittens, they were, in fact, keeping two. When Gemma and Kit had taken Erika in to see them before lunch, she had admired the little calico female.

But then she'd asked if she could hold Xena, and the tabby

had settled in her lap as if she belonged there, gazing up at Erika with her luminous golden eyes.

"This one," said Erika, "the little mother," tracing the white blaze on Xena's face. "Are you set on keeping her?"

Gemma glanced at Kit before she spoke. "We want her to have a good home. People are usually more willing to take kittens."

"I'm not quite certain I can keep up with a kitten." Erika stroked Xena's silky back. "But this one, we understand each other. She knows what it is to be abandoned, and to have found friends and safety again. I think we would do well together. And the two little ones"—she nodded at the black-and-white boy and the calico girl—"they will be playmates."

"Poor Sid," said Gemma, laughing, "outnumbered once again." And so it was settled, and Gemma thought Kit was happy with the decision.

Now Kit turned to Bryony. "When can Hazel and MacKenzie take their kittens?"

"Most people give kittens away at six weeks, but in my opinion that's too young. I think eight weeks is much better for both mother and babies. And believe me," Bryony said with emphasis, "by that time you'll be glad to see two gone."

Gemma rolled her eyes. "You're telling me I have rampaging kittens to look forward to?"

"A little like curtain-climbing Mongol hordes," answered Bryony, grinning.

They had reached the tea and cake stage—the cake a beautiful pear torte Wesley had brought from Otto's café—when someone's phone buzzed.

"It's mine," said Duncan, checking it. "It's work. Sorry. I'll just take it outside."

The text had been from Simon Gikas, asking Kincaid to ring him back.

Kincaid let the dogs out the French doors into the garden.

He stood for a moment, admiring the view and the day. The grass was a brilliant green, and it seemed as if the tulips had sprung up overnight and the fruit trees had burst into bloom. The trees had not yet come into leaf, and against their still-bare branches, the sky was a brilliant, crystalline blue.

He could hear the laughter and voices from the dining room through the closed doors. For a moment, he was tempted to put off returning Simon's call, but he knew his crime scene manager wouldn't have rung unless it was important.

Kincaid punched Return on his phone, and when Simon answered, said, "What's up?"

"Hated to bother you on a Sunday, Guv. But I'd come in to check something and saw that the forensics had come back on the grenade fragments. I thought you'd want to know."

"Don't keep me in suspense, then." Kincaid could hear the satisfaction in Gikas's voice.

"Ariel Ellis's DNA was on the grenade. More, they think, than if she had just handled it casually, which will probably be her barrister's argument. It's not foolproof, but added to the other things it might be enough."

Paul Cole's journal had been filled with his doubts about Ariel. He knew the embankment where Wren had been killed, and had never been comfortable with Ariel's account of Wren's death. When he'd learned that Ariel had lied about her miscarriage, he'd borrowed his mother's car and had a look at the scene of Wren's accident for himself. He'd found it hard to believe that Ariel had intended to tag a spot where the fast trains came through on their way into London, or that Wren had accidentally fallen.

Had the scrawled page in his notebook been meant as a threat to Ariel? Had his need for attention and power, and his desire for her, overcome his suspicions? If so, he had underestimated her, to his ultimate cost.

. . .

Kincaid had been in touch with Nick Callery, letting him know that although they might need to worry about a protester selling military-grade weapons, it looked as if Paul Cole's death had not been connected with any terrorist objectives. The search for the man who had sold Matthew the smoke bomb, and might have sold Ariel the grenade, had been turned over to SO15.

"Thanks, Simon," said Kincaid now. "Good work all round. I'll see you tomorrow."

As soon as Kincaid hung up, he rang Doug and relayed the news. "Can you tell Ryan?" he asked. "He'll want to know it looks like we may be able to make a good case without him."

"He's gone to Hackney," said Doug. "This morning. He and his wife have been talking, making some sort of a plan, I think. But he said he needed some things from his old flat."

"Do you have the address?" Kincaid asked.

"He gave it to me. He had me check on it earlier in the week, just to see if everything looked okay."

"Text it to me, then. I want to tell him the news myself."

He waited until the guests had left and he'd helped Gemma with the washing up before asking if she minded if he went out for a bit. When she'd raised a questioning eyebrow, he'd said, "I'll tell you later."

"Don't be too late, then. The kids want help with their homework."

He'd kissed her cheek and slipped out of the house. He drove the Astra—back on the road thanks to a new battery—to Hackney.

The sun was setting and the evening drawing in as he found the estate. The buildings were comfortably ordinary, two story, brick and shingle, with tidy front gardens. He guessed the estate was probably still, at least in part, owned by the council.

He saw the reflection of the flashing lights before he turned into the section that housed the address Doug had given him.

His heart came into his throat when he rounded the corner and saw what lay before him. A half-dozen blue-and-yellow-liveried panda cars, lights flashing. An ambulance. A crime scene van.

He found a place to pull the Astra over. When he got out, he realized he was shaking. Walking up to the temporary cordon, he showed his warrant card to the officer. "What's going on?" he asked, making an effort to keep his voice steady.

"Suicide," said the uniformed constable, sounding bored. "Some bloke with a gun. Hence all the bells and whistles."

Light spilled from the doorway of the flat that was marked with the number Doug had given him. "Mind if I have a look?" Kincaid asked, struggling to keep his voice level.

The constable shrugged. "Not exactly your patch, but what-ever turns you on."

"Thanks." Kincaid walked on, trying to still the voice in his head that said *it must be the wrong flat, the wrong man.* He waved his warrant card at the constable on the door and walked in.

"You the detective?" asked the overall-suited crime scene tech, bending over the form on the floor.

"Not on this case, no. Just passing. Stopped to see if I could help."

"Not much you can do for this bloke," the tech said, and moved aside.

There was no doubt that it was Ryan. And there was no doubt that he was dead.

He lay on his back on the carpet. There was a neat hole in his forehead. Below it, his face was now clean shaven. His blue eyes were open. They were just beginning to turn milky, and the bloodstain behind Ryan's head looked fresh.

A small-caliber semiautomatic handgun lay next to his shoulder, beside his curving, open fingers.

"Had a bit to drink, I think we'll find," the tech said, gesturing at the bottle of Bell's and the empty glass on the coffee table.

All Kincaid could do was nod.

Later, he would remember every detail of the flat. The things that were there, and the things that were missing.

Now, he knew only that he had to get out. "I'll leave you to it, then," he said to the tech.

He walked out and back to his car, trying not to weave or stumble, raising a friendly hand to the perimeter constable as he passed him. He hoped neither officer had really looked at the name on his warrant card.

Once in the Astra, he managed to get the key in the ignition and start the car. Pulling away, he drove as carefully as a drunk, taking turn after turn until he had lost himself in a maze of unfamiliar streets, far away from the flashing lights.

He stopped then, turned off the engine, and put his head on the steering wheel he still gripped with both hands.

What the hell had happened? What the hell was he going to tell Doug? What the hell was he going to tell Melody? And, oh, dear God, what was he going to tell Christie Marlowe?

Worst of all, had anyone connected him with Ryan Marsh?

ABOUT THE AUTHOR

Deborah Crombie is a native Texan who has lived in both England and Scotland. She lives in McKinney, Texas, sharing a house that is more than one hundred years old with her husband, two cats, and two German shepherds.

R2200/740220

12/01/41